Guy
Staight

TESTAMENT

Published by whitefox on behalf of Guy Staight

This edition published 2014

ISBN 978-0-9930910-1-8

Printed and bound by CPI Group (UK) Ltd, Croydon, CR0 4YY

1 3 5 7 9 10 8 6 4 2

Author's Note

I have clear childhood memories of my grandfather, from afternoons when he showed me his medals to times when my grandmother left the room and he rolled up his sleeve and displayed the tattoo on one of his arms. The sight of the long dark-blue snake winding down from his inner elbow to his wrist both fascinated and frightened me.

After he died I found out more about his extraordinary life and decided to try and write a book about it. I started many years ago, stopped for a while, but felt compelled to carry on and tell his story. I have tried to replicate events as faithfully as possible, drawing upon family stories and my own research. There are a number of areas where the facts are impossible to verify and my imagination has had to fill in the gaps, particularly in relation to the officers who commanded him. Their names and characters are fictional.

Now that so many people are reflecting on the outbreak of the First World War and remembering those who were wounded or died, and the toll it took on their families, it seems the right time to tell my grandfather's story to the wider world.

This is the tale of one man from Worcestershire, and his First World War spent in Egypt and Turkey.

ଚ୬

Chapter 1

Manor Farm, Stoulton, February 1905

Tom awoke with a jolt and for a moment was uncertain why, until he heard the sound of weeping coming from his sister Jane's room.

'Mother!' she cried. He thought her voice sounded more husky than usual.

There was a pause while they waited for the familiar creak of their mother's bedroom door. Nothing happened.

'Tom?' Jane said hesitantly, and he could sense her straining to hear a reply. He swept back his bedcovers and made his way to her room, kicking his brother Hender's bed as he passed.

There was a faint milky glow on the landing cast by the full moon shining through the skylight. He pushed open Jane's door. The end of a candle was guttering on its saucer on her bedside table, sending irregular bursts of light across her bed. He could see that her pretty, round face was flushed, and beads of sweat covered her forehead. Jane had been ill with scarlet fever for four days and Tom, along with his other sisters and brothers, had been forbidden by the doctor from having any contact with the sick child as the illness was so contagious. Their mother Nora wasn't someone you disobeyed and Tom worried about entering his sister's room, fearful of the reaction if his mother were to wake and catch him there.

'How are you feeling?' he asked his sister, lighting a new candle from the stub of the old one. He melted a little wax to fix the candle in place. Jane's bedroom was stuffy and smelt faintly of herbs and mothballs.

'I feel hot...very hot,' she whispered hoarsely.

Tom took the flannel from the bowl on the washstand, dipped it in cold water and wiped her forehead. Then he held a cup to her cracked lips. Her dark curls stuck to her clammy skin and her pale-blue eyes looked sunken and tired.

'Thanks, Tom. I've missed you. But perhaps you'd better go now,' she said, with a weak smile. She had a maturity and presence unusual in a girl of ten and Tom, at fourteen, often found himself taking her advice. She also had a way with their mother, seemingly indifferent to Nora's bad moods and bouts of melancholy.

'Call again if you need me,' he said, tucking in Jane's sheets and smoothing her eiderdown. He knelt by her side for a few minutes longer, watching as her breathing slowed and she fell asleep.

He settled back into his still-warm bed, listening for a while in case she woke again and called for him, but she was sleeping peacefully. Outside the wind whistled through the orchard. He heard the branches groan and stir in protest. He imagined the whole house breathing in and out as the dark of night closed in.

Tom woke to hear screams coming from Jane's room. He rushed down the corridor and saw his father Reg standing at the open door. There was a smell of smoke and the screams seemed endless: piercing, fearful, agonising. He stood at the door and saw flames leaping from Jane's bedclothes. Her hair was on fire. Tom's father was throwing water on her from the jug he carried in his trembling hands. When that was empty he snatched a spare blanket from the corner of the bedroom and used it to smother the flames. Tom ran back to his own room, waking his brother, and brought their water jug, which his father threw over Jane before sweeping her up in his arms in the dripping blanket. He pushed past Tom and Hender, who stood by shocked and silent.

'We must take her straight to hospital, Nora,' shouted their father. Their mother had appeared from her own separate bedroom and was tying her dressing gown around her. The adults hurried downstairs, leaving Tom and Hender staring into the empty room. Wisps of smoke from the charred bedclothes curled out on to the landing.

Tom felt as though his life had been suspended. All feeling seemed to have been sucked out of him. He stood watching ash settle on the charred bed and the floor beneath. There was a bitter taste in his mouth from the burnt wool and his eyes began to water. He felt the tears come from deep within him.

Slowly awareness returned to him, and with it the realisation that the candle he had lit had caused the fire. The thought of his sister in hospital, horribly burnt, made him run to the corner of his room and vomit into the washstand. Afterwards he wiped his face and sat on his bed, staring down at the floor. Thirteen-year-old Hender came back in and sat beside him, still sobbing in the way children do long after they have stopped crying. Tom put his arm around his brother.

'We'd better try and get some sleep.'

Hender nodded and slid under the covers. Tom climbed into bed and closed his eyes, but could not erase the image of his sister with her hair aflame or the agonising sound of her screams. Eventually, as it started to become light, he fell into a restless sleep.

Tom and his family lived on a mixed farm in Worcestershire. They kept cattle, some pigs and hens. There were also a number of working horses and two or three hunters for Tom and his father to ride. The farmhouse had an old orchard at the back with a mixture of apple and pear trees, which had aged gently, lichen sprouting like ragged beards from their trunks. The morning after the fire Tom went out to the stables to feed his pony whose full name was Lord Pantingham but whose nickname was Pants. Tom gave the pony's warm sweet-scented neck a hug and tried to find comfort in the familiar morning routine.

His father had agreed to take Pants from another family, the Caldicotts. Their son Harry was a good rider but kept being bucked off. When, after yet another fall, he broke his arm, his father decided Pants had to go. Reg told Tom not to ride the new pony. He planned to send him to a dealer in Wales, who had a reputation for taking on half-mad beasts.

But Tom had gone to the paddock every day, carrying carrots. He was fascinated by this jet-black pony with a white star on its forehead. For the first week Pants tried to kick or bite him, but slowly Tom gained his trust. After a month he was leading the pony around the field with a bridle and saddle on. On a day when his father had gone to Worcester market, Tom decided to try and ride Pants. To his amazement all went well. He rode round the paddock at a walk, then a trot, and finally a canter. There was no sign of rearing or bucking, and Tom prompted Pants to jump the low post-and-rail fence out of the paddock and then back in again.

Tom was ecstatic. He had grown to love this mad black beast. Of course, when his father found out he was furious, but he eventually calmed down when he saw that Pants was perfectly behaved with Tom. He thought it best to let the Caldicotts know of the change in their pony, but when Harry came over to ride him accompanied by a friend of his, both boys were bucked off in seconds. After that Tom became known as a lad with a 'gift with horses'. He was asked to ride all manner of crazy animals but his father gently refused most requests, except from a handful of friends locally. Nevertheless Tom's reputation for being able to cure a horse or pony of all sorts of problems spread by word of mouth.

On that terrible morning after Jane's accident Tom cleared droppings from the stable, scooping them into the wheelbarrow in his usual way. As he walked back to the house, racked with guilt and close to tears, Reg appeared and came shuffling across the yard.

His cap was pushed back on his head. He looked drained, rubbing his neatly clipped brown beard that was flecked with grey, stubble shadowing the rest of his face. He wore a shabby tweed jacket with gaping pockets, and hobnail boots that rang out against the stones. When he saw Tom he swiped one sleeve against his eyes and, for the first time in years, bent down to hug his son. Tom knew then that Jane had died. He sobbed against his father's shoulder. Tears that had been held back until now poured out like a dam giving way.

'Your sister died early this morning, Tom. The doctors at Worcester Infirmary could do nothing to save her.'

'Father, it's my fault! I put a new candle by her bed…it must have fallen over. I did it,' Tom wailed.

Reg put his hands on Tom's shoulders and held him away so that he could look his son in the eye as he spoke to him.

'Now, Tom, you can't think like that. It was a dreadful accident. Sadly these things happen. This was none of your doing, lad. Any one of us could have gone into Jane's room and put a new candle by her bed. She is with God now and at peace.'

He saw that his father had been crying too. Tom ran inside, past his mother in the kitchen and up to his bedroom, where he buried his head in the pillow. He could not understand how Father could appear so composed. His daughter had died and yet he'd appeared more upset when his old hunter had been put down last year. Tom was angry with himself but even more so with his father's calm acceptance of the tragedy that had befallen them.

The next three days were a whirl of activity with plans being made for Jane's funeral. This was held in the church opposite their farmhouse in the village of Stoulton.

On the morning of the service Tom put on his school jacket and a pair of grey flannel trousers that were still far too big for him in spite of having been bought eighteen months before in the expectation he would soon be tall enough to wear them. He stood in front of the mirror, combing his hair. His normally cheerful face was drawn and blotchy and his brown eyes were still red from crying. He had been unable to eat for days.

Tom, his remaining sisters Birdie, Mary and Phyllis, and his brothers Hender and Ray, walked up the aisle behind their parents. A small coffin rested on a pair of trestles at the top of the nave. There was a wreath of white lilies laid on it. After the service the family moved to the graveyard behind the church where a mound of freshly dug brown earth marked the site of Jane's last resting place. Tom felt sick to see it. He stood taking in deep breaths, hoping the day would end soon and everything would go back to the way it used to be before his sister's death.

The congregation walked quietly back down the road to the farmhouse and into the garden. It was a cold, clear spring day and a number of them stayed outside, wrapped in their black coats, afraid that within the house the sadness would be overwhelming. Tom shuffled round with a plate of sandwiches, moving silently from person to person and avoiding eye contact. His father offered beer to the men, while most of the women drank tea. In the hall, Tom became trapped between the stairs and two tall men who stood talking to his mother.

'I'm sorry for your loss, Nora,' said one of their neighbours. 'Tragic for you all.'

'Yes, it is. Of course it was Tom who went into Jane's room during the night and replaced her candle. The one he lit must have fallen on to her bed. An accident…yes, that's what it was,' she said, in a tone that implied he was fully to blame. Tom was now convinced that he had caused his sister's death and felt over-whelmed with guilt. He put down the plate and ran up the back stairs to his room. Hender appeared after nearly an hour, unaware that Tom had been lying on his bed for so long.

'I don't know how life can ever get back to normal for any of us. Jane was such a good, kind girl,' said his brother, sitting down on his bed and taking off his thick-lensed spectacles to polish them. He wiped his eyes again and blew his nose, saying afterwards, 'You seem pretty quiet.'

Tom jumped up and launched himself at his brother, punching his head and back as Hender wrapped his arms protectively around his ears.

'Watch my glasses! You'll break them.'

Tom carried on hitting him until gradually his punches lost their power and he collapsed on to the floor.

'It was all my fault,' he said in a hoarse voice.

'It was not your fault, it was an awful accident. I think Jane must have knocked over the saucer in her fever. It had nothing to do with you or how you fixed the candle,' said Hender, starting to cry again.

'That's not what Mother thinks. She even said as much to two people downstairs.'

'You know what she's like, just ignore her,' his brother hiccuped, burying his head in his pillow, shoulders heaving.

Their mother Nora was widely recognised in the area as a 'difficult' woman. Reg had been married before, and Nora seemed to nurse a grudge against him and her own eldest children for that very reason. His first wife had died in childbirth along with their baby daughter and both of them lay buried in Herefordshire. Reg made no secret of the fact that he had adored his first wife and every year, on the anniversary of the deaths, would travel to the next county to place lilies of the valley on their graves, to Nora's deep displeasure.

Reg's second marriage and the tenancy of Manor Farm, Stoulton, had been arranged through a family friend. Nora had beaten Tom when he was younger, and all the older children were aware of the favouritism she showed towards Phyllis, Jane and Ray. Jane and Ray, in particular, could do no wrong in their mother's eyes.

This was the main reason Tom had become involved with horses, and spent so much of his time outside, riding or schooling them. Reg loved all his children equally but Tom was very aware of the sadness and loss that his father still carried within him. Though his parents rubbed along pretty well, it was more out of a sense of duty than from love.

Nora was sharp-tongued and unsympathetic, but maybe this time she was in the right. Lying back on his bed, Tom thought it best not to discuss his feelings with anyone. He followed a crack across the ceiling with his eyes, tracking it up and down. Tom listened to Hender's muffled sobs as he himself dug his nails into his palms, refusing to shed any more tears.

Over the next few weeks the family tried to get back to normal as best they could. Reg spent more time on the farm and stayed out of the kitchen as much as possible. Nora busied herself baking and cooking, telling them all that life must go on.

One afternoon seemed to typify this. The rest of the family were all out or still at school when Tom came into the kitchen and found his mother sitting at the table pouring tea. She was straight-backed and stiff-shouldered as usual. Her mousy brown hair was drawn into a tight bun. She had a pinched face with a small, slightly upturned nose. The lines around her eyes and mouth seemed to pull together in a permanent scowl. She always wore a long-sleeved dress and kept a small lace-edged handker-chief tucked into one cuff. She seemed to have a permanent nasal problem and sniffed every minute or so, pulling out the scrap of white lace and dabbing her nose, as if to emphasise the fact that no doctor was able to cure her.

'So, Tom, how are you feeling now?' she asked, dabbing and sniffing.

'Better, thanks, Mother,' he lied. He felt worse now than he had immediately after Jane's death, having recently begun to suffer from nightmares filled with ghastly images of that terrible night.

'Good. I knew you would get over it in time, as we all must,' said Nora in a dismissive tone.

Tom told her he had homework to do and retreated to his bedroom. He was finding it hard to concentrate and knew his schoolwork was suffering, but his teachers had been very understanding so far. Pants had been his saviour, welcoming him every morning and seeming to sense his low mood.

The other blessing in Tom's life was his friend Sid. He was only a few months older but a lot taller than Tom. He was very broad for a teenager, with a mop of light-brown curly hair that always looked uncombed. As he told his exasperated mother, brushing it made no difference. Sid had a rather hooked nose and piercing blue eyes. He had an air of confidence about him that Tom had always admired. His friend would chat away to teachers and parents with a self-assurance that was sometimes viewed as cockiness. He was very good at maths and his parents wanted him eventually to go to university. Sid had other ideas as, with his mathematical skills, he had become fascinated by the study of the turf and gambling, something his father was less than keen to encourage. Sid had recently lost money on a horse at Worcester races, having persuaded a bookmaker to take his bet by saying he was over eighteen. The horse wandered in at the rear of the pack and thankfully this had cooled his interest in racing for the moment.

Tom and Sid were both the sons of farmers and were as close as brothers. The Parkes family lived in a small village called Pinvin, five miles from Stoulton, and had a good market-gardening business growing lettuce and fruit.

Tom walked across the fields to Stoulton station every morning to catch the train to the grammar school in Worcester. In the winter months he crossed wet ploughed fields and his boots were soaked through by the time he got to the station, never really drying out for the whole day. He'd ride in the same carriage as Sid, who had joined the train two stops earlier, and every morning was greeted with the words: 'All right, matey?'

For the first two years Tom sometimes reached the train sporting cuts and bruises or a black eye, as a result of fights on the way to the station. A group of local boys who had already left school thought any grammar-school boys easy prey. Tom learnt he either had to run fast or suffer a good kicking. But last year, when he had just turned thirteen, Tom had been persuaded by Sid to fight back and show the three hobbledyhoys who tormented him what he was really made of.

Sid came to stay with him the night before they went back to school for the start of the autumn term. They cut two staves from an ash tree on the farm and left for the train as usual. They each carried a small canvas bag containing some bread and cheese and set off together, walking through the orchard at the back of the house. It was about seven-thirty in the morning and already the sun was warm. Many of the fields had been cleared of wheat and only golden stubble remained. Skylarks were high above, invisible but singing, and droplets of dew on the hedgerows were clearing as the boys headed down the narrow track and across the fields to the back of the station.

As Tom and Sid approached, three boys stepped out from behind the tall hedge bordering the track. Tom had been feeling confident with Sid alongside him, but now that confidence melted away. If Sid and Tom had grown during the summer then these three boys looked as though they had been eating steak for every meal. The leader of the group was called Jimmy Finch. He stepped out boldly to block their path.

'Well, well, well. Two grammar-school boys for us to help to school today…what a treat,' he snarled sarcastically.

Sid stopped a few yards away from him, leaning on his stave with one hand gripping the top of it.

'Piss off, Jimmy,' he said in languid tones. Then, before Jimmy could reply, he flicked the stave up, hitting the bigger lad as hard as he could around the knees. The bully fell to the ground, and the second blow came down on his head. Blood began to pour into his eyes from a huge split over the front of his scalp. As Jimmy moaned, clutching his head in both hands, his two accomplices ran away.

Tom never had another problem going to school, and his and Sid's friendship became firmer than ever.

One afternoon they walked to the football pitch in the village and practised shooting, each taking a turn as goalkeeper for fifteen or twenty minutes.

'Right, time for a rest, I'm knackered!' Sid sat down and wiped his forehead with the hem of his shirt. 'I'm hopeless using my left foot, but Father says all the great players can kick just as well with either foot.'

'Yes, that bloke Alfie Burnet at school is just as good with both feet and they say the Aston Villa scouts are after him already. He's tiny, but last week against Bromsgrove he dribbled round half their team and scored,' agreed Tom.

'That's all very well, but he's thick as shit.'

'You'll be telling me he can't even play chess next,' said Tom, laughing.

'You're right, he can't.' Sid paused, looking at the stitching on the old football he had brought with him. 'How are things at home?'

'Bloody awful. Strangely, Mother seems to be the most cheerful one of all of us. It's really odd.'

'That's no surprise since it's her,' said Sid, pulling a face.

'I'm still feeling bad about Jane. I keep remembering how I changed that candle,' said Tom, pulling at a piece of grass so as not to have to meet his friend's eyes.

'Look, Tom. I know your mother's a cross to bear, but no one else blames you. Here, have one of these,' said Sid, holding out a small bag of sweets.

'What are they?' said Tom, popping one into his mouth and whirling it round with his tongue.

'Humbugs. My uncle Alec brought them over last week; he eats bags of them.'

Tom sat sucking hard for a while, making noises of approval and smacking his lips loudly.

'They're scrumptious. Can I have another?'

'Sure, help yourself,' said Sid, realising that his friend had a big smile on his face for the first time in weeks.

Sid visited Tom every few days over the next two or three weeks, taking him away from the atmosphere at home. Some days they played football or else went down to the brook and built dams using bits of scavenged wood and small rocks. On others they took their bicycles and explored the neighbouring villages. Another boy began to join them on their excursions. Alf Busk was fifteen, a little older than Tom but shorter, with very wiry fair hair. He had a large unruly cowlick and his hair shot out horizontally from the right side of his forehead. He was lean, muscular, and noticeably bow-legged, which caused him to walk with an unusual rocking gait. Alf had already left school and had started smoking and drinking, sometimes bringing stone jars of cider with him that he had 'borrowed' from his father's barrel. His teeth were quite yellow and stuck out at odd angles as though too many of them had been squashed into his mouth.

Alf had come to the farm with Sid, and Tom was already outside waiting for them.

'Hello, cocker, how are yer?' asked Alf, who had begun to call Tom that all the time now.

'Fine, thanks. What are we up to today then?'

Alf smiled and reached down the back of his trousers, pulling out two catapults. Tom took one and turned it round in his hand. It was home-made, two long pieces of rubber secured in a 'V' of wood and bound with string. The wood was freshly cut and had a shiny layer of bark, which appeared to have been polished by hand. The two lengths of rubber were attached at the other end to a small sling made of leather.

'I made this one specially for you, Tom. Sid doesn't need one as he prefers maths and chess, the daft bugger.'

'No, I don't,' protested Sid. 'These are good though, really powerful. We had a go with them on the way over.'

Alf led the way down to the brook where they found some small round pebbles. Tom fitted one into the catapult as Alf sat on the grass bank and lit a cigarette. He started coughing and laughing as Tom fired his first pebble into the air. It shot upwards, disappearing into a speck in the sky before dropping down behind some trees. 'That's bloody good,' said Tom, laughing. Sid kept busy meanwhile trying to find flat stones, to see whether he could skim them across the water.

Tom's arm ached after a while, so they sat down with Alf on the bank and drank some of his cider. It was pretty rough and made them cough, but as Alf said, his father would miss even tiny amounts of his whisky being stolen, but not his rough cider. Tom passed around his bag of humbugs, having found a sweet shop in Worcester that was able to satisfy his new craving.

'Thanks for coming round,' he said, filled with the warmth of the cider and flushing with embarrassment.

'Think nothing of it. We're glad to see you're feeling a bit more chipper, aren't we, Sid?'

'Yes, it's good to see Tom here with some colour back in his cheeks, although if we give him any more cider he'll look like a bloody clown!'

Alf took back the jar and drained the last of the cider before lighting up again. He offered the cigarette to Tom, who had never smoked before.

'Just take a deep breath in, cocker,' Alf instructed him.

Tom took the cigarette between his fingers and looked at the unlit end. A shred of tobacco hung out and he could see the faint line of moisture from Alf's lips. He took a deep drag and almost instantly began coughing furiously. Alf grabbed back the cigarette and thumped him on the back.

'That's bloody awful,' Tom gasped between coughs.

'I said, take a puff, not your last bloody breath,' said Alf, laughing.

Chapter 2

Manor Farm, Stoulton, July 1914

Reg Bomford filled up his pewter tankard with more cider from the wooden barrel in the pantry. He picked up the newspaper from the kitchen table and settled down in his high-backed wooden chair, taking a long, satisfying swig. He wiped his beard and slowly pulled on his wire-framed spectacles. He held the paper close to his nose and squinted through his glasses, ensuring that the evening sunshine caught the front page. Tom sat by the sideboard, polishing his black boots, while his mother fussed around the stove, putting potatoes on to boil and shelling some peas from the garden.

Since leaving school Tom had worked on the farm with his father and Hender. He had settled into the rhythm of country life, growing corn and rearing sheep and cattle according to the seasons. He had become even closer to his father and they had enjoyed many days' hunting together through the winter months. Tom had developed a good sideline for himself, buying young horses, which he then schooled, hunted and sold at the end of the season.

'I don't like the sound of this business in Europe, Tom. Since this Archduke fella has been shot in Serbia all hell has broken loose. Where in Hades is Serbia anyway?' His father paused and read on. 'Anyway, looks like Germany may try to pick a fight with France now.'

'Sid said the Austrians are stirring it up as well, and we might get dragged into it too,' said Tom, finishing off his boots with a duster and admiring the sheen.

'Well, if we do, I'm sure that as a Territorial reservist you will do your bit, lad.'

Tom was now twenty-three and had joined the Territorial Reserve some years before. He had come to enjoy the weekends away on exercises, and firing practice on the ranges. There had seemed little prospect of ever fighting in earnest. Most of the talk had been about the Boer War, campaign stories passed on by the regular soldiers who trained them. Tom had found these weekends a welcome change from his life on the farm. Although camping in Devon could be a miserable affair, at least it took him away from his mother whom he still chose to avoid whenever possible.

A sense of guilt over his sister's death had become deeply embedded within him. His sleep was still disturbed by images of flames and the memory of Jane with her hair ablaze. He would be down at the pub, having a pint and enjoying a joke, when without warning he would feel as if his stomach was being gripped by a steel claw. Sid now knew when this had occurred. He would see a look of anguish appear on his friend's face. Tom's smile would become rigid and fixed, and Sid would watch as his mate disappeared into the lavatory, waiting until the feeling passed or he had vomited up his beer and supper. He would then quietly rejoin the conversation but leave early with an excuse about being needed at home.

His mother avoided mentioning the subject directly, but instead would make pointed comments. One evening, for instance, she asked Hender to check that the candles were out downstairs as she went up to bed, saying in a loud whisper that was clearly audible to Tom that she'd best not ask him in view of his problem with them.

'The bloody cow! She keeps on doing that. When is she ever going to stop?' he said later to his brother when they were in the room they shared.

'I'm sorry, Tom, she's twisted. It's not your fault. Try to get some sleep.'

Hender had been working on their farm but also for other farmers in the area, helping with sheep-shearing and mending bits of machinery that had broken. He had always looked up to Tom, and these conversations were difficult for him. Hender felt just as helpless and frustrated by the situation as his brother did. Tom was grateful he understood, but Sid was the one person who properly appreciated the depth of the misery his friend continued to suffer.

He lay gazing at the ceiling, unable to sleep, certain that the only way to break the hold his mother had on him was to leave home. He thought about working on a farm somewhere else. In the autumn there were numerous places looking for men to help with cultivation and planting; Tom was sure to find work. It was just a matter of broaching the subject with his parents. But then he imagined going off to war instead, a cast-iron excuse to leave far behind his mother and the memories that haunted him.

August 1914

It was a warm late-summer evening. Sid had called for Tom and came into the house for a drink. Reg sat in his usual armchair with his tankard of cider beside him and asked them both to join him. The tall sash windows stood wide open, allowing the evening breeze into the room.

'Evening, Mr Bomford. How are you? Has the harvest gone well?' asked Sid.

'Yes, pretty well, thanks, Sid. The weather's been good and the yields have been fair. How's your father doing? He must be having a good summer for the fruit…all this sunny weather.'

Sid had never gone to university. After leaving school he had helped his father at home, expanding the business so as to grow a variety of fruit and vegetables in the spring and summer, leaving Sid with time to play football for Pershore during the winter months.

'Tell me, what news of those buggers across the Channel?' asked Reg.

'Last I heard, Germany had declared war on Russia. That was a couple of days ago now,' Sid commented.

'Yes,' said Tom, taking a long drink of cider, 'doesn't sound too good at all.'

'I told you, Tom, those Germans are like border Welshmen – they can't be trusted. D'you remember that Welsh chap down in Monmouth who tried to sell us a hunter last year? He told us it was only five and the moment I looked in its mouth it was obvious it was nearer ten years old. Still, we got a good deal in the end, didn't we?' said Reg, winking at his son.

'Yes, we did. What do you think will happen next then, Sid?' asked Tom.

'I'm not sure, mate, but I can't see Britain allowing Germany to trample over Europe. More importantly, Tom, did you hear about Emily Turner from Pershore? The girl you fancied at the Football Club dance last year? Well, she's got a bun in the oven and she's not sure who the father is. You were lucky there.'

Tom blushed before laughing along with his friend. Reg stopped them both with a disapproving look and a shake of his head. 'Not very good news for Emily's parents, though, is it?'

At eleven o'clock that night, 4 August 1914, Britain declared war on Germany.

Waking early the next morning and heading straight out, Reg Bomford was unaware of events unfolding across Europe. Tom had helped him feed the horses and check their water, and was sweeping the yard when Sid rode up on his bicycle, panting from his exertions.

'Morning, Tom. Morning, Mr Bomford. Have you heard the news?' he said. 'We've declared war on Germany.'

Tom looked at his father, who had taken off his cap and was scratching his head.

'I thought as much. Those bloody Germans, trying it on,' said

Reg, almost spitting with rage. 'You boys will join up, I hope. It's your chance to make men of yourselves.'

'Yes, 'course we will, Sid, won't we?' said Tom, jumping at the chance to leave home with his father's blessing. Away from his mother, away from the memories, at last.

'That we will, Mr Bomford. Men will be joining up all over the country. Me and Tom better head over to Worcester tomorrow, to the Territorials' headquarters.'

'Come by here tomorrow morning and we can cycle in together,' Tom said.

Sid touched his cap and swung his leg back over the saddle of his bike, ringing the bell as he cycled out of the yard. For the rest of the day Tom felt fidgety, trying to keep himself occupied by grooming the horses and sweeping up. He spent a good two hours in the tack-room, cleaning the saddles and bridles with saddle soap. He enjoyed the scent of leather and had always been fascinated by the huge variety of bits attached to the bridles, all with strange names such as snaffle, Pelham or Kimblewick. The bridles were gleaming by the time he finished and shut the door, heading back to the house for tea.

The following day Sid and Tom cycled to Worcester to go through the formalities of enlisting. As they were both in the Territorial Reserve it took no time to sign the papers and receive their orders. They were to report for duty in just four days' time.

Tom came home and found Hender in the garden, picking raspberries for supper.

'Howdit go, Tom?' he said, popping a raspberry in his mouth and peering at his brother through the misted glasses perched on the end of his nose. Hender's vision was so poor there was not a hope of his ever being allowed to join up.

'Very well. I'm now a soldier in the Queen's Own Worcestershire Hussars,' he said, saluting. 'Sid and Alf have joined up too.

We leave in four days to start our training. To be honest, I'm bloody relieved to be getting away. Not from you, mind, but I think I need a change.' He picked some raspberries and ate two before putting the rest in the basket. Then took one that was over-ripe and squashed it in Hender's ear.

'Thanks very much,' said his brother, smiling as he picked out the pips. 'This is a good thing for you, Tom. Father and I will be able to manage here, don't worry.'

'That's my only real concern,' he admitted with a frown.

'There's plenty of help nearby if we need it.'

The QOWH, also known as the Yeomanry, was a cavalry regiment that dated back to Napoleonic times. A large number of Tom's old school friends from the area had agreed to join up together.

Many of them had ridden since they were young. Tom knew that the riding involved in regimental life would pose no problem, for him at least. He had ridden ever since he could remember and won numerous prizes at local shows, moving from leading-rein classes in gymkhanas to showjumping as a teenager. He had hunted for some years, was a reasonable shot, and had fired a rifle on the ranges as a Territorial soldier.

The next two days were very busy for him. He helped with his usual jobs on the farm and instructed Hender on those he would have to take over, such as feeding the horses each day. His younger brother had spent much of his time during the summer months earning good money by travelling through Worcestershire and Herefordshire as far as the Welsh borders, shearing sheep. He cycled the shorter distances, and for longer journeys he and his bicycle hitched a lift between villages on lorries and horse-drawn wagons. Hender had endless stamina. In spite of his thick-lensed glasses misting over from the heat and humidity, he would stead-ily shear sheep all day, inflicting barely a nick on their thin skins.

Tom would miss his brother. He and Hender shared a love of

football, both playing for Pershore, the nearest town to their village. Tom had always been very protective towards Hender but the previous season had perhaps taken this too far.

Evesham Town were their greatest rivals and this particular match was set to be another hard-fought game. It was played at Pershore in a fine drizzle, which rendered Hender, playing at right back, almost completely blind in his glasses. Tom played at centre half and was set to mark Buller Nutting, an enormous centre forward who worked as a slaughterer in the local abattoir. The first half proceeded uneventfully with no one able to control the ball well in the wet conditions. But Buller Nutting had fouled Hender twice in the first half and Tom was becoming more and more angry.

As the second half began, Buller Nutting ran on to a loose ball, which was close to Hender. The whole team shouted 'Yours!' but poor Hender had no idea where the ball was. Nutting hurtled down the left wing, flicked the ball past Hender and deliberately shoulder-charged him. Hender was thrown backwards, his head hitting the turf and glasses flying into the air. Nutting ran on and scored, while Hender lay groaning on the pitch. Tom was livid. As Buller Nutting celebrated, Tom swung a huge punch which connected with Nutting's jaw and laid him out flat, only yards from where Hender knelt on all fours, groping round in the grass, trying to find his glasses. The referee ran over, waving his arms and trying to separate the teams as a riot broke out. Tom was sent off and the match abandoned.

He was issued with a two-shilling fine by the County Football Association, which he refused to pay. He thought it only proper that he had defended his brother and made a stand against a bully and a thug. As war was declared the case was still continuing, with Tom being threatened with a lifetime ban. He'd come a long way from the boy who'd regularly turned up to grammar school with cuts and bruises inflicted by bullies.

Tom went upstairs to get ready for the final family supper before he left in the morning. He opened the window in his bedroom before stripping off his shirt and trousers. His forearms and the V at the front of his neck were tanned but the rest of his body was pale, a classic farmer's tan. He wetted his comb and studied himself in the mirror as he swept back his dark hair, parting it on one side. He wondered how he would look with an army short back and sides. He remembered Emily Turner saying at the Football Club dance what lovely hair he had, and that with his brown eyes he looked quite cheeky. He wondered what army training would involve, and whether he could actually kill a man if called upon to do so. Still, he knew that he was taking the right course in leaving home, while also doing his duty towards his country.

Hender came in then, knocking over the chair standing at the end of his bed.

'Damn it, I always does that,' he said, righting it. He had picked up some local quirks of speech from the Herefordshire farmers he worked for, which infuriated his mother.

'All set for supper then?' he asked. 'Mother isn't taking it very well, you know, Tom. She's been crying all day.'

'I noticed; she couldn't look at me when I came in, but there's no going back for me now. She'll just have to get used to it. Mind you, she'd be *really* worried if darling Ray decided to join up, wouldn't she?'

Hender laughed as they both knew their younger brother Ray was their mother's favourite. He was only thirteen but seemed totally unlike his elder brothers. He disliked football and much preferred growing vegetables and dead-heading roses with his mother.

As they came out of their room, their sisters Birdie and Phyllis appeared on the landing. Phyllis was seventeen, six years younger than Tom. She was pretty and petite, her brown hair tied back with a ribbon. She linked her arm through Tom's as they walked down the stairs together and into the kitchen. Birdie had fairer hair and a pair of striking green eyes in a round face. Now twenty-five, she had trained as a secretary. Tonight she was wearing a fetching green floral dress and heeled shoes, making her almost as tall as Tom.

Their sister Mary was standing over the sink washing pans. She was nearly twenty and still unmarried. Like Hender she had very poor eyesight, and like their mother an almost permanent frown. She wore very dark-rimmed round glasses, a brown dress stretching down to her ankles, and a pale-grey pinafore. Out of earshot she was usually referred to as 'poor Mary'.

Phyllis and Mary served the joint of ham as they all sat around the table. Reg was at the head of it, a glass of whisky in front of him. Birdie was next to him, then Tom and Hender, Mary, Phyllis and Ray sat on the other side, and Nora at the bottom of the table. There was home-made bread and pickles, and a jug of cider for Tom and Hender. Nora said grace and they all began to eat.

They chatted about the village and a dance that was being held in Pershore Town Hall in two weeks' time. Birdie teased Hender that there was a girl who worked in the grocer's who was hoping for a dance with him. He blushed and began polishing his glasses at a furious rate.

'Do you remember last year's dance, when Tom met that girl from London?' said Birdie.

He laughed and nodded his head. 'She was lively! Her mother was Indian and she was staying with her uncle locally. Her father had been stationed out in India with the army.'

'You didn't stop dancing with her for about an hour, it was *so* embarrassing,' said Birdie.

'She told me I needed more dancing lessons and that she'd arrange some if ever I went down to London.' Tom winked at Hender, who snorted in disbelief. 'But I seem to remember that you, Birdie, had your card full that whole evening. The men were queuing up to dance with you.' He remembered how lovely she had looked in a new dress, and how proud he'd been of his elder sister that night.

'I did enjoy that evening, we all seemed to have a wonderful time. Do you remember Phyllis dancing with Billy Trigg's son? And how he fell over and pulled the vicar down on top of him!'

'Alfie Trigg had been on the cider, and of course the vicar was furious. I thought he was going to hit Alfie, but thankfully he stuck to very strong language instead,' said Phyllis.

'I shall miss those evenings,' said Tom wistfully.

'I spoke to Bill Coggins last week and he reminded me about you and Hender playing some trick on him,' Birdie said.

Tom and Hender both started laughing.

'What's this all about, Tom?' Reg asked, sounding intrigued.

'We were quite small but you used to take us down to Pershore for "meetings", as you called them, although they usually seemed to be in the Miller's Arms.' Reg smiled guiltily and glanced at his wife, who for once smiled with him. 'Hender and I got bored with waiting, so one night we took down some black cotton thread and went round the corner to Bill's house and tied it to the door knocker. We hid in an area just below the front door, and then pulled on the thread. Bill came to the door and opened it. "That's queer, I'm sure someone was knocking," he said. We carried on doing this three or four times more and he started to get pretty annoyed, shouting that if there were ghosts bothering him, they should bugger off. We thought we'd better leave then, we were laughing so much, and Hender was about to wet himself.'

Hender had tears of mirth rolling down his face now and was wiping his eyes with his handkerchief as he said, 'I think he saw us running off because after that he used to make jokes about ghosts and front doors whenever I saw him.'

''Course he knew it was you. He told me he recognised Father's pony and trap – that pony was trained to stand outside the pub for hours without moving,' said Birdie.

'Very good place for doing business though,' said their father, standing on his dignity.

After the plates had been removed Reg stood up and cleared his throat. He stroked his beard, coughed theatrically and addressed them in a broad Herefordshire accent. Tom knew the signs. It was plain to him his father had drunk a little too much whisky tonight.

'In the morning Tom'sh off with the Yeomanry. We'll all pray for his shafe return and I'm hoping it won't be too long before he's back with ush. The Germans won't last long, the buggersh, not againsht the likes of ush,' he said, shaking his fist. Nora looked on disapprovingly as he continued.

'Tom, your mother and I would like to give you a present to take with you.'

He passed over a parcel wrapped in brown paper. Tom opened it and found inside a small leather-bound book, which fitted comfortably into the palm of his hand. On the front, written in gold leaf, were the words New Testament Bible. On the inside, in distinctive handwriting, was the inscription:

Tom Bomford
Stoulton
Worcester
With Father's and Mother's love and prayers for a safe return

Tom thumbed through the finely printed pages, which were interspersed by colour plates of biblical scenes. He looked at his father and mother, who both had tears in their eyes. That the book was given by both of them, with love, meant more to him than anything.

'Thank you, it's beautiful,' he said softly.

They sat and chatted for a while longer. Eventually his parents and Mary left for bed. Ray pleaded to stay up a little longer, and as usual their mother agreed to his request. He sat on Tom's lap at one end of the table while they all finished the cider.

Afterwards Tom wandered outside to spend some time alone. The night was still warm and he could hear a horse snorting in the paddock near the house. The moon was a reddish-brown colour and for a moment he felt uneasy about leaving home. He dismissed this and convinced himself he had made the right decision by joining up.

Tom felt a little drunk but contented as he climbed the stairs to bed. The floorboards creaked in the usual places as he tottered down the landing and with the cider inside him, he knew he would not need a blanket. As Tom slid under the sheet, Hender was already asleep, snoring quietly. Although he would miss his family, Tom hoped his spell in the army would shift his life in a new direction and provide him with a release from the past. He heard an owl hoot nearby before sleep claimed him.

Chapter 3

Tom woke early and lay in bed listening to the birdsong coming from the orchard at the back of the house. His mouth felt dry from the cider the previous night. Hender snored lightly beside him.

Tom got quietly out of bed and packed his battered brown case, carefully placing the new Bible on top of his clothes. He went down to breakfast and sat with the rest of the family, listening to them loudly crunching toast. After breakfast Sid arrived at the farm with his father, who was going to drive them both to Pershore station. All the family stood waiting to say their goodbyes, with Tom's brothers and sisters hugging him through their tears.

He said his farewells to his parents then, receiving a long hug from his father and a quick peck on the cheek from his mother, and then with a last wave through the car window they were gone, through the gate and away to the station.

'Well, Tom, this is it!' Sid yelled over the noise of the car's engine. It was obvious he could hardly contain his excitement, as he slapped his friend on the back and ruffled his hair. Tom felt there was no one he would rather be joining up with than Sid.

They boarded the train at Pershore along with many other recruits all heading to Worcester to form 'D' Squadron of the Worcestershire Yeomanry. The train was packed, with the men all trying to look out of a window to wave a last goodbye to their families. There was a whistle from the engine and in a cloud of steam the train set off. Three children ran alongside, waving and shouting, until they reached the end of the platform where they came to an abrupt stop. The train rumbled on through the countryside, with men in the fields shouting and waving at them, and Tom sensed the huge amount of goodwill that the whole country felt towards those who were enlisting early. He settled back to join in the nervous chat and affected bravado of the young men he was travelling with.

They stepped off the train at Worcester and Tom immediately recognised more familiar faces. He thought one of the men might have been Jimmy Finch, who had confronted them on the way to school all those years before. Alf Busk, as ever with a cigarette tucked in one corner of his mouth, greeted Tom with a slap on the back.

Alf had been working for a small business selling farm machinery. He had good contacts in the area and had been surprisingly successful as a salesman.

'Hello, cocker, how are yer? Ready for some army food? I have come prepared,' he said, pulling a bottle of whisky from his knapsack.

Dick Edwards was another old friend from Pershore where his father owned a men's outfitter's on the High Street. He was tall and slim with fair hair and a long narrow face, and had a passion for fishing. He had often called on Tom on a Thursday after school with two rods, and they would cycle down to the River Avon to fish together. Tom would sit on the bank, chatting away and never catching much, while Dick would land perch and on one occasion a large pike. He'd worked for a time in a department store in London before returning to work in his father's shop. He was always smartly dressed, and today was wearing a tweed sports jacket.

'Bloody hell, Dick,' said Alf, 'we're not off to a garden party, you know.'

'I know, but that doesn't mean I've got to look like a tramp either,' Dick said, holding Alf's lapel between finger and thumb, and frowning in disapproval. It was stained with food and had bits of ash stuck to it from Alf's ever-present drooping cigarette.

They were then asked to form up in small groups and march to the barracks in the middle of Worcester. The marching, or rather the lack of it, was the first sign of how much they had to learn.

The next week left them all too busy to think. They had to grow accustomed to officers barking orders, their new haircuts, the issuing of uniforms and their introduction to army rations, which Tom found surprisingly palatable and somewhat better than those he had tasted with the Territorials. Their uniform was traditional khaki with a short jacket plus breeches worn with leather boots covering the ankle and webbing above. Spurs were standard attire, and they were issued with a Lee Enfield rifle and leather holster that was designed to be strapped behind their saddles. They slept in some wooden barns with straw scattered on the floor and the farmer who owned them kept appearing to warn the new recruits not to smoke, which irritated Alf enormously.

After a week, they were ordered to transfer to Newbury by rail. Having arrived at the station it was obvious that the three carriages were far too small to take such a large number of men, so carts were requisitioned to assist with the transport. Sid, Tom and three other soldiers rode on a horse-drawn milk float, which took most of the day. The milkman was muttering the whole way about loss of earnings, the milk going off and how tired his horse would be, while the men in the back smoked, sang and watched the countryside pass by as the remains of the harvest were being brought in.

During the day soldiers arrived in small groups at, where a huge tented area had sprung up near the barracks. The Worcestershire Yeomanry joined up with the Yeomanry from Gloucestershire and Warwickshire, and there were many faces that Tom recognised from the hunting field. His first night there was spent in wooden barracks with most of the windows broken but Alf found some spare blankets to put over the gaps, which kept out the fine drizzle that had started to fall.

Tom slept fitfully and dreamt of riding on the farm with his father, jumping the big hedges in the fields at the back of the house. He was already awake when the morning call sounded. He put on his uniform and stepped outside for the first parade of the day. After a breakfast of porridge and tea they were ordered out to the long lines where the horses were tied up.

There were at least eighty of them lined up, tethered to a post by a rope in front of them with a small rope set at right angles to separate each horse from the next. Most of the grass near the horses had been grazed flat. Tied near their heads were small nets of hay that some were chomping on. Others dozed in the weak sunshine, often with one leg cocked. Tom smelt the familiar mixture of dung, hay and the salty odour of horsehair.

He at least felt more at home here. The huge numbers of soldiers, noise, barking of orders and general disorder of army life had unsettled him. Many of the new recruits had never ridden, and others not for years, but they were told the training would make cavalrymen of them all. The men marched down the line and were ordered in turn to stop behind a horse. Not every soldier had a mount, but Sergeant Vint began barking orders for them all to groom the horses and then to saddle them up. Vint was a little older than the lower ranks and had joined the army nine months before war broke out. He was stocky with huge shoulders and very dark in complexion, looking almost Italian with his olive skin and brown eyes.

One well-worn brush lay beneath each horse's hay net, along with a bridle and saddle that had seen better days. Many men had no idea what to do so Tom and Sid moved down the line, showing them how to fit a bridle and to tighten up the girth of a saddle properly – do up the girth and then, as the horse thought you had finished, a gentle knee in the ribs usually allowed you to tighten it one or two holes more, which at least prevented the embarrassment of falling off the moment you tried to mount. Eventually, after a long delay, the horses were made ready.

Captain Smith Maxwell rode down in front of the line and ordered them all to mount up and ride round in a large circle. Smith Maxwell looked young but had managed to produce a small moustache. He was quite thin, with reddish-brown hair. His accent gave away his public school background and he had a slight stammer. Tom could immediately tell that the officer was an accomplished rider. As they circled, one or two horses bucked, getting rid of their riders. Smith Maxwell yelled, 'Hang on to their reins!' so none got loose.

At the walk, most of the men looked passably competent, but once they started trotting it was soon obvious who had ridden before. Twenty or thirty riders were bouncing uncontrollably with pained expressions on their faces. Most of them were trying to hang on to the front of the saddle, which only worsened the pain. The Captain separated out those who had ridden before.

'You! Wh-what's your n-name?' he asked Tom.

'Bomford, sir.'

'Right, t-take that lot over there and t-try to t-teach them some b-basics. In three months they need to know h-how to gallop straight and mount a c-c-cavalry charge.'

The Captain wheeled his horse around and left Tom in front of twenty men, all looking to him pleadingly for relief from the pain they were feeling.

They stopped during the day for some bread and cheese and to water the horses. Then Smith Maxwell circled around, continuing to bark orders: 'Come on, g-grip with your legs! Gentle on the h-horse's mouth…c-cavalry? This is a bloody joke.'

Tom tried to help as best he could but the combination of many young horses with novice riders made progress impossibly slow. The older horses could sense an inexperienced rider and would plant themselves, refusing to move, leaving the rider sitting motionless shaking his reins and pleading with his mount to walk. Smith Maxwell would inevitably be drawn to the noise of laughter from the other soldiers and would appear in a cloud of dust.

'Bomford, ch-change horses!' came the order, and Tom would swap his horse for the recalcitrant one, dig his heels into the new mount's side and use the reins to slap its neck until the horse moved forward with a look of blameless innocence. There were usually telltale flecks of green in its mouth from the illicit mouthfuls of grass it had managed to grab while the inexperienced rider was powerless to stop it.

The training went on, day after day, with men developing appalling blisters on their hands and legs. One man fractured a wrist falling off, and another was so hopeless he had been transferred to an infantry regiment after Smith Maxwell lost his temper with him yet again.

Five days after their arrival Tom and Sid lay in their tent one evening talking over the events of the day. It was nearly ten-thirty. Tom had just read a short passage from his Bible and blown out their candle when the shouting began. They hurriedly pulled on their trousers and ducked out of the tent. There was some light from the moon, which lit a scene of complete chaos. Two horses galloped past them, joined by a length of rope with two stakes dragging behind. Loose mounts were everywhere and men were running around trying to catch them. Smith Maxwell appeared in trousers but no shirt, his red braces glowing in the moonlight.

'It's a st-stampede, B-Bomford. Absolute disaster! T-try and c-catch as many as you can and f-form a new line. J-just tie them to any st-stakes or rope you can f-find,' he yelled.

Tom and Sid made their way from the tents to the picket line.

A few pieces of rope and an occasional broken piece of wood, with head collars lying on the ground, were the only evidence of where an hour before nearly two hundred horses had been tied up. They gathered some rope and head collars and headed out into the night.

It took the men two days to round up their horses. To the amazement of the locals, at least forty had galloped down Newbury High Street. Some were found grazing on the racecourse and Tom and his fellow soldiers were ferried there with saddles and bridles to ride them back. They usually rode one horse and led two with a leading rein in each hand. Amazingly all but ten were rounded up and returned to their lines.

The morning after the stampede Smith Maxwell called Sergeant Vint into his tent.

'H-how the hell did those horses st-stampede, Vint? I w-want to know why the sentries d-didn't stop it happening,' he shouted.

Vint looked straight ahead without blinking. 'Yes, sir. I will conduct an investigation, sir,' he replied.

'You'd b-better, Vint, you b-bloody idiot. N-now get out and f-find me some answers.'

Vint saluted and turned on his heel to march out of the tent. He had not enjoyed the grilling and was in fact deeply uncomfortable around horses. He had joined an infantry regiment, but as a regular soldier with some limited experience had been transferred to the Worcestershire Yeomanry to help them train their men. He had only sat on a horse for the first time three months before, and was painfully aware that a number of the recruits under his command had ridden all their lives. He felt it undermined his command.

He called his company together in front of their tents. Vint had beads of sweat visible on his brow and was frowning darkly.

'The Captain is pretty furious with this bloody mess and wants to know how it happened. Who was on duty last night?'

'I was, sir,' replied Alf Busk.

'Busk! I might have known it. Too busy having a smoke, I suppose,' screamed Vint, by now purple in the face and pacing up and down in front of them.

'No, sir. A dog came down the far end of the line and started barking very close to the horses. Once one was spooked it just set them off. There was nothing any of us could do, sir.'

Sergeant Vint muttered under his breath but thought this story about a stray dog might at least be some sort of answer for Smith Maxwell.

The Captain ordered more patrols at night and greater separation of the lines, to ensure there was no repetition of the shameful incident. Tom avoided Vint whenever possible but one particular event was especially difficult.

Vint had ordered an inspection one morning of uniforms, tents and bedding to ensure all was 'shipshape' as he put it. Soon after dawn they had lined up outside their tents with everything laid out in front of them. Vint marched up and down, finding fault wherever possible in the row just in front of Tom and Sid. Tom was already beginning to feel anxious and had rechecked his kit two or three times. Eventually Vint paused in front of Tom, who held his breath.

'Ah, Farmer Bomford. This should be interesting.'

He picked up Tom's bedding and stepped inside the tent, poking around in there before coming out again holding up Tom's blanket. To his horror there was a huge wet stain in the middle of it. Vint was smiling and Tom felt the dread of imminent humiliation.

'Bomford,' he said slowly, relishing the moment, 'I see you have had a little accident during the night.'

He held the blanket up, showing the assembled men, who were laughing, just as Tom feared. 'It seems poor Bomford is missing home, but as his kit has failed the inspection,' Vint paused, ready to deliver his sentence, 'he will stand on sentry duty all night tonight.'

Tom was boiling with anger. He had been set up completely but knew there was nothing he could do. Vint had thrown water on his blanket when he was in the tent, which only showed how low the man would stoop to humiliate him. Sid picked up the blanket and ducked back into the tent.

'Don't let him get to you; we've been through this before. Just try and rise above it.'

'The bastard! I was this close to hitting him,' said Tom, seething.

'Tom, I know you are good with those fists of yours but that would mean a court martial. Give it time. He'll switch to bullying someone else, you'll see.'

The following morning, after completing the usual sentry duty and his punishment, Tom collapsed on to his bed and took out his New Testament Bible. He had hardly glanced at it in the last few weeks and felt a pang of guilt. He opened the pages and began to read. He slowly began to feel less anxious and flicked back to the front page again to read the words his parents had written. He pictured them both, the farm and the rest of his family. He had only written to them once and determined to write again the following day to tell them how he was getting on. He closed his eyes and began to recite the Lord's Prayer in a half whisper. For the first time in his life he prayed with absolute conviction, asking God to protect him and his family and friends.

The heat of the summer continued throughout August as their training went on six days a week. Sunday was a rest period when the horses at least could recover a little. For Tom, Sid, Alf and Dick, each day was similar. They were woken at six-thirty and went to feed the horses with hay and half a bucket of oats, and to check their water. Then they walked to the mess tent where they had breakfast consisting of fresh bread and occasionally bacon and eggs. By nine o'clock they were mounted in ranks for training. Both Captain Smith Maxwell and his superior Colonel Jeavons were obsessed with drill and being able to fight as a cavalry unit. They wanted perfect lines at walk, trot and canter, and the ability to wheel and charge at speed.

At one o'clock sharp they would break for lunch for an hour and then start their training again, usually finishing with a full charge at the gallop across the showground. The horses by this time were sweating profusely and, at about four o'clock, returned to their lines, where they were washed down and fed again. The men were then free to wander back to the mess tent for some supper.

At the end of August the brigade was called together by Colonel Jeavons. He told them that Lieutenant Colonel the Earl of Dudley was due to inspect them the following week and Jeavons wanted them as smart as possible. The Colonel had been in the army for years and had risen through the ranks slowly, in stark contrast to his whisky drinking which was rather faster. He had a large bulbous nose tinged with purple and his cheeks were deep red with numerous broken veins. He had short black hair, greying near his sideburns, with a centre parting, and a thick bushy moustache.

'I want uniforms cleaned, metalwork polished and tack gleaming. Lord Dudley will not tolerate sloppy second-rate soldiers. He wants to see a proper cavalry brigade.' The rumour among the men was that Jeavons was still desperate to resurrect his army career, and thought commanding the Yeomanry a retrograde step.

The Earl of Dudley was an unusual man. He had taken over the regiment from Sir Henry Grey in November 1913 and for some time, contrary to popular opinion, had been convinced that a European war was approaching. He had gained first-hand knowledge of warfare from the Egyptian campaigns where he'd fought as a cavalry officer.

Before the outbreak of hostilities in Europe he recognised that the Worcestershire Yeomanry had many deficiencies as a cavalry regiment so set up a number of military schools, recruiting instructors from the ranks of the regular cavalry and building training grounds. The main school was at Dudley and he bought twenty special training horses for this, dramatically raising the standards of the regiment's horsemanship. He was very committed to it and popular with all its officers.

The following week the men paraded as Lord Dudley arrived in his open-topped Rolls-Royce. A small platform had been built and he mounted it briskly, conveying a sense of urgency and energy. He saluted the other officers and turned to face the men. He brushed his large moustache with a bent forefinger and adjusted his peaked cap. He wore full dress uniform, had a long cavalry sword swinging from his hip and wore beautifully polished boots. Colonel Jeavons and the other officers stood behind him on the platform.

Lord Dudley coughed loudly and began to address them all.

'Good morning, officers and men. It's good to see a few familiar faces. The Colonel tells me your training is going very well.' His voice boomed out across the ranks and Tom was amazed by how easily they could all hear him.

'I can assure you I take no pleasure in having my worst fear of a war in Europe being realised, but I am sure that with the type of men the British Army has, this war will be won quickly and decisively. I have no doubt that the cavalry will play an integral part in this victory and so it is with great pleasure that I am presenting each of you today with a new cavalry thrusting sword.' The last three words were delivered with great pride.

There was a huge cheer from the men and Dudley smiled. He held up his hand for quiet.

Tom turned to Sid and whispered, 'I was running short of blades for shaving, this sword should save me a few bob.'

Dudley gave them his valediction. 'I wish you good luck, and may God bless you all.'

Colonel Jeavons stepped forward, his voice almost muffled in contrast to Lord Dudley's parade-ground tones.

'Three cheers for the Earl of Dudley!'

Three hip-hip-hoorays boomed out across the parade ground. Lines then formed as the men stepped forward to receive their swords, one by one. Tom, Sid, Alf and Dick stood and saluted before strapping on their belts. The swords felt remarkably heavy and they were immediately given strict instructions by Sergeant Vint never to draw the weapon unless commanded to do so.

After the presentation, Lord Dudley saluted the regiment and stepped down from the platform. His chauffeur held open a door to the Rolls and he slid into the passenger seat. The engine rumbled and the car glided away across the burnt grass of the parade ground, eventually obscured by a cloud of rising dust.

Tom had enjoyed his training, largely because he was spending so much time with horses and his three good friends. He had become very attached to his mount, a bay mare called Bessie who was always pleased to see him. He had not missed home. Although he had wondered how his father was coping without him on the farm, he had felt less guilt-ridden than in the recent past. He had laughed more in the last few months than he had for years. The sole concern he had was the simmering anger directed towards him by Sergeant Vint, who seemed deeply to resent not only Tom's riding skills but also his success in teaching the other men. Tom had a feeling that his superior's irritation was building to a dangerous degree. They paraded every morning and Vint always took issue with some detail of Tom's uniform.

One morning he stopped in front of Tom, who gazed ahead into the distance, feeling sweat forming around the rim of his cap, his mouth drying. He had a strong sense that this time Vint was in an even more aggressive mood than usual.

'Ah, Bomford, the man who thinks he's a better rider than anyone else.'

'He is!' a voice shouted from a few rows back.

'Silence in the ranks! Another word and the whole bloody lot of you'll be in front of the Major. Bomford, you look a mess,' Vint sneered, as he kicked some dust over Tom's boots.

'Yes, sir,' shouted Tom, still standing rigidly to attention.

'You're always scruffy and this is not what the army expects, Bomford. D'you hear me?' he bellowed straight into Tom's ear. He felt a spray of spittle hitting his cheek and half turned away, partly to avoid Vint's foul breath.

'Don't you turn away from me, Bomford,' bawled the Sergeant, his face now contorted with fury. 'You will run round the ground with a full pack and rifle directly after parade.'

'Yes, sir.'

Tom knew there was nothing he could do except comply and get through the punishment as quickly as possible. It was similar to being bullied at school and he felt the same helplessness, although in this instance he had the full support of his friends. After parade he reported to Vint, who had a smug expression on his face.

'Right, Bomford, you piece of shit! Get running until I tell you to stop.'

Tom set off at a steady jog, holding his rifle in front of him. It was very warm. Thankfully Sid had encouraged him to drink plenty of water beforehand, as within minutes sweat was running down Tom's face and stinging his eyes. He had never found running easy, and with a full pack on his back he soon began to feel very breathless. The stiff khaki uniform was already causing soreness between his legs. After one lap, Vint was standing with hands on hips ready to meet him.

'No slacking, Bomford, keep going,' he chuckled, lighting a cigarette and enjoying every moment. On the far side of the parade ground Tom ran behind a small hedge, which shielded him from view, and dropped to a walk, struggling to get his breath back.

'Bloody hell, cocker, you look buggered,' said Alf, holding out a water bottle. Tom stopped, gasping, and took a long drink.

'Thanks, Alf, I'm hoping this is the last lap.'

He staggered round to Vint, who stopped him and stood enjoying his moment of supremacy. Tom bent over, hands on knees, gasping for air.

'Bomford, don't you ever give me your stuck-up look again or I will break you. D'you understand?'

'Yes, sir,' Tom said, standing to attention as sweat dripped off his chin and on to his jacket, which was already soaked through. Vint turned on his heel and marched off, leaving Tom to collapse on the ground and recover. Sid walked over with more water for him.

'He's a bitter, angry bastard. Don't let him get to you, matey.'

Tom was too tired to respond but as ever Sid was there to support him. Tom was embarrassed to admit how much that meant to him.

As October arrived, the trees turned from green to golden-brown and the early mornings became colder. Training continued with increasing monotony as drills were repeated over and over, and Sergeant Vint grudgingly admitted to Sid that they were starting, but only starting, to look like proper cavalry.

In mid-November the first frost came and the flimsy canvas tents provided very little warmth or cover. More blankets were issued but it was so cold that on many nights sleep was virtually impossible. Tom, Sid, Alf and Dick were huddled in one tent. It was two in the morning and below freezing outside. Wrapped in blankets, they sat crowded round a small hurricane lamp, which provided very little heat. Alf sucked on a half-smoked cigarette that had gone out some time before.

'Smith Maxwell says they're getting some news from France. It's settling into trench warfare there,' said Tom.

'So much for "it'll all be over by Christmas",' said Alf grimly.

'Well, if they called it off now and told us all to go home, I'd be happy,' said Dick.

'What about some action since we've come this far? I wouldn't mind going over to France, at least to see what's happening,' said Sid.

Tom shook his head. 'I don't think it will be much fun and cavalry would be useless in trench warfare, according to Smith Maxwell.'

'Well, at least I've learnt to ride a bit better,' said Dick, adjusting a rather elegant woollen scarf he had tied around his neck.

'Nearly riding as well as me now,' said Alf encouragingly.

'You have improved, Dick. You were a bloody joke when you first got on though,' said Sid.

'I think we'll have Alf out hunting with us next season. You might have a chance of jumping Bow Brook this time,' said Tom, joking with him.

'Sod off, cocker,' laughed Alf.

Alf Busk had come out hunting with Sid and Tom once before when he was seventeen and the Croome Hunt were meeting just outside Pershore. What Alf lacked in style he made up for in daring, and he was prepared to jump anything. The hounds had found a fox after about an hour and ran towards Stoulton. They had jumped four or five big hedges, which Alf had managed to scramble over, when they galloped down towards Bow Brook. There had been a lot of rain so the water level was high. In summer it was very easy to wade across the brook when it was six or eight feet wide and quite shallow, but now it was in full spate.

Tom yelled back to Sid and Alf that if they kicked on they would clear the obstacle easily. The hounds were already over and the huntsman in his pink coat could be seen cantering up the bank away from the brook, blowing his horn. Tom and Sid met the jump on a perfect stride and landed safely with their horses' back legs just on the bank in shallow water.

Alf's horse stood off much too far and landed only two-thirds of the way across, in a huge explosion of water. Alf disappeared and emerged five or six yards downstream, gasping for air and clutching his hunting cap in one hand. Tom and Sid had pulled up their horses and were holding their sides laughing. Alf scrambled up the bank and lay on his back with his legs in the air to allow all the water to drain out of his boots. His horse had scrambled out meanwhile and was shaking its head to clear water from its ears. Alf squeezed some from his coat sleeves and got hold of the reins, jumping back on and yelling, 'I'm all right, lads, let's just kick on again,' and then he'd cantered up the bank, his boots squeaking on the sides of the wet saddle.

Remembering it in the light of the hurricane lamp now, Alf said, 'It was a great day, Tom.'

'I'll never forget the look on your face when you realised the horse was not going to clear that brook,' he laughed.

They stayed up talking and laughing until they felt tired enough to try and sleep for a few hours before dawn.

The following morning on parade they were told that the regiment was being moved to an undisclosed destination to complete their training. Four days later they rode to Newbury station and loaded horses and equipment on to the train for their mystery journey. There was a long line of wagons with ramps in front, and officers shouting at men and horses. Tom's mount Bessie, although a little reluctant at first, loaded easily, and he went back down the line to help load Sid's, who had planted and refused to move. He reared and kicked out but eventually, after Sid had fallen into a large pile of droppings, was loaded and tied up. The men were packed into carriages with next to no seats and then, with a whistle, the engine slowly pulled out of the station.

There was much speculation that this might be the final preparation for a move to France but after many hours of travel the train came to a stop. The wagons groaned and clanked as the engine hooted. Tom looked out of the small window set high up in the carriage's wooden door. A grey dawn with a thin mist clinging to the ground surrounded them as the doors were opened and the horses led down the steep ramps. The men were puzzled to read the sign painted on the side of the platform which read 'Welcome to Sheringham'.

'Where the hell are we?' asked Alf, rubbing his sticking-up hair.

'I think Sheringham is in Norfolk,' said Dick. 'We came near here for a family holiday once when I was about eleven. My sister almost drowned when the tide came in; it was so fast we had to run to escape it.'

'Run from a tide? You're having us on,' said Tom.

'No, it's true. Good job we're on horses, I reckon.'

Colonel Jeavons called them together to address them.

'Now, men, you may wonder why we have come halfway across England to Sheringham in Norfolk, which is even further from France than Newbury.' There was a low rumbling from the ranks indicating they were indeed somewhat surprised.

'Army headquarters has good information that Germany is considering invading England, and Norfolk is a likely site for this. Some heavy artillery will be arriving here in the next few days and we have been ordered to patrol this area, ensuring that anywhere that German troops land they will be met with stiff resistance.'

Tom and Sid roared their defiance with the others, although they were not entirely sure how they would manage to repel any invaders.

'You will start patrols this evening and continue your training here over the next month until we receive further orders.' Jeavons turned back towards his staff car.

Sergeant Vint then ordered his section to mount up ready for their first patrol in the Norfolk countryside. Tom walked back to Bessie, who was tied up to one of the wagons of the train. He had become very attached to her over the last few months. She was now standing with her near foreleg raised slightly off the ground, he saw. He untied her and walked her up and down, which revealed what he feared. She was obviously lame. The vet was called and confirmed that she was unfit for duty and would need some weeks off, so Tom would be assigned a new mount the next day. He was sure the injury was caused by a knock received on the long train journey.

That night he went to his quarters feeling very low. He had become accustomed to Newbury, and the change to new barracks near King's Lynn was unsettling. The threat of a move to France hardly helped matters. Sergeant Vint still continually belittled him at the slightest opportunity and it had started to get to Tom. Now the horse that he had done all his training on to date was lame, and he had no idea what Bessie's replacement would be like. For the first time he was missing home.

Chapter 4

Ivy Lodge, Stourbridge, December 1914

Eddie Williams awoke with a surge of excitement. It was Christmas Day 1914. Even though he was fifteen years old and had long ago abandoned any belief in Father Christmas, he still looked forward to this special day of the year and the excitement that always filled the house. He lay in his warm bed, the heavy blankets pressing down on him. Faint grey light began to fill the room, filtering through the heavy green curtains. The walls were painted the colour of cream, with a picture rail in dark brown. A picture of a Scottish loch hung over his bed, and a small table and cane chair stood in one corner. He heard the clock downstairs chime eight o'clock and his sisters Daisy and Dolly giggling in the next room. Eddie's third sister Marjorie, known as Madge, whom he adored, had the bedroom on the other side of theirs, which overlooked the garden. Daisy and Dolly were very close in age and had always had an intuitive understanding of each other.

There was a faint knock on the door and his younger brother Dick was suddenly bouncing on the bed, clutching a bulging Christmas stocking to his chest. Eddie jumped out of bed to pull on his thick dressing gown. Flattening his blond hair with his hands, he turned back to the excited child.

'Eddie, Eddie, I think there's a proper cricket ball in here!' said Dick breathlessly.

Eddie had a feel and nodded slowly. 'I think you're right. It'll make a change from those manky old tennis balls.'

Dick, like Eddie, was cricket mad and the boys spent many

hours in the garden, taking turns to bat and bowl. Eddie was a very good footballer and had already been spotted by an Aston Villa scout. This caused huge problems within the family as older sister Daisy was a fanatical West Bromwich Albion fan, and as their house was in Stourbridge they had already been to watch the team four or five times at their ground, The Hawthorns.

The siblings all trooped downstairs to open their stockings by the Christmas tree. Their mother Marian was already up and dressed. She held out her arms to her children.

'Happy Christmas, my darling boys and girls,' she said as she hugged each of them in turn. Marian had a trim figure, and a head of curly brown hair tied back into a loose bun. She wore a pin-tucked blouse and blue cardigan over an ankle-length serge skirt, and as ever managed to look stylish. Although not tall, she towered over her husband, Harry French Williams, who was only five foot three inches. His hair was already grey and he had a large moustache that was turning slightly yellow at the edges. His bushy eyebrows often shot upwards in mock surprise. He always sat in a huge armchair in the sitting room and loved having his children perch one by one on his knee, laughing and joking with him. Eddie always thought of him as an immensely warm and loving man, and whenever he hugged him smelt the mixture of old cigars and whisky, which seemed to have soaked into his father's moustache.

They all sat on the floor around the tree and began to pull beautifully wrapped parcels from their stockings. Dick cheered when he found his cricket ball and Eddie unwrapped a penknife with a mother-of-pearl handle. Daisy sniffed one of her presents and smiled as she showed everyone a bar of French soap. Dolly had a book of recipes and Madge a pair of gloves, which she slipped on to show Harry.

'Thank you, Father, they're lovely,' she said, hugging him.

'I'm glad you like them. Are you happy, Dolly?' he asked. He worried about this child of his, who was bright, studious, but always so serious. He longed for her to show some of the enthusiasm and joy of her two younger sisters, but knew deep down she was unlikely to change.

'This is a proper cricket ball, Father, isn't it?' said Dick anxiously.

'Yes, my boy, it is. Five and a half ounces. It'll seem a bit big at first, but you'll soon get used to it.'

'Main thing is, try not to bowl too fast to start with, otherwise you'll lose your line and length,' said Eddie. Dick was stroking the new ball and turning it over in his hands, a look of sheer joy on his face as he sat surrounded by discarded wrapping paper.

The excitement continued after breakfast. Harry was being scolded by his wife for playing catch indoors, and Daisy and Dolly were discussing their presents.

Eddie was carrying a secret, which he had shared only with his father, and his enjoyment of the day was tainted by the fact that his brothers and sisters knew nothing of it. He was desperate to join the army and fight in France and, grudgingly, his father had agreed to let him go in spite of his being only fifteen years of age. At sixteen a father could provide a letter giving his consent to his son enlisting. Eddie knew his mother would be horrified by his leaving home to fight, but he also knew she would not contradict her husband.

They all moved through to the dining room for their traditional Christmas dinner, which was enjoyed by all the family. As they sat around the fire in the evening Harry glanced across at his eldest son with a mixture of concern and pride.

Three days later Eddie set off early by train for Birmingham carrying with him his birth certificate and a letter of consent from his father. He'd managed to alter his date of birth on it from 1899 to 1898 the forgery was unlikely to be noticed by army officers desperate to enrol men into the war effort. Eddie's problem, however, was that he was very short. He had often stuffed paper into his boots at school to make himself look taller and had thought about trying this again in Birmingham, but decided against it. Although undersized, he was very wiry and surprisingly strong due to the amount of sport he played. He had blond hair and blue eyes, a mischievous grin, and his school reports usually had the words 'cheeky and bright' in them. On one occasion he had climbed the outside of the tower above the main school building, scaled the flagpole and replaced the flag with a pair of his mother's bloomers. He had been found out and punished, but once his father had been suitably cross in front of the headmaster they had laughed for nearly half an hour on the way home. Eddie was a risk taker and relished the chance of travelling abroad with the army.

There was a short queue at the Yeomanry recruiting office when he arrived. A group of seven or eight men stood stamping their feet and blowing into their hands, breathing smoke from their cigarettes into the frosty air. When it was his turn to enter Eddie marched into the office. It was lit by a single bulb and had a small round table set in the middle of the room. There was an empty chair opposite the one occupied by a Sergeant Major who rose to greet him.

'Morning, young man, come to join up?' he asked with a somewhat forced smile.

'Yes, sir,' replied Eddie, trying to make his voice sound a little deeper and to lengthen his spine by standing as straight as possible.

'Ever ridden before? You know that the Queen's Own Worcestershire Hussars is a top cavalry regiment?' said the Sergeant Major.

'Yes, a bit, but I haven't really sat on a horse for a while now,' replied Eddie.

'No need to worry, plenty of training will sort that out. You'll be as good as bloody Wellington by the end of it. Just sign here, sir.'

With a signature and a handshake Eddie Williams was signed up with the Queen's Own Worcestershire Hussars and ordered to report for duty in Birmingham in five days' time.

Chapter 5

Norfolk, December 1914

Tom had experienced a cheerless Christmas. If there was one event that was guaranteed to worsen homesickness, it was the holiday season. A number of men could be heard sniffling in their beds at night and, although there had been a reasonable army attempt at a celebratory dinner with turkey and Brussels sprouts (Tom always thought Christmas was not Christmas without sprouts), it was certainly not like being at home.

He had received a small parcel and a letter from Stoulton. It contained some of Phyllis's apple chutney, which was well known locally for regularly winning first prize at the village fete. There was also a letter from his sister Birdie.

> *Dearest Tom,*
>
> *I hope all is still going well with your training. We miss you so much at home and Christmas will not be the same without you. The weather has been rather cold and damp here, but Father is relieved that most of the winter ploughing has now been done.*
>
> *I hope you remember John Guilding, whom you briefly met before you enlisted. He works at the City and Midland Bank in Great Malvern and his prospects seem very good. I have been seeing a lot of him and I am already very fond of him. I have never felt like this before and would have loved to have told you all about it face to face. Father and Mother have met him on a number of occasions. He calls Father 'sir', which makes*

*us all smile, and leaps up whenever Mother comes into the
room. He has just enlisted with the Worcestershire Regiment
and is due to leave for France in the next month.*

*Tom, as he is leaving soon, we have secretly become
engaged. I have told Phyllis but no one else knows as we felt
it best to wait to announce it until John returns home. Now I
am worried sick about his safety and pray the war will end
soon so we can marry and be together.*

*Phyllis is as busy as ever at school and has been planting
the garden ready for spring. She still visits Mrs Jeffers, who
used to work in the house, in the village every day, cooking a
little lunch for her in the holidays, and taking in some bread
and milk from the farm.*

*I hope you have a reasonable Christmas in the
circumstances and I send you all our love.*

Happy Christmas and best wishes for the New Year.
With love,
Birdie

There had been a short Christmas service in a makeshift chapel in
one of the wooden barracks, and Sid had borrowed Tom's Bible to
read the lesson of the shepherds and the Angel Gabriel. Tom made
his traditional prayer for each member of his family, including of
course his sister Jane.

Tom had now taken possession of his new horse, which he called
Duke as it looked just like one of his father's favourite hunters.
The horse was only five and already nearly sixteen hands. He was
a dark bay with a dash of white over one fetlock and a very short
tail that looked as though it had been chewed off by another horse.

The first time Tom had put a saddle on Duke it was clear that he
had barely been broken in. He arched his back and began snorting,
and when Tom swung his leg over the horse's hindquarters, Duke

put in an enormous buck, catapulting him into the air, to land on his back on the frozen ground. Thereafter Tom had proceeded more carefully. He kept a supply of sugar lumps in his pocket and fed them regularly to the horse.

Duke soon became a joy to ride. His trot was performed with such elegance he seemed to float over the ground. There were two problems with him, however, that became obvious rather quickly. If anyone tried to touch his ears he would bite, and bite hard. The second problem was that when a hand was placed on his hind-quarters behind the saddle it often resulted in a huge buck. Tom had once or twice felt something akin to flying as a result of this. Still, Duke learnt faster than many of the older horses, and was soon responding well to neck reining and galloping in a straight line in tight formation.

On 31 December the alarm sounded, indicating a possible invasion. Captain Smith Maxwell had become increasingly uneasy and paranoid about the prospect of a German expeditionary force, with his stammer worsening considerably whenever the alarm sounded.

'C-come on, men, m-mount up as quickly as possible. Busk, stop smoking! This is n-not the time for smoking when we could be invaded at any m-m-moment.'

Alf Busk was a little shorter than the rest of the men so had some difficulty mounting his horse at speed. Sid Parkes was trying to haul him into the saddle from his own horse, stammering the whole time in imitation of the officer. The unit formed up and cantered off to Cromer beach. The tide was out, leaving a vast expanse of sand shimmering in the sunshine.

'What a beautiful day,' said Sid. They all gazed out to sea, watching a small fishing boat bobbing on the horizon. The sun gleamed on the surface as waves rolled gently up the beach, sweeping carpets of water across the sand. Seagulls bobbed out at sea, occasionally dipping their heads beneath the surface and flicking water away from their beaks as they reappeared.

'Don't forget the tide; it comes in here so fast,' said Dick, gazing anxiously up and down the beach.

'Dick, we're on horses, relax.'

'Yes, sorry, Sid. I know it seems a bit silly, but she did nearly drown.'

They continued patrolling for a full two hours, still with no sign of imminent invasion. Captain Smith Maxwell now seemed rather cross about the lack of confrontation.

Their training continued over the next few months as the weather began to improve. Smith Maxwell had by now realised that an invasion was unlikely and his focus was on the war in France, which appeared to have reached an impasse. There were rumours amongst the men that he had requested a transfer so he could be more directly involved in frontline action.

A rapid British victory was now a distant dream. It was difficult to be sure how many men had been killed as news from the front in France was very carefully controlled. There were stories of many wounded men with ghastly mutilating injuries, who had been seen being transported to hospitals in Norwich.

One March day Tom and Sid were granted a pass for a night off. They took a bus to Sheringham in the early afternoon and found a small pub called the Duke of Norfolk. They ordered their pints and settled by the fire, enjoying the warmth. After ten or fifteen minutes a young man of about twenty hobbled in on crutches. He propped himself up on a bar stool and ordered a light ale. Sid, who was wearing uniform, got up to help him carry the glass and bottle back to a chair and table next to theirs.

'Mind if I join you?' the young man asked.

'Come and have a seat. I'm Sid Parkes, and this is my old mate Tom Bomford.'

Tom held the new arrival's crutches for him and shook his hand. The soldier leant back and then dropped down heavily on the seat. Sweat beaded his forehead and he looked pale. His face was peppered with scabs and there were healing cuts over both of his hands.

'Sorry about this, still trying to get the hang of them. I'm Stuart...Stuart Ross. Where are you boys stationed?'

Tom and Sid told him about the Yeomanry and their transfer to Norfolk, to combat the threat of invasion there. They even hinted that they were keen to get to France and at least test their skills.

Stuart took a long drink of his light ale, which left a line of white froth on his top lip. His hands were shaking slightly as he gripped the glass. 'You stay here as long as you can. France is sheer hell and I should know, that's where I was injured,' he said.

'What happened to you then?' asked Tom, rather tentatively.

'I have to be careful what I say,' said Stuart, lowering his voice. Then it all came out in a rush. 'I was a Territorial, so I thought I'd be enlisted for Home Service. We went into intensive training in September and were given the opportunity of volunteering for active service. Nearly the whole battalion agreed to go, and we were soon shipped off to France.'

He took another long swig of ale before continuing. 'Within six weeks nearly four hundred of us were either sick, wounded or dead. We were moved to Ypres in Belgium at the end of October. There was heavy gunfire throughout the whole of the first bloody night. I never slept a wink. The next day we began marching forward. There were smashed vehicles on the road and dead horses lying in ditches. The ground was just mud, deep mud. Everything sank into it...men, vehicles, horses. We were losing men as we advanced to Jerry's Jack Johnsons.'

'What the hell are they?' asked Tom.

'Those are the Jerry shells and they're bloody awful. There's no warning and you never know where they'll fall. A single shell will kill two or three men and wound many more. We advanced at a crawl, digging shallow trenches and then creeping forward. We were pretty close to Jerry at times but often they would counterattack and we'd have to fall back over the ground we'd just taken. There were so many wounded everywhere. I was sent forward to try and retrieve some of 'em and as there were no stretchers we used a door we'd found lying in the mud. We managed to get ten or so back to an old cottage with the roof blown off but there was little in the way of treatment and most of 'em died where they lay in that hovel. I buried one outside with the help of two other men but the following day there was nothing but a shell hole where we'd dug the grave. The rest of him must have been scattered over the whole bloody field.

'This went on for two weeks non-stop. The trenches were full of water and the cold at night was terrible. Some of the men found some wood and a bit of old paper and managed to start a small fire, which meant we could make some tea and fry up some bully. My foot was getting bloody sore but I daren't take my boot off 'cos of the cold. There was a bit of a smell from it and when we were relieved in mid-November I had it seen to in a dressing station. The whole foot was black and gangrenous. The surgeon took one look and said, "That is coming off or you'll die."

'I don't remember much for a week or so after that. They gave me plenty of morphine, and then shipped me back here to my parents. I'm useless for manual work any more but maybe I can find a job in an office.'

Tom and Sid had been listening in a state of shock, staring at the crippled man in disbelief. Their image of war and how the fighting in France might still involve cavalry charges across open fields had just been comprehensively shattered. They both realised their training was hopelessly inadequate for this type of conflict.

'I'm really sorry, mate,' said Sid. 'It doesn't sound good at all over there.'

'Well, let's get another beer and we can buy you a pie, Stuart,' said Tom, hoping they might be able to change the subject. He did not want to admit it to Sid, but even life with Sergeant Vint sounded better than life in France.

'Thanks, that'd be grand.'

Tom, Sid and Stuart carried on drinking late into the night and ended up getting very drunk.

As spring progressed, the weather was growing warmer. Duke was beginning to lose his winter coat, and each time Tom brushed him over in the morning, more hair came off in the curry comb.

'Why d'you spend so much time grooming your horse, cocker?' Alf asked him one day.

'He enjoys it and it keeps me away from Vint. It seems to calm me down, being around horses. I suppose it always has done.'

'Well, I don't blame you. Things weren't ever easy at home for you. I think your mum felt I was a bad influence; she never really spoke to me much. Your old man was a good 'un, though, always asked me about the family. Fine rider too.'

'Alf, how do you feel about going to France?' asked Tom, brushing Duke's head and carefully avoiding his ears.

'Bloody worried, to be honest. Half the blokes are spouting rubbish about finally seeing some action, but it sounds like hell to me.'

'I know we aren't meant to mention it, but I wonder how I'll cope with it.'

'Tom, you aren't the only one who wonders, and I'm damn' sure Smith Maxwell is more frightened than the two of us put together. I hope if you're stuck in it with your mates, it won't seem quite so bad.'

Tom gave Duke a pat on the neck and turned to look at Alf, who stood thoughtfully blowing smoke rings.

'Let's hope so.'

The whole regiment was ordered to get ready for parade and full inspection the following day. Tom and Sid were up early, even before the first call, polishing their boots and saddles. Thankfully the weather was dry and after breakfast the regiment mounted up and formed ranks.

An open-topped car glided across the parade ground, its passenger door opened by a soldier almost before the vehicle had come to a complete stop. The regiment's Honorary Colonel, Viscount Cobham, got out and straightened himself slowly as if unlocking his back. Lady Dudley accompanied him, wearing a long dark-blue coat plus a small hat and short veil. They both climbed the steps on to the platform and shook hands with Colonel Jeavons, who saluted and then bowed low as if before royalty.

Jeavons then turned and addressed the ranks. He had a strong voice but appeared a little nervous before such distinguished guests.

'Good morning, men. Viscount Cobham will shortly be carrying out an inspection, but before that I have some very good news for you. Orders have arrived here indicating that we are being shipped overseas to join the British Mediterranean Force. I can't give you any more details at present, but your training is now complete and I feel sure you will conduct yourselves with great distinction wherever you are posted. I trust you will act to the honour of the Worcestershire Yeomanry, as so many men have done before you.'

There was a loud cheer at this, which was quickly silenced by Colonel Jeavons raising his hand for quiet.

'As you may know, some years ago the Yeomanry served as the Imperial Yeomanry in South Africa. Before they departed Lady Dudley presented all the ranks with a sprig of pear blossom, and she will do so again today.'

'Fat lot of good it did them against the Boers,' muttered Alf.

'Still, nice touch, with the pear being on the Worcestershire coat of arms,' said Tom.

'You soft sod, we need more than pear blossom where we're going.'

'As long as they need cavalry I won't mind. It sounds like horses are no use at all in France,' replied Tom.

The parade lasted nearly two hours while they were inspected by Viscount Cobham, closely followed by Colonel Jeavons, who seemed satisfied with their general turnout. They then slowly filed past the platform and the large table covered in pear blossom. A small sprig was pinned to the regimental badge on the pocket of each man's jacket by two corporals, while Lady Dudley gave encouraging waves from time to time. Tom and Sid filed past and saluted, while Alf Busk managed to wink at Her Ladyship – thankfully none of the senior officers spotted it.

The rest of the day was taken up with stowing tents and ensuring their packs and supplies were in order. They cleaned their rifles and sharpened their swords, the atmosphere in the camp now charged with expectation and excitement.

The morning of 8 April was fine and still. A thin mist slowly burnt away as the sun rose over the Norfolk countryside. Tom went to saddle Duke, and fitted his rifle into the sheath behind the saddle. He carefully attached his pack. The whole regiment then mounted up and rode to the nearby station. Many of the local people lined the road to see them off; they would be missed because of the business the regiment had brought to the area. The butcher and baker had been especially busy and handed out sandwiches and pies to the men as they passed.

It took some hours to get all the horses on to the wagons as one or two were very reluctant to walk up the steep ramps, needing considerable persuasion. The men eventually boarded the train and settled down for the long journey.

The following day they arrived at Avonmouth in South Gloucestershire. It was a small dockland town and they had been told they would be boarding a horse transport boat called the SS *Eloby*.

The station was very near the docks. As Tom led Duke down the ramp from the train a wall of noise hit him. It felt deafening after the quiet of the Norfolk countryside. Dockers in flat caps were pushing trolleys laden with sacks. Soldiers were everywhere, some trying to hold on to horses' heads as they reared and whipped round, frightened by the noise; other men were carrying two or three packs on their backs. There was a smell of sea, mud and horse droppings. Tom patted Duke's neck, quietly talking to him and trying to keep him settled.

Sergeant Vint ordered them to follow him from the station, down the walkway and between some redbrick warehouses. Some had company names painted on walls that were weather-beaten and peeling. As they walked the first few hundred yards away from the platform, between the buildings Tom glimpsed a large black funnel with smoke drifting up from it. They rounded a corner and arrived at the quayside to find the dock laid out before them. Three ships could be seen moored alongside, the nearest with the name SS *Eloby* painted on her bow. She sat very high in the water, her black hull showing patches of rust near the waterline. Either side of the funnel, fore and aft, were two low masts and a large bridge with a row of portholes propped open, glistening in the sun. Tom had once visited the docks at Gloucester to see the loading of some grain ships, but this vessel was huge by comparison.

'That's your ship, boys,' shouted Sergeant Vint. 'Line up on the side here; we'll start loading before too long.'

They brought their mounts forward and stood watching the semi-organised mayhem in front of them. Horses were being winched by crane into the air, legs flaring out, before being lowered into the holds of the ships. There were two more vessels tied up nearby, where men with large backpacks were filing slowly up gangplanks, swaying from side to side and clutching the rope set to one side as they went.

Captain Smith Maxwell marched up and addressed them. He looked excited, his face flushed.

'Good morning, men. We shall be boarding the SS *Eloby* before too long. You'll be sleeping on the ship tonight and we hope to sail tomorrow at high tide. The other two ships you see moored here are the *Wayfarer,* which will be transporting the Warwickshire Yeomanry, and the *Saturnia,* which will take the rest of the Worcestershire Yeomanry. The *Eloby* is a first-rate ship. She's a steamer, so not the quickest, but she is big…six and a half thousand tons. She is taking most of the horses so every man here will have to feed and tend three or four on top of his own. Boarding will begin in one hour. At ease.'

Smith Maxwell saluted, turned away smartly and strode off to give orders to another group of men.

Alf pulled a cigarette from his top pocket, struck a match and lit up, puffing hard.

'Good news…mucking out four or five bloody horses each. That's really going to help my seasickness,' he moaned.

'Looks like our ship is a bit more solid than the others. I think that might be better if we come across any German boats out there,' said Sid.

During the rest of the day, men, horses and supplies were loaded on to the ships. Most of the mounts seemed remarkably relaxed as a sack or two of grain was strapped on to their saddles and they were then lifted high into the air and swung into the hold. Duke looked around the dock as he travelled slowly through the air, gently rotating, and appeared unconcerned when he was lowered down next to Tom, stationed deep in the front hold. It was gloomy down there. Lines of rope had been erected on wooden boards where the horses were tied. Each had a small area so they could lie down comfortably, with a net of hay tied in front of them, a water bucket and a second empty bucket for the daily ration of oats as extra feed. The air was already stale and hot, but Tom hoped this would clear once they set sail.

By nightfall everyone was on board with the horses safely stowed in the holds. The men shared four to a cabin with a variety of short beds and hammocks for sleeping. That night they discovered they were sailing for Egypt as part of the Egyptian Expeditionary Force. Most of the men knew nothing about the war outside Europe as the little news they had heard concentrated on France. Sergeant Vint explained there was a large Turkish force stationed in the Middle East and that the Yeomanry were likely to be up against them. He knew little more than that, but having fought in South Africa, he warned the men of the obvious: it was going to be 'bloody hot'.

Tom was woken soon after six by the ships' horns all sounding at once. He climbed the metal stairs and went out on deck with Alf, who had already lit his first cigarette of the day.

'Smell that sea air, cocker,' he said, as he inhaled smoke deep into his lungs, and then laughed as a fit of coughing overcame him. A small tug had manoeuvred into place to take the bow line from the *Eloby*, ready to tow her out from her mooring. The bow and stern lines to the quay were released, and the ship started to head slowly towards the open sea. Tom had imagined sailing from England many times, picturing the quayside lined with his family and the soldiers on deck all waving and cheering. In reality there were only a few dock workers, who had already turned their backs on the departing ships for a chat and a cigarette with their mates.

Sid and Dick had joined them on deck. They leant on the rail, gazing back over the buildings around the dock to the country-side beyond.

'I wonder when we'll be back here,' said Dick.

'Or whether we'll ever be back?'

'Oh, thanks, Alf, bloody cheerful that is,' said Dick.

'Alf's right, you know,' said Tom, 'we have to face the possibility. But for now let's hope and pray we all return safely. Now, I think it's time for breakfast. Alf needs something to line his stomach if he's not going to be seasick.'

The SS *Eloby* headed out into the Bristol Channel with the *Wayfarer* some way ahead of them and the *Saturnia* at their stern. A destroyer accompanied them as there was the ever- present threat of being torpedoed by a German submarine. The convoy of ships headed west into the Atlantic Ocean and the following morning the destroyer left them. Tom realised then how vulnerable they were out on the open sea with no protection.

The weather was fine although there was a good breeze. The ship was rolling over the waves, but making steady progress. There were whitecaps reflecting the sun and still one or two gulls wheeling over the stern of the ship, which seemed rather odd to Tom considering they were so far out to sea. He gazed out over the rail, inhaling the salty smell which brought back memories of holidays in Cornwall, with rock pools and sandcastles. Dick was already feeling very seasick and spent much of the day bent over the rail, dry heaving repeatedly. Alf, much to his surprise, was perfectly well, but put this down to his smoking.

'Dick, why don't you try a fag? It might help the seasickness.'

'Bugger off, Alf,' he said briefly, looking up at the horizon, 'I couldn't face it.'

'I've heard lying down below can help a bit,' said Tom. Dick nodded and Tom guided him down the steps below as if helping a drunken man to bed.

Late that afternoon, their fears of attack were confirmed as they passed the *Wayfarer*. She was leaning heavily to port, having been hit by a German torpedo. A pump was spouting water overboard and men were throwing supplies over the side to reduce her chance of sinking. A small ship was standing by to transfer men and horses off, but later that day they heard she'd managed to limp into Queenstown, a port on the southern coast of Ireland, where repairs could be undertaken.

The days assumed a steady routine; the men rose early and went down to the hold to check the horses. They filled the water buckets, gave them hay and oats, and mucked out each stall in turn. Conditions in the hold were not good; it was very hot, and the overpowering smell of manure and urine was barely stirred by the faint breeze that drifted in through the portholes. The horses developed a stance to prevent them falling when the sea got rougher. They leant back in their head collars and planted their legs as wide as possible, which allowed them to sway and keep their balance reasonably well.

Sadly, during the first spell of rough weather, two horses slipped and went down on the boards and, in thrashing viciously to get up, each broke a leg. There was no option but to shoot them and winch up their bodies to drop them over the side. Tom and Sid stood watching by the rail as they hit the water. An extended hoof was the last thing to disappear beneath the surface.

Over the course of the next five days Tom met some of the crew and found they were mostly from Scotland or the north-east of England. Their heavy accents made conversation slow but they had all travelled widely around northern Europe in the years before the war. They had a variety of tattoos, including anchors, ships and snakes on their forearms, which marked the ports they had visited. One sailor had a picture of a prison in Argentina where he had spent a month before he was released, half-starved. Another had the face of a beautiful woman tattooed on his back, who he insisted was his wife although the other sailors said they had only ever spent one night together. Tom thought their work in transporting troops was almost as dangerous as being in the trenches in France.

As they sailed south the weather grew warmer and the crew reassured them that the threat from submarines would be a lot less until they got to the Mediterranean Sea, where it would increase again. Each night Tom retrieved his Bible from his pack and read a few verses, praying for his safe return and that of his friends. He prayed for his family too and thought of his father back on the farm. At this time of year the lambs would be a good size and they would be preparing to cut grass for hay in the next three or four weeks.

As the temperature rose Tom's chief worry was the condition of the horses. The heat in the hold in the middle of the day was unbearable and the horses would stand with their heads down, sweat pouring off them. It was hard to keep up with the amount of water they drank. Tom and Sid were continually throwing seawater over Duke and Billy, Sid's horse, to keep them cool. Duke was losing weight but he was eating well and Tom assumed it was the heat that was causing so many of the horses to lose condition. He tried to discuss the problem with Sergeant Vint, who had himself been feeling sick for much of the time.

'Sir, the horses are suffering badly in this heat. Is there anything you want us to do?' Vint had just come from the stern of the ship and Tom could see some vomit on his jacket.

'Just get on with it, Bomford. We've plenty of fresh water so make sure they're not short,' said Vint, still looking rather pale. Tom had seen very little of him since they had been at sea, which was a relief, and slowly he had begun to seem less threatening. Tom even felt a glimmer of sympathy for the man, watching him trying unsuccessfully to conceal his seasickness from the lower ranks, while bent over the rail pretending he was admiring the view.

There was one man who came to check his horse twice a day without fail and Tom and Sid came to know him well. Dr Oskar Teichman was the regimental doctor and became close to many of the men during the voyage. He had been a member of the Royal Army Medical Corps before the war and was only thirty-four years of age. He'd studied at Cambridge and ridden in a point-to-point there against Oxford. In 1903 he'd travelled across Russia with his father. He had brought with him to Egypt a bay hunter called Nemo that he had owned for many years. Whenever Teichman appeared in the hold, Nemo would start to whinny in expectation of some extra feed.

'Good morning, Bomford. Morning, Parkes,' he said one day as they were giving the horses their morning feed.

'Morning, sir.'

'It's getting a lot hotter down here now.'

'Yes, it is. Some of the horses are getting pretty distressed. They're drinking gallons of water.'

'Bomford, would you mind keeping a careful eye on Nemo for me and letting me know immediately if there is any problem?'

'Yes, sir. We'll keep throwing water over him and try to keep him cool. He's a grand sort, you must have had some fun with him.'

'I have, he's a brilliant hunter. Never refused a fence in his life. I bought him as a three-year-old and he is the best horse I've ever had. I'm not sure he is a cavalry horse, but as a doctor I hope they won't need me charging across the desert.' Teichman laughed and made his way back to the ladder out of the hold.

They sailed into the Mediterranean. As they passed the Rock of Gibraltar the sea became calmer and the air even warmer. There was more shipping, with many fishing boats from North Africa, their large sails flapping in the light winds. The local fishermen had their heads wrapped in white and orange cloth and waved frantically at the steamer as it slowly passed by. The rock loomed above them, thin cloud clinging to the upper slopes, and Tom was amazed by the narrowness of the straits.

Within hours of passing the Rock, a number of the horses began coughing and some became unexpectedly breathless and feverish. One morning Tom came into the hold with Alf to water and feed them and found three horses lying dead in their stalls. Tom feared for a second that one of them was Duke but found that he was still alive and well. Tom hugged him and fed him some extra oats from his pocket. He assumed that the stagnant air was causing some type of equine pneumonia but there appeared to be little anyone could do to prevent it.

On 21 April 1915 the ship reached Malta and docked in Valletta harbour. Several more dead horses were taken out of the hold and dropped on the quayside, covered with tarpaulin sheets. Their hooves poked out as a grim reminder of how the war was claiming the lives of animals as well as men. More water and food was taken on board, and within hours of docking the *Eloby* was ordered to proceed as quickly as possible to Alexandria in northern Egypt. All the men were relieved. Tom estimated they had lost over twenty horses on the journey already, and they were worried about losing more in the appalling conditions below decks. The sooner they could disembark on to dry land in Egypt, the better for everyone.

Almost as soon as they left Malta Dr Teichman's horse began coughing. It was nearly midday and Tom found the doctor in the small ship's hospital treating a patient. He waited until Teichman had moved away from the bedside.

'Doctor, it's not good news. Nemo has started coughing.'

'Thank you, Bomford. I was dreading this. I'll come with you now.'

They went back down into the hold and found Nemo standing with his head a few feet off the ground, coughing. He rallied a little when he saw his master.

'Hello, old boy,' said Teichman, patting him on the neck and rubbing his ears. 'He's not good, is he?' the doctor asked Tom.

'No, sir. We'll keep cooling him with seawater and hope he pulls through. There have been a few that have recovered.'

'And plenty more that have died. No need to pretend, Bomford.'

That night and the next the doctor came and stayed with Nemo, washing him down with water and trying to give him some feed. After two nights, the horse collapsed and his breathing became

70

more rapid. He lay on his side with Dr Teichman cradling his head and stroking his ears, talking quietly to him. Tom could see Nemo growing weaker. His flanks were heaving as he desperately tried to suck in more of the stale air. The doctor sensed his breathing beginning to slow and then stop. He patted the warm neck as tears ran down his own face on to the horse's head. 'Goodbye, old friend,' Teichman told him.

Tom gripped the doctor's shoulder as he sat with Nemo's head cradled in his lap.

An hour later Tom and Sid stood with Teichman as his beloved Nemo was dropped over the side, quickly disappearing beneath the waves.

After another three days they were all on deck when Egypt came into view on the horizon. As they approached the dock there was a brown haze hanging over Alexandria, caused by a mixture of sand carried on the wind and smoke from the many household fires as the first tea of the day was brewed. Tom and Sid were excited about the prospect of setting foot on land once again. They had no idea what to expect. Dick appeared, looking green and feeling only marginally less sick than when they had set out from Avonmouth two weeks before.

'Dick, you still look bloody awful,' said Sid. 'How much weight have you lost?'

'Too much, I've hardly kept anything down. It's been the worst two weeks of my life,' he said, utterly dejected.

'We'll be on dry land soon so you'll get your balance back then.'

Dick did not look convinced and staggered away.

'He never was the bravest, you know, Tom. Do you remember when he fell over in the playground at school and hurt his wrist? His mother came to school to ask the headmaster to speak to us about being too rough. I wasn't sure who was more embarrassed, Dick or the headmaster,' laughed Sid.

'You're still miffed about him dancing with Alice Dallimore at the big dance last Christmas,' said Tom, grinning.

'Well, maybe. Anyway, welcome to Egypt,' said his friend sheepishly.

'I never thought we'd end up out here when I joined up last August. Did you?'

'Not a chance. I wonder whether we'll get a look at the pyramids.'

'Guided tour from Sergeant Vint? No bloody chance.'

Tom could only imagine what Egypt might be like from the pictures in his Bible. One showed the Hall of Kings in Karnak and under the picture was written 'The Treasures of Egypt'. The image conveyed a sense of majesty. Another picture was entitled 'A Samaritan Village', and showed in the foreground a woman in long robes carrying a water vessel on her head and holding a small child by the hand. In the background, under the walls of the town, was a shepherd with a small flock of sheep and a man leading a donkey out of the city. Sid and Alf had looked through the Bible pictures, too, and felt they were being transported back thousands of years.

The SS *Eloby* docked in Alexandria and the men transferred to Chatby Camp, about a mile outside the town, near the beach. It was a joy to be on dry land again, although it took some days before Dick stopped feeling sick. Nobody had warned him that he could also suffer from land sickness.

The horses too were in a piteous state. When winched ashore they found great difficulty in walking, and many of them had lost a significant amount of weight. Out of the nearly two hundred that had begun the journey, about thirty had died of pneumonia and other injuries.

Chapter 6

Chatby, Egypt, April 1915

Two days after the SS *Eloby* had docked, the *Saturnia* arrived safely and the whole regiment set up camp at Chatby in a sprawling mass of tents near a small oasis. The heat was intense. None of the men had ever experienced anything like it in England. It sapped them of all energy and for the first week Tom was permanently thirsty. He sweated throughout the night except for an hour or two before dawn, when the temperature dropped a little, but once he was up he felt as if he was working in a furnace. The tents, although they provided shade, were unbearably stuffy, and the desert wind provided no relief.

To make matters worse, Alf for some reason felt completely at ease there and wandered around quite unruffled, saying how nice and warm he felt. He was hardly bothered by the flies that were an additional curse. They landed on any bit of exposed skin, buzzed around eyes and nostrils, and drove Tom half wild with frustration. The men were issued with khaki shorts and pith helmets, which Dick thought were rather smart, and that helped a little. At least in the evenings there was a slight breeze from the sea, which provided some respite.

Sergeant Vint had reverted to his usual unpleasant self once again and was totally dismissive of their suffering.

'This is nothing, Bomford. It's like winter now, just wait till we hit summer *then* you'll know how hot it really gets. You are the feeblest excuse for a soldier I think I've ever met.'

At least the horses were recovering. Duke had gained weight, and with some extra corn had begun to get a shine back in his coat. Tom and Sid often took the horses down to the beach in the afternoons and rode them into the shallow water to cool them off.

Their training was intensive. The day began with breakfast at six and they were out on exercises by seven before the day grew too hot. They usually broke at noon to return to what shade they could find before further exercises and parade later in the afternoon. Their skin, initially very sunburnt, was now turning a deep brown and even Dick Edwards was beginning to look a little healthier. His eczema had finally settled after large flakes of skin had peeled off along with his sunburn. Alf was down to his last few British cigarettes and had begun trying some of the local brands, which smelt like burning spices and made him cough furiously.

In late June Captain Smith Maxwell brought the men together to tell them they would be transferring twelve miles away to a different camp called Aboukir Bay. Camels were loaded with supplies, tents packed away and horses saddled for the ride across the desert. News of the campaign at Gallipoli in southern Turkey was coming through on a regular basis. It was clear that the losses there were very heavy and the wounded were being landed in Alexandria for treatment. Sadly, many men died on the crossing and there was an ever-expanding military cemetery.

Smith Maxwell had explained that the campaign in Gallipoli currently involved infantry and he doubted whether there would be any need for cavalry at all. After their training, however, many of the men were curious at least to see action.

On 13 August 1915 the division was ordered on active service as infantry and deployed to the Dardanelles in Turkey, despite the fact that they had only ever trained as cavalry. The Worcestershire Yeomanry were instructed to leave behind one hundred men and four officers in Egypt to look after the horses. Tom, because of his experience with horses, was told to stay, while Alf, Sid and Dick were all ordered to collect infantry equipment from the stores. No one knew how to fit any of the new kit, and it took some time before they were ready for parade. Tom helped Sid and Dick adjust the webbing and other extras that had been issued. The men lined up, ready to march back to Alexandria, leaving the camp and their horses behind.

Tom stood in front of his three friends and wished them luck. Sid clapped his old mate on the back.

'We'll see you soon, Tom,' he said.

'Yes, see you in a few months. Just look after yourself...and these two as well,' Tom told him.

'Bye, Tom,' said Alf, cigarette still wedged in the corner of his mouth, though it had long since gone out.

'Tom, good luck, old mate.' Dick was shaking as he held out his hand in farewell.

'Bye, Dick. It won't be so bad on the ship this time,' said Tom, trying to reassure him.

'It's the worst bloody feeling in the world,' his friend replied.

Tom patted him on the back and they all fell into line. He stood alone as his three closest friends turned and marched away, wishing more than anything that he was going with them. Suddenly he was struck by the fear that he might never see any of them again and felt a tightening in his chest as he tried to keep his emotions in check. The Sergeant Major's order for them to fall in and march echoed across the desert. The division began its journey back to the transport ship, HMT *Ascania*, that awaited them at Alexandria. Tom felt tears prickle in his eyes, which he immediately suppressed, worried that Sergeant Vint would see how upset he was.

He knew how difficult life was in the Dardanelles. After the valiant Anzac attacks in April and May, with terrible loss of life, a type of stagnation had set in with Turkish troops in prominent positions on higher ground and Allied troops dug in below, hoping in vain to make some type of breakthrough.

The camp seemed strangely quiet as Tom walked back between the canvas tents towards the lines of horses. Duke whinnied as he approached and Tom patted him on the neck, stroking one ear before the horse tried to nip his arm. It had now turned into a game where Tom would try to touch each ear and then pull away before Duke could sink his teeth into his arm or nip his shirt.

'Just you and me for a while now,' said Tom.

'And me, Bomford, don't forget that,' said Sergeant Vint. Tom started and stood to attention.

'Come on, man, at ease, it's going to be a bit quieter here for a while. You and me are going to have to exercise quite a lot of horses. These hunters may be fine for jumping hedges in the Worcestershire countryside but they're not suited to the desert.' Vint seemed a little friendlier and Tom hoped that this might signal some kind of shift in his behaviour.

As August ended, the heat in the middle of the day was beginning to ease a little. The number of horses dying had dropped off too and Tom would now arrive at the lines in the morning with less anxiety. Only a month before, as he'd walked down to check the horses first thing, every tenth horse would be lying dead on its side with clouds of flies gathering around its head.

Captain Smith Maxwell was worried about the losses. It was a morning in early September when Tom met him on the lines. He had fed and watered most of the horses with the other men when the Captain stopped to talk to him.

'Ah, Bomford, just the man. Didn't you break horses back home in England?' he asked, with no trace of a stammer. He seemed more confident and self-assured.

'Yes, sir, I did. Not that many, but my father bought a few horses as youngsters and sold them on after they had been broken in.'

'Good. Headquarters are worried that the number of horses we are losing will affect our ability to work as a cavalry regiment. It was bad enough having half the men shipped off as infantry to the Dardanelles, but when they return we will need more horses so that everyone is mounted. We have some new mounts arriving in the next week to boost the numbers.'

'Where are they coming from?'

'They are being shipped from New South Wales, Australia. They're a very tough type of horse, used to the heat, so they should do a bit better than these British horses that are more used to the mud of the Croome Hunt!' Captain Smith Maxwell laughed, delighted with his little joke.

'How many are we expecting?'

'God knows,' replied Smith Maxwell, flicking his moustache. 'They are all unbroken, which is where you come in. The Australians call these horses "Walers" and say they're not completely wild but...how shall I put it?...quite spirited. I found another chap to help you, Walter Garland, who says he can break horses too. I'll send him up to meet you.'

Tom returned to watering the horses as they were due on patrol in an hour and he wanted to check Duke and saddle him up in good time. It was now nearly nine and the day was becoming uncomfortably warm. A light breeze stirred the dust around the horses' hooves. The sky was a silver shade of blue and the sand dunes shimmered on the distant horizon. Tom untied Duke as Sergeant Vint shouted for the patrol to form up. He swung his right leg over the saddle and gave Duke a pat on the neck. He rode to the end of the line and formed up as a pair in front of the Sergeant.

'Bomford, you are riding with Garland today. The Captain asked for you to be paired as you will both be getting bucked off those new horses pretty soon anyway.' Vint laughed unsympathetically and threw his cigarette butt into the sand. Tom leant over and shook Garland's hand.

'Hello, mate, Tom Bomford.'

'Walter Garland, good to meet you.'

Tom looked across at Walter to check his appearance on a horse. He hoped Captain Smith Maxwell was right and that this man could ride. It was going to be very hard work to try and break even ten or twenty horses, and no one had any idea how many of them were due to arrive.

Walter rode quite short but did not look as though he was much over five foot seven standing off a horse. He was redheaded and very freckled. He was trying to grow a moustache but there was only a small amount of reddish-blond hair on his top lip. He held the reins very lightly in his left hand while the right checked his rifle and pulled his jacket straight. Tom noticed he was relaxed and entirely at ease. An Egyptian ran from behind one of the palm trees near the oasis and started waving. Walter's horse jumped sideways but his hands stayed still as he sat into his mount and allowed his body to sway upright. Tom could see that the Captain's judgement of him was entirely accurate.

Walter nodded as his horse whipped round again. 'This thing seems a bit lively. I'm from Ledbury, near the Malvern Hills. Father farms there. How about you?'

'We're farming too, near Pershore. You've ridden a bit then?'

'Fair amount. We've always had horses about and I've hunted with the Ledbury for years. I've heard some of the officers have been trying to start a hunt out here, though what they'd hunt I've no idea.'

'I've not seen many foxes, now I come to think about it,' said Tom, laughing.

The camp was situated to the east of the Suez Canal, to provide a large force to defend it from Turkish forces. The Turks had spent a good deal of time and money building a railway line from Damascus, all the way across Palestine, and down across Jordan to Medina and Aqaba. This allowed them to reinforce from both ends of the long line as they controlled the port at Aqaba. It had taken many months to build and the Allied forces had considered a number of ways of disrupting it to interfere with the supply route. In recent months there had been sightings of Turkish troops advancing towards the Suez Canal in small patrols, and Tom had seen some mounted units in the distance. As soon as the Allied troops began to advance the Turks always galloped away, much to the annoyance of Sergeant Vint who was keen 'to get stuck in to the bastards'.

This morning's patrol was no different from the previous week's. They had formed up at the edge of the camp, near the larger oasis fringed by numerous palm trees and thick green vegetation. They were ordered to fill their water bottles and allow the horses to drink, before remounting and checking their rifles. The standard-issue Lee Enfields were heavy but fairly reliable. There were five bullets in the small magazine and a cacophony of clunking rang out as the men checked the bolt action. They all flicked on the safety catch and sheathed the rifles in the holsters behind the saddle as Captain Smith Maxwell ordered them forwards.

The column of thirty men and horses walked out of the camp. Three young local boys ran beside them in long white robes, waving at them. An hour went by as they followed a firm track through the vast tracts of sand. The terrain here was rough but had been worn flat by previous patrols and camel trains. Sweat was running down Tom's back and face, stinging his eyes. The heat of the sun was relentless. The patrol halted to allow the men to drink water from their canteens; Tom sipped from his and the fluid resembled warm tea. He wiped his eyes and noticed the Captain climbing the side of a small, steep sand dune, holding his binoculars in one hand. He lay down just below the ridge and peered over. Almost immediately he ducked back down and ran back to the patrol.

'Men, quiet...quiet!' he said in a hoarse whisper. 'There's a

Turkish unit over the hill, ten or fifteen cavalry. We can take these buggers.'

They all mounted as quickly and quietly as possible. Duke suddenly seemed aware of the tension in the air as Tom shortened his reins and pulled out his rifle.

'Men, this is your first piece of proper action; you've trained hard for this. I want you to form a line to my right as we round this hill and we'll canter towards them. On my order, charge and begin firing,' said Smith Maxwell.

Sergeant Vint wore a slightly crazed smile on his face as he turned towards Tom and Walter. 'All right, lads, nice and steady.'

Tom nodded. He could feel the pulse beat at his temple and the butterflies in his stomach. He leant forward and allowed his left hand to press quickly against the Bible in his breast pocket.

They trotted slowly and quietly around the low ridge of sand. The horses were almost completely silent on the soft surface, the only noise the clinking of their bits. They spread out into a line, with the outer horses breaking into a canter as they rounded the ridge. A huge flat expanse of desert spread out before them and Tom suddenly saw the group of Turkish troops. There were fifteen mounted cavalry walking slowly away from them, about eight hundred yards distant. He heard one man laugh, throwing his head back. Captain Smith Maxwell drew his sword. Sun flashed off the blade as they cantered forward with the sun slightly behind them. Duke was keen and Tom had to sit back in the saddle to hold him.

They had managed to cover another fifty or sixty yards before one of the Turks looked round and saw them. He began yelling and almost as one the remainder of the men turned, saw the British, and began to kick their horses into a canter.

Smith Maxwell shouted 'Charge!' and the line started to quicken into a gallop. The Turks were desperate to flee. Their reins were flapping madly as they crouched forward shouting at their horses, legs pounding, urging their mounts to go faster.

'Fire at will, lads,' shouted Sergeant Vint. Captain Smith Maxwell was leading on the right with his sword pointed to the horizon in front of him. One Turkish soldier was dropping back as his horse appeared to be slightly lame. The Captain reached him quickly and slashed him across his left shoulder and back, looking as though he would slice him in two.

Tom cradled his rifle over his forearm and was aiming at one of the Turkish soldiers ahead when he heard a popping noise and realised he was being fired at. The noise reminded him of cracking walnuts at the end of autumn, back in Worcestershire. Being fired on made him realise this was war, and as his rifle bobbed on his left forearm, he pulled the trigger. The shot disappeared into the air above the Turkish soldiers' heads. Trying to shoot at full gallop seemed almost impossible. The Turks were by now almost out of range. Captain Smith Maxwell held his arm upright and ordered his men to halt.

Tom leant back in his stirrups and pulled Duke up. He slowed to a trot and then turned and walked back into line. The Captain had dismounted and stood over the dead Turk. He lay face down in the sand and Tom could see a gaping wound on his neck, shoulder and back. Dark blood oozed out on to the sand. His cap lay twisted on the back of his head with the chinstrap pulled tight.

'Right, Garland, Bomford, off your mounts and cover this man with some sand and rocks. We don't want to leave his body out in the open, that's not the British way,' ordered Vint, still quite breathless.

'Typical, he picks us to demonstrate British good manners,' muttered Tom.

Tom and Walter dismounted and dragged the dead man to some softer sand about ten yards away. They began scraping at it with the short shovels they carried behind their saddles. Until now they had only used these for filling the hundreds of sandbags that surrounded their camp. Tom felt rather foolish that he had never imagined he would use the tool for digging a grave.

Within ten minutes sweat was pouring off the end of his nose. He and Walter had formed a shallow grave. They rolled the body into the hole before shovelling sand back on top. Walter placed the man's cap under a small pile of rocks as Tom and the other men crossed themselves. Smith Maxwell said a short prayer before they mounted up for the ride back to camp.

'These Turkish johnnies are starting to get a lot closer to us, sir,' said Sergeant Vint.

Captain Smith Maxwell mopped his forehead with his handkerchief.

'Yes, Sergeant. They're getting a bit too cocky. They might just be pushing on towards the canal.'

Tom could see no sign of any reaction from the Captain, though as far as anyone here knew he had just killed a man for the first time. Tom felt a shift happening within himself too. He had been brought up around animals. He was used to lambs going to be slaughtered, and had been involved many times in putting animals down when they had been injured, but this was very different. A man had died, not by Tom's hand, but he had fired with the intention of killing a Turkish soldier and they had been trying to kill him. The brutality of war had contaminated him as though an infection had begun to take hold. He felt it was inevitable that it would spread. He just hoped that friendship and humanity would act as an antidote to prevent it from taking him over completely.

They rode back in silence, with the horses cooling off very slowly as the full heat of the day began to build. The Captain dismounted immediately they arrived back in camp to report on their patrol to Colonel Jeavons. Tom led Duke back to the lines, washed him off with a bucket of water and then fed him. There was thankfully shade for the horses under canvas strung between poles.

The camp was soon buzzing with news of the patrol and the possibility of the Turks pushing towards the Suez Canal. There were also rumours of heavy losses at Suvla Bay in the Turkish Dardanelles. Tom wondered about the men transferred there, who were now rumoured to be embarking on a tough campaign of trench warfare.

Sergeant Vint appeared at the end of the line of horses.

'Bomford, the Captain wants to see you.'

'Yes, Sergeant, I'll go straight away.'

Tom set off for the Captain's tent where the officer was sitting outside writing notes. He stood up as Tom stopped and saluted, standing to attention.

'At ease. Bomford, you are showing great promise as a cavalryman and I have some good news. You are being promoted to Lance-Corporal. Well done.'

'Thank you, sir.'

Tom shook his hand. He wondered how this would change anything; he knew his pay would increase marginally but he was more curious as to how Vint would receive this news. He felt sure the Captain must have discussed it with him so perhaps life would be a little easier if he was wearing one stripe on his arm.

Tom saluted and marched back to his tent to tell Walter.

The last week of August saw more patrols into the area east of the canal and the arrival of more horses. The first group of thirty from Australia arrived in the camp ready to be broken by Tom and Walter. The 'walers' looked very different from the British mounts. They were smaller, had short necks and were a variety of colours from bay and chestnut through to grey and roan. They proved to be very tricky to break in. Although some could be backed and ridden in a few days, others proved almost impossible. There was one chestnut horse in particular that Walter had nicknamed Tiger. He had seemed fairly quiet when they had walked around the fenced area built for the purpose of breaking in, and Tom had put a bridle on him which Tiger appeared to tolerate well.

The saddle was more difficult. As soon as Tom laid his body over it, Tiger careered off around the ring, bucking and kicking. Tom hung on as long as possible before being launched into the air. His left hand caught one of the fence posts on the way down, sending a jolt of pain lancing up his arm. He lay in the sand, spitting dirt out of his mouth, and looked at his hand. There was a long cut on the back of it and blood ran down freely. He quickly applied pressure to it.

Walter arrived beside him. 'Hell, Tom, that's a bad cut.'

'That bloody horse! He knew what he was doing.'

'I'll get you to the doctor. Come on, let me help you up,' said his friend, offering his hand.

'No, don't fuss, I'll be right enough. Let's just strap it up and I'm sure it'll heal,' said Tom, wincing with the pain.

'Stop being a bloody fool, you need a doctor for this.'

Tom struggled up and made his way to the medical officer's tent. It was a very basic unit where Dr Savery treated patients for minor injuries and referred on more serious cases. He had been a GP for many years and had volunteered soon after war broke out as he was unmarried and only twenty-nine. All the men liked him for his cheerfulness. He smoked a small straight-stemmed pipe and was sucking on this when Tom walked in and sat down on the single chair by a flimsy table.

'Bomford, isn't it?' said Savery, dribbling slightly as he put his pipe down on the edge of the table. 'What have you done to yourself?' He sat back in his canvas chair, smoothing back his black hair with both hands. His jacket was undone and he had a small tear in his shirt, which made him appear rather scruffy in this military setting.

Tom explained and very slowly removed the bloodstained handkerchief from his left hand. Thankfully the bleeding had nearly stopped and Dr Savery examined the wound, gently probing it with a piece of gauze and some forceps, which he lifted from a steel kidney dish on his desk.

'Hmm, it looks pretty deep. I'm worried about the risk of infection here, Bomford. I'm going to ship you back to the small field hospital about an hour away where they can treat this properly.'

Tom screwed his eyes up and shook his head. 'Surely a few stitches in this and it'll be fine?'

'No, Bomford, sorry. If infection gets hold then you could lose your entire damn arm from gangrene. We can't take that chance.' Dr Savery turned away and marched out of the tent to arrange transport to the hospital before Tom could argue any more. He sighed but realised the doctor was right, there was little point in arguing. Dr Savery returned after a few minutes.

'Now, before you go I need to give you an anti-tetanus injection. Roll your sleeve up.'

'What's this for, sir?' asked Tom.

'This is a new injection that stops you getting lockjaw; it's been used for about a year now. We've been ordered to give it to anyone with a deep wound.'

Tom had heard of lockjaw or, as it was properly called, tetanus. As a boy he had become very friendly with their gardener Cyril, who had worked part-time for his father for nearly twenty years. He lovingly tended the roses and mowed the grass. One day when Tom was out trying to help Cyril, but really just chatting and wasting his time, the gardener had tripped and gashed his arm on a long climbing rose. Cyril had sworn; Tom clearly remembered him saying 'bugger that'. The cut did not seem very serious and Tom thought little of it, until Cyril did not appear for work the following week.

Tom's father took him to one side a few days later to explain that Cyril had died of lockjaw. He said that the manure spread around the roses carried a high risk of tetanus, and the cut had become infected.

Tom had cried and hugged his father. It was his first experience of losing someone he was close to and he'd hung around the garden, listless and sad, for days, wondering whether it was his fault Cyril had died.

Tom flinched as Dr Savery pushed the needle into his upper arm and injected the anti-tetanus serum. There was a slight ache as Savery rubbed the area and then dropped the syringe back into the dish of sterilising fluid on the table. Tom smelt alcohol wafting up from his arm and felt the cooling effect on his skin.

The journey to the military hospital took over two hours as the ambulance bumped over the rough track, heading westward towards the Suez Canal.

A nurse in starched uniform welcomed Tom to a ward on the ground floor of the shabby mud-brick building. The roof appeared only half finished but the ward looked spotlessly clean. Tom was asked to remove his boots and lie down on the bed. Half an hour later the surgeon breezed in on his ward round. He nodded at Tom and quickly removed the dressing. He mumbled some orders to another doctor behind him, then to the nursing sister, and finally turned to the patient. Tom was struck by how young he looked, barely twenty-five, with a boyish face and no sign of ever having shaved.

'Nasty wound that. We'll clean it thoroughly and then stitch it up but we will need to observe you to ensure that you don't develop an infection.' The doctor smiled briefly and walked on to the next bed.

There then followed the painful process of the wound being meticulously cleaned in the makeshift operating theatre. There was a significant amount of sand and two small wood splinters that had to be removed before it was stitched up, all carried out with no anaesthetic. Tom tried to direct his mind back to the farm and riding across the fields after the harvest, but it only partially diminished the pain.

When he returned to the ward he found an extraordinary rig

above his bed, which was designed to hold his hand high in the air, to reduce swelling and also the chances of infection developing.

He spent the next few days being very bored, chatting to the other men on the ward. There was a soldier from London called Billy who had a very strong cockney accent. He had broken his leg, which was also suspended in the air. He rather annoyed Tom by continually saying 'stop waving at me' and then laughing uncontrollably.

In the end Tom snapped and told him to shut up, which was a little out of character for him. In hindsight he realised it was the first sign of him becoming more unwell. The fever began that night. He shivered and called to the nurses for more blankets in spite of the intense heat. His temperature soared and the sheets were soaked through to the mattress with sweat.

Dawn came and he woke feeling a little cooler, but now he was aware of an intense pain and deep throbbing in his hand. He found he could barely move his fingers due to the swelling. The nurses had already called the surgeon who came to inspect his hand.

'Bomford, your hand is infected. We will bathe it every six hours and you must keep it elevated. Hopefully this will settle but if it worsens overnight I may have to operate.'

The surgeon looked grim-faced and turned with a small shake of his head to the nurse, which Tom recognised signified real concern. Once they left, Billy started chatting again.

'Bloody 'ell, Tom, sounds like the boss is a bit worried. I hope you're still waving at me in two days,' he said. 'Might be your ticket home though, eh?'

Someone told him to shut it and Tom was grateful as he was now more than worried that he might lose his arm.

The pain worsened that day and he felt every pulse in his arm as an explosion of agony. He could not move his fingers at all and it was obvious that the redness had extended to his wrist. His temperature continued to fluctuate wildly throughout the afternoon and night. He was given morphia every six hours, which thankfully kept him in a haze. The surgeon visited again the following day and indicated that they might have to operate if things did not stabilise. Tom muttered that he thought the pain was better, in the vague hope that a little more time might help the situation.

That night the fever and rigors appeared to worsen. He shivered, and suffered appalling hallucinations. A nurse sat by his bed most of the night, bathing his head with cool water and trying to comfort him.

It was now two days since his admission and Tom woke with a sense of resignation. He was facing surgery. He could not imagine life with only one hand; the impossibility of ever farming or riding again, and the prospect of never marrying. He tried to sit himself up in bed to drink some water as it was impossible to quench his thirst. When he pushed up, leaning on the sling around his left hand, he felt something give in his hand. He thought he had torn the bandage but felt a strange sensation of wetness under the dressing. He called the nurse over and asked if she could check his bandages. She immediately summoned the surgeon and a few minutes later he arrived. The young man looked exhausted, his lids heavy and dark rings under his eyes.

He gently removed the bandage and Tom watched his face carefully. His demeanour was grim. As the final piece of dressing was removed a disgusting smell rose from it. The surgeon immediately grinned and started nodding his head in approval.

'You, Bomford, are a lucky man. This wound has just burst. What you felt was pus discharging. This should be the end of it. Your hand is safe; you just need some more time here for us to keep it clean and allow it to heal properly.'

'Thank you, sir. That's wonderful news. I can move my fingers a little more easily already,' said Tom, smiling and sinking back into his pillow. The ceiling fan whirred, barely stirring the heavy air but casting a slight breeze over his skin, which felt sticky with sweat. It was perhaps too soon to notice anything, but it felt as though his temperature had just dropped a few degrees as well. Tom waved at Billy, who gave him a thumbs up in return.

Tom's hand now healed quickly and after three days the skin had begun to close. He felt drained of energy, though, and short walks left him feeling breathless. The surgeon had advised a period of recuperation and Tom was transferred for the next week to a smaller camp, closer to the canal.

The weather here seemed cooler and he swam in the river every day, gradually regaining his strength. His hand felt better, although the skin around the wound was very pink and that over the rest of his arm and wrist, which had been inflamed, had now begun to peel.

Finally, at the end of September, he was transferred back to his unit, feeling as though he had at last recovered. He was looking forward to seeing Walter and even grumpy Sergeant Vint once more.

Chapter 7

Ivy Lodge, Stourbridge, September 1915
Madge drew the curtains back, letting the grey morning light fall across her bed. She pulled on her dressing gown and splashed her face with cold water from the jug. She glanced out of the window and saw Burt Deacon, their gardener and part-time chauffeur. He was already in the garden with his hoe, slowly scratching up and down the lines of vegetables, occasionally pulling out a weed.

Madge's father Harry liked to wander out to talk to Deacon before breakfast and let him know what time he wanted to leave for work. Deacon would soon disappear into the garage and reverse the Austin out into the drive ready to depart. His boots and smock would have been discarded and replaced by the jacket and cap of a chauffeur.

Harry was a successful man, but not quite at the stage where he could employ both a chauffeur and a gardener. His brewery, Smith & Williams, had grown steadily and now owned two pubs. The local foundry workers had good thirsts and, so far, the war had only served to increase sales.

Madge woke Daisy. Dolly was already up and helping to prepare breakfast. Madge dressed quickly and brushed her hair. It was brown, shoulder-length but quite bushy, and she usually tied it up in a loose bun with lots of clips, to try and gain some sort of control over it. She smoothed down her dress and smiled into the mirror. She had very clear blue eyes, which seemed all the more striking against her dark hair.

She passed Eddie's room and felt a pang of loss. She missed

her brother so much and wondered where he was at this moment. She would write to him when she had finished breakfast, with news of her new admirer.

Downstairs, her father was sitting at the head of the table behind his paper. He dropped it and peered at her over his steel-rimmed glasses. 'Good morning, Madge. Did you sleep well?'

'Good morning, Father. Yes, I did, thank you,' she replied.

Dolly served up fried eggs and Madge cut some bread with the old knife that her mother was so fond of using, in spite of the fact that half the handle was missing. Dick appeared in his school uniform and shorts. He wore the Aston Villa scarf that had been knitted for him by Dolly as a birthday present, and was bubbling with enthusiasm.

'Father, we have our first match today,' he said excitedly.

'Who are you playing?'

'Dudley Grammar. We beat them last year, three-nil. I'm playing inside right.'

'Good, you might even score then,' said his father, smiling with pride.

Dick was very keen but had so far never quite matched Eddie's skills on the football field. But whatever he lacked in dribbling and goal-scoring ability, he more than made up for in enthusiasm. Madge helped her mother clear away the breakfast things and then went up to write to Eddie.

Dear Eddie,

I do hope all is well with you and that the training is not too exhausting. Life here goes on as usual although we all miss you very much. Dick has a match today against Dudley Grammar and is very excited. I have some exciting news to tell you too.

Two weeks ago we were all invited to a reception at the town hall held by the mayor. You know Father knows him well and he insisted we should all attend. I was rather dreading the prospect as these affairs are normally very dull, but while I was standing waiting for Daisy to leave her coat with the attendant, a man began talking to me.

He is a local doctor called Timothy Parkes. He was quite shy, but even though we'd talked for only a few minutes he said what lovely eyes I had! I blushed and felt rather embarrassed. Daisy then came up beside me and started quizzing me as he walked away. I said nothing but I think she suspected something as I still looked rather red in the face. I did not see him again that evening, but he dropped a note at the house asking me to tea at the Brierley Hill Hotel. We sat and had sandwiches and chatted for nearly two hours. He works as a GP in his father's practice and trained in London at St Bartholomew's Hospital. He looks at me so kindly I find myself telling him all manner of nonsense, which he says he loves to hear. We are meeting again this weekend when he wants to take me for a drive and picnic in St Mary's Park.

Daisy thinks it is all very exciting as Father knows nothing of it. He would only begin questioning me about Timothy's character and intentions if he did. Dolly is still working very hard at Father's office and even at home she rushes about with papers in a very important way.

We all send our love and pray that God will keep you safe.

Your loving sister,

Madge

P.S. I will write again after my picnic with Dr T!

Madge took the envelope downstairs and gave it to Deacon to post at lunchtime. She felt quite excited to have written about Dr Parkes, and went out into the garden for a walk before lunch. Daisy came out to join her, a basket over one arm, and asked Madge to help her dig some potatoes for supper.

'So how is the wonderful Dr Parkes?' she asked mischievously.

Madge bent forward, worried that someone else might overhear her secret.

'I'm seeing him again at the weekend. We do get on so well, Daisy. He's very kind and I can see why he is so popular with his patients. He tells me his father is due to retire in the next two years, so Timothy will need to find a new junior partner. He's very handsome too and tells me how much he likes my hair…' Madge stopped talking and giggled with embarrassment. 'We've only been out together on our own once but…well, it's just very exciting.'

'I have certainly never heard you talking about a man like this before,' said her sister with a smile.

'You make it sound as though I have been out with lots of men,' protested Madge. 'I've led a very sheltered life so far, as you well know. Father is very protective of us all.'

Daisy put down her basket and began digging. As she turned the soil, Madge lifted the potatoes out of the ground and brushed off the earth before dropping them in the basket.

Daisy stopped digging and looked at her sister.

'I hope he treats you well. Dear Madge, you deserve to be happy.' She seemed concerned for her sister.

'Daisy, we've only known each other a month and I would never dream of committing myself to anyone while Eddie was away, even if we do get to that stage,' Madge told her.

Chapter 8

Aboukir Camp, Egypt, September 1915

Tom rejoined his unit on 30 September. It felt as though he had been away for months rather than a little over two weeks. He arrived back in camp late at night and it seemed hotter than ever. He found it hard to sleep, waking at five and opening the flap of his tent. The dark-blue sky was clearing as the first light in the east spread upwards. There was a gentle breeze, relieving the stuffiness around him. It was a time of day he enjoyed. The camp was quiet and he often lay looking out across the desert, absorbing the sounds of Egypt coming to life. There were shouts in Arabic, and groaning from camels reluctantly rising to begin work. The call to morning prayer cut across the sounds of men snoring and horses snorting in the lines. As the sun rose its glare and heat began to build, a relentless, physical force exerted against eyes and body. The hopeless daily challenge of trying to keep cool began.

Sergeant Vint seemed genuinely pleased to see Tom at breakfast, which was somewhat unexpected, but there was no doubt that Walter Garland was overjoyed. A group of men gathered round to greet Tom, a number showing surprise that he was still alive.

'Thank the Lord you're back! Twenty more horses arrived this week, although they don't seem quite as wild as the last lot,' Walter told him.

'How's Duke?'

'He's fine, been doing well. The farrier reshod him this week and said his feet all looked grand.'

The men knew that many of the horses had awful problems in

the desert, which varied between soft sand and jagged pieces of rock that could easily punch a hole in the underside of a horse's hoof. Tom finished breakfast and went down with Walter to the lines. The familiar smell of horse dung and semi-dried grass rose to meet them.

Tom saw Duke and gave him a hug round the neck. Tom had some extra oats in his jacket pocket and the horse whinnied, nuzzling close and rubbing his head on his master's jacket, nearly pushing him over. He then licked Tom's hands clean of all the oats. The pink area of scarring on his injured hand felt particularly sensitive.

The rest of the morning was spent breaking the Australian horses. It went well, but Tom was more wary than usual. It would take a while for him to regain his confidence. At midday they broke for water and a rest in the shade. The wind had picked up but provided little respite as it was so warm. Walter sat next to Tom under the shade of the palm trees, the coarse dry leaves rustling above them.

'Any news on the Turks?' asked Tom.

'No, it's all pretty quiet again. Smith Maxwell thinks they are building up for a big push to try and capture the canal, so it might get a bit lively.'

'Walter, has anyone heard anything from Suvla Bay? I was wondering how Sid, Alf and the others were doing.'

'It's not good up there, Tom. They've been dug in for weeks and a lot of men have been killed or wounded. There's nothing official, but it sounds too much like bloody France all over again.' Walter tipped some water over his face and rubbed his eyes.

They were quiet for a while, listening to the wind in the trees and brushing flies away from their faces. Tom realised that one of the joys of the hospital had been the lack of flies, and he wondered how they'd managed to keep them away. He had hardly thought about Sid and Alf while he was in hospital, but now longed for some reassuring news from the Dardanelles. He instinctively touched the Bible in his pocket and said a short silent prayer for them.

'Right, Walter, enough of this moping. Let's get some lunch.' Tom got up and shook the sand off his breeches. They walked to the dining area. Lunch usually consisted of some rice with a few shrunken bits of meat and some stale bread. There were normally plenty of bananas, which Sergeant Vint bizarrely thought were the answer to a whole range of problems from cramp through to syphilis. It was a camp joke that he thought they could cure anything.

That afternoon the wind seemed even stronger as Tom went down to the lines to check the horses. Duke seemed quiet and relaxed, but some of the younger horses were jittery, pulling back on their head collars. Tom tightened the hay nets and loosened the ropes on their head collars a little.

One of the local Egyptian workers who helped carry feed for the horses was sitting with his head cloth wrapped around his face and only his small dark eyes showing. Tom recognised him as Mustapha, who was always cheerful and had an excellent way with the horses.

'Are you well, Mustapha?' he said, slowly and very deliberately.

'Very bad, Mr Tom, very bad,' he said as he pointed up to the sky.

'Is there going to be a sandstorm?' asked Tom.

'Yes, yes, very bad.'

Tom was not really sure he had understood. But he had been in a few sandstorms before and the wind seemed stronger today, as if it had been building for hours.

He set off back to the main camp. He now had to lean against the gusts, and sand was being whipped up around his waist. As he reached his tent, three camels came loping towards him. Their riders wore army trousers and boots but had white robes wrapped around their upper bodies and Arab headdresses. Tom saw the leading rider raise his thin guiding rope and bring his camel to a stop. He tapped the camel's shoulder with a short cane and the animal dropped down on all fours. Tom went over to them as the two camels behind also dropped down on all fours, allowing their riders to dismount.

The leading man stood upright. His white robe dropped back and Tom saw the Captain's insignia on his shoulder, so came to attention and saluted.

'At ease, Private,' the Captain drawled. 'Will you take me to your commanding officer?'

The Captain dropped the camel's rope and pulled off a dusty leather saddlebag. He then allowed his headdress to drop down and Tom was struck by how short the man was, certainly no more than five foot four. The Captain smiled and his jutting lower jaw became more obvious. He had bright green eyes that were very noticeable in his sand-encrusted face.

'Yes, sir, follow me,' said Tom as he led him through the driving wind to Colonel Jeavons's tent.

Tom pulled back the flap of the outer part and waited for the order to enter the inner tent of his commanding officer.

'Sir, I have an officer to see you, a Captain...' Tom turned around.

'Lawrence. Captain Lawrence,' said the new arrival. Tom stood back to allow the Captain to step forward. The newcomer shook Colonel Jeavons's hand rather than saluting him. Jeavons eyed him askance.

'Thank you, Bomford. Wait outside, will you?' ordered the Colonel.

Tom stood in the outer section of the tent, peering outside as he awaited further orders. The wind was howling and sand was being thrown against the canvas, creating a strange drumming noise. The leaves of the tall palm trees were being plucked out and fired like spears through the air. A few men were running back to their tents with arms cradled around their heads, bent double as if carrying huge invisible packs on their backs. Tom ducked inside again, shaking the sand off his face.

Ten or fifteen minutes passed before the order came for Tom to re-enter the inner tent. Colonel Jeavons looked up and tapped out his pipe into the ashtray on his desk.

'Bomford, will you escort Captain Lawrence to your tent? It's not too far to go in this sandstorm and you can double up with Garland. Have you eaten, Lawrence?' asked the Colonel.

'Thank you, Colonel. I carry supplies with me,' he replied.

'Good, good. Before you turn in, I would like you to meet Captain Smith Maxwell. He's a decent chap and needs to hear all this. Thank you for your information, very useful indeed, and we shall be on the alert. Good night, Lawrence.'

Captain Lawrence then saluted and turned to duck through the tent flap, with Tom following close behind. The sandstorm hit their faces like a slap. Tom's cheeks began to burn and his eyes and mouth filled with grit. He tried to shield his face and turn his back to the wind. Lawrence pulled up his headdress and walked behind him, seemingly unconcerned.

Visibility was very poor but they eventually found Smith Maxwell's tent where on the windward side a small pile of sand was building up against the canvas. Tom pulled the flap open and they both felt the instant relief of shelter. Tom saluted and stood to attention while Lawrence dropped his headdress. Smith Maxwell looked confused until he saw Captain Lawrence's army insignia and then shook his hand.

'Smith Maxwell, good to meet you.'

'Lawrence, good to meet you too,' he said, sitting down in one of the canvas chairs. 'The Colonel asked me to come and fill you in about the Arab tribes and so on.'

Lawrence then laid his saddlebag by his chair and took off his headdress, folding it neatly and leaving it on top of a small camping table.

'Have you heard much about the war out here and how things are going?' he asked Smith Maxwell.

'They're going pretty well, I hear,' said the other Captain, sitting down in the chair opposite his. Lawrence laughed and shook his head dismissively.

'Don't believe anything you hear from those on high, they're fools. They'd like you to believe all is going well in the Dardanelles as well as here in Egypt, but the reality is very different. I have seen their incompetence for myself on numerous occasions.'

Tom coughed nervously, not sure whether he should be listening to this.

'Bomford, stay here for the moment so you can take Captain Lawrence to his tent later. The storm is too bad for you to stand out there,' Smith Maxwell said, shooting him a look that implied what he was hearing was for his ears alone. Tom nodded.

He understood that what the ordinary private was told was very limited, but Lawrence's view was at best disloyal; at worst, if voiced in front of Jeavons, it could result in his court martial. There was an arrogance about this man that made Tom feel very unsettled.

'Let me tell you a little more about the situation we face. The generals out here have no idea how to defeat the Turks. They sit around playing cards, drinking whisky and sending each other memoranda. They will never defeat the Turks without the cooperation of the Arab tribes. There are nearly two hundred and fifty of them, stretching across Egypt, Arabia and Syria. Every one of these tribes controls their own land and will not allow British troops, let alone Turkish soldiers, to wander around doing what they please on it.'

'How long have you been over here, Lawrence?' asked Smith Maxwell.

'I first came to Syria in 1911 and then worked as an archaeologist in Egypt for a year. That's where I polished up my Arabic. When war broke out I returned to Oxford. They wouldn't allow me to join up because of my height, so they sent me to London to help with drawing up maps. However, headquarters in Cairo were finding life a little difficult, so last Christmas they sent me back out and gave me the rank of Captain. Meaningless really as I would never attend their ghastly dinners and I'm beginning to do more work with the Arabs than the British. Mark my words, the Arabs are the answer to winning the war here. They despise the Turks, who treat them like savages. They know the desert better than anyone, and camels are the answer to fighting here, not horses.' He half suppressed a yawn and rubbed his eyes but Tom could see he was still fired up with enthusiasm for his subject.

'I have interrogated some of the Turkish prisoners myself and many of them have been forced to fight after threats were made against their families. There are some local Arabs in the pay of the Turks, who inform on anyone in their own tribes who questions Turkish rule. These "rebels" are then arrested and just disappear, which only increases the resentment felt towards the overlords. Prince Faisal is the one man who can change this and possibly unite the tribes. Have you heard of the Arab revolt?'

Smith Maxwell shook his head.

'Grand Sharif Hussein is the guardian of the holy city of Mecca and in June he entered into an alliance with France and Britain against the Ottomans. The British High Commissioner in Egypt is a man called Henry McMahon and he had the sense to ensure Hussein came over to our side, admittedly with the promise of an Arab empire after the war. Now, Hussein has two sons, Ali and Faisal, and they attacked the Turks in Mecca. The Arab forces were huge in number, and poorly armed, but by God can they fight! Thankfully, with Egyptian artillery support they eventually took the city, but the Turks had done a lot of damage. As this was the Holy City of Islam, it has not gone down well with the Arab tribesmen.

'My plan now is to meet Faisal and try to help coordinate the Arab attacks against the Turks, using British support, but I'm not sure our command is very sympathetic to my advice. They are most concerned with guarding the Suez Canal, and think of little else. But if the Arabs can unite and create a force of, say, fifty thousand men, all armed with rifles and mounted on camels, then the Turks will be defeated and the Arabs can rule their own lands once more. The railway is key to the campaign. It runs from Damascus to Medina and supplies the Turkish Army continuously. We have to disrupt their supply line if we are to defeat them.'

Lawrence paused to sip some water. He reached into the large saddlebag he had brought with him and pulled out a piece of cloth, which he unwrapped. He began to chew some dried dates. There was a strong smell from the wrapping of camels and stale sweat.

Tom was bewildered. He had heard no one talk like this since his arrival in Egypt.

'So what about us here, will we just stay guarding the canal for the next year?' asked Smith Maxwell.

'There has already been a lot of activity in the area, and the Turks are determined to try and take it. I am informed that now the Senussi tribe has been defeated west of the canal, there are plans for the British to begin pushing east towards Gaza. If the Arab forces can then be mobilised from Arabia and to the east of the railway, we could push the Ottomans back into Turkey. The Turks will not give up this land readily. They have ruled here for hundreds of years and their armies are well organised. They also have German and Austrian advisers, who have added an edge to them tactically, but we have time on our side. The Arab tribes may well need more persuasion and certainly money to convince them to unite against the Turks, but I am convinced that they will in the end see it as the only option if they want to rule their own lands once more.'

Lawrence leant back in his chair and yawned. 'Now, I think it is time for some sleep.'

'Certainly. Bomford, will you escort the Captain to his tent? Thank you, Lawrence. That was most informative,' said Smith Maxwell, sounding unconvinced.

Tom nodded, pulled back the flap of the tent and stepped out into the sandstorm, which appeared stronger than ever. Lawrence ambled after him, his head once again fully covered. Tom found his own tent and showed the Captain his bed, before stumbling, half blind, into Walter's tent. His friend was asleep, head buried under the thin blanket, a small patch of ginger hair just visible.

Tom lay awake next to him, in the dark, listening to the wind howling and the sand beating against the canvas. Lawrence had shifted Tom's whole understanding of the war and how it should be fought. There seemed little doubt that there was going to be a lot more activity here if the Turks were going to push towards the Suez Canal. Tom felt a pang of anxiety. The thought of fighting seemed to generate a mixture of fear and excitement in him. He wondered about his own death, now more than ever, and what would happen to his beloved horse Duke if camels were to be the way the war was won.

He woke and realised the sun was beginning to rise and the wind had dropped. Tom turned his boots upside down to ensure nothing had crept into them overnight and quickly pulled them on. He pushed open the tent flap and kicked sand away from the entrance. The sun just topped the highest sand dunes and was lending some heat to the early morning. He walked towards the line of horses and checked Duke and two or three others next to him. They all had water, although the buckets had at least an inch of sand in the bottom of them. Just beyond the lines he saw Lawrence and his two Arab tribesmen mounting their camels. Tom hurried over to them.

'Good morning, sir,' he said, saluting.

'Oh, stop that bloody nonsense. No problem sleeping through

the sandstorm, I see.' The camel lurched upright, with Lawrence rocking forward and back, showing that he had done this a thousand times before.

'Goodbye, Bomford. Good luck.'

Lawrence had already turned and began to head back out into the desert with his two tribesmen following close behind.

'Goodbye, sir,' said Tom, and stood and watched until the riders had disappeared behind a low-lying dune.

Chapter 9

The weather was cooling as they entered November, and the temperature in the middle of the day becoming more bearable. Tom and Walter were still based near the Suez Canal, on the eastern side, patrolling the desert of the Sinai Peninsula on a regular basis. They would usually leave early in the morning and ride out on a large loop into the interior, travelling four or five miles east before sweeping back in a circle towards their camp.

Sergeant Vint was always with them. With his skin burnt darker than ever, he looked as though he could have been born in the Middle East. Captain Smith Maxwell would lead, peering through his binoculars, ever ready for Turks to appear on the horizon. There was occasional shellfire to the north and from time to time they saw small pockets of Turkish cavalry in the distance, but these normally galloped off once they had been sighted.

Tom and Walter enjoyed patrols. Their horses were well trained, sound, and seemed to revel in their daily exercise. As they rode back one morning, Sergeant Vint announced to all of them that they could have a night's leave in Port Said.

'Bomford, I'll allow you to go as well, although it might be a bit racy for you,' he said contemptuously.

'Leave him be, Tom,' murmured Walter. 'He's not worth the trouble.'

Tom grudgingly agreed and turned his horse off to one side while he allowed his temper to cool a little.

For the rest of the day Walter grew steadily more excited. 'What are we going to do in Port Said?' he asked nervously.

'Nothing that'll get us into trouble. The regimental doctor has enough to do without treating you for some bloody infection.'

'I've never been with a girl,' said Walter, blushing. His red hair and freckles made him look nearer fourteen than twenty.

'Well, lad, there's not much to it,' said Tom. He did not want to admit that fumbling at a young farmers' dance when he was seventeen was the extent of his experience.

'I think we'll see the town, have a drink or two, and they say there are some belly-dancing clubs that might make your face go redder still.'

'That sounds just the ticket.' Walter grinned sheepishly and trotted forward to discuss plans with another soldier.

That evening at just after five, having checked the horses for the night, Walter and Tom received their passes from Sergeant Vint.

They boarded the train to travel to Port Said. They passed the big tanks by the side of the sweet-water canal, where the domestic supply was stored. Because the local water contained the parasite that caused bilharzia, to render it safe it had to be pumped into tanks and allowed to stand for forty-eight hours.

The train rumbled on down the line, hooting regularly. Large groups of young boys appeared out of small mud-brick houses and ran by the side of the track, waving furiously and shouting: 'Hello, hello! Mister, you have money?'

Tom and Walter waved back through the open windows. Particles of soot from the steam engine blew in through the windows, landing on their faces. Brushing this off produced black smudges, so that by the time they arrived in Port Said they looked as though they had just emerged from a coal mine.

It was beginning to get dark and the call for evening prayer could be heard echoing over the city. The station was teeming with people. Two beggars sat on the platform holding out their deformed fingerless hands. Tom tossed a small coin into the hat near a shrivelled foot.

Dogs sniffed about for scraps of food and porters weaved in and out of the crowds, carefully balancing cases and parcels on their heads.

'Watch your pockets, lad,' Tom said to Walter as they pushed their way through the crowds. An Egyptian face brushed past, grinning, showing a pair of blackened teeth. Tom winced as he caught a brief whiff of the man's breath. They eventually managed to wrestle their way through the crowds and climbed into a horse-drawn taxi. Tom showed the driver the address that another soldier had recommended to them.

The streets were quite wide and the buildings all looked to be in good order as the town had only really developed with the building of the Suez Canal. Tom and Walter paid the driver and walked into the bar, to be greeted by a huge, bearded Egyptian man standing waiting for them with open arms.

'My friends, you are very welcome. This way, if you please,' he said, speaking English with a very strong Egyptian accent. He ushered them into wicker chairs set against the wall, with a small wooden table in front of them. The air was thick with the blue haze of smoke and there was a strong smell of spices emanating from the kitchen. Two beers arrived and their host, Sallahdin, fussed around them. They ordered a selection of dishes recommended by their host and before long Walter had ordered more beers and was fully relaxed and Tom had got past the stage of worrying about him. Walter started singing and four other soldiers nearby joined in. More beers were ordered. Even Sallahdin was clapping along; desert patrols and the Turks seemed like a distant memory. Tom ordered himself a whisky, deciding they had time for one or two glasses before they needed to leave the bar. An hour later he felt the room spinning around him as he turned to check on Walter, who was now standing on his chair conducting the communal singing.

'Come on, Walter, it's time we went,' slurred Tom.

'Right you are,' said his friend, and fell off the chair into Tom's arms.

They made their way back to the station, having promised with the certainty of two very drunk men that they would come back and see Sallahdin one day. They found that the train was delayed by nearly two hours and, as they staggered off the heaving platform once more, Tom spotted a small shop offering tattoos.

'Walter, come on, let's have a look. I've always wondered about a tattoo.'

'Why not?' said his friend, almost falling through the door of the shop after him.

The Egyptian owner welcomed them and asked them to sit down. The walls had peeling yellow paint and there were a few crudely drawn illustrations of the tattoos that were offered. Walter pointed to a large anchor while the Egyptian cleaned the inside of his left forearm with surgical spirit.

The next memory that Tom had was of waking up on the train back to the camp. It was pitch black outside and there was a small flickering oil lamp hanging from the roof of the carriage. Walter was groaning in the seat opposite and Tom's headache was the first warning sign that all was not well. There was a pulsating ache behind both of his eyes, but more painful still was his left forearm where a bloodstained bandage had been wrapped. The ghastly realisation of what had happened flooded back as he saw Walter's bandaged left arm hanging over the edge of the seat, dried blood covering his hand.

Tom belched and smelt a faint odour of whisky. He was desperate for water. Thankfully, fifteen minutes later, they were off the train and back in their tents at the camp. Tom poured water into Walter's mouth. He muttered his thanks and Tom drained the rest of the canteen before falling back on his bed in a deep sleep.

Morning roll call was a very painful business for both of them. Their heads throbbed and the light was savagely bright. Tom's arm felt as though it had been scraped with sandpaper; the bloodstained bandages had dried and were now a faint brown colour. They cautiously removed them and inspected the tattoos. Walter had indeed got an anchor. Tom's tattoo was rather grander. A serpent twisted up the inside of his left forearm, with zigzag patterns down its back and a long forked tongue protruding from its mouth. Both images were covered in bloody scabs. They thought it best to leave the bandages on for another day or two until their arms had healed.

Sergeant Vint was amused and enjoyed their evident discomfort. 'Well, lads, you're a pretty sight, and by the look of your arms you managed a visit to the tattoo parlour by the station. At least when you're blown apart and I pick up a few bits of you, I'll know which arm belonged to who. That should make life a bit easier.'

Tom and Walter looked at each other sheepishly.

Sergeant Vint called them to attention as Captain Smith Maxwell marched over for inspection, swinging his arms jauntily, which always gave him a vaguely comical look. He cleared his throat and ordered them to stand at ease.

'Now, men, I have some good news for you. Although the war in the Dardanelles has not gone entirely to plan, the rest of the Yeomanry will be returning to Egypt in the next few weeks. In fact some men are already on their way here as I speak. Sadly, as I am sure you will have heard, there were heavy losses and this means that the Turks may well start to concentrate on the Suez Canal, so things could get a bit livelier in the next few months. General Mortimer has requested reinforcements and we hope to have an extra two hundred thousand men here in the next four to six months.'

The men murmured their approval, both at the return of their friends and for the promise of extra troops.

Smith Maxwell cleared his throat again and continued, 'You will be issued with new orders in the next few days as men arrive back at camp. It is essential that the canal should remain fully protected. Germany has now taken Serbia and Bulgaria, which means they'll be forging even closer links with Turkey.' He nodded at Sergeant Vint, who bellowed at them to stand down.

Tom wore a huge smile as he looked forward to the possibility of seeing Sid and his other friends again. But there was also the worrying prospect of the war escalating from the quiet standoff that had developed over the last few months.

Five days later the first troops from Suvla Bay arrived back at camp. Sid was not among them as they were mostly members of the Warwickshire Yeomanry. Many looked very dejected and disheartened, and Tom was shocked to see how thin and unwell many of them appeared. Although many men had died in action, they found out huge numbers had also died from disease, and Walter discovered that an old friend of his had died of typhoid fever.

The morning of 30 November dawned with a spectacular sunrise, produced by a fading dust storm in the eastern sky. By mid-morning Tom had heard that the troops from his regiment had landed in Egypt and hoped to be back at the camp within a day or two.

The following morning, after he and Walter had fed and watered the horses, streams of soldiers began to arrive back in camp. The men looked tired, unshaven and drawn; a number of them had arms supported in slings or bandages wrapped around wounds. A few acknowledged Tom with a nod, but most of them looked more interested in finding a tent to sleep in.

Suddenly, he thought he saw Alf some thirty yards away, puffing on a cigarette.

He had his face turned to the man beside him and was laughing. Tom ran forward trying to push his way through the men. He shouted out. Alf turned, recognised him, and they shook hands and slapped each other on the back, laughing.

'How are you?' asked Tom.

'Not so bad, cocker, not so bad. It was pretty grim up there,' said Alf. Tom felt a tap on his shoulder and turned to see Sid Parkes standing in front of him, arms outstretched.

'Me old mate, how are you?' he said, giving Tom a short powerful hug.

'Very well, Sid. It's grand to see you. But where's Dick? Isn't he with you?'

Sid shook his head and looked down at the ground as they walked on together. There was a brief silence and Tom feared that Dick was dead.

'We were stuck in trenches for weeks on end and poor Dick was hit when a shell landed next to him. Two men nearby were killed but he was pretty badly wounded with shrapnel in his arm and back. He was shipped back to Blighty on one of the hospital ships. He should recover, in time. He was having a bloody awful time out there. With his skin weeping and oozing, he was in a lot of pain even before he was injured. But typical Dick...he was more worried about how his uniform looked.'

Sergeant Vint marched up to them.

'Chatting away, Parkes and Busk, I might have guessed. You still have duties, you know. Drop your packs back in a tent and report to me at 1600 hours. We're going to have some fun digging trenches. Now...move!' he shouted at them.

'Well, we thought we'd be coming back for a holiday in the desert, didn't we, Alf?' commented Sid.

'Aye, that we did,' he said, repeatedly striking a match to light his cigarette.

They all marched through the camp to find their billets. Tom held open the flap of a tent and, as he did, Sid spotted his friend's tattoo.

'What's this?' he asked, holding up Tom's arm and laughing.

'I had a few too many whiskies in Port Said,' he said, although secretly he was now rather proud of it. His arm had healed fully and the tattoo was a deep-blue colour. The snake appeared slightly threatening and he had already noticed nosy local Egyptian children peering at his arm and then running away in terror.

'It looks pretty good, Tom, although I'm not sure what your

father and mother would say about it,' said Sid, laughing and shaking his head. Tom agreed, knowing his mother especially would be horrified.

The heat at midday was uncomfortable, and as they tried to find shade flies descended on them, buzzing around their faces, landing on any bare patch of skin. If anyone breathed in too sharply it invariably meant inhaling a cloud of them, provoking an attack of coughing and spitting. Most of the men snatched some sleep after the long voyage and were woken mid-afternoon.

At 1600 hours they formed up for Colonel Jeavons to address them.

'I would like to welcome you all back to Egypt. I'll be straight with you: the Dardanelles did not work out as planned, but now we have to concentrate on defending the Suez Canal. We have good information that the Turks are being advised by German officers, and at the very least will be trying to disrupt shipping through the canal, if not to capture it. We have orders to extend our defences into the desert, so we'll be digging trenches and fortifying bridgeheads to strengthen our positions. We'll also be increasing our patrols to pick up any Turkish movements and I trust you'll be ready to fight and repel any advance they attempt. Dismissed.'

Tom explained to his friends about the patrols and their one piece of action so far. There was no doubt the Turks were edging a little closer to the canal, but the logistical problems of marching a large army seven hundred miles south from Turkey and another one hundred and fifty miles into a desert, and keeping them supplied with food and water, were considerable. Sid and Alf had already seen that Turkish soldiers were tough and very well trained, and that the British could expect a difficult time in combat with them. There had been a big drive to try and recruit more camels to the British side along with camel drivers. Many Egyptians were already working for the army, transporting supplies around the camps, such as food and water for the horses.

They were paid a pittance, but Tom had come to know a number of them and they were always cheerful and keen to help.

Recently the Egyptian Labour Corps had formed, and with the increase in the numbers of camels being utilised it had produced an offshoot called the Camel Transport Corps. The animals were being used to carry water to troops stationed in the desert to the east of the canal. They also provided primitive transport for the wounded, using wooden boxes or chairs that were strapped to each side for movement across the desert. Tom thought this seemed a good idea but had met a wounded soldier who had endured nearly two hours in one of these cribs, and said the camel's uneven rocking stride made every step agony.

The men were now issued with shovels and marched out into the desert to begin digging trenches. The sun was still strong and within minutes of starting the march Tom felt sweat running down his back and forehead, stinging his eyes. Sergeant Vint laid out the plan for the trenches and told them to strip down to their shorts and start digging. They worked in teams of four, digging a wide hollow about fifteen feet across. Sand refilled the ditch very quickly, so they had to put in battens with canvas backs and anchor them before refilling the space behind with the excavated sand.

Alf caught the canvas with his shovel, causing a tiny hole. Within a few minutes a pile of sand had begun to fill the bottom of the trench. Vint spotted it straight away and Alf, swearing and cursing, had to start again. Camels brought up empty sacks, which, once filled, reinforced the front of the trench as sandbags.

At the end of two hours' exhausting digging, a small section of trench had been prepared to Vint's satisfaction, and the men were allowed to rest their aching backs. Tom's hands were reasonably hardened from years on the farm, but the digging had already brought up small blisters over his reddened palms. After draining their canteens, they trudged back to the camp for the usual evening meal of bully beef and some solidified rice.

At least the evenings were cooler. The men not on sentry duty lay chatting outside their tents. Tom was anxious to know what life had been like at Gallipoli, and although Sid and Alf were somewhat reluctant to say too much, they agreed to give him an outline.

'The journey over was bloody rough. We were in this old ship, HMT *Ascania,* which anchored up off Mudros. We were then transferred to another ship…a cruiser, I think. What was she called, Alf?' asked Sid.

'HMS *Doris.* I had a grandmother called Doris, who was almost as big.'

Sid went on, 'She took us to Suvla Bay. The first sign that things could get hairy was when the padre read out the Twenty-third Psalm. There were boats everywhere: British and French battle-ships, cruisers, mine-layers, mine-sweepers, colliers, and masses of Greek sailing boats too. Well, we should have known then that this was no surprise attack. The Turks were shelling us the whole time, and when we transferred into these small craft I was terri-fied. Huge fountains of water erupted when a shell landed and the whole bloody boat rocked as if it was going to capsize. One took a direct hit and there were bodies all over the place. Everyone was killed instantly, poor buggers.' Sid paused, the horror of the memory making it hard for him to continue.

'It took two days for the whole division to get ashore and the attack to be launched. You could tell it was going to be nigh on impossible. Scimitar Hill in front of us looked to be bloody well defended. Colonel Dudley had to stand down because of his gammy leg, so Major Gray-Cheape took over to lead the attack.

'On the twenty-first of August it began; I remember the date because it's my father's birthday. There was heavy bombardment with artillery first, and half an hour later we were ordered to advance up Chocolate Hill. Odd name for a hill. We were spread out in columns at twenty-yard intervals, but had only gone about fifty or so before we came under artillery fire. There was nowhere to go except upwards, to try and find some cover. I was terrified. I think I aimed my rifle and fired off a single round, but I just wanted to get clear of the shrapnel that was flying everywhere. Harry Sansome took some in the leg just in front of me. Tom, you know him, his family own Oak Farm.'

Tom nodded. Harry was a superb rider, a little older than Tom, who had studied in Worcester.

Sid went on, 'So I managed to get Harry under some cover and we fitted a tourniquet around his knee to try and reduce the bleeding. He was very matter-of-fact, laughing and saying, "They'll probably take my leg off now". Eventually some stretcher-bearers reached him but there was nowhere for us to go. The Turkish machine gunners went on firing at us and we just kept our heads down. The heat was dreadful and we lay there in the sun with all our water gone. There were a lot of dead men lying in the open ground behind us and I felt bloody helpless. The sun went down and it got a bit cooler. We passed around some biscuit and waited for orders. The Turkish fire lessened and then stopped. They knew we were going nowhere so probably went off to have a bit of supper. We waited until it was really dark and after midnight we were ordered to withdraw. We went back over the same ground and passed those poor men who lay there gazing blankly at the sky. Major Gray-Cheape came round the following morning and told us how well everyone had done in difficult circumstances, but we all knew it was a bloody disaster.'

'More like bloody impossible,' interrupted Alf, rolling his cigarette in his fingers and looking like thunder.

'We found out later that nearly a third of the division had been wounded and over forty killed…We were ordered to dig trenches and so weeks of back-breaking work started, under continuous fire from the Turks above. Dick was injured a few weeks later and shipped out to hospital on a tiny boat. I'm sure hundreds of men died because it took so bloody long to get them to the hospital ships.

'The next few months were dreadful. There was almost no shade during the day and we had to sleep when we could on small steps built into the trench. There were some basic latrines but they became infested with flies and the smell from those and the decomposing bodies in front of us was bloody awful. At night a few brave souls crawled out to try and retrieve what was left of the men for burial and to collect their leather tags.

'We were all ill at some point with Turkish belly, as we called it. The doctors said it was dysentery due to the flies, and a lot of men died of that. Some just wasted away and you found they had died in their sleep.' Sid stopped and looked down, lost in his thoughts.

Tom put his hand on his friend's shoulder and encouraged him to take his time to recover. Alf took over the story then.

'The machine guns had a huge range, and if they hit you would destroy an arm or leg. The other problem was the snipers. One poor bugger woke up one morning, stood up, stretched, and… bang! His head just exploded. Those Turks were good shots and they used this German rifle, a Mauser, which had a massive range. There were a load of Irish boys who lost a lot of men to sniper fire, and one morning we could not work out where it was coming from. There was no flash or puff of smoke. But then one of the officers spotted a cave set into the cliff and thought it must be coming from there. The sniper would have climbed down the cliff in the night to hide. He asked Harry Green, who was a brilliant shot, to try and hit the cave. It was bloody difficult, especially with a Lee Enfield rifle, and he had to fire across a small valley. The first shot caused a puff of smoke above the cave. He adjusted his sights and fired twice more and hit just inside. We saw a bit of rock drop down. There was a cheer from all of us watching and then, just as he was about to fire again, a Turkish soldier appeared in the mouth of the cave waving a white flag.

'Harry Green asked the officer whether he should shoot the sniper. The officer said no, and shouted to the Irish boys up ahead to open fire. They all did so at once and the Turk fell down into the valley below. A huge cheer went up, which did not seem right, as he was flying a white flag, but we had a terrible time from sniper fire and there was very little else to cheer about.' Alf sat back, shaking his head.

'Did you just stay there for the next three months?' asked Tom.

Sid spoke up again. 'Yes. There was the occasional attempt to attack the hill again, but each time the Turks opened up with machine guns and artillery and we had to retreat. Major Coventry arrived to take over from Gray-Cheape during that time, and I think he probably realised how hopeless our position was. At the end of October we were pulled off the beach and taken out to sea again. Alf and I nearly wept when we left that place. We smelt like hell and the whole place was thick with flies, so that it was almost impossible to eat. I know that we may be involved again down here, but anything would be better than being stuck on that beach in Suvla Bay.'

'How about you, Tom, what's been happening here?' asked Alf.

'It's been pretty quiet really. This lad Walter Garland and I've been breaking in horses, which caused a few problems.' Tom recounted his time in hospital to them. 'Now I hear we're moving towards camels to replace the horses. More than anything I'm missing home and the farm. I wonder if they're able to cope without me there to do the heavier work. It's been quite a while since I had a letter from anyone, although I did hear there's been a lot of food rationing. Hopefully they'll not be too short, what with the vegetable garden and fruit trees. Father is not the greatest shot but perhaps the men on the farm can shoot the odd rabbit for them, if meat is rationed.'

'Tom, stop worrying about the family, I'm sure they'll manage. You need to look after yourself and make sure you get home safely,' said Sid.

116

Tom returned to his tent, still thinking of his family. He worried about Birdie, Mary and Phyllis, but they were all sensible girls and more than capable of looking after their father and mother. Hender would also be able to help out if he was not working at another farm in Herefordshire. Ray, as his mother's darling, would always be fine. Tom's lamp was still flickering so he took out his Bible and said a short prayer, thanking God for the safe return of Sid and Alf and also asking for Dick's recovery. He then read a few verses from St Luke's Gospel before falling asleep.

He dreamt of home. He was walking on the farm with his father and looking at the sheep fencing to check it was all secure. His father turned to him, smiled, and Tom felt the unspoken bond between them. Then they were riding across the land, jumping a low hedge. It was summer. The corn had been cut and sheaves of wheat were scattered across the fields ready for thrashing. It was Tom's favourite time of year...

His dreams of home were all too soon interrupted by the morning call.

Over the next few weeks they continued digging trenches in the desert and preparing for a Turkish advance. Tom's view of the Turks as incompetent and cowardly had been debunked by Sid and Alf, and he was worried about the action to come.

Christmas was approaching and Tom hoped for a letter, or possibly a parcel, from home. He thought endlessly about all the preparations that would be going on without him. His father normally fattened four turkeys, selling three to friends locally and keeping one for the family. Phyllis and Birdie would be having whispered discussions about what presents to buy everyone and Ray would be dreaming of some new book or game. He still believed in Father Christmas, which Tom thought very strange for a boy of his brother's age. No doubt the Christmas stockings would be brought out ready for their yearly outing.

In the week before Christmas it appeared that Turkish artillery had been moved closer to the canal as there was shelling on an almost daily basis. The missiles were landing well short of their camp but Colonel Jeavons was concerned and moved British artillery up to return fire. These were heavy guns. After a day of fire being returned by the British there was no further attack from the Turks.

On Christmas Eve Tom's prayers were answered. He received a small parcel from home. A huge shipment of mail had arrived from England; over two-thirds of the men received either a letter or a parcel. Tom's was wrapped in thick brown paper and tied neatly with string. A label had been glued to the outside and he immediately recognised the neat, slightly sloped writing of his sister Phyllis. He opened the parcel and found a letter along with a packet of biscuits and a flat box containing five apples. Three of them looked brown and shrunken but two were still quite firm and he inhaled the familiar smell before biting into one of them. He opened the letter and began to read.

20 November 1915

Dearest Tom,

I hope all is well with you. We so enjoyed your last letter. With Christmas approaching we think of you constantly and pray that the war is over soon. You asked for news, so I will try and tell you how we all are.

Birdie is working at Norton and cycles there every day. She's a secretary. She is so in love with John Guilding and cannot wait for his return so that they can marry. He is fighting in France. Although his letters are cheerful, conditions in the trenches sound very hard. He has a delightful batman called Harold Harris who looks after him, making tea and cleaning his uniform. John says he has an endless supply of rather risqué jokes, which keep all the men amused.

Hender has had a very busy time, working on the farm and

helping out all over the county as there is such a shortage of men. He has just travelled back from Leominster where he was helping out with some ploughing on the Bryans' farm.

Mary and I are busy at home. We are never short of work in the house or garden. Mary milks the cow twice a day now, and is making a lot of butter. I help Father a little on the farm but mainly grow all the vegetables and pick fruit from the orchard. We had a wonderful crop of apples this year and your favourite Cox's are safely stored in the loft. I have enclosed some with this letter and hope they survive the journey. Mother thought it the most ridiculous idea!

Raymond is due to start at Wycliffe School next year, but he is already rather worried about being away from home. Father says it will be the making of him, but Mother, although she says very little, I think would prefer him to stay at home. He also spends a lot of time in the garden, growing small flowers and planting seeds such as radish and cress.

Father says quietly that he longs to see you again and misses your advice on both the farm and the horses. He and Mother spend little time together except at supper when we all sit down to talk about the day. She sends her love as well. I know you found her very difficult before you left, but I really do think she misses you dreadfully.

We send our love and prayers for this Christmas and for a more peaceful 1916.

Phyllis

Chapter 10

Kantara, Egypt, December 1915

Eddie Williams too was struggling in the heat of Egypt, in a camp a little to the north of Tom's but still close to the Suez Canal. He missed home far more than he'd ever imagined he would. His riding skills had developed from virtually hopeless to basic competence, but he still felt nervous when going any faster than a trot. Being the smallest member of his company, this resulted in an endless stream of jokes about his height. He had found a fellow soldier, Bill Green, who defended him when the jokes became a little too personal. Bill was over six foot tall and had huge hands that were more like spades. With his large nose and broken blood vessels on both cheeks, he was a dominant and slightly intimidating figure.

Bill Green had been in the regular army for five years, from around 1907, but the dates always seemed to vary when he talked about his previous service and Eddie wondered whether he had left under a cloud. Since he had rejoined, Bill had been promoted to Corporal, but his trenchant views and plain speaking to all ranks occasionally irritated his superiors. On one occasion Bill told a Second Lieutenant, as he towered over him, that he did not know what he was doing and was incompetent. He was reported to the Major, who thankfully was old school and just tore a strip off him without further punishment.

Eddie thought Bill could be part gypsy as he had an encyclopedic knowledge of the countryside. He appeared never to have had a regular job but survived by poaching and trapping animals and then selling them in local markets. He told Eddie there was a mass of food in the countryside and no one need ever go hungry. He had often eaten squirrel and hedgehog but preferred other game such as hare and rabbit.

The contrast between Eddie's privileged background and Bill's life could not have been greater, and yet Eddie never tired of hearing these stories of surviving in the countryside and Bill's narrow escapes from local gamekeepers.

Christmas dinner was no different from lunch on any other day: bully beef with plenty of congealed rice. A few of the men had been sent some biscuits and sweets, which were shared round. There was at least an afternoon off from the endless digging of trenches and filling of sandbags. The men lay around in the shade, trying to keep cool and chatting about the feasts at home that they were missing, lovingly describing different types of stuffing and sherry trifle. They were all championing their mother's cooking, which in Eddie's case was a little difficult as his mother had never fully mastered anything more than a simple roast and a huge array of different jellies.

In the evening they all assembled for a short service conducted by the army padre. He had a pronounced lisp, which was a little distracting when it came to 'Hark the Herald Angelth Thing' but everyone enjoyed joining in with the familiar carols. Eddie imagined his family, clearing snow from the driveway and making their way to church, wrapped in thick coats and scarves.

At last, three days after Christmas, he received a small parcel containing some humbugs, a jar of strawberry jam and a fruit cake that had become a little dry on its long journey from England. He shared it all with Bill Green, who adored humbugs, and then settled down to read a letter from his sister Daisy.

Dearest Eddie,

I do hope you are keeping well and not suffering too much in the heat. Thank you for your last letter. We all read it endlessly and know that you are restricted in what you can tell us. We have heard of the sad losses in Turkey, especially of the many brave Australian and New Zealand men who died.

We are well here, although Mother has had a nasty cough for some weeks and is performing her usual regime of daily inhalations, which give off the most dreadful smell, filling the house for hours.

Father is very busy with the brewery and tells us sales of Smith & Williams best bitter are doing surprisingly well considering so many men are fighting abroad. He has found that a number of women who work in the factories have taken to buying one or two bottles of stout to drink at home. One of the local doctors has advised some of his patients to take a glass or two in the evening to help them with tiredness!

Dolly still works on the accounts and reads the papers from cover to cover for every piece of news relating to Egypt. Madge is very taken with a local doctor called Timothy Parkes, who calls on a regular basis to take her out for tea and drives. He works in his father's practice and seems charming and smartly dressed, always wearing a tie and jacket. Madge usually finds a delivery of flowers for her on Fridays and blushes madly whenever he calls to pick her up.

Dick is well and playing a lot of football. Sadly for him there is no league at present as many of the players from the main clubs have joined up. He is hoping for a new ball for Christmas and is very excited as always about Aston Villa.

Do write again soon. I hope this cake and a jar of your favourite strawberry jam help a little. Everyone here sends their love and prayers for your safety and wishes you a Happy Christmas.

With love,
Daisy

Eddie folded the letter and placed it carefully back in the enve-lope before tucking it into the side pocket of his pack. He picked up the jar of jam and looked at Daisy's elegant writing on the label, with the year 1916 inscribed beneath the heading Straw-berry Jam. He pictured the long rows of strawberries, carefully tended by Deacon, the straw beautifully arranged around the plants. When he was twelve he had once helped to pick straw-berries with Daisy and had eaten so many he'd had to hide behind the summerhouse to disguise the awful stomach pains he had developed. After a while, following a large amount of belching and one explosive episode of wind, he had ventured back into the kitchen where his mother and Daisy exchanged knowing looks, fully aware of his problem.

Eddie missed them all dreadfully but still felt he had done the right thing in enlisting. He was sure that his mother would have insisted on him working in the brewery with his father if he'd stayed at home, and how then could he have held up his head before men who were fighting for their country?

Bill Green as a more experienced soldier seemed to know rather more than anyone else about what the regiment was supposed to be doing. As he and Eddie climbed up on to the open railway wagons he pulled a pack of cigarettes out of his top pocket and struck a match, inhaling deeply.

'From what I've heard this railway from Kantara is going to stretch east, out into the desert, up to a place called Romani where there is another oasis. They can then transport troops, food and water up there to reinforce the positions. I hear they're even planning to lay pipes for water and lines for the telephone. These locals are going to be kept busy for a while.' Bill nodded to the railway truck behind him, packed with Egyptians dressed in white robes with scarves wrapped around their heads. They were talk-ing loudly and waving their arms. Eddie caught sight of one man laughing and then coughing furiously, before producing a huge lump of sputum, which he spat into the sand below. He saw Eddie and began waving and laughing even louder.

Eddie knew that the bulk of the work involved in laying the railway line and pipeline would be done by locals, and that camels would be needed to bring forward water and food until it was completed. The job of the Yeomanry was to guard the track and to build lines of defence around the oases to ensure the Turks could not mount any unexpected attacks.

The train trundled slowly out into the desert, the old wagons squeaking and rattling in complaint. The men sat leaning against the sides. Squinting into the sun, they looked out across the endless rolling expanse of sand. The horizon shimmered with heat. Three camels loped slowly along in the distance.

'So what are we going to do after the war, Eddie?' asked Bill.

'Go back to junior school,' laughed Bert Hopkins, who always seemed to take special pleasure in making jokes at Eddie's expense. He rolled his eyes and Bill intervened to defend him.

'At least he will be bright enough to go back there, and on to university if he so chooses. What about you, Hopkins? Back to the butcher's shop or helping Mother with the washing?' Bill laughed, and Bert blushed and shook his head. His family lived in Worcester next door to a local butcher, and Bill knew Bert's father was a drinker. It was his mother who made ends meet by taking in laundry at home.

'I'll eventually go into the family brewing business, providing I make it back,' said Eddie, touching the wooden side of the wagon. 'Although if there was a chance, I might try and play some more football and go for trials with one of the Birmingham teams. I was asked to do a trial by the Villa scout, just before I joined up.'

'Not bad, not bad,' said Bill, and even Bert Hopkins nodded grudging approval. Eddie knew Bert supported Aston Villa, so felt this unusual lapse into boasting was justified if it would give him a slightly easier time.

The train shuddered to a halt, brakes screeching and engine hooting. The soldiers swung over the sides of the wagons, passing down packs and rifles to each other, while the Egyptians began unloading spades and pickaxes. It seemed as though they had hardly travelled any distance into the desert, as the palm trees and smoke from fires at the Kantara camp were still visible behind them. They formed up and marched forward to the front of the train. The engine was puffing steam with the driver sitting on the step smoking. The rails finished twenty or thirty yards in front of the train and local workers were carrying pieces of timber and rail forward to lay track in front of the engine.

Eddie was ordered over to one of the clumps of sandbags, placed either side of the line, to provide some cover from marauding Turks.

'Don't forget the wire, lads,' shouted Bill. Because the area could suddenly be enveloped by fog, particularly in the mornings, the men were ordered to check the ground around the wire where an area was kept swept flat to show any footprints. The wire was strung so tightly that any Turks stumbling into it at night would alert the British lines and thus prevent a surprise attack. Eddie marched out past the shallow trench with the bank of sandbags in front, pacing out the fifty yards until he came across the wire. It was so thin you could not see it until you were right on top of it as the posts were well camouflaged with sand-coloured paint.

He walked down the line for a hundred and fifty yards, occasionally stopping and staring out into the desert to check for the presence of Turks. He had seen, over the last week or so, small groups of cavalry drawing steadily closer, but not near enough to be in range of the British rifles. Once they knew they were observed they would quickly disappear behind one of the sandy hills in the distance. Eddie's mouth was already dry and he took a short sip from his canteen. The water it contained had a faintly salty flavour and he was always relieved that he was unable to see its colour. He turned back towards the trench and the babble from the Egyptians grew steadily louder. They seemed to work at the same slow, steady pace, whatever the weather and regardless of orders from British officers for them to work harder and faster.

He stepped down into the shallow trench and balanced his rifle over the top layer of sandbags. He sat down next to Bill, on the plank that had been laid down as a type of step. If they crouched slightly, it allowed them to survey the ground in front with their eyes just level with the top sandbag. There were four men in the trench, Bill Green, Bert Hopkins, Eddie and Frank Folkes. Frank, with his dark hair kept trim with a centre parting, was only twenty but seemed older than his years. He had joined up at the same time as Eddie and they shared a passion for cricket, both their fathers having taken them to the picturesque ground at Worcester overlooked by the cathedral where King John lay buried. Frank was a left-handed batsman who had opened the batting for Worcester Grammar School and had made a hundred in his final match before he left.

He was also a very good artist, drawing caricatures of many of the soldiers and somewhat risqué cartoons of their senior officers, which produced a modest income as men liked to send the pictures home to their families. He would bring an old book out of his pack at any quiet moment. He had at least four leather-bound volumes and Eddie had discussed one or two of the titles with him. Frank's favourite was *The Oxford Book of English Verse 1250–1900*, edited by Arthur Quiller-Couch. There was a bookplate glued to the inside of the cover, displaying a school crest and, in spidery italic writing, the inscription 'The MacNamara English Essay Prize, 1914'. Eddie was always amused when Frank lent it to him, as Arthur Quiller-Couch had dedicated the book to the president, fellows and scholars of Trinity College, Oxford, as well as 'my most kindly nurse'. Frank and Eddie wondered quite what service Quiller-Couch's nurse had performed, to rank alongside the presidency of Trinity College, Oxford.

Every night, before falling asleep, Frank read at least three or four verses of Thomas Gray's 'Elegy Written in a Country Churchyard'. Frank insisted he slept better after he'd read this but Eddie thought it rather depressing, arguing that Tennyson's 'Blow, Bugle, Blow' was far more uplifting. In fact he thought that the first verse was one of the best in English poetry:

> *The splendour falls on castle walls*
> *And snowy summits old in story:*
> *The long light shakes across the lakes,*
> *And the wild cataract leaps in glory.*
> > *Blow, bugle, blow, set the wild echoes flying,*
> > *Blow, bugle; answer, echoes, dying, dying, dying.*

Frank also had books by Charles Dickens and William Makepeace Thackeray but it was the poetry that they discussed most regularly. Frank told Eddie that his father, who was a railway station master, had read poetry to him as a child. Although at the time Frank had rather dreaded his father sitting on the bed and opening the anthology, he felt that the verses had become part of him so that now he was almost dependent on his daily ration of verse.

'Right, lads, get those rifles cleaned,' said Bill Green. Eddie had already found out that the sand played havoc with the Lee Enfield rifles and every spare moment was taken up with cleaning them to ensure the action was pristine. Frank and Eddie chatted away about their favourite home-cooked meals while they cleaned the barrel with the pull-through and ensured the bolt action was working perfectly.

'This could save your life,' Bert chimed, in imitation of Bill Green. Bill shook his head, as he had been about to repeat an oft-told story of how his rifle once jammed and his life had been saved by a fellow soldier, who had always taken more care of his. Bill realised he must be repeating himself rather too often.

The four men sat in the shallow trench as the sun rose higher throughout the morning; their pith helmets provided the only shade from the relentless heat. Eddie licked the sweat from his top lip and tasted salt. He leant back against some sandbags, feeling slightly drowsy. There was a gentle breeze blowing across the desert but it did little to cool them down. Bill had his elbows resting on the top sandbag and was gazing out over the desert. He was the first to see some movement on the horizon.

'Lads, have a look over there,' he said.

Eddie squinted but could only see shimmering and the ever-present mirage of water close to the horizon. A few minutes passed and then, sure enough, blurred at first but growing more distinct, a group of Turkish cavalry appeared. Eddie realised his heart was pounding and his thumb was sliding back and forth over the safety catch on his rifle. The Turkish cavalry halted about six hundred yards away. Bill Green stood up to obtain a better view.

'What the hell are they doing?' He scratched the back of his neck and turned to check on the railway behind them. The Egyptian workforce continued in their state of semi-organised chaos, unaware of the Turkish presence. Bill sat back down.

'We'd better just keep an eye on them,' he said, a moment before there was a boom behind them and a plume of sand shot into the air.

'They're shelling us! That's a piece of artillery they've brought up,' yelled Bill. 'Open fire. They may not realise there are troops guarding the line.'

Eddie and Frank rested their rifles on the sandbags and aimed slightly over the heads of the Turks, to allow for the distance over which they were firing. Another shell landed behind them and the workers around the line were by now shouting, screaming, and running in all directions. An officer standing on the wagons pulled his pistol from his holster and fired into the air to try and restore order. Eddie slipped the safety catch off and looked down the sights, which were bobbing in time with his pulse. He took a deep breath in, exhaled slowly and squeezed the trigger. There was the familiar jolt in the shoulder. This was the first time he had ever fired at a person, as opposed to the rocks in the desert.

He kept looking down the sights as he had been taught, while he reloaded and fired again. Frank's rifle shot echoed in his left ear. Eddie felt exhilarated, and for a fleeting moment was aware that this was the reason he had enlisted. Another shell exploded behind them. All four men continued to fire but could not see whether they had hit anyone.

'Keep firing, boys,' Bill yelled. 'If they hit that engine we're in trouble.' Eddie reloaded with some difficulty as his hands were shaking from the adrenaline pumping through his body. He realised that the shelling had stopped and some of the Turks were turning away. One man fell from his horse and was dragged with his foot caught in the stirrup.

'We got one,' shouted Frank. They ceased firing and stood up in the trench. The artillery piece was being towed away and, after a few seconds, all they could see was the desert skyline flickering in the heat once more.

They all climbed out of the trench and ran back to the railway line. There were shallow craters where shells had exploded. Egyptians were running down the line shouting while a British officer was ordering them back to work, holding his pistol in the air. Two white-robed bodies lay on the ground close to a shell hole. One lay twisted at a strange angle, his white robe bloodstained and the whole of his right lower leg missing. Another man knelt near the body wailing, and Eddie assumed they were related. Bill went up to the grieving man and laid a hand on his shoulder. The bodies were wrapped in some spare robes and lifted reverently by numerous outstretched arms, then laid in a wagon. They were all ordered to get back on the train but it took twenty minutes to cram everyone aboard before the engine began gasping and squeaking back down the line towards Kantara.

Chapter 11

Aboukir Camp, Egypt, March 1916

It was nearing the end of March and the camp at Aboukir was expanding day by day. Tom had noticed a huge increase in troops and especially in engineers, busy planning the laying of water pipes, communication lines and the railway east into the desert. The days were now getting longer and, more importantly, as far as the men were concerned, the nights were less cold. Throughout January and February, Tom and Sid had both slept fully clothed, curled up under their thin blankets. There were many nights when they had been unable to sleep but had lain awake talking, through lips numb with cold.

Captain Smith Maxwell had reminded them, after one night when frost had formed on the tents, that at least it was better than the trenches in France, where men waded through knee-deep water and were shelled continuously throughout the night. The horses had grown a thicker coat, if a little less full than it would have been in England. There was plenty of feed for them. Duke had taken an instant dislike to camels, though, as there were now huge numbers of them tied up quite near the horse lines. Leaving on patrol often required Tom to use his spurs to get him past them and out into the desert.

On 29 March, after they had returned from their early-morning patrol, Colonel Jeavons called them together in the large flat area which doubled as a parade ground.

'Good morning, men. You will have already gathered that the Turkish presence to the east has increased dramatically in the last few months. They are deploying more troops and artillery so it's essential that we prevent any further advance, which may threaten the Suez Canal. There are a number of oases to the east, which could provide important staging posts for them to launch attacks, so you are being ordered to Qatia to prepare defences and repel any further advance. Good luck to you all.'

Sergeant Vint shouted them to attention as the Colonel saluted and turned away. The next twenty-four hours were spent packing up supplies and dismantling the heavy canvas tents, which were then strapped to the sides of camels.

Two days later the whole regiment began the march to Qatia. They set out just as the sun was beginning to appear over the hills to the east. Tom, Sid and Alf were mounted and rode as part of 'D' Squadron. Duke had hardly been exercised so was on his toes, bolting sideways whenever he caught sight of a camel. Tom felt anxious about the move; he had been in the area of Kantara for just over six months and there was a familiarity to his daily routine there he had come to enjoy. He was aware that the forward positions were likely to be more active and hoped that his friends' prior experience in the Dardanelles would help calm his nerves.

'Tom, you seem a bit quiet,' said Sid. 'We'll be safe as houses up there. The Captain says it's not a bad spot and we'll have two squadrons to make sure Johnny Turk doesn't get too cocky.'

'It seems strange to be leaving this place but I know Qatia well; we've patrolled around there before. I just hope those Turks think Alf is too terrifying to bother attacking us,' said Tom.

Alf turned round laughing and raised his arms, sniffing beneath them. 'They get downwind of this, they'll gallop back to bloody Constantinople '

The column of horses and camels marched up the railway line where the Egyptians were working. Some paused, straightening up and waving as the riders passed by. Tom saw one or two familiar faces and shouted back to them.

The column continued into the desert for nearly two hours, stopping occasionally so that scouts could patrol ahead. They passed the first oasis of Romani to their left and could see the small collection of palm trees marking Qatia a few miles ahead. Further to the east lay another oasis, Oghratina. Once Major Wiggin, their new commanding officer, was happy that there were no Turks in the area, they dismounted by the oasis at Qatia. Tom led Duke down to the side of the water and let him drink. The water looked quite cloudy but none of the horses seemed worried. Tom leant against the saddle, patting Duke. His neck had sweat drying on it and he occasionally looked up, shaking his head to keep the flies away.

Over the next few hours a camp slowly took shape. Lines for horses were formed to the west and to the east, and they were ordered to begin digging shallow trenches to make a simple defence, which could then be reinforced over the coming days. Smith Maxwell was in his element, rushing about issuing orders and then scurrying back to Major Wiggin to report on progress. It was almost dark by the time they had pitched tents and were ordered to line up for supper, tired and dehydrated.

Tom woke the following morning to shouts from near his tent. Sergeant Vint was screaming at one of the camel drivers and slapping him around the head. Tom pulled on his boots and asked if he could help. Vint picked up a bucket in each hand and hurried off, shouting over his shoulder, 'Bomford, stop bloody gawping and get digging trenches.'

Tom walked over to the horse lines and found Alf and Sid convulsed in laughter.

'Tom, d'you see Vint with some buckets?' asked Alf.

'Yes, he was giving one of the camel drivers a slapping and saying something about it being fresh,' said Tom.

'He's taken the bloody bait. Follow me, lads,' wheezed Alf, still laughing. They made their way back around the palm trees to where the officers' tents were pitched and saw Vint, now walking more slowly, carrying the two buckets in a rather deliberate way, as if trying not to spill anything. He stopped outside Major Wiggin's tent and straightened his uniform.

'Good morning, sir, Sergeant Vint reporting,' he bellowed. Major Wiggin ducked through the tent flap and saluted. He was young for a Major, with broad shoulders and a thick brown moustache. All the men spoke of his open manner and concern for their wellbeing, which was rare for an officer.

'Good morning, Vint. How are you today?' he said, flicking his moustache and looking the Sergeant up and down, and then gazing with a more puzzled expression at the buckets.

'Bloody hell, Vint, what's in there? They stink.'

'As you ordered, sir, I have brought camel's urine to soak your painful ankle in, and I can guarantee it's fresh this morning, sir,' said Vint, saluting again with a big smile on his face.

'Stop bloody saluting! What are you talking about, man? My ankle is perfectly sound,' said Wiggin. Vint's expression began to change with the faint realisation that all was not well.

'I had a message last night, sir, from Captain Smith Maxwell, ordering me to collect two buckets of fresh camel urine this morning for your bad ankle and to bring them to your tent,' spluttered Vint, looking panic-stricken.

Wiggin shook his head and began laughing.

'Vint, you mug, it's the first of April. You've been completely had,' said the Major as he marched off to the officers' tent, still laughing.

Alf, Tom and Sid ducked out of sight quickly before their laughter gave them away. Alf explained that during the last day or so Smith Maxwell had been issuing huge numbers of bits of paper with written orders on them and Alf had obtained a blank sheet from his tent, written the order for Vint and forged the Captain's signature. He had then asked one of the other soldiers to deliver it to Vint's tent when most of the men had fallen asleep. Apparently he had read it immediately and begun cursing the Captain, calling him every name under the sun, but Alf had spotted him in the early hours with one of the camel drivers, waiting patiently in the lines for any camel to help fill his bucket.

Alf was lucky Sergeant Vint never found out who the joker was.

During the next week, both squadrons were deployed building defences and filling sandbags. The trenches were quite shallow, as there were areas of rock where they were only able to dig two to three feet down, which spared them some sweat. They patrolled each morning and it was soon obvious there was far more Turkish activity in this area than back in Aboukir Camp.

The force in the area was officially the 5th Mounted Brigade, which was made up of eight squadrons of cavalry from the Warwickshire Yeomanry, Gloucestershire Hussars and the Worcestershire Yeomanry. Tom and Sid recognised a few familiar faces among the Warwickshire Yeomanry. Bobby King had hunted with the Warwickshire since he was a child. His father Albert was a farmer and horse dealer, often travelling over to Ireland and bringing back six or eight horses as three- and four-year-olds, to break in on the family farm. Bobby's job was to take the horses out hunting and develop them over a couple of seasons. He was a confident rider, to say the least, and knew that horses would jump well for him. He had almost been lynched at a point-to-point before the war when he had stopped riding and lost the race on a red-hot favourite in the Croome Hunt open race. A huge crowd of punters who had backed the horse Bobby was riding tried to find him, but he managed to slip away across the fields to safety. This narrow escape had resulted in a new degree of humility in him, which was welcome, although Tom had always liked him and respected his skill as a horseman.

Tom had been out with the Warwickshire in the winter of 1913 when Bobby, in full view of all the other riders, galloped across three fields of grass, jumping on the way three of the biggest hedges and ditches that Tom had ever seen. Bobby's father, Albert, happened to be standing next to one of the joint masters, who made a substantial offer for the horse and bought it then and there.

A week after they had arrived in Qatia, Tom saw Walter Garland in company with a small group of men, talking very excitedly. The group dispersed and Tom went over to him.

'Are you all right, Walter?' he asked. His friend looked flushed and his ginger hair was stuck to his scalp, with sand matted around his ears.

'Tom, we have just come back from patrol and ran into hundreds of Turks…hundreds of them,' stammered Walter.

'Slow down, man. Where was this?'

'We were about fifteen miles east of here, near Bir-el-Abd, when Smith Maxwell spotted them. There were at least two hundred and they had machine guns and artillery. We dismounted and ran forward to a small ridge and fired off ten rounds. Then they set up the machine gun. The bloody noise! Our rifles seemed like pea-shooters by comparison. We remounted and got the hell out of there. Forty or fifty cavalry galloped after us but we fired at them and they pulled back. I think they've got something planned, Tom.'

'Sounds like it. How's your horse?'

'Well, thanks. Plenty of feed, although we seem to be a bit short of water.'

'Apparently there are some engineers trying to dig wells to increase the supply.'

Word of the skirmish soon spread around the camp at Qatia, while officers met in their tent to discuss the events. They had hoped to obtain reliable information on the number of Turkish troops from the Bedouin in the area, but since their arrival very few tribesmen had been seen, which was suspicious. For the next week the camp was on high alert, with sentries doubled and more patrols sent out each day.

Palm Sunday came on 16 April, and the chaplain held a short service close to the oasis. He asked all the men to approach the makeshift altar and presented them with pieces of palm leaf to mark Jesus's journey into Jerusalem on a donkey. Tom had read the passage in Matthew's Gospel the night before and realised how close they now were to Jerusalem itself. He thought back to Easter in Pershore Abbey, when as children they'd brought small crosses they had made at school from pieces of bark or reed.

The chaplain spoke of the difficulties that Jesus had endured and the courage he had shown in facing his accusers. He likened Jesus's struggle to that of the British in Egypt, and asked them all to remember their families at home and to pray for their safe return. They then filed forward to receive Communion. Tom noticed the thin smear of sand on the side of the chalice as he bowed his head to receive the Blood of Christ and noticed the grit in his mouth as he took the bread on his tongue.

On 20 April 'D' Squadron was told they would be moving the following day, five miles east of Qatia to Oghratina, another oasis, where there was an opportunity for a party of Royal Engineers to dig more wells. Tom was by now used to packing up their kit and, as ever, Vint provided a certain amount of entertainment, marching around the small camp, ordering men to continue what they were already doing. Tom was not so afraid of him now. He appeared less vindictive and seemed to ignore Tom most of the time.

'Bomford, Parkes, have you packed up your supplies?' he asked them late in the afternoon, wiping his brow and appearing rather agitated.

'Yes, Sergeant. Would you mind if I had a quick pee?' said Sid, smirking.

'Don't get smart with me, Parkes, you little shit,' said Vint through gritted teeth. He turned away and stalked off to his own tent.

Chapter 12

Kantara, Egypt, April 1916

Eddie Williams was lying stretched out in the afternoon sun. His head was in the shadow of his tent, resting against his pack, and his legs were comfortably crossed. They were darkly tanned except for the area of white skin where his shorts had ridden up. Bill Green wandered over to the tent, flicking a cigarette end into the sand and exhaling smoke behind him as he went. Frank Folkes lay beside Eddie, puffing on a cigarette and whistling between breaths, his book of poetry held in one hand. His legs extended well beyond Eddie's, as he was nearly six inches taller.

'So, Bill, what's the gossip?' asked Frank.

'We're being moved forward soon; the order is being given tonight.'

'Where to?'

'Qatia, apparently. The Turks have this new German commander. Those on high think he knows what he's doing, so they want a few more boys up there to help out,' said Bill.

The following morning they were ordered to leave their horses behind in Kantara and transfer as far as possible by railway, marching the remaining distance across the desert. Both Frank and Eddie were secretly relieved to leave the horses. Eddie was more comfortable on foot and still felt ill at ease mounted on his horse, Ginger. He was a chestnut and, according to Bill, at least ten years old. He showed very little interest in Eddie, or anyone else for that matter, except when he was being fed. For most of the time, including when he was being ridden, he walked with his head down, and to keep him from stopping completely Eddie had to kick him continuously. Trotting and cantering needed even more effort, with the reins flicked down on his neck like a whip. With very little warning Ginger would often stop walking so that Eddie was catapulted forward around his neck, hanging on grimly to stop himself from sliding off, in which he was not always successful.

Eddie was rather envious of the men who were better mounted and had become fond of their horses. He feared that, even in the heat of battle, Ginger would be far too slow and he and his rider would end up being cut down by Turkish cavalry.

Before he left, Eddie walked down the lines of horses to check that Ginger had enough food and water. He patted him on the neck as the horse continued to munch on his hay, ignoring him.

'Cheerio, old mate. I'm not sure when we might see each other again,' Eddie said, pulling on one of Ginger's ears. He recognised then that this rather unloved horse had allowed him to admit the risks that faced him and the real possibility that he might be killed. He tried to grasp what death would mean and found himself feeling strangely indifferent. He knew his family would be devastated but felt resigned to whatever lay in store for him.

Eddie met Frank as he walked back through the lines to board the train. As usual the area was heaving with people and there were many members of the local Egyptian Expeditionary Force (EEF) who were working on the railway. Supply camels were being loaded and unloaded, and there was a small winch lowering sections of rail on to a truck. Eddie could smell camel dung, spices, and the familiar smell of unwashed men. They walked down the track, climbed up on to an open wagon and sat down to wait for the train to depart.

Frank pulled out his sketchpad and started drawing an Egyptian wearing a large turban. He puffed on a small hand-rolled cigarette and was smiling at them, saying, 'Hello, hello, British very good,' flashing one or two brown teeth. The engine whistled, the wagons began to whine and clank, and with a shudder the train moved forward. Their speed picked up, which gave them a rapid snapshot of the camp. Rows of tents, water tanks, lines of camels led by turbaned men, a company of soldiers marching through the camp in time, save for one man who skipped every third step to try and fall back in line. Towards the outer edge of the camp was an area where the Egyptians slept under canvas sheets. Eight or nine of them sat around a small fire with a steaming pot over it. They turned and waved, one of them brandishing a stick he had just lifted out of the vessel. The train rattled on past the huge, sprawling expanse of their incursion into the desert.

Eddie pulled out his last letter and began to read Daisy's very neat forward-sloping writing. The paper was cream woven and almost as thick as parchment.

Frank looked up from his book of poetry.

'So what news from the Williams family then?'

'Well, my sister Madge is still seeing quite a lot of a local GP, Dr Parkes, who visits her every week and either takes her out to the local tearooms or for a drive in the country. My father believes he has good prospects and that Madge needs to settle down before too long. He thinks she is not getting any younger, so if Parkes asks for her hand she should accept.'

'I'd imagine the doc will be on bended knee soon,' said Frank.

'Daisy says Madge is not sure about marrying him, although she thinks they could be happy, but she says she won't do anything until I get back from the war.'

'If any of us ever do get back, that is,' said Frank, shaking his head. He tucked his book of poetry back in his pack and leant forward, which Eddie had come to realise usually meant a short lecture was coming.

'As I see it, this push into the desert is just what these bloody officers want. They're itching to start charging across the sand, waving their swords, while us lot are blown to pieces by artillery. Those generals underestimated the Turks in the Dardanelles and I'm bloody sure they will do the same in Egypt if we don't watch our arses. Bill should know – didn't he fight in the Boer War? Well, he says most of them are out here because of some family connection to Lord Dudley or something.

'Sorry to go on, Eddie, but I'm fed up with this place…bloody sand, flies, filthy water, and food that you wouldn't feed to animals back home. The only highlight is the cake you kindly share with us that Daisy somehow manages to send out to you. That is proper stuff. I bet if it took twice as long for it to get here, it would taste even better.'

'Don't worry, the desert's getting me down too. Maybe Beersheba will be full of bars packed with belly-dancers,' said Eddie, chuckling.

Chapter 13

Ivy Lodge, Stourbridge, April 1916

Harry ate his last piece of toast and marmalade and put down his paper.

'Well, if rationing has stopped them making marmalade, I shall miss it on my toast in the morning. I find Mrs Deacon's strawberry jam a little too sweet.'

'Now, Father, don't be so ungrateful. It's lovely jam and very kind of her to make it,' said Madge.

'I know, Madge, but they are *my* strawberries, don't forget.'

'Now, dear, you have remembered we have Aunt Frisky coming to lunch today, haven't you?' his wife Marian asked him.

'I had forgotten, but it will be good to see her. I have to go to the brewery for a few hours but I'll be back in time for lunch. Have we got enough sherry in the house?' Harry said, laughing.

'Father, don't be rude! She is my favourite godmother and very good fun too,' said Madge. 'I haven't seen her for ages.'

Madge's godmother, Frisky Bentall, was by any definition a character. She was thought to be in her early sixties, although no one knew her exact age, and had been a friend of the family for ever. She was very large, had a round smiling face, and drank copious amounts of gin and sherry. Her cheeks were always rosy and she generally wore a hat, often with elaborate decoration in the form of feathers, flowers or fur.

Madge cleared the breakfast things and started preparations for lunch. She peeled some potatoes and picked broccoli from the garden. Meals had become increasingly difficult with rationing in force, and although with their large garden they were well supplied compared to most, cooking had to be planned carefully.

She changed into a pale-blue dress and pinned up her hair. She was coming down the stairs as her father returned from work.

'All well at the office?'

'Yes, thank you. I shall bring up a barrel of sherry for Aunt Frisky.'

'Oh, Father, she's not that bad.'

Madge checked the dining room. The table was laid and there were some daffodils on the sideboard in a crystal vase. The grandfather clock in the hall chimed midday, and as it did Madge heard the clip-clop of hooves out on the road. She hurried out of the front door and there was Aunt Frisky in her pony and trap, drawing to a stop. She was wearing a wide-brimmed felt hat that she had tied under her chin with some string. She also had on a large, heavy, tweed jacket, a green skirt, knitted brown stockings and thick-soled brown brogues. She jumped down from the trap, brandishing her whip, and hugged Madge.

'Darling Madge, it's lovely to see you. How is my favourite goddaughter?'

'Very well, thank you. How are you, Auntie?'

'Very well indeed,' Aunt Frisky replied, turning to Deacon and handing him the reins.

'Thank you, Deacon. You look very well, I must say,' she boomed. 'Would you give Jenny some water? There are some oats in the back of the trap.'

'Yes, I will, with pleasure,' he replied, smiling. He remembered Aunt Frisky always tipped him generously.

Madge led the way into the hall and took her godmother's coat. The rest of the family were all in the drawing room, which was bathed in sunshine. Aunt Frisky swept in and hugged them one by one.

'No problems with your trip, I trust?' asked Harry, as he poured her a large glass of sherry.

'No, none at all. Roads very empty actually. Well, lovely to see you all,' she said as she raised her glass and took a generous gulp of sherry. 'Rather thirsty, as it happens,' she said, laughing.

Madge and Daisy adored seeing Aunt Frisky. She was amusing, energetic and always interested in what they were all doing. The first sherry disappeared at speed and Harry soon topped her up as she told them she was thinking of becoming a spy.

'Woman of mystery, I rather fancy the idea,' she said mischievously.

'Auntie, don't you think it might be hard for you to work in disguise? You are rather unforgettable after all,' said Daisy.

'You may be right, my dear. This rationing's a bit difficult, isn't it, Harry?'

'Yes, it is. Coal is about to be rationed too and allocations will be linked to the number of rooms in your house, I hear.'

'Not really a problem for me. As you know, I can't stand too much heat. If it's cold I put another coat on. Lovely sherry, Harry,' said Aunt Frisky, holding up her empty glass.

'We're going to get some chickens to keep in the garden, aren't we, Father?' said Daisy.

'Yes, although Deacon will not be too pleased.'

They made their way in to lunch and Marian served a lamb stew with vegetables.

'How is Eddie? Do you have any news?'

'He has written to say he's in Egypt guarding the Suez Canal. He seems well although the heat is difficult for him,' answered Marian.

'You poor things, you must be so worried. As you know, I only have godchildren to care for, as I never found the right man, but I pray every night for his safe return. Delicious stew, Marian, thank you.'

Daisy cleared the plates and brought out their dessert. Aunt Frisky looked round, trying to check what was being served.

'Don't worry, Auntie, it's your favourite,' said Madge, reassuringly.

'I was a little worried for a moment, I have to admit. Marian, your sherry trifle is still the best I've ever tasted,' she said, sitting back and rubbing her hands together.

They talked of fishing in Scotland where Aunt Frisky had been for three months, looking after an elderly relative who had died. She'd stayed on, catching four salmon in the River Tay, and, having smoked two, emptied the railway carriage by the time she arrived home. Then they moved on to the recent bombing attacks on London by the German zeppelins, which utterly disgusted Aunt Frisky. Harry was worried about the ever-increasing price of food, as imports were restricted by attacks on merchant shipping by German U-boats. He thought he might have to provide extra food for some of the brewery workers if supplies worsened.

'More acts of cowardice by the Germans with these heinous attacks by submarines. They really are a shower, aren't they?' Aunt Frisky said, looking round the table for support. There was a general nodding of heads in agreement.

'Well, I must away before Jenny stiffens up too much. Rather the same with me,' she said, slapping Harry on the back. 'Next time, perhaps I can meet Dr Parkes, Madge.'

'Yes, of course, you must.'

Aunt Frisky met Deacon outside. He touched his cap as she slipped some money into his hand. She slowly pulled herself up into her seat and the trap shook as she sat down heavily. She tied on her hat, pulled on her gloves and took up the reins.

'Goodbye, my dears, lovely to see you all,' she shouted, as she cracked the whip and hurtled out of the gate.

'Father, why is she called Aunt Frisky?' asked Madge.

'I'll tell you one day, it's quite a long story,' Harry said, as he puffed on his cigar and headed back into the house.

Chapter 14

Oghratina Oasis, Egypt, Good Friday 1916

Tom woke long before the morning call. It was still dark outside and he gazed at the roof of his tent in the moonlight. He heard a sentry shout, 'Who goes there?' and the reply of 'It's me, you bloody fool,' followed by a laugh. Sid snored beside him, mouth wide open and a blanket pulled up to his chin.

It was Good Friday and Tom thought of home and of his family preparing to go to the early Communion service. His father would be following his yearly ritual of abstaining from beer from Shrove Tuesday through to Easter Sunday, when he would return from church and open the bottle which had been carefully placed on the kitchen table in readiness that morning. Tom thought of his mother, sitting at the table sniffing and dabbing her nose with her hand-kerchief, which always used to annoy him although he surprised himself this time by remembering it fondly. He pictured Hender, and Ray, and each of his sisters. Lastly he allowed himself to think of Jane. He remembered her always sharing her Easter egg with him and smiling to reveal teeth blackened by chocolate. He realised she would want him to return home safely to the family.

He felt Sid shaking his arm as he had obviously dozed off again. Tom pulled on his boots and stepped out of the tent into the cool of the early morning. Men were scurrying around the camp, making ready for the march to the oasis of Oghratina. Tom and Sid dismantled their tent in a well-practised routine, and folded it up to load on to a camel. They had filled their water bottles already and had some stale bread in their packs. Tom saddled up Duke and fitted his rifle into the holster, checking once more that the safety catch was on; he had an irrational fear of shooting the horse by accidentally firing the gun while mounting. The two squadrons assembled and began the short ride from Qatia to Oghratina.

Captain Smith Maxwell was one of four officers at the head of the column. He was very nervous, stammering commands to Sergeant Vint and the other men. Tom had always wondered how he would handle the pressure of being attacked by a large force of Turks as opposed to small groups of cavalry who were always heavily outnumbered.

Alf was riding just in front of Tom and Walter, and was perched on the edge of the saddle at a strange angle.

'Alf, what's the matter? You look like you've got a carrot stuck up your arse,' shouted Tom.

'It's my bloody piles, Tom, they're killing me. I've had it with the bully beef – and before you say anything, I don't want to see another date for as long as I live,' said Alf, trying to shift position once again.

The sun was now well above the horizon and Tom started sweating. The uniform began to itch across his back, where it stuck to his skin, and the tinkling of water canteens as men drank to try and quench their almost permanent thirst.

They rode over firm sand on a slight track formed by the regular Bedouin caravans, which travelled from oasis to oasis. They must have been about halfway when Tom saw a hill to their left, rising quite steeply to about a hundred feet high. The sand was perfectly rounded on the slopes but there was a flat outcrop of rock at the top. It appeared a perfect viewpoint from which to survey the area and he was sure a good number of them would be marching up there before the day was out. On the shimmering horizon a few palm trees appeared. Sergeant Vint suggested calling a halt to send scouts ahead to check the oasis, which had obviously not occurred to Captain Smith Maxwell.

'Yes, yes, good idea, Vint. I was about to order just that,' he blustered. Ten men were sent ahead while the two squadrons dismounted to rest their horses.

Tom pulled some biscuit from his pocket to give Duke, who nuzzled into his hand looking for more. The whiskers around his nose always tickled Tom's hand, making him chuckle.

'Well, me old lad, what d'you think of this place then?' said Sid, patting his neck.

'He's pretty relaxed about most things,' said Tom.

'You really love that horse, don't you?'

'I do, Sid. He's been with me since nearly the beginning. Every morning he's pleased to see me, and unlike Vint he doesn't talk rubbish and scream abuse at me the whole time.'

After thirty or forty minutes two scouts reappeared and told the Captain all seemed quiet up ahead. Smith Maxwell turned his horse and addressed the men.

'Seems like the Turks have disappeared, clearly not at all keen to take on British cavalry and their swords.' He laughed confidently.

Sid turned to Tom, shaking his head.

'He hasn't got a clue, has he? Typical toff. Those Turks are pretty sharp, and if they have German officers as well we could be in a bit of trouble if they appear in numbers.'

'We all know the Captain's father is friendly with Lord Dudley, and that is how he got his commission. Still, he wouldn't be the first officer to find his way into the regiment through the old boys' network,' said Alf, who found the need to take orders rather harder than most. Tom reminded him of the time, during training, when Alf had refused to lead the Captain's horse home in the rain while Smith Maxwell rode in Colonel Jeavons's car. Alf was hauled in front of the commanding officer and punished with two weeks of lavatory cleaning. This foul duty wasn't helped by the fact that there had been an epidemic of diarrhoea sweeping through the regiment at the time.

They reached Oghratina and were ordered to pitch tents and prepare defences. The oasis itself was filled with brackish water but they were told that as long as it was well boiled it would be perfectly safe to drink. There were a few palm trees fringing the water; otherwise desert stretched away from them in every direction. Tom tied up Duke to lines that had been hastily erected to the west of the small camp.

They began digging trenches on the eastern side, but found that after about a foot they hit bedrock. They all knew that this made them very vulnerable to attack. The only option was to try filling sandbags as soon as possible but this was much more time-consuming. Tom and Sid stripped off their shirts and began laying out sacks. It was back-breaking work and the day was still very hot.

They had been digging for nearly an hour and had paused for a drink of water when Walter spotted a small group of Bedouin, with their camels, meandering across the desert from the east towards them. The men moved behind the low wall of sandbags and got their rifles ready while Alf went to alert Sergeant Vint. When the Bedouin were thirty yards away a warning was shouted for them to halt. One of them stepped forward, dropping the rope attached to his camel's head.

'We are friends of British, we have no guns. Down with Turkey!' shouted the Bedouin leader in a thick accent, prompting cheers from the rest of his band. Vint ordered the men to approach the lines slowly, and as he did so muttered quietly, 'If you spot even a bloody pea-shooter, lads, open fire.'

Tom slipped off his safety catch and moved his right forefinger on to the trigger-guard, ready to fire. His temple pulsed steadily as the Bedouin came to within ten yards of them. Walter and two others were ordered to search them while their leader, who called himself Moussa, jabbered away in broken English about their hatred of the Turks and how they all loved the British.

They were carrying no weapons, and Walter together with two

other soldiers escorted them to the west of the oasis near the lines of horses. Tom and Sid returned to filling sandbags before stopping for the night. They walked to the water and bent down to wash. Sand and sweat was caked around their arms where the wind had blown it, forming layers of crust. The water was a faint brown colour and smelt slightly of salt. They rubbed their heads with their shirts and shook off some of the water.

'I think we've another day of that tomorrow,' said Sid.

'We need it. If the Turks attack now we've almost no cover at all,' said Tom. 'Just over a hundred of us here, lying round some filthy water...we're like sitting ducks.'

'Have you seen any Turks around? It seems quiet to me.'

'Quiet right now, but we haven't got three regiments out here, have we?'

They walked to the mess tent for some supper and then collapsed in their tents. As it was still Good Friday, Tom took out his Bible and, by candlelight, read a passage on the crucifixion of Jesus. He rubbed the Bible's leather cover and then tucked it back in his jacket before closing his eyes and praying silently that they would come through whatever was ahead of them the following day.

The next morning they were woken well before sunrise and went to check the horses, carrying their rifles with them. Moussa and the other Bedouin waved to them and Tom saw that Walter was already standing by their camels, joking about with them as Moussa patted him on the back.

Walter ambled over to join Tom. 'They're a laugh, that lot. Not keen on the Turks or the Germans. Moussa told me half their camels have been stolen and that his brother was shot only a month ago.'

'Walter, you just be careful. They look like those gypsies who come round all the farms in the spring...bloody shifty,' said Tom.

'Tom's right. They'll say anything they think you want to hear,' warned Sid.

Walter seemed slightly hurt that his judgement had been questioned. Tom looked back and saw Moussa and his friends all huddled together, heads down, deep in conversation.

A slither of orange light was appearing over the hills to the east. The sky was beginning to change colour as they finished breakfast and went back to their tents to clean their rifles. Captain Smith Maxwell appeared with Vint, looking sweaty and rather pale.

'Good morning, men. I've heard overnight that there is a lot of Turkish activity in this area. The remainder of "A" Squadron will soon be joining us to reinforce this position. Keep working on our defences...and keep those rifles clean! Anything else, Vint?' asked Smith Maxwell, as he turned to the Sergeant. Tom could see the officer's hands shaking slightly.

'No, sir, but our trenches are very shallow as there's only a thin layer of sand before we hit rock, so the lads have been filling sandbags. It's pretty slow work,' warned Vint.

'Well, best for you to get digging as well and help them out then, Sergeant,' said Smith Maxwell, missing the point. Vint rolled his eyes and realised it was hopeless to protest. Sid and Tom smiled and held out two shovels for him to choose from. They didn't say anything: Vint's expression was menacing.

They spent an hour working on the defences, filling sandbags and using rocks to raise them a little higher. It was beginning to get unbearably hot for digging, the flies had started to appear and they were all desperate for water. Vint had been almost completely silent during the process, except for a lot of puffing, blowing and repeated halts to mop his head with a stained piece of cloth that Tom assumed had once been a handkerchief.

Tom walked over to the horses and checked Duke's water. He was dozing in the sun, chewing on the occasional piece of feed, eyes half closed. Tom gave him a pat and rubbed his face, which led to Duke's eyes closing completely in pleasure. The Bedouin called over to them, signalling for them to come towards the camels, which were lying on the ground in a semicircle.

'British very good, Turkey bad, we not like Turkey,' shouted Moussa, before turning to the other men who all started nodding in unison. Tom lost patience with them. The relentless heat was making him tetchy. He walked towards Moussa.

'Hello, British, very welcome, very welcome!'

He surveyed the line of men all grinning at him. 'Why don't you all just piss off back into the desert?'

He turned away and stalked back towards the oasis, leaving Moussa looking puzzled. Sid put his arm round Tom's shoulders as they went back to the camp. 'Hey, mate, that's unlike you. What's going on?'

'This bloody heat and shovelling sand day after day, I'm fed up with it. We've sweltered out here for months and those Bedouin are just sitting about shouting. Well, it got to me. Why don't the lazy devils come and give us a hand?'

'Now, you know that's never going to happen. Let's go and get some food and water.'

After eating they sat in the shade of the palm trees, smoking and chatting, while other men were on sentry duty. At around three in the afternoon the remainder of 'A' Squadron arrived to reinforce the position. Although everyone welcomed the extra numbers, their defences seemed even more inadequate then, with another hundred men and horses to safeguard. Captain Ward who commanded 'A' Squadron informed the men, again, that there was a lot of Turkish activity, but the numbers involved were difficult to estimate.

Tom immediately liked Ward. He was young, enthusiastic and seemed competent. He walked around the squadron, having a quiet word with many of the individual soldiers.

One of the men from 'A' Squadron asked Alf for a light and they started talking.

'So, how long have you boys been out here?' the new arrival asked, puffing hard on his cigarette, trying to get it to burn properly.

'Only arrived yesterday morning, otherwise we would have sorted out a welcome party for you. So what's your Captain like then?' Alf queried.

'Great bloke, tough as hobnail boots. He'll dig trenches along with us and he's got some fists on him too. There was a Corporal back in Kantara who returned from leave really drunk one night and took a swing at Ward. Well, that was stupid because next thing the Captain plants one on his chin, and the Corporal's out cold.'

'At least we've got one officer who knows what he's doing then,' said Sid.

That evening they checked their equipment and cleaned their rifles again. They were issued with more ammunition and sentries were doubled. Tom lay in his tent fully dressed, dozing and waiting for his duty at two o'clock. It was quiet outside with no wind and he occasionally heard the deep groans of the camels and mumbling as men changed duties and tried to get a little sleep.

Easter Sunday, 23 April 1916
'Bomford, Parkes, sentry duty! Get out there, you lazy bastards,' said Vint, peeling back the tent flap.

'Yes, sir,' said Tom, sitting bolt upright, instantly awake. Tom and Sid slid out of the tent into thick fog. Sid coughed as the cold air hit his lungs.

'We won't see much in this, mate,' he said, pulling on his pack and slinging his rifle over his shoulder.

'It's bloody thick, like being on the river Avon in Pershore on a November night,' agreed Tom.

They made their way to the shallow trenches to the east of the camp and took up position, listening for any noise. The chill fog swirled around them. It had a shimmering, ghostly quality. At least the cold kept them awake. It remained quiet in spite of one scare – straining to hear, both men thought they heard a sound like the rattle of a horse's bit, but nothing materialised.

Soon after 4 a.m. the whole camp was called to arms and Tom and Sid were relieved. As they were walking back to their tent they heard a thumping noise coming from the south, which sounded like water pumps. Captain Ward and two other men passed them, heading out of the camp to investigate. Tom and Sid waited on the edge of the camp, straining to hear. The rhythmic thudding of water pumps could be heard quite clearly now, and a number of men stood by, rifles at the ready, desperate to see anything through the thick fog. The visibility was no more than ten to fifteen yards.

After five minutes Captain Ward appeared, having shouted a warning to the sentries. He was breathless and agitated. 'Men, quickly, there's a group of Turkish soldiers down there pumping water. Bring your rifles and follow me.'

Ward disappeared into the fog with a group of men. There was a pause and then rifle fire and shouting broke out, before more fire some minutes later that appeared to be at a distance. Tom and Sid waited, rifles pointing out into the fog. The tension was palpable. They both imagined enemy horses and men rushing out of the shifting, swirling fog in front of them. Minutes passed, there were more shouts, and then Ward suddenly reappeared out of the fog. He was breathless and sweating.

'There's a mass of Turks down there, back to your positions!' he gasped.

Tom and Sid ran back to their trench as Ward went to find Smith Maxwell to discuss the defences.

'Where the bloody hell have you been, lads?' asked Alf, who was sitting casually on a pile of sandbags, picking grit out of his hair.

'Alf, get yourself down in this trench! There's a mass of Turks just over that hill,' said Sid, pointing over his shoulder. Alf jumped up, scratched his groin, and sat down in the shallow trench.

'Thanks, Sid, that's all I need to know right now. Time for a smoke,' he said, fumbling in his breast pocket, his hands shaking. Many of the men were still in their tents, sorting out packs and cleaning their rifles, and as Tom looked back to the palm trees there was shouting and four or five soldiers came running across the sand. One of them was Walter, clutching his bloodied left arm and limping badly.

'Tom, it's the Bedouin. They've started attacking us,' he shouted. He was sobbing and shaking his head.

'Don't worry, we'll sort those devils out,' said Tom, leading him across to the doctor, who pulled a field dressing out of his jacket to apply to Walter's wounds.

Vint appeared at Tom's shoulder, running through the men who were fleeing towards them, shouting, 'Lads, follow me! Fix bayonets, time to sort out those bloody Bedouin once and for all. I knew we should have shot the buggers when we first saw them.'

They rounded the palm trees to find a scene of horror before them. Moussa and his accomplices were running from tent to tent, stabbing wildly at the canvas with their curved daggers. Tom saw three soldiers lying dead with a shredded tent half covering their bodies.

'Finish British, finish British! Turks Kantara! Turks Cairo!' Moussa shouted, as he waved his dagger in the air.

Vint half turned towards his own men.

'No firing, lads, too dangerous. Just run 'em through.'

Vint then took off at a sprint, closing in on Moussa. The Bedouin turned and there was a moment of realisation when triumph turned to terror. Vint's bayonet pierced the Bedouin's stomach. Vint carried on running as Moussa was lifted off the ground and hurled on his back. It took very little time for the remaining Bedouin to be found and killed, but they had wrought havoc on the camp.

It was now just before five in the morning and Captain Smith Maxwell ordered about sixty men out to the most easterly trench to take up defensive positions. He warned them that the sound of gunfire would have alerted all Turkish troops in the area, and that they should expect an attack before too long. Walter Garland, despite his injury, insisted on staying in the second line of trenches, saying he would be able to fire his rifle, resting it on the sandbag in front of him.

'Well done, Garland, do the best you can,' said Smith Maxwell, patting him on his injured left shoulder and causing Walter to wince in pain.

'What about saddling up the horses, sir? The men could ride out to meet them,' said Walter.

'We've got the engineers to think about, Garland. We can't just abandon them here.' Smith Maxwell strode off to the forward trench. A few wisps of residual fog blew across the desert, temporarily engulfing him. Walter leant back in the trench, his arm throbbing so much he was feeling nauseous.

Tom and Sid were crouching in the shallow forward trench, rifles propped on the top sandbags. The sky was lightening as the sun began to rise in front of them. Other men lined the defences but no one was talking. There were a few muffled orders from the oasis behind them and Tom heard a horse neighing. His mouth was dry and he realised he'd had nothing to drink since last night. He twisted his pack off and offered some water to Sid.

'Thanks, that's better,' whispered his friend as Tom took a long drink himself. 'We're going to be under attack pretty soon, you know.'

Tom nodded. 'I never thought we'd be in a trench like this. I always thought I'd be mounted and we'd be taking on their cavalry out in the open. How are you feeling?'

'Scared shitless. My hands are shaking so much I'm not sure I can hold the rifle.'

'Me too. I'd feel a lot safer with Duke, somehow.'

'Well, let's hope and pray we all survive this,' said Sid.

As he finished talking there was a loud explosion behind them and Tom saw a cloud of sand billowing ten or fifteen feet in the air. Then there was another explosion and he realised it was in the middle of the horse lines about a hundred yards behind them.

'Bloody hell, they're shelling the horses! Look over on that hill,' said Sid, pointing to the ridge to their left. Tom glanced up and could see the barrels of three pieces of artillery positioned above them, in clear view. They both realised it made no difference whether they were visible or not as the British had no artillery themselves. Tom was frantic with worry for Duke but realised he was powerless to do anything. He knew if he left the lines Sergeant Vint would have no hesitation in shooting him for desertion, so he concentrated even harder on scanning the horizon. There was no chance of a retreat on horseback now and every chance this was going to be the place where his life would end.

A myriad of thoughts flashed through his mind, of his family, the familiar fields around Bow Brook and the farm, but he realised that his friends were here with him, and if he was going to die, he was in the best place to do it.

The artillery fire continued and Tom could now see the regular bursts of flame from the guns, followed shortly after by an explosion behind them. There was shouting, and frenzied whinnying from the horses. Tom had only heard this once before, when he and Hender had been called to a neighbouring farm whose barn was on fire. By the time they arrived the flames had spread to the stables and terrified horses were whinnying and kicking frantically at their doors to try and escape. Hender had poured buckets of water over Tom and himself. They crawled towards the fire and managed to unbolt the outer door to release three horses, who careered across the yard, one with its tail on fire. The flames and heat were too much for them then and Tom had had to drag Hender away as five more trapped horses were burnt alive.

'Right, lads, look lively. Hold your fire until they're within killing range,' shouted Vint from the end of their trench. Tom could see nothing initially and then, at a nudge from Sid, saw Turkish cavalry advancing from behind the ridge. More and more men appeared at a trot, until they numbered at least six hundred. They were out of range for rifle fire but advanced steadily, spreading out into a long line of khaki across the horizon.

Tom flicked off his safety catch and felt the hard ridged metal under his thumb. The Turks were now four or five hundred yards away, and although he was still angry over the shelling of the horses, he felt panicky as he saw the overwhelming numbers of the enemy.

'Wait, lads. A hundred yards more, then let the bastards know we're here,' shouted Vint.

The Turkish cavalry began to canter. Tom realised that several of the advancing horses were very lame, which filled him with disgust, and many of the riders were bumping about in the saddle, indicating their inexperience. The first shots came from the Turks as their commanding officer fired his pistol and other men began firing their rifles. Tom knew how hard it was to fire at a canter and hoped that, at least, would give them some advantage.

He lined up one Turk who began to charge at them and could see his mouth open to shout, with his rifle held pointing upwards. The man in his sights leant forward and Tom squeezed the trigger. The recoil jolted his shoulder and he saw the Turk slump on to his horse's neck. Tom aimed, fired again and missed. Slow down, he said to himself, breathe. The Turks were now very close, about fifty yards away, and were splitting to gallop down their flanks.

Tom fired again and a Turk fell off his horse and was trampled by two horses behind.

The enemy now surrounded them. Tom turned around, leaving Sid behind him to fire at the Turks to his right, but as he did so he saw the British soldier next to him lying dead. His face was white and his hands were clutching his throat as if he had been trying to stem the bleeding. Tom fired again into the back of another man, who fell just as Tom felt a bullet thud into the sandbag next to his left arm. The enemy were now wheeling away ready to form up again and mount another charge. Tom thought the British trench must have inflicted heavy casualties, but it was unlikely to make much difference in the long run when they were heavily outnumbered. His eyes were stinging from sweat. He wiped them and turned to Sid.

'You're not hit, are you?'

'No, mate, but we can't hold out here; just look around you,' he said.

'Fall back, lads,' shouted Vint.

Tom scrambled to his feet, keeping his rifle clear of the sand, and glanced up and down the trench. There were bodies everywhere; men lay twisted at strange angles and Tom was shocked to see how many had been killed. He saw a flash of red hair only a few yards away and recognised Walter Garland's head. He ran down the trench and lifted Walter to his feet. Tom slung both rifles over one shoulder, wrapped an arm round Walter's waist and dragged him back to the next trench.

He laid his friend down gently, leaning his head against a sand-bag that had been knocked into the trench. Walter's eyes were closed and he looked very pale. Tom saw the wide bloodstain over his lower jacket. He unbuttoned it and there was the neat bullet hole entering his abdomen just below his right ribs. Blood pulsed out on to Tom's hand as he tried to apply pressure. Walter groaned and Tom realised it was pointless to try and stem the bleeding.

'Walter, Walter, can you hear me?' he said, close to his friend's ear. Walter opened his eyes and looked straight at him.

'You'll tell my mother, won't you?' he whispered. Tom held his hand tight as Walter's eyes closed. After a minute his grip relaxed and his mouth dropped open. Tom laid him flat and closed his eyes. He felt a strange emptiness, as though any feeling was blocked. Walter had become a good friend to him, an open, trusting man whom he would miss.

'They're coming back again, boys,' shouted Captain Smith Maxwell. Tom turned and looked out to see the Turkish line re-forming. The artillery had stopped firing but there were loose horses galloping everywhere. Tom could see that a good number of them were British as they had no bridles or saddles. He thought he saw Duke galloping past the palm trees but could not be sure. He felt ashamed to think that he was worrying as much about Duke as about his fellow soldiers.

He crouched again, looking out across the sand as the Turks made ready. The trench was crowded and they were packed elbow to elbow. He did not know the soldiers to his left, though to his right he knew Len Page slightly. Tom looked down and saw Page's huge rough hands clutching his rifle. They looked like farmer's hands.

Tom thought this trench seemed a little deeper, as he found he was kneeling on the floor of the trench cradling his rifle on top of the sandbags. The sun had risen and a light breeze was dusting sand across the desert in front of them. Even more Turkish infantry had joined the attack and Tom thought they must number nearly two thousand. They were vastly outnumbered. Unless help arrived from Qatia very soon, the situation appeared hopeless.

The Turkish cavalry began to move forward at a trot. The sun behind them made their uniforms even darker and their faces hard to see.

'Come on, you buggers,' Tom muttered under his breath. Page

heard and turned towards him. He had a very square chin covered in black stubble. He grinned, flashing large prominent teeth.

'May as well take some of them with us, I reckon,' he said, and looked back down his rifle sights.

This time the Turks came at them more quickly, breaking into a gallop very early and crouching over their horses' necks. Tom saw the leading officer, who was brandishing a cavalry sword, plunge forwards out of the saddle. His sword tumbled behind him as he fell and was trampled under the charge. Tom started firing, reloading as quickly as possible. Large numbers of Turks were being killed but it seemed to make no difference to the lines of men that galloped towards them. There was screaming from the trench further down, a man terrified and in pain. Sand kicked up in front of them as bullets thudded into the ground and smoke swirled around their heads. Tom turned again as the Turks wheeled past them, firing down the trench. Len Page was hit in the thigh but hardly flinched, continuing to fire as the horses flashed past. His trousers were ripped by the bullet and blood was now staining the khaki. Tom ripped some material from the tattered trouser leg and tried to fashion a tourniquet but he had nothing with which to apply any pressure so could only tie it in a rather feeble knot.

'Sorry, mate, that's the best I can do,' he said, wiping his hands on his trousers. He noticed the blood felt slightly sticky and warm as he tried to brush it off on the sand.

'That'll do well,' said Page, breathing heavily.

The Turkish infantry were spread out in front of them. Tom saw they were now surrounded on three sides. The artillery began firing again, the whistling followed by the explosions behind. The noise was deafening and Tom could feel bullets thudding into the sandbags. Page was hit again, in the shoulder, and slumped back in the trench. The man on the other side of Tom collapsed, face down on a sandbag.

'Fall back, fall back!' the order was passed down the trench.

Page was unconscious and there was no way Tom could carry such a large man, so he picked up his rifle and, crouching as low as possible, began running back to the main line of defence close to the oasis. He weaved across the sand, expecting to be hit at any second. Two men fell in front of him and he scrambled over the small wall that formed the last defensive line.

Tom dropped behind it, blowing hard. He slowly got his breath back. His mouth was dry and he felt sand round his teeth. The noise was even more intense here, with rifle fire and exploding shells close by. He looked out across the sand to where the Turkish infantry were positioned. Dead men lay everywhere. Many were spread out in the trench in front of them, some shot while retreating.

Two soldiers were crawling slowly across the sand, their legs trailing uselessly behind them. Tom saw a man jump back over the wall, running towards the furthest man who was making painfully slow progress towards them. Tom recognised Vint from his broad shoulders and the rolling gait that was so pronounced when he was running. The rifle fire increased as Vint bent down and lifted the injured man in his arms to start the run back to safety. Men started shouting encouragement while the remainder tried to give some covering fire. Thirty yards, twenty, ten. Vint was almost there when he stopped and stumbled as though he had dropped something. He had been shot in the leg but somehow managed to hobble the rest of the way as two men helped the injured man over the wall. Whatever Tom had thought of Vint before was replaced by admiration for his amazing bravery. The man had delighted in ridiculing Tom at any opportunity, and he had come to enjoy the moments when Vint had been made to look like a buffoon in front of the senior officers, but perhaps the Sergeant had had his men's interests at heart after all.

Vint was dragged back over the wall clutching his thigh. A dressing was produced and his leg bandaged, but he had been hit by a round from a heavy machine gun, which had smashed his knee and was causing severe blood loss. The machine gun was now dominating the battle and the ceaseless juddering and shower of bullets was shattering the rocks and stones in front of them. Four men were ordered to try and make their way around close to the oasis to see whether they could direct fire at the machine gun but they were soon spotted and picked off by Turkish snipers.

There was an occasional let-up when Tom presumed the belt of the machine gun jammed, and at each pause they cautiously peeked over the wall and opened fire. The Turks were about fifty yards away and with the first volley from the British line a number of them fell, but within moments the machine gun resumed its rain of death once more. He was sure that a message would have been sent to Qatia, requesting reinforcements, but that would take far too long to save them if the firing continued at this intensity. Vint was still barking orders but was getting weaker.

'Come on, lads, keep firing. Pick your targets and don't rush the shot.' He was cursing and clutching his knee, trying to grip the muscle above it to relieve the pain. After a time he stopped barking orders.

Tom moved down the trench and found that Vint had collapsed. He could see blood oozing from the knee and realised there was no kneecap left. He tried to apply pressure to the leg, but as he did so another soldier leant over. 'It's no good, mate, he's stopped breathing.' Tom looked into Vint's face, pale now and strangely peaceful. Tom felt a sob well up in his chest and then tears mixed with sweat as he was overwhelmed by fear and sadness.

He was shocked back to reality by the sound of rifle fire next to him. The sandbags were beginning to break up and he cowered lower. He peered through a narrow gap between bags and managed to slot the barrel of his rifle through it. The lines of Turkish troops were even closer. Tom's tongue was completely dry and felt swollen. He found he could not reload his rifle; the bolt action was jammed, and as he frantically worked it backwards and forwards he realised the firing had died down.

'Cease fire. Cease fire, lads. It's no good, we'll have to surrender.'

The voice came from behind Tom and he looked round to see an officer waving a white flag above his head. He was tall and had lost his cap, but from his uniform Tom assumed he was a Major. His face was smeared with sweat and dirt and he slowly walked forward, waving the flag. There was now an eerie silence as, one by one, British soldiers stood up, throwing their rifles down in front of them and raising their hands in the air.

As Tom stood he saw the tiny number of men left. No more than thirty or forty were left standing. There were bodies scattered across the desert and wounded men were lolling against sandbags, some barely conscious, others groaning in pain.

The Major handed his sword over to a Turkish officer as the remaining Turkish troops kept their rifles trained on the British soldiers. The officer stepped forward, and with a grandiose sweep of his arm announced to them in a heavy accent that they were now prisoners of the Ottoman Empire. He ordered his men to give everyone water once they were seated on the ground.

Tom found the water very salty but at least it cleared the sand from his mouth. He could still smell the cordite from the rifle fire and looked around to see whether he could locate Duke. There were no loose horses now. All he could see were bodies and wounded men all around him.

Tom felt a hand tap his shoulder and turned round to see Sid's familiar face. He looked utterly exhausted and drained.

'What a disaster, we've lost hundreds...' His voice trailed away as he wiped his eyes and shook his head.

'We never had a chance against that many Turks,' replied Tom. 'Walter's dead, Vint was carrying a man back when he was shot. I should have saved Len Page…I left him there, I could have saved him.' Tom gazed down, filled with a familiar feeling of guilt and remorse.

Sid put his arm round Tom's shoulders. 'Don't say that. We could all have saved men out there.'

Chapter 15

Qatia, Egypt, Easter Saturday, 22 April 1916

Eddie Williams and Frank Folkes fell into their tent exhausted. They had been digging trenches for most of the day and their blistered hands were swollen and red. There were nearly forty dismounted Yeomanry, and it appeared that they were carrying out the majority of the digging. The Gloucester Hussars had been patrolling on a regular basis and were reporting increasing numbers of Turkish troops in the area.

It was the evening before Easter Sunday and they were resting as the sun began to sink behind the hills to the west of the camp. Captain Lloyd-Baker strode towards their tent. Eddie had noticed that, when he was nervous, the officer rubbed his thumb and forefinger together as if rolling tobacco. He was rolling his fingers vigorously as he approached them.

'Evening, men, all well?' he asked.

'Nothing a cold beer wouldn't sort out, sir,' said Frank.

'Very good, Folkes,' he replied, forcing a smile. 'The whole camp will be on standby early tomorrow as we are expecting the Turks to advance. Clean your rifles and make sure you're ready.'

Lloyd-Baker marched off, rolling furiously. He was one of the less intelligent officers and Eddie had no respect for him. The Captain was one of those who had little time for the lower ranks and spent far too long talking about what he had planned for when he was next on leave in Port Said. Lloyd-Baker's one habitual command was 'clean your rifles', which made him an easy target for ridicule.

'Clean your rifles! They've not the slightest clue what they're doing, Eddie,' Frank complained.

'Well, they've got more idea than me. I'm not even sure which direction the Turks are coming from.'

Frank laughed and took a long drink from his water bottle. 'When I joined up I really thought we'd be commanded by the cream of the British Army. I thought we'd meet officers who were naturally intelligent, with real insight into the dangers we were likely to face. Instead we've these buffoons who are more interested in Egyptian whores who'll give them syphilis and make them even more stupid than they are now.'

'Well, Frank, at least I'm clear on how you feel,' said Eddie, smiling. He valued Frank for his forthright views, but found his friend's pessimism only fuelled his own misgivings about going into action. As the threat of attack increased, Eddie was feeling far more nervous and wondering whether he would be able to conduct himself well in combat. They settled down in their tents as the air cooled and talked of home. Frank's mother was a very good cook, and he liked to create his perfect dinner menu.

'Eddie, tonight I'm going to start with fresh asparagus and ham, followed by lamb shank. Mother does it perfectly. She leaves it in the oven to cook for hours so it just melts in the mouth. For pudding, I'll have treacle tart with plenty of really thick cream. What about you?'

'Well, I love grilled mushrooms so I'll have picked them myself this morning. Then I'll have roast beef, really rare, with Yorkshire pudding, mustard and lots of gravy. Mother makes the best gravy, really dark with all the juices from the meat, then after that I'll get some bread and soak it in the juices...bloody fantastic.' Eddie sighed with pleasure at the thought of it. Frank began snoring gently and soon Eddie was asleep himself.

Easter Sunday, 23 April 1916

They were roused shortly after three-thirty. It was dark, with limited light from the moon penetrating the dense fog. They were ordered to the forward trenches where Bill Green, Frank and Eddie settled down to prepare for attack.

After an hour the sound of gunfire could be heard coming from the direction of Oghratina.

'Look out, boys, here we go,' said Bill. Eddie peered into the darkness. There was almost no wind and the fog floated in front of them, creating bizarre shapes.

'Will it be a cavalry charge, Bill?' asked Eddie.

'No, lad, they might try to soften us up with some artillery first. With any luck the Gloucesters will be able to engage them before they get too close.'

Bill seemed relaxed, which helped to calm the butterflies in Eddie's stomach.

Frank was drawing patterns in the sand with a stick and seemed uninterested. 'Not much we can do until they get here, and something tells me we'll know soon enough when they do,' he said, stifling a yawn.

It was starting to get light and the heavy gunfire continued in the direction of Oghratina. Bill, who had gone for a pee, came back saying word had come through that the British there had managed to beat off a Turkish attack. He had also heard that another camp to their rear at Dueidar had been attacked. Eddie sat up in the trench and stretched his legs. The mist had almost cleared and the sun was beginning to warm his stiff body. The gunfire had stopped and he saw a patrol mount up and head out into the desert. Eddie sat back down and looked out to where the sand rolled away into the distance, merging with the sky. He rubbed his chin and felt the soft stubble that usually took some days to develop into anything that really needed shaving.

'It's getting pretty hot again…so windless,' said Frank, wiping his forehead with a blue spotted handkerchief.

'Maybe the Turks will think it's too hot to do anything today and go back home,' said Eddie hopefully.

'No bloody chance, the heat at Gallipoli was never a problem for them.' Frank opened his canteen and offered Eddie water. It was one of the things that Eddie found so considerate about him. There was never an issue made of it, but whenever he himself wanted water, Frank always offered it to Eddie first. He would have been embarrassed if Eddie had ever mentioned it, but the gesture meant a lot in the rigid and dispassionate military world they now inhabited. Small acts of kindness counted.

They talked about home once more, and Frank went back to talking about his elderly parents and his father's poor health. Frank's father, Arthur, had worked in service for many years and had contracted tuberculosis at the age of forty. His employer, Lord Norton, who had also employed Frank's grandfather, had sent Arthur to London to see a leading respiratory specialist. He'd advised that Arthur should be admitted to a sanatorium for complete rest, and there he stayed for the next nine months. He made a good recovery and went back to work for Lord Norton, but over the next five to six years his breathing had grown steadily worse and he was diagnosed with lung fibrosis. Lord Norton reluctantly accepted that he could no longer work, and provided Arthur and his family with a small cottage on his estate. Arthur was now too breathless to leave the house but doted on his son, following his progress and sharing his love of poetry.

'If anything happened to me, Eddie, it would finish the old chap off, you know.'

'Don't talk like that. We'll get through this,' he said.

Artillery suddenly thundered ahead of them. There was a pause and then loud explosions behind the lines. Frank turned around, straining to see where the shells were landing. Clouds of sand were drifting into the air. There was shouting from men near the lines of horses and orders for them to mount up. Eddie saw an animal thrown into the air before crashing to the ground. It was clear that the Turks were intentionally shelling the horse lines, which meant that retreat for many of the men was impossible. Eddie felt the hum of bullets near him and ducked down in the trench. He glanced over the sandbags and saw hunched figures two or three hundred yards away, steadily moving forward as they fired.

'Eddie, they're getting closer! We'd better return fire,' shouted Frank. Eddie nodded and together the line of British soldiers popped up and began firing. The advance slowed and a few Turks fell forward, clearly hit. A cheer went up and the firing intensified. Bullets hit the sand in front of them, causing small eruptions. Eddie was breathing hard, filled with a mixture of dread and excitement; he was firing as fast as he could. He dropped down to reload. He turned to Frank and froze. His friend was lying back, face up in the sand. Around his left shoulder his jacket was a mass of blood; his eyes gazed sightlessly at the sky. Eddie bent over him.

'Frank...Frank, can you hear me?' he said, his voice shaking. But even as he asked he knew there was only one answer. Eddie thought of Frank's father sitting at home, frail and breathless, and realised he would have to go and visit the family himself if he survived. He pulled his friend's book of poetry from a jacket pocket and tucked it into his own. Then he turned to the front and started firing again, revenge driving him. The artillery fire continued but the British forces were managing to hold their own. Eddie was shocked to realise that his gun barrel was too hot to touch from repeated firing.

They were ordered to retreat to a trench closer to the palm trees. Eddie could see Turkish troops closing in on them on three sides. Captain Lloyd-Baker had realised the danger of the camp becoming surrounded entirely. Camels had already been dispatched back towards Kantara, carrying as many wounded men as possible, and cavalry were escorting men away from the oasis under heavy fire. Eddie found himself close to Bill, which gave him some hope of surviving the battle that was raging around them.

'Eddie, keep firing as best you can and await orders for the retreat. We'll be lucky to get back to Kantara in one piece,' Bill said. His red face was shining and he had black marks around his nose and mouth from the repeated firing. He had lost his helmet and his short hair was stiff with sand and sweat.

A man collapsed next to Eddie, shot through the head. There was another explosion near their trench and Bill threw himself on to Eddie and slowly looked up. The intensity of the rifle fire had suddenly increased.

'Bill, where's that coming from?' gasped Eddie.

'They're bringing snipers forward, lad. These Turks are good marksmen,' said Bill. More shots rang out and Eddie waited for him to make some further comment. He felt his friend's weight grow heavier, and wondered why Bill had not moved. Eddie lay still, listening to the crack of rifle fire, and suddenly he was certain that Bill was dead. He pushed up on his arms, twisting the lifeless body off him, and saw blood seeping from the back of Bill's head.

Eddie's stomach churned and he was overwhelmed by panic. His closest friend and confidant was dead. He knelt there frozen, gazing down at the face which was rapidly draining of colour. The sound of machine-gun fire jolted him back to the present, and he grabbed Bill's leather tags from around his neck, pulled the letters from his breast pocket, and, crouching as low as possible, sprinted for the palm trees some thirty yards back.

The firing was continuous, and he was aware of sand being kicked up around him from sniper fire. Eddie glanced up. He could see men ahead of him in the trench, shouting to him, urging him on, but he could not hear their individual voices. It seemed to take an age to reach them; he felt as though he was running through thick mud. He threw himself over the low wall of sandbags and collapsed, gasping for air, his mouth full of sand. He felt a pat on his back and rolled over to bring up his rifle to point over the sandbags. He pulled the bolt back but felt a grating and saw the chamber was clogged with sand. He dropped the weapon and crawled along behind the line of men, crouched or lying, all firing at the Turkish line. He felt a stab of pain in his hand and saw he had caught it on a spike of rock. As he cursed and wiped his hand, the soldier next to him slumped forward, shot through the chest. Eddie checked for a pulse and could feel nothing. He eased the rifle out from the dead man's hands, trying not to drop it in the sand. The barrel was too hot to touch but he laid it on a split sandbag and began firing. The Turks were pressing forward in huge numbers and Eddie was aware of more and more men lying dead or injured.

He felt detached from the battle raging around him. Sounds were muffled, although he was aware of his own irregular breathing, like old bellows wheezing away. He ran out of ammunition and lay on his back, fumbling to fit his bayonet before the inevitable charge from the Turkish troops, which would mark the final chapter in his life. He felt resigned and strangely calm. On the right flank he saw Turks charging and could hear their shouts as they fought hand to hand with British soldiers.

The firing had stopped. He could see men further down the line slowly standing up, with their hands in the air.

'It's no good, boys. Throw down your rifles,' said Captain Lloyd-Baker. The Captain slowly walked forward, arms raised, waving a white handkerchief in his right hand. Eddie was struck by how white it was and imagined the Captain carefully washing it on a regular basis. Men were now following him, slowly venturing forward from the trenches to surrender.

Eddie was relieved but felt as though he had betrayed Frank

Folkes and Bill Green, who were both lying dead along with so many others. Eddie tossed his rifle down as the Turks slowly advanced towards them, rifles waving from side to side, waiting to fire.

Eddie gazed around him to see smoke curling upwards and realised that many of the tents were burning. There was a strong smell of gunpowder in the air and flies had begun to visit the dead bodies that lay scattered over the sand. He slowly turned his head to try and gauge how many men had survived. There looked to be about sixty to seventy standing up and, in addition, some wounded were being carried forward for treatment.

He felt an overwhelming sense of sadness. It was as though he was suddenly inhaling air that was saturated with grief and now this was circulating through his body. He had lost the two men he'd depended on the most, and he reflected on the way they had provided him with a sense of stability and a replacement family. Bill Green had looked after him from the very start of his time in the army, and had saved his life here in the desert. Frank Folkes, whom Eddie had seen every day for the last year, had made him laugh and shared stories with him of home life, cricket and poetry. Eddie closed his eyes for a moment and thanked God for their lives, praying that they were now at peace. He squeezed his eyes shut a little more tightly then slowly opened them, surveying the scene of defeat all around him.

Chapter 16

Oghratina Oasis, Egypt, April 1916

Tom was exhausted and growing more annoyed with every prod between his shoulder blades from the Turkish soldier's rifle. He shuffled forward, his mouth dry and lips sore from the deep splits in them. There were thousands of Turkish troops now camped around Oghratina and he saw how utterly hopeless their idea of defending the oasis had been. Artillery pieces and machine guns were laid out before him and Turkish soldiers were cleaning and oiling the guns. The British prisoners had spent the last two hours burying their dead comrades in large, communal graves. There were far too many familiar faces, as Tom, Sid and the other prisoners laid the men beside each other. Alf was resting. He had been hit by shrapnel in the shoulder and forearm. Fortunately, although he was in pain, a Turkish doctor had said it would heal fully.

Strange memories were triggered in Tom of football games, farmers' dances and parties with classmates from school, all now lying dead. He was thankful when the Turkish commander ordered them to start shovelling sand over the bodies to hide their faces. Out of twenty officers and two hundred and thirty other ranks, only nine officers and fifty-six men were left, many of them wounded.

The prisoners were ordered to sit in rows and Tom received yet another prod in the back. He turned and raised his fist in retaliation, hurriedly dropping his hand as the guard lifted his rifle to Tom's head and began screaming threats. Tom sat down quickly in the sand.

'Steady, old lad, you don't want to get yourself shot on the first day after capture,' said Sid, in a whisper.

'You're right, it was daft.'

'You always want to get the old fists out, mate. Let's just see how these buggers treat us first.'

They sat waiting in the full heat of the day while their Turkish guards wandered casually about, smoking and occasionally pointing their rifles at them and pretending to fire, then laughing. Nearly an hour passed before a Turkish officer approached them and began speaking in remarkably good English, albeit with a heavy accent. He was tall, painfully thin, and, with his large hooked nose, very striking.

'Gintleman, you are now prisoners of the Ottoman Empire and you will be treated well. We are Muslims and respect Christians. Though you have tried to conquer these lands before, you will fail again. As this battle has shown, Turkish soldiers, together with our German allies, are a match for anyone. Qatia has also fallen, so you will be joined by other prisoners from there.' He paused and brushed his thick moustache with his forefinger.

'That's a disaster, Tom. We had even more men there. If they've been defeated at Qatia that means something has gone badly wrong,' whispered Sid. Tom just shook his head and wondered whether any of their commanding officers would have to answer for this defeat.

'Gintleman, we will bring you water, food and some ciga-rettes. Soon we will be marching you to a prison camp for the rest of this war, which we will win very soon, I am sure. Thank you.' The officer bowed low, saluted in a rather theatrical way and marched away.

'That sounds a little more hopeful,' said Sid, smiling faintly.

'I'm not so sure. Their officer may be all charm and smiles but these other soldiers don't look quite so friendly,' said Tom, glancing towards a group of Turks, who gazed back at them with looks of sheer hatred.

After another long wait the prisoners were escorted towards an area where a large group of camels lay in a circle. A group of Bedouin tribesmen had lit a fire under a huge metal cauldron and were eating bowls of rice. Most of the captured men had not eaten since the previous night and the smell of cooking made Tom feel nauseous with hunger. Sid had managed to get back to his tent and find a few ginger biscuits, which he passed round. He gave one to Alf, who was sitting, half propped up against some sandbags, clutching the wounded arm that was supported in a bloodstained sling. Sid sat down beside him and held another biscuit to his mouth.

'Slow down, Sid, my mouth is so dry I can't eat that fast,' he slurred, spitting out bits of biscuit.

'How's the arm?' asked Tom, peering at the makeshift bandage around Alf's elbow.

'Not too bad, to be honest. Quite sore but I got lucky.'

'Lucky means you can still light a fag, I suppose,' said Tom. Alf shook his head, chewing on his last bit of biscuit.

'Lucky means staying alive, cocker. Looking at all those bodies you buried brings it home. So many men killed. Before I came out here I'd never seen a dead body. But now…' Alf's voice trailed off and he gazed at the sand by his feet. 'I've seen enough to last me a bloody lifetime.'

They had still been given no water when a Turkish doctor came round, checking on injuries and seeing which wounded men were able to walk. One man had clearly fractured his leg and was told he would ride on a camel. A crude wooden splint was tied to his leg. The doctor applied traction to his foot with no pain relief. Tom winced as the man screamed in agony.

'The bastard. What the hell's he doing, Sid?'

'Tom, at least they haven't taken him over the sand dunes and shot him,' said his friend wearily.

Later on the day of the battle they were ordered to form up and march east. Most of the men had lost their supplies and many had shed their jackets during the day in the intense heat. As the sun sank below the dunes the temperature dropped rapidly and a cold wind began to blow. The men were exhausted and found walking over the soft sand almost impossible. Tom was falling every ten or fifteen yards as they stumbled forward in the dark. Every hour they stopped for five minutes. As soon as the order was given he dropped on to the sand, desperate for rest. On one occasion he fell asleep instantly and was woken by a guard standing over him, shouting, '*Hadi, hadi!*' and prodding him in the back with his rifle. An hour later, Tom found Sid apparently asleep in the sand and shook him awake as he was afraid the Turks needed very little excuse to shoot anyone.

'Don't worry, lad, I'm awake. Too frightened to sleep,' said his mate.

'Do you think we would have any hope if we tried to escape back towards Kantara?'

'Only if you fancied a bayonet up your arse or a bullet in the back.'

'Only joking, Sid. Might cure Alf's piles though,' said Tom.

It was still dark when they were ordered to halt and Tom assumed they must have reached Bir-el-Abd. They collapsed and sat huddled together, backs to the wind, their trousers and shirts flapping, waiting for the sun to rise on Easter Monday.

Breakfast consisted of some dry biscuits with a small amount of very salty water that was drawn from a well nearby, but at least the sun had risen and begun to warm their stiff bodies. Shortly after breakfast there was some noise to the east and another group of prisoners appeared from the direction of Qatia. Tom, Sid and Alf, cradling his arm, lined up on the edge of the camp to greet them. They were shocked by the men's appearance. Many of them were badly injured, hobbling or being half carried by their fellow prisoners. Some had dirty bandages wrapped around their heads, which were bent forward, eyes turned to the ground in front of them. Two men were shuffling at the back of the group and three or four Turkish guards were slapping their heads and hitting them with their rifle butts.

One British prisoner near the back stopped, turned and went over to the last two men to try and help them, pleading with the Turkish guards to leave them alone. He was beginning to get angry, waving his arms and pointing at the prisoners. He grabbed his cap and threw it on the ground in frustration, but as he bent down to retrieve it the Turkish guards set on him, kicking him repeatedly in the ribs and legs. After nearly a minute they stopped and spat on him as they turned away, leaving a cloud of dust and the British soldier groaning and clutching his ribs.

Sid and Tom ran over and slowly sat him up. His face was covered in sand and his eyes were tightly shut. He was grimacing in pain.

'Are you all right, lad?' asked Sid, wiping the other man's face with his shirt.

'Yes, I think so,' he groaned as he opened his eyes. 'That was pretty silly of me, wasn't it?' he said, beginning to smile.

'Bloody brave, but daft,' said Tom, laughing. They both hooked an arm under his and hoisted him up. It was immediately obvious how small the man was and how young he looked.

'What's your name, lad?' asked Tom.

'Eddie. Eddie Williams,' he said, holding out his hand.

'Tom Bomford, and this is Sid Parkes. Good to meet you. We'd better keep an eye on you, before you get in any more trouble.'

'Thanks very much,' said Eddie, blue eyes shining out of his sand-covered face.

They walked back together to where the prisoners from Qatia were now joining up with those captured at Oghratina. Many men recognised one another and were talking about the last few days and their survival, as well as the many friends they had lost.

Eddie sat with Tom and Sid, explaining what had happened at Qatia. He went over the details of the battle and the fact that his friend Bill Green knew their chances of survival were limited once the Turks had begun shelling the lines of horses. They all found it extraordinary that such a large force of Turks had attacked and overwhelmed them without any warning.

'I think we all imagined there'd be just one big cavalry charge, us against lines of Turkish cavalry, but that German commander must be good. He knew that machine guns and artillery would be far too tough for us to defeat,' said Eddie, realising that he was sounding rather like Bill Green.

'You're right. Still, we need to concentrate on how we're going to survive as prisoners. Food and water are our main worries now, and if they march us north it'll be cold too,' said Tom.

At around midday the Turks gave all the prisoners some rice with a few small bits of meat in it. It was slightly spicy and as they were all very hungry every last grain was eaten.

'Well, I've tasted worse,' said Alf.

'That's saying something from the fussiest man I know,' said Tom.

'I'm just used to my mother's cooking, that's all. A lot of what she uses in her food is very good for the heart.'

'Not dandelions and dock leaves?'

'That was the one supper when you came round and she was experimenting. I admit, it wasn't very good.'

Alf's mother was obsessed with using herbs and other unusual ingredients, which she collected from the hedgerows and fields near their house. He was always fiercely loyal about her cooking, but Tom and Sid had dreaded being asked to Alf's house as they usually ended up having to leave the table, unable to control their laughter.

'Is that one of ours?' said Sid, pointing to an aeroplane flying directly towards them. The drone from the engine increased and as it banked they saw the distinctive colouring of a British plane. A few men cheered as it flew lower but then there was a sudden loud blast, followed by three more, and they realised they were being bombed. Turkish soldiers were running around, shouting and shooting at the small plane. Tom looked up, shielding his eyes from the sun, and saw the plane make another turn and begin to fly straight towards them. There was a strange knocking noise as it came lower.

'The bloody idiot is shooting at us!' yelled Tom as they all crouched down, trying to find non-existent cover behind small depressions in the sand. The Turkish guards were screaming and poking the prisoners with their bayonets so that it was impossible to avoid the fire. Tom shrank down, expecting to be hit any second. He held his head in his hands and looked up at a Turkish guard a few yards away, to see his head suddenly jerk back and blood spray from his neck. A British prisoner a few yards on began screaming and clutching his leg. Some men stood up to hurl abuse at the pilot as he flew away back towards the British lines, and none of them could believe that he had not seen they were prisoners.

They lay in the blazing sun with no water for the rest of the afternoon. A British aeroplane appeared again, but the Turks had set up two anti-aircraft guns and the moment they opened up the pilot turned away, much to the relief of the prisoners.

'Up, up, up!' shouted a Turkish soldier, waving his arms at them as evening fell. He was scurrying round the prisoners like a sheepdog. They formed up in ranks of four, with the Turkish guards pushing them into position. Tom felt oddly light with no pack or rifle to carry as they began marching away from Bir-el-Abd.

It was another painful night marching over soft sand and his feet were feeling very sore, but that was nothing compared to his stomach, which was cramping. Every hour or so he suffered a bad attack of diarrhoea. Sid was vomiting, and only Alf, shuffling along clutching his arm, seemed to be free from symptoms. The following morning they arrived at Maza and managed to rest for most of the day. There was plenty of water, which Tom was desperate to drink, but it was so salty it seemed only to increase his thirst. There were a few areas of canvas rigged up, so they slept with their heads in the shade.

After a week, they had made painfully slow progress north-east. Tom estimated they were covering fifteen to twenty miles a day, with numerous stops to tend the wounded and to encourage them forward, even when they were begging to stop. Water rations had increased and were becoming slightly less salty, and Tom was slowly growing accustomed to the combination of heavily spiced rice and chunks of very stale biscuit that had to be sucked over several minutes or dunked in water to prevent one's mouth drying out completely.

The British officers were mounted on a variety of captured horses. There were only fifteen or twenty of them. The Turkish officer who had addressed them at Oghratina after the battle had been nicknamed The Sultan, due to his regal bearing. On the first night of their captivity he had demonstrated his eccentric behaviour. He had called all the British officers together and apologised for the inadequate washing facilities, saying that he would at least provide them with a change of underwear. He then ordered all the Turkish officers back to their tents and told them to return with a clean pair of underpants for each British officer. Only a small number actually wore them, but all of them at least showed their gratitude with profuse thanks and bowing while the rest of the prisoners laughed for the first time in days.

It was the only trace of humour for the next week. Each morning one or two of the wounded were found dead, usually succumbing to overwhelming infection from their wounds. Many men pleaded with the Turkish doctor for extra help when he appeared, but he just shrugged and walked on, indicating there was nothing more that he could do.

Eddie stayed close to Tom and Sid as they stumbled across the desert. He told them how he had joined up underage after always being desperate to leave home for some sort of adventure. They all talked of their families, and realised how much they would miss the occasional letters and parcels, which had provided a reminder of the life they hoped eventually to see again. Tom especially missed his Bible, which had been taken by one of the Turks soon after their capture. He felt as though a part of him had been removed.

When the Turk had searched him, looking for any valuables, he had initially appeared uninterested in the Bible. Tom had made the sign of the cross and pointed at the sky to try and indicate the book's religious significance, and then the Turk had laughed and put it in his pocket. Every night now Tom dreamt of finding the soldier and stealing it back from him. The small pictures of biblical scenes and his parents' message in the front had been a comfort to him and he felt increasingly pessimistic without the Bible in his possession, wondering whether he would survive the war at all.

They eventually marched into El Arish where a large Turkish force was stationed. A group of local Arabs lined the road ahead of them.

'Is this a welcome party?' said Sid.

'They don't look very happy to me,' said Eddie.

As they marched through the town, Tom saw low mud-brick houses and some children, who ran past throwing stones at them. Most of the townsfolk seemed to be on the streets. They began shouting abuse and spitting on the prisoners as they passed. Tom looked ahead, trying to ignore them, but Alf shouted back.

'Bugger off, the lot of you! You won't be so chirpy when the British march through here in a few months' time.'

They washed for the first time since the battle with buckets of warm water that had heated in the sun, and even managed to sleep under cover. The drinking water was fresh and Tom thought it was the best he had ever tasted. His cramps and diarrhoea had settled and he was feeling a little stronger. They had been ordered into a long barn that looked as though it was normally used for storing grain. Straw had been scattered over the floor. Although Tom still felt very low he was at least warm. Cushioned by the straw he fell into a deep sleep. His dreams were composed of battle flashes interspersed with visions of Duke, turned out in one of the paddocks on the farm in Worcestershire, enjoying his retirement.

They stayed in the town for two nights while some of the wounded were offloaded from camels and admitted to a Turkish military hospital where The Sultan assured them they would receive the best possible treatment.

Chapter 17

England, May 1916

Madge Williams sat fiddling with her brown leather handbag while glancing out of the kitchen window. It was a sunny Saturday morning, and Dr Timothy Parkes was due to take her out to lunch with his parents. Madge was so nervous she wondered whether she would be able to eat anything, but hoped a glass of sherry before lunch might help settle her butterflies. She had briefly met Timothy's father Bernard some months before when she had visited the surgery. As she opened the door, he had stepped out of his consulting room on his way to a home birth. He'd raised his hat to her and told her how pleased he was to meet her after hearing so much about her from his son. Madge thought he seemed very kind and polite. She was more worried about meeting Timothy's mother.

Edith Parkes had always wanted a large family but sadly, after delivering Timothy, problems had led to an emergency hysterectomy. He'd recounted how she had cried for months after that and had always bitterly blamed the surgeon involved in her care. This left Madge with the impression of a woman nursing a lasting sense of bitterness, and overprotective of her one and only child.

There was a short toot on a car horn and Madge could see Timothy's Austin pull up outside the gate. She jumped up, checked her hair which she had carefully pinned up under her hat, and called goodbye to no one in particular.

'Have a lovely day, my dear,' her father shouted back from his chair in the sitting room. She dashed across the small yard at the back of the house and saw Timothy standing by the car smiling at her. She gave him a peck on the cheek while he walked her round to the passenger side to open the door for her, ever the gentleman.

'Madge, you look lovely. How are you feeling today?' he asked.

'A little nervous.'

'Oh, you'll charm them both. Father is terribly easy. Just ask him about the practice. And with Mother, it's gardening and anything to do with fairies.'

'I forgot about the fairies. Doesn't she think they come out at night in the garden?' Madge giggled.

'Yes, she does, but do not, whatever you do, laugh about it because she will be dreadfully upset,' said Timothy, rather disapprovingly. Madge realised, there it was again; just when she thought they should both be sharing the humour of the moment, Timothy would become rather serious and somewhat critical. She loved him dearly but he could be so pompous at times. She had talked to Daisy about it and she had told Madge it was a minor thing and she should not worry; he was such a kind man and so obviously adored her.

She settled into the passenger seat as Timothy started the engine.

'Well, it's sunny at least, and thankfully Father is on call for the day,' he said.

'Oh, that is kind of him. Perhaps we can go for a walk after lunch,' suggested Madge.

'I'm sure that would be possible if Mother does not have any jobs for me. We may have to drive her home if Father is going on a visit. Mrs Chambers our housekeeper is answering the phone while we are at lunch.'

Madge was amazed to learn that the practice phone was usually manned by Timothy's mother, and wondered if that would become her role as the young doctor's wife.

Bernard and Edith Parkes were already seated in the restaurant when Timothy and Madge were escorted to their table. Bernard stood up with his hand outstretched and greeted them both warmly.

'Mother, may I introduce Madge?' Timothy said, sounding as nervous as Madge felt.

'How do you do?' Edith said, extending a white-gloved hand. She nodded at Madge, adjusted her napkin and returned to gazing out of the window.

'You are a little late, Timothy,' she said, without looking at her son but with a note of reproof in her voice.

'Yes, I-I'm sorry, Mother,' he stammered.

'I think we should order some sherry. Is Tio Pepe to your taste, Madge?' asked Bernard.

'That would be lovely, thank you.'

Edith turned slowly towards Madge and clasped her hands together in front of her. Madge stared in disbelief at her gloves, which glowed white and perfectly matched her complexion. A waiter placed a menu in front of each of them, which diverted Edith's stony gaze for a second.

'Timothy tells me you are helping your father at home,' she said, looking as though she had just swallowed a wasp.

'She is a huge help,' he said, trying to be supportive.

'And I hear you are a keen gardener,' said Madge to Edith, changing the subject.

'Yes, I am very interested in all things botanical.'

'Timothy tells me you are interested in fairies too.'

'Yes, I have always been interested in them and have collected books about them for many years. Have you heard of Andrew Lang?'

Madge shook her head.

'He compiled short stories about them. My favourite was *The Blue Fairy Book*. My mother read them to me and, when I slept, I dreamt I was reliving them. It was wonderful. The images were

187

so real, you see. I believe fairies may be visible to us at certain times.' Edith paused, as if wondering whether to continue. 'Many people think that sounds ridiculous, but I have created a garden which provides a haven for them at night.'

She gazed thoughtfully out of the window again while Madge suppressed a smile. Timothy appeared unaware of how ridiculous it was to hear a middle-aged matron talking about fairies coming out at night. Madge tried to kick him, missed, and the table shuddered.

The inquisition resumed over lunch, but thankfully Madge felt a little calmer after her sherry. The tomato soup was cold and the chicken dry and shrivelled. Timothy helped her through the ordeal, always portraying her in the most positive light. It was clear that this began to annoy Edith more and more, and her snide comments even brought some signs of disapproval from Bernard.

At one point Madge said they were growing vegetables in the garden to give to the men at the brewery along with eggs as food supplies were so restricted.

'All very well for some, getting all they like,' said Edith, sniffing and turning to look out of the window again.

'Now, dear, that's not very fair,' Bernard reproved her.

Sherry trifle was chosen by all of them for dessert. Bernard seemed far more interested in that than he did in their discussion about Stourbridge. Madge suspected that they all wished they were somewhere else.

From time to time Timothy looked longingly at Madge, trying to catch her eye. Though she was aware of this she felt she needed to keep her gaze fixed firmly on Edith or Bernard. At last the bill was paid and Madge thanked them both for a delicious lunch while Timothy telephoned the practice to check that there were no emergencies to attend. His father patted him on the back to reassure him all was well, and he and Madge finally left the dining room with Timothy glancing back over his shoulder to wave to his mother.

'I am sorry, my dear. I hope that was not too awful for you,' he said as they settled back into the car.

'No, it was as I expected. Your father was kind and friendly. I felt I didn't impress your mother as much as she or you would have liked, though.'

'No, no, you were wonderful, Madge.'

They settled into silence as they drove out into the country to some woods where they enjoyed walking. Timothy touched her hand as he drove and she squeezed his in response. They parked the car and got out. There was a stiff breeze and the sun appeared occasionally from behind the clouds, making it quite warm. The beech trees sighed in the wind. Madge's hair began to slide free from its pins.

They strolled down the side of the wood on a flat grass track. Timothy took Madge's hand again. She felt more relaxed now and began to swing his arm higher and higher as they walked. Timothy carried a tartan rug under one arm. He spread it on the grass at the edge of the wood. They sat there and chatted, laughing about his mother's interrogation of her.

'Madge, you know I adore you, don't you?' he said, lying back so he was looking up into her eyes.

'Yes, I know you do, and I have deep feelings for you too, my love.'

'Well, would you do me the honour of becoming my wife?' There was a pleading expression in his eyes, which reminded Madge of Eddie when he was asking her to bowl at him in the garden, desperate to play cricket.

'Timothy, you know I can't give you an answer now. I must wait until we have news of Eddie. It wouldn't be fair on Mother or Father for me to leave home now. They worry so much about him. I hope and pray that when he returns home safe and sound I can give you the answer you hope for.'

She looked into his eyes and could see she had hurt him by not falling in with his plan at once. She kissed him and his response surprised her by its urgency. He seemed reluctant to break the kiss. When he wrapped his arms around her and lay back on the rug, Madge did not resist.

Some hours later Madge pushed open the front door. She paused for a moment to look at herself in the hall mirror, desperately trying to restore the pins which had fallen from her hair.

'Hello, I'm home,' she called up the stairs. There was silence, which immediately struck her as odd in a house where there was usually a buzz of conversation and noise.

'We're in here, dear,' called her father from the sitting room. She went in and the air of sadness in the room was palpable. The whole family had assembled there. No one spoke as Madge came in; they barely looked at her. Harry beckoned her over to the small stool by his leather armchair. He stood up and hugged her and she was aware of the familiar faint smell of whisky.

'Sit down, dear. We have had news of Eddie.'

Madge felt sure this meant that her brother was dead, and was instantly overcome by sobs. Her father held her tight and reassured her Eddie was not dead but they had received a telegram informing them that he was missing in action. It was believed he had been taken prisoner. He held out the telegram for her to read.

She looked at the piece of flimsy brown paper that was dreaded by every serviceman's family and checked the name Edward Williams printed at the top. A jumble of words below – 'missing', 'prisoner', 'presumed', 'action' – all added up to the fact that her darling Eddie was not coming home. She was frantic for more facts. What had happened to him? Where was he? What chance was there of him being alive somewhere still as a prisoner-of-war? Madge began crying in earnest, tears rolling down her father's tweed jacket as he held her tight and stroked her hair.

The tension of their months of fearfulness and uncertainty overwhelmed them all then. The family cried and comforted each other. Daisy hugged her mother, Dick sat on Dolly's lap, and Madge held on to her father as he tried to soothe her. She wiped her eyes and looked out into the garden. As she did so she saw Deacon standing holding a rake and watching the scene inside the house. He crossed himself, turned away and returned to work.

At Manor Farm, Stoulton, Tom's sister Phyllis was clearing away the breakfast things. Birdie was washing up when, through the kitchen window, she saw the postman arrive.

'Phyllis, the postman's at the door,' she said.

'Yes, I'll just clear the last of the plates to be washed up.'

Phyllis opened the door with the postman's hand still poised over the knocker.

'Good morning, Albert,' she said cheerfully.

'Morning, miss, I have a telegram for you,' he replied, looking at his feet and pushing his thick glasses higher on his nose.

Phyllis knew immediately why he felt so uncomfortable. Poor Albert had already delivered far too many telegrams to distraught relatives containing news of their sons' deaths. His mother had told Phyllis that he had thought of resigning from his job but his poor eyesight would limit him in any other work. Phyllis took the telegram with a sense of dread.

'Shall I wait for a reply?' he asked.

Phyllis shook her head and thanked him as she closed the door. She went through to the kitchen and Birdie immediately saw that something was wrong. They sat down with the telegram between them on the table. Phyllis knew they would have to open it. Their mother was in bed – she usually rose late – and their father was out on the farm helping Hender with some fencing. They read the telegram together.

'Bomford, T. R., Worcestershire Yeomanry', was written along the top in black ink. Beneath in rather child-like writing: REGRET TO INFORM YOU THAT LANCE-CORPORAL T. R. BOMFORD IS REPORTED MISSING IN ACTION

23 APRIL 1916. There was a small illegible signature under a Ministry of Defence stamp.

They held hands while they slowly absorbed the news.

'We must hope he's a prisoner. At least they haven't found his body. Mother will be distraught.' Phyllis began pacing the room, bunching her apron in her fists.

'I know. She's been depressed enough with Tom being away, although she could hardly say a kind word to him when he was here. Mother is tough enough to cope, though. It's Father who'll really need our help,' said Birdie.

Mary came into the kitchen then, carrying a pile of washing. She sat down at the table while her sisters gave her the news, tears of anguish slowly sliding down behind the thick-lensed spectacles she wore.

'We'll tell everyone at lunch and leave Mother to sleep as long as she wants,' decided Phyllis, wiping her eyes with her handkerchief. A bright morning, a visit from the postman, and they knew that family life might never be the same again. Tom was the eldest son but it was more than just that; he provided humour at times of tension, calmed his father and supported his siblings. He even managed to deal with his mother's continual sniping and sullenness.

Birdie looked out of the window at the garden where rows of vegetables of all varieties were flourishing. She took enormous pride in growing carrots, radishes and runner beans, not just for the family but for other people in the village too. She felt overwhelmed suddenly by a sense of hopelessness and tears began rolling down her face on to the tablecloth.

Phyllis wrapped her arms around her sister from behind and hugged her.

'This isn't just about Tom, is it?' she asked. 'You're worrying about John too.'

Birdie wiped her eyes and nodded.

'Yes, I can't bear the thought of losing them both. I've not heard from John for a few weeks but that's not unusual as the post from France is so haphazard. I've often wondered whether it would have been better for us to have trained a carrier pigeon to deliver our letters,' she said with a little smile.

'We must hope and pray they both return home safely and that this wretched war ends as soon as possible,' said Phyllis, beginning to busy herself around the kitchen.

Birdie nodded and went upstairs to her room, taking some of the washing that had been brought in by Mary from the line. She sat at her dressing table and looked at the photo of John Guilding, which she kept tucked into the frame of the mirror. It was a formal black-and-white portrait that had been taken in a studio in Malvern. John was wearing his officer's uniform and sitting rather stiffly, gazing past the camera. His hands were folded in his lap, and his boots and belt gleamed in the flashlight. Birdie had spent hours lovingly examining every detail of the photo, wishing she could have him beside her just for a few minutes. His parents had long suspected they were secretly engaged, and John's mother had taken her to one side shortly after he'd left and whispered her blessing on the relationship.

John's letters, which had initially been very positive about an early end to the war, had more recently been less upbeat, although with the censors vetting every word it was hard to ascertain the real situation. It was now over eighteen months since she had seen him. If it were not for one of his sweaters which she kept in a drawer at her bedside, she feared she would lose any sense of him at all.

Birdie brushed her hair and tied it up in a small bun, using hairclips to hold the rest in place. She decided she must continue to keep busy and went into the garden to dig some potatoes for lunch. Somehow she was convinced that Tom was still alive. They had always been close and Birdie thought back to the time when her brother had fallen while out hunting and been knocked out for over five minutes. They had been late home and she was sure there had been some type of accident. Tom eventually appeared, clutching a bloodstained rag to his head but still grinning, although a little unsteady on his feet. Their mother had panicked and called the doctor, while their father had retrieved the whisky bottle from the living room and prescribed his own dose of medicine.

She busied herself around the garden, tying up the broad beans and weeding some of the borders, postponing the moment when they would have to break the news to Nora.

Reg and Hender appeared with one of the working horses from the field, unhitched it and parked the trailer in the yard. They took off their boots and came into the kitchen for lunch. There was a delicious smell of fresh bread, and slices of cheese were laid out along with some cold potatoes and home-made chutney.

Once they had finished eating Birdie cleared her throat and told them she had something to say to them all. The men sat silently as she slowly described how Albert had delivered the telegram that morning and that Tom had been reported missing. Hender leant forward with his head in his hands while Reg crossed himself and held the hands of Birdie and Phyllis for comfort. They were all waiting for their mother's reaction. She began to take deep breaths and then her chest heaved with spasms of sobbing and she ran from the room. They all heard her thumping up the stairs and a door slam behind her, followed by a strange mewing sound.

Birdie repeated her conviction that Tom was still alive, which seemed to comfort her father who gazed at the table and played with a small pile of crumbs. Mary began to clear away and tackle the washing-up to keep herself occupied.

'Well, we just have to hope that he's not badly wounded and that Birdie is right,' said Reg finally.

Chapter 18

Beersheba, Palestine, May 1916

Tom woke early with the sun rising over the hills behind him. The nights had become warmer but the prisoners were still huddled together so he lay still, trying not to wake his neighbours. Men snored. There was a strong smell of sweat and unwashed bodies, and none of them had shaved for two weeks. Tom rubbed his chin and felt the unfamiliar stubble and his dry lips. Every morning there was a sprinkling of sand over everything. As they got up a cloud of dust billowed around them.

Food supplies were reasonable, if tasteless, with dry biscuits in the morning, water throughout the day, and in the evening rice and a watery stew with a few bits of meat in the bottom of the bowl. All the men were losing weight and Alf in particular was looking gaunt. He was suffering from recurrent diarrhoea and had been stopping five or six times each day and diving behind the nearest rock. Initially the horrendous explosions had caused laughter, with the Turkish guards finding it amusing, but before long Tom grew increasingly concerned for him. One guard gave Alf more water and Sid and Tom helped support him a little with an arm under each shoulder. Over the last three or four days he'd slowly recovered.

They had lost count of the date since their capture, but close to midday, after travelling through hilly country for some hours, they stopped to rest and saw a vast flat plain in front of them and, for the first time, the walls of Jerusalem in the distance.

The Sultan soon appeared to lecture them again.

'Gintlemen, as Christians I am sure you will enjoy the sight of the Holy City over there. Sadly for you, we will be marching you through it as prisoners, but I hope you will enjoy your visit as the first Christian prisoners to enter the city since the Crusades.' He smiled triumphantly and bowed low again, just maintaining his balance as his horse whipped round.

'He may be a pompous ass but he can ride a bit,' said Sid.

'Is that right, the first Christians since the Crusades?' asked Eddie.

'I'm not sure, I was never much good at history, but there hasn't been much fighting out here since then that I can think of,' said Tom.

'It's strange to think of us travelling through the Holy Land, possibly walking in the steps of Moses and men from the Bible. Perhaps Jesus himself,' said Eddie, gazing around.

'I would prefer a bed and some decent bloody food rather than a walk through history,' said Alf, who thankfully had perked up.

'Alf, good to hear you're feeling better and can have a moan again,' said Sid, slapping him on the back.

'Yes, apart from an arse that feels like the ring of fire, I am on the mend,' he said proudly as he stood up and stretched his arms in the air. His shirt hung off him, more like a dressing gown, and his cheekbones protruded from his sallow face.

It was good to see him feeling better but Tom knew that he also needed to build up his strength and gain weight, and was sure this would not be the last episode of gastroenteritis any of them would contract.

The order came for them to form up in pairs for the march to Jerusalem, which was a new formation designed, Tom thought, to increase the dramatic effect of a body of prisoners being marched through the city. They had been marching for over a week and his feet were aching and swollen. As they approached Jerusalem the walls rose up before them, white and arresting, and they realised that the road leading to the southern gate was only really wide enough for two men on horseback to pass through. A few local men stood and stared as they walked by, their donkeys completely uninterested in the spectacle. There was a brief pause for water before they entered the city. Then, as they marched through the main gate, the old weather-beaten buildings rose around them.

After a few minutes the road widened and the noise increased. More and more people lined the streets, banners flew from the rooftops and maroon and red flags were draped over window sills, flapping above the men as they passed. After two or three hundred yards the street opened out into a rectangular square, lined by a series of raised seats. Tom looked up and saw a large number of women smiling and waving at them. One particular face stood out from the crowd, a woman wearing a scarf draped loosely over her head. She had dark eyes and one of the most beautiful faces he had ever seen. She smiled at him and moved her hand in a slight wave before brushing back her scarf to reveal long black hair tied at the nape of her neck.

Tom was mesmerised by the sight and turned his head as they walked past to try and prolong their eye contact. For a moment he wondered about a life spent living with this beautiful woman in Jerusalem, not considering the impossible gulf between them of language, culture and religion. He allowed the fantasy to linger and savoured the thought of waking up next to her rather than alongside a mass of stinking comrades in the open air.

The long column of men passed slowly through the centre of the city with The Sultan sitting on his horse, saluting the crowds and acknowledging their cheers as though this was his personal victory. He saluted the captured officers also, who responded with cold stares. Occasionally, to prolong his moment in the spotlight, he stopped the column to insult one or two British soldiers dressed in rags.

They marched on through the magnificent city, occasionally glimpsing church towers alongside minarets and tiny cobbled streets snaking away from the main highway. The crowds thinned and eventually there was only the noise of boots clicking against the cobblestones as they marched out of the northern side of Jerusalem.

They stopped outside its walls and camped for the night, where they heard The Sultan would be escorting the officers to a different camp in the morning. Tom found the idea of being separated from them disturbing, not from any notion of needing officers around to issue orders and direction, but from the sense of vulnerability that came from their departure – the idea that the Turkish might be more cruel towards ordinary soldiers.

Sadly, his fears were soon realised. A new, more junior officer took over from The Sultan. He appeared keen to exert complete control over every prisoner under his command. He was short with a narrow forehead beneath a head of thick dark hair, which extended almost as low as his eyebrows. His face was heavily pockmarked and his skin greasy. He preferred to command from horseback whenever possible. He rode with a very long stirrup, and Tom suspected he was frightened of riding because he shouted at his horse continually and yanked hard on the reins, often drawing blood from its mouth. He carried a short thin whip, which was unusual in that the top was bone-handled and quite elegant, but the lower part thinned down at the tip to a piece of multi-knotted rope. He once struck his horse behind the saddle with such force that blood oozed from its hindquarters. As a horseman, Tom despised the man immediately and loathed his cruelty.

Over the next few weeks they continued to march through hilly countryside and small villages, which looked as though they had changed little since biblical times. They were all exhausted from the endless marching and poor food. Since Jerusalem it had deteriorated in quality and quantity. Men glanced at trees and bushes, looking for nuts or fruit that they could snatch as they passed, but this was highly dangerous as the Turkish guards had already whipped one man who had been caught stealing an orange, and had threatened to shoot anyone else who attempted the same.

In one village the sight of a large group of thin prisoners, wearing tattered uniforms and with their feet bound with rags, stirred some of the local people to pity. They had thrown pieces of bread when the guards had ridden back down the line.

The march north continued day after day through soaring temperatures. They usually rested in the shade in the middle of the day, to drink and eat a small amount. Every day men collapsed on the road through sheer exhaustion, and more than once were loaded on to mules and disappeared off the road. The prisoners were told the men would be looked after but Sid was convinced they'd been taken away and killed. They were all determined to help each other as best they could, as it seemed unlikely they would survive if they fell behind. Turkish guards shouted and prodded them with rifles or beat them with sticks, and Tom found it increasingly difficult not to react against this treatment.

The Turkish officer, who had now been nicknamed The Weasel, was relishing his command. They had skirted Damascus and were travelling up the west side of the Syrian Desert. The pace of the march had been slowing steadily. It was now nearing the end of the first week in May and the heat was increasing. One night the prisoners woke to the sound of shots being fired, and a full riot broke out with Turkish guards beating prisoners with sticks and firing into the air. When the situation was eventually brought under control, the men were ordered to form up and forced to remain at attention, in the dark, for the next hour until the sun rose. Every five or ten minutes there was a gentle thump as a man fainted and dropped to the ground. A guard would then be sent over by The Weasel to beat him until, with hands wrapped around his head to protect himself, he slowly struggled back to his feet.

'The bastard! How long are we going to stand here?' hissed Tom under his breath.

'He's a vicious little sod. Must have had a father that beat the living daylights out of him,' whispered Sid.

Down the line, the story came that a prisoner called Arthur Weeks had become delirious during the night. He had been developing a fever over some days and his friends had begged the guards for treatment but they'd merely laughed and dismissed the request. It was thought that Arthur had woken during the night, hallucinating and confused. He'd wandered away from the camp and been challenged by the guards. He'd not replied but continued to stagger around in the dark until two guards had opened fire and killed him.

'You will all learn lesson from me,' The Weasel shouted in his heavy Turkish accent. 'The man tried to escape so he was shot.' There was a murmur of protest from the British, but no one dared to voice their real feelings.

'Quiet! You are now prisoners of the Ottoman Empire and you obey us,' shouted the Turk, spraying spittle over the front rank of soldiers. 'You are now dismissed.' And he waved his whip, yanked his horse round and rode back to his tent.

Chapter 19

'Well, Tom, another day of digging for us,' said Sid, sitting up in bed and stretching.

'Do we have to get up straight away?' groaned Eddie, pulling the thin blanket back over his head.

'Yes, lad, we do. You know The Weasel is returning from leave so our little holiday from the bastard is sadly coming to an end. Something tells me he'll not be bringing us back any presents,' said Sid.

'He's right, Eddie. I feel as though I've been at home on leave myself with him away. The guards are different too. More food, more breaks on the work details, and the whole camp seems more relaxed. Not to mention you, Eddie. You seem like a new man without him picking on you the whole time,' said Tom.

'He seems to detest me because I'm the only man in the camp shorter than him,' said Eddie. 'Tom, don't intervene, though. I can sort myself out. You shouldn't keep challenging him or he'll have you shot.'

They rolled out of their bunks and into the chill of the autumn morning. Their camp was perched on a rocky outcrop of the Taurus Mountains in southern Turkey. Each morning after breakfast, any prisoner passed fit after roll call would march the two miles to one of the entrances to the tunnel they were digging under the mountains. They had been told by a friendly Turkish guard that the journey by rail south to Jerusalem would be shortened considerably by passing through the mountains rather than diverting around them, and that this would help the supply route to the south.

They had been at the camp now for some months and a routine of sorts had developed. They paraded shortly after sunrise and then had a reasonable breakfast, which varied from porridge laced with large quantities of cinnamon to fried eggs and bread. They were then marched to the tunnels where they would dig into the mountain and transport earth and rock away in small wagons towed by mules, which looked to be better treated than they were. They had a short break around eleven o'clock and then worked for a further two hours before returning to the camp for some food. In the afternoons they either rested or, for those feeling more energetic, there was sometimes football or cricket.

Eddie excelled at football and Tom immediately recognised his extraordinary skill. He could dribble round the whole team and walk the ball across the goal line if necessary, but more usually tried to set someone else up to score. On occasion the guards would join in, but tackles usually then became a little too heavy and the game would often break up with a scuffle and threats from the Turkish soldiers.

In the evening, they were given rice and usually some type of stew containing a small amount of meat. They were allowed to sit out on a grassy bank overlooking the valley, with spectacular views to the mountains, watching the sun set in a blaze of orange and crimson. Alf would save one of his cigarettes for this time. Somehow he had persuaded several friends to pass over their ration of four cigarettes a day to him, which resulted in him being submerged in a cloud of smoke for most of his waking hours. He claimed it kept the flies at bay.

Tom was desperate to write to his family and let them know he was a prisoner in Turkey as he was sure he would have been listed as missing and they would all be terribly worried about him.

It had taken weeks of persuasion for The Weasel to allow any letters to be written, and he had informed them that the mail would be heavily censored so no details of their location or activities could be mentioned. They all felt it unlikely he would pass on any letters from Britain to them, as he took immense pleasure in depriving them of any hope of release.

Their biggest problem was medical treatment, or the lack of it. There was no doctor at the camp and any treatment was provided by a guard who told them he had never been to medical school but that his father had been a surgeon. They nicknamed him 'Bill the Pill' as he handed out a variety of pills with little idea of what they were. Tom sometimes thought he himself knew more about medicine. 'Bill' was, however, very caring, and when Alf injured his hand on a work detail, the Turk ensured it was properly cleaned and dressed each day to prevent infection. He even obtained extra rations for Alf.

In mid-October, shortly after The Weasel had returned from leave, there was an outbreak of dysentery at the camp. All bar a handful of men went down with severe diarrhoea and there were no work details at all for nearly two weeks. Tom and Sid recovered after eight days but Eddie and Alf hardly moved from their beds, except to visit the overflowing latrines. The smell was horrendous. It was hard to get enough water to keep them hydrated. Alf, thin at the best of times, shrank to skin and bone. His fever fluctuated wildly and he was passing large amounts of bloody diarrhoea. Tom and Sid took turns to sit with him, bathing his head and encouraging him to sip water and try to eat small amounts of rice.

'It's no good, lads, I'm done for here,' he said, on the tenth day of his illness.

'No, we are going to see you through this,' said Tom, though for the first time he had serious doubts as to his friend's chance of survival. Alf's skin was wrinkled and his eyes were sunken. His mouth was dry and his tongue had swollen and looked like a piece of dry chamois leather.

Eddie was still very weak but now walking about. He went to talk to Bill the Pill. Bill was passionate about football and Eddie used their shared interest to try and persuade him to get some medicine for Alf from a neighbouring camp. Eddie knew this was dangerous as The Weasel disapproved of outside help. He would have Bill court-martialled and shot if he found out. Eddie pleaded for help but Bill left him, muttering and shaking his head.

The following day only a quarter of the men were deemed fit to work. Eddie was chewing on some bread and talking to Sid at breakfast, relieved that they would all be having another day off from working in the tunnels. They glanced up and saw Bill walking past looking guilty and gazing across the room at the far corner. As he passed them he bent forward, brushing Eddie's shoulder.

'For your friend, Eddie. Good pill, I think,' he said.

Eddie looked up, nodded and smiled, mouthing 'thank you'. He stuffed the small paper parcel in his pocket. He wandered back to their wooden barracks and past the latrines, which were being cleared by some local farm workers who wore scarves tied around their mouths. Eddie tried to hold his breath as he passed by, but the smell was overpowering and he found it hard not to vomit. He went straight to Alf, who lay on his bed bathed in sweat. His mouth was open and he was panting through cracked lips.

'Hello, Eddie,' he rasped, in a voice barely above a whisper. 'How are you?'

'Alf, I've managed to get some pills for you. I think Bill took quite a risk as he had to go to another camp, but I hope they'll sort out your gut.'

'Well done, Eddie,' said Tom, 'that's wonderful; let's hope this works.'

Tom took a pill out of the paper bag and placed it on Alf's

tongue. He sat him up and gave him some water. Alf coughed but managed to force down the tablet before flopping back on the bed. Tom slid the other pills under the straw mattress, ready for the next dose.

That night, long after they had fallen asleep, The Weasel called for an inspection of their barracks. They scrambled out of their beds and stood at the ends while he strode around shouting for the guards to search everyone.

'You have weapons here, I know, so tell me where they are and there will be no problem,' The Weasel shouted, slamming his stick down on the beds as he marched up and down. He stopped in front of Tom and lifted his chin with the bone handle of his stick. Tom felt the man's breath on his face. It smelt of stale garlic. He tried to avoid looking into The Weasel's eyes. He stepped away and turned towards Eddie, who stood as tall as possible with his head bowed.

'So, little man, what have you hidden here?' he sneered. Eddie was shaking and kept his eyes fixed on The Weasel's belt.

'Nothing, sir,' he murmured. The stick slammed against his shoulder.

'What you say, little man? I not hear.' He towered over Eddie who had slumped to the ground, groaning and trying to suppress the searing pain he felt.

'Get up, get up!' screamed his tormentor.

Tom, although desperate to try and help Eddie, realised that the guards had stopped searching and were looking on open-mouthed, which reduced the chances of the medicine being found. Eddie slowly climbed to his feet before The Weasel struck him again on the side of the knee. This time he managed to stay standing, which riled The Weasel even more. He struck again at the front of Eddie's legs. There was a loud crack like a whip and Eddie went down, curling up into a ball and sobbing with pain. The Weasel appeared satisfied with the level of punishment inflicted, turned on his heel and marched out of the room.

Tom rushed to Eddie and helped him sit up. Silent tears streamed down his face as he rubbed his thighs. The other men gathered round in support. There were cries of 'Don't worry about that bastard' and 'We're with you, mate'. Tom helped Eddie back to his bed.

'I'll tell you now, Eddie, just to make it plain, that bastard never does that to you again.'

'Thanks, Tom, but there's bugger all you can do,' Eddie replied. 'He can't stand me, and when he gets mad, I'm usually on the receiving end. At least he didn't find the medicine.'

Alf recovered quickly over the next few days. Whatever was in the pills, it appeared to be working rapidly. Several men sacrificed some of their food at each meal to help him gain some weight. The camp returned to the usual routine of morning working parties and relaxed afternoons.

The Weasel was spending at least half his time at another prisoner-of-war camp nearby, which meant they saw a lot less of him. Tom often wondered about his mental state and upbringing. At best he cared little for the prisoners, at worst he had a horrendous temper which resulted in numerous vicious beatings. None of the guards knew anything about his personal life but there were rumours that his parents had both died when he was young and he had joined the army at sixteen to save himself from destitution.

Chapter 20

Manor Farm, Stoulton, October 1916

The weather had changed in a week, from sunshine in September to thunderstorms and strong winds that had ripped the roof off Bert Alvis's barn at Drakes Broughton. Reg was grateful that the harvest was safely completed and most of the ploughing done. He still had two fields where the stubble had changed from golden yellow to dirty brown, and these would be planted with spring barley instead of winter wheat, as he had no hope of horses being able to pull a plough through ground sodden by rain. There was little work to be done in this weather, but Hender, who loathed being in the house before evening, had started cutting hedges around the fields. His father had been cleaning the stables, and painting the wood inside while the horses were turned out during the day.

Reg sat at the kitchen window, watching the rain lash against the glass. He could see the horses now in the small paddock, grouped together, their hindquarters turned into the wind, water running off their backs, looking very miserable. He knew that as soon as the rain lessened they would have their heads down, munching on the lush grass. The horses had lost weight during the ploughing and planting as the hours had been long. Reg had insisted on finishing the latter late one night as he'd been sure the weather was about to change. The elegant needle on the old barometer hanging in the kitchen had begun to swing, slowly edging from sunshine to showers.

His wife was still spending most of the day in bed. She struggled with the uncertainty of her son's fate in Egypt, forgetting, for the time being, the resentment she'd felt towards him while he was growing up. Phyllis and Birdie were tidying the kitchen behind Reg, chattering about the harvest festival planned for the following Sunday in the parish church. Birdie had gathered and stored fruit and vegetables, along with some wheat, which would be tied in bundles and placed near the altar.

There was a knock at the door and as Reg opened it he saw the postman huddled in the porch, sheltering from the rain.

'Morning, Albert. Come on in out of the rain for a moment and have some tea,' said Reg, ushering him into the kitchen.

Albert shook the rain off his coat, spraying a mist of water into the air. 'Thanks, Mr Bomford, I think I will,' he said, water dripping from his chin. He slipped off his boots and shuffled in further, holding the postbag in both arms.

'Letter for you, Mr Bomford. Looks like it's from London,' said the postman nervously. He knew the significance of any news from there and rummaged in his bag for the missive. Reg took the brown envelope and sat down with Phyllis and Birdie at the kitchen table. He scanned the contents and broke into a smile.

'Tom's alive! He's alive, girls.'

Phyllis and Birdie leapt up and hugged each other, laughing. Reg hugged Albert, who looked bemused but relieved it was not news of another death.

'What does it say, Father?' asked Phyllis.

Reg sat down again and unfolded the letter.

10 July 1916
Dear All,
I have written once before but do not know whether you will have received my letter. I am being held prisoner in Turkey and am being well treated. We were captured in a battle near Qatia on Easter Day and were marched north to this camp.

The food is good and I am in good health, as is Sid Parkes.
All the letters are checked so I am unable to say much more.
I hope you are all well and that there are no problems on the
farm.

I send you my love and hope that the war is over soon.
Tom

There was a tick in red ink at the bottom of the letter indicating the Turkish censors had passed it, and a separate note from the Ministry of Defence in London stating that the status of Lance Corporal T. R. Bomford was now registered as that of prisoner of war.

Phyllis sat smiling, holding her father's hand, while Birdie wept, her face in her hands. Albert sipped his tea, shuffled his feet and coughed.

'I'm very pleased for you, Mr Bomford, and glad to hear Mr Tom is safe. The rain seems to have stopped so I'd best be on my way.' He touched his cap and let himself out.

Phyllis and Birdie took the letter and ran up the stairs to wake their mother. They burst into the room and found her sitting up in bed reading. The heavy curtains were open a little, letting a shaft of light fall on the corner of the bed. She slowly peeled off her wire-framed spectacles and set them down on the bed.

'Good morning, my dears,' she said with a forced smile.

'Mother, it's such good news! We have had a letter from Tom. He is being held prisoner in Turkey,' Phyllis said breathlessly.

Their mother patted the bed and asked them to sit down. 'Now, slow down and tell me exactly what has happened.'

Birdie told her about the letter, while Phyllis watched her face closely for any sign of a slight clearing in her depression and a change of mood. The atmosphere at home had been oppressive and sad for so long, she desperately hoped this would mark the beginning of an improvement. Her mother checked the facts again and closely examined the letter, as if unsure whether to end her period of mourning or not. She finished reading, put the letter down and then held each of her daughters by the hand.

'Girls, this is wonderful news. Dear Tom is alive so we must be grateful for that. I am going to dress and would like you to accompany me to church so we can give thanks to God and pray for Tom's return.'

She kissed them both on the head, swept back the bedclothes and opened the curtains, allowing sunshine to fill the room. Phyllis heard her mother give a sigh of happiness as they left her to dress for church.

Chapter 21

POW Camp, Turkey, February 1917

Tom woke, shivering, and realised it was still pitch black outside. He had slept heavily but knew he would not get back to sleep again. The wind howled outside and the door of the wooden barracks rattled with each gust. A few men snored as Tom curled into a foetal position to conserve heat.

The snow had arrived with a sudden drop in temperature in mid-November. One morning, as they marched towards the tunnels, one of the guards had stepped off the edge of the path, which was covered by a snowdrift, and had disappeared. The prisoners were ordered to search for him by one of the other guards, the man's brother. They lined up on hands and knees and crawled through the snow, scooping handfuls behind them as they inched towards the edge of the path following his tracks. The whole snowdrift in front of them suddenly gave way, revealing a sheer drop into the valley below. The brother began wailing and shouting as the men slowly backed away from the edge. More snow was falling heavily, like hanks of wool dropping from the sky. It was so dense that the prisoners were ordered back to camp for the day.

There had been little change in their rations with the cold weather, and the men were losing considerable amounts of weight. Alf once again looked skeletal, with sunken cheeks and ears that looked far too big for his head. In spite of this he was still cheerful and made light of how weak he felt, laughing and joking with the guards.

As the temperature dropped, more and more men began scratching. During the summer they could wash and dry their clothes in the sun. Now the blankets they needed for warmth at night were riddled with lice. The guards ignored the men's pleas for new blankets and thought it amusing to see them all itching. The Weasel, who had insisted they keep working on the tunnel, enjoyed beating men who scratched when they paraded each morning.

Within three weeks of the start of the cold snap, men began to complain of shivering and searing headaches. They suffered with leg pains and work was impossible. After four or five days of illness they appeared to recover, only to relapse again a week or so later.

The Weasel was convinced the prisoners were malingering and insisted they return to work. But when the first man collapsed and died, he finally accepted that they were ill. Bill the Pill was baffled and managed to persuade a doctor to visit the camp. He was an Austrian who had travelled widely around Europe during the war, working for the German Army. He had a kindly face, and wore a small neat grey beard and a monocle. He visited each of the barracks and spoke to the men in remarkably good English, making notes as he went round the camp. After an hour he went to The Weasel's office and informed him there was an outbreak of Trench Fever.

He ordered all blankets and clothes to be burnt in a huge fire, and all the men to have their hair cut as short as possible and to wash thoroughly before putting on fresh clothes. The Weasel was furious and took this as a personal slight on his command, but had little choice but to follow the senior doctor's orders.

After five days there were no new cases, and mercifully fewer beatings on parade as the itching completely cleared.

In late-February there was a break in the weather and the snow began to melt. Tom was sitting in the sun one afternoon on a small rock outside his barracks when he heard a trickle of water as the melting snow began to fill the small stream nearby. The trickle developed into a steady flow and over the next hour built into a current of water. Tom enjoyed the feeling of heat against his legs and felt relieved that they had managed to survive the ferocious cold of a winter in the mountains.

'Looks like winter might be easing a bit, Tom,' said Eddie, drawing patterns in the remaining snow with a small stick.

'Yes, it's warmer and I think we're through the worst. I wondered if any of us would survive when the first snow came. I felt sorry for the guard who fell off the path but maybe him losing his life saved a few of ours,' said Tom.

'The Weasel seems a bit quieter too.'

'Now, lad, don't get your hopes up. He's just worried about some inspection, according to the guards,' said Tom.

Over the following two weeks it became obvious that an inspection of the camp by a senior ranking officer was due. The Weasel arranged for the barracks to be cleaned, the latrines were cleared, and a coat of paint was applied to doors and fences around the camp.

The food improved, with regular supplies of lamb and more rice and potatoes. Men began to gain a little weight despite the resumption of working parties.

One morning when they were standing on parade The Weasel appeared wearing gleaming brown boots and a peaked cap, the brass buttons of his jacket shining. He puffed out his chest and clicked the heels of his boots together.

'Men, the camp will be inspected tomorrow morning by Major-General Sorpen. He very important man.'

Tom remembered The Weasel's English faltered badly when he was nervous.

'He ask you many question about the camp and I want you tell him how good camp is and how food also good. If you do, food will stay good and I very happy man.'

He bowed to them and walked back into his office.

'The bloody bastard! If he thinks, after everything he has done here, it is going to be that easy, he can bugger off,' said Sid.

'Bloody right,' said Eddie. There was a rumbling through the ranks of men and Tom felt nervous that the inspection might lead to a mass protest.

They had another good meal that night, of what Alf was certain was goat but Sid thought might be horse, as one of the guards had indicated with sign language that The Weasel was rather partial to horse meat. Tom blocked the thought from his mind and ate as much as he could in case the menu changed in the next few days.

The meat caused many of them to suffer from indigestion, which was why Tom was talking to Eddie in the early hours of the morning.

'What should I say if this officer asks me about The Weasel and the camp?' asked Eddie.

'Tell him the truth but speak quickly, quietly, and hope The Weasel isn't listening. We can't let the bastard bribe us so he gets promotion. We need to remember what he has done to you and that poor bloke last year he had flogged and we never saw again. I know everyone feels the same so we're all prepared to go back to the old diet. With any luck we might even get him transferred.'

They were hustled through breakfast and ordered on to the parade ground. They stood to attention for nearly an hour, then as there was no sign of Sorpen they were ordered to stand at ease. As Tom stretched his legs, he saw on the road below them a plume of dust winding up the valley. The Weasel spotted it too and began running around outside his office, barking orders at his officers.

A magnificent open-topped car purred through the gate and swung to a halt in front of The Weasel, surrounding him in a cloud of dust. He coughed and waved it away before saluting as

Major-General Sorpen stepped out of the car. He towered over The Weasel as he acknowledged the salute, and then stood back to survey the camp. He had a huge moustache that was perfectly groomed and almost covered his mouth, but his eyes lingered on some of the men and Tom felt hopeful that he at least appeared sympathetic. The Weasel began chattering away and ushered Sorpen into his office with a toadying smile. The door slammed shut and the men waited. The sun was now warm and it was turning into a beautiful spring day with just a faint chill still in the air.

One of the Turks barked the order for attention as the Major-General reappeared and began to inspect the men, slowly marching up and down the lines. A few men saluted and occasionally Sorpen stopped to talk to one or two of them. The Weasel was looking pleased and all appeared to be going to plan. The men were then dismissed and returned to their barracks to prepare for the march to the tunnels. Eddie was a little late forming up so Sid and Tom, from habit, hung back to diminish the chance of The Weasel attacking him. This meant the three of them were a little detached from the main group and The Weasel was ahead, ordering the other prisoners to line up in tight ranks. Sorpen glanced over at the stragglers, and with one of his junior officers walked straight towards them.

'Good morning, men. I was hoping to speak to you about life as a prisoner of the Ottoman Empire,' he said in perfect English, and with a hint of sarcasm in his tone. 'You, what is your name?' he asked Eddie.

'Eddie Williams, sir,' he replied, saluting.

'Do not worry about that,' said the senior officer, waving a gloved hand dismissively. 'Tell me about the Captain, is he a fair man?'

'No, he's not. He is vicious, violent, and he beats us. Our food is terrible but he has improved it over the last few weeks to bribe us. He knew you were coming and wanted us to tell you how good it is here. Men have died digging those tunnels,' Eddie waved towards the mountains ahead of him, 'and he could not give a damn. If you could have him transferred to the trenches in France, we would be very happy.'

Sid and Tom nodded in agreement as Sorpen smiled. He shook Eddie's hand and nodded, just as The Weasel came bustling up behind them looking anxious.

'Well done, Eddie, that was bloody brave and just what the bastard deserved,' said Sid, keeping his head forward so he could not be observed talking.

That day at the tunnels was like any other; a morning spent digging rock and loading wagons to bring the rubble back out was followed by bread and water and a rest in the shadow of the mountain. They all worked on for another hour at a gentle pace and then marched back to the camp.

Major-General Sorpen's car had gone, but worryingly there was a lot of shouting coming from The Weasel's office. The door opened and one of the Turkish Corporals staggered out, clutching a bloodstained ear. The whole camp was ordered on parade and Tom sensed things had not gone well. Eddie stood between Tom and Sid right at the back, hoping they were hidden behind the ranks of men.

The Weasel stood in front of them with his stick in one hand. His face was flushed and his uniform had large sweat stains under both arms. He began pacing up and down in front of them, hitting the palm of his hand with his stick in time with his steps.

'This not good day for me. The General not happy and he say camp is not good. I tell you good food will stay but you tell him lies about camp,' he yelled. He marched down the lines of men, stopping every few yards and shaking his head, muttering to himself. Tom was instantly filled with fear; The Weasel was looking for someone and it could only mean the three of them.

Tom kept his head down and saw the familiar brown boots appear in front of Eddie and himself.

'It was you, little man, who speak to General,' said The Weasel, his spittle spraying Eddie and Tom. His stick came from nowhere and struck Eddie on the side of the face. He rocked back on his feet but stayed staring forward, defiantly. The Weasel brought his knee up hard into Eddie's groin and, with a cry of agony, he fell to the ground. The Weasel stood over him, ready to strike again.

Tom felt something shift inside him. Principle mixed with anger forced him to take a step forward. The effect was instantaneous. The Weasel stood stock still, hardly believing that a prisoner could defy him so openly by stepping out of line. He turned slowly and that was when Tom attacked.

He leant back slightly and then swung his right fist as hard as he could into The Weasel's jaw. He felt a cracking sensation as his fist followed through, twisting the man's head violently backwards. The Weasel fell to the ground and there was a moment of silence, when time felt suspended, before a roar erupted from the camp. Tom was grabbed by two guards who held his arms while The Weasel was helped away, unable to speak, with blood pouring from his mouth.

The guards managed to manhandle Tom through the crowd of prisoners, who all cheered and tried to shake his hand or slap his back. Tom's hand was throbbing with pain from the blow but he could move his fingers and was certain nothing was broken. His hands had become very strong from heaving rocks on to the wagons in the tunnel. He hoped that had helped prevent too much damage.

Tom knew where he was being taken as soon as they passed The Weasel's office. There was a small brick block that looked as though it might have been an old cow shed. It now served as the punishment block.

The heavy outer door was unlocked and Tom was marched past a table and chairs towards another door with a small grille set in the middle. The block smelt of stale urine and, as the door was opened, a rat ran over Tom's foot. The cell was very small with a low ceiling, forcing him to crouch. As his eyes grew used to the dim light, which filtered through a tiny slit high up in the wall, he saw a wooden pallet on the floor and a bucket on its side in the corner. He was thrown to the floor, his confidence and elation draining from him. He was now alone and at the mercy of The Weasel.

He barely slept that night as the cold ate into him. In the morning, stiff and sore, he was brought water and hard bread, which he tried to suck on then broke apart to chew in very small pieces. The rest of the day passed slowly and he realised how important the routine of the camp was and the company of his friends. Tom made a vow to God that if he survived, he would treasure his friendship with Sid, Alf and Eddie for the rest of his life.

That second night he was exhausted enough to sleep on the wooden pallet, although when he awoke the following morning his right arm was completely numb. He heard the door grinding open and shouts for him to stand up. His clothes stank, having absorbed the ghastly smell of stale urine and the contents of his bucket. As he stepped outside a rat ran back into his cell, which made him smile for the first time since he had broken The Weasel's jaw.

It was a cloudy day as he was marched outside, wind buffeting the men's shirts on the parade ground. The whole camp was lined up in front of him but there was no sign of The Weasel.

A large plump officer came out of The Weasel's office. His waist bulged over his belt and the buttons of his jacket were straining against the pressure from his enormous abdomen. He waddled over to stand beside a wooden box that had been placed in front of the men. He spoke in Turkish while Bill the Pill translated.

'I am sorry to tell you that the Captain has been taken to hospital after the violent attack from a British prisoner and will not be returning.' A huge roar went up from the prisoners. The officer waited patiently for silence.

'Because of the attack, Lance-Corporal Bomford will be flogged, receiving twenty lashes.'

There were cries of 'Shame' and 'Disgusting'. Tom could see Sid in the front rank, shouting encouragement, while his friend was dragged over and tied to the wooden box. It reminded him of the horse that they had used for vaulting in the gymnasium at school. His shirt had already been removed and he felt his arms and legs being secured to the four corners of the box.

He looked down at the patch of grass in front of him and tried to prepare himself for the pain to come. His mouth was dry and he found it impossible to swallow.

The first blow fell with a crack of noise followed by a wave of pain that spread over his back. He could not breathe. The agony was so much worse than anything he'd imagined. While he was trying to collect himself, the next blow struck.

It went on and on. Tom felt his brain fill completely with pain; there was no room for any other thought or idea.

Finally, the end did come but the agony if anything was worse. Tom thought it would lessen but he could feel blood running down his sides and knew that his skin had split in numerous places. Two guards cut his ties and carried him back to his cell. Tom was semi-conscious, unaware of the fact that every single prisoner stood to attention, saluting him as he was dragged away.

Tom lay on his pallet and dared not move. He felt resigned to the fact he could die here. Unaware of time, he drifted in and out of consciousness.

Some time later he heard the door grind open and Bill the Pill bent down beside him.

'Tom,' he whispered, 'I have come to bathe your back and apply some cream to help the healing. My mother makes the cream, it is very good.'

'Thank you,' he groaned. He felt Bill's hands gently applying the cream, which felt cool. As it was rubbed on to the bloody lines across his back, he felt his skin loosen a little. It was still sore but he thought he might be able to move around his cell a little now.

Bill continued to come every day to apply the cream and Tom began to heal slowly but surely. The cream smelt of eucalyptus, which kept the flies away, and after a week he could wear a shirt without the agony of removing half the skin on his back along with it. Tom found the separation from his friends just as hard to cope with as the pain. He missed Eddie's cheerful demeanour and Alf's cynicism. He could still picture Sid on parade as Tom was about to be flogged, his gaze determined and unwavering, instilling in his friend the strength to survive.

Despite Bill occasionally smuggling in food for him, Tom was only given water and dry bread and his weight was falling dramatically. The skin on his legs hung in folds and he was losing all the strength in his arms. He had developed a cough, which was at its worst when he lay down. He lost track of time, with no idea how many days he had been held in solitary confinement. He grew a beard, which itched.

The weather began to get warmer and in the middle of the day the heat in his cell was stifling. He persuaded a guard to bring him a bucket of water so he could lie on the stone floor, splashing himself and trying to stay cool. He knew he was very dehydrated as his urine was becoming darker and darker. After several days of this heat he felt unable to move, lying still in utter exhaustion. His mouth was permanently dry and he drifted into bizarre dreams where he was floating on clouds over the Malvern Hills. Bill had not visited him for some time as his back had very nearly healed. He had no appetite at all and found it hard to get up off his pallet. He was sure he was dying of dehydration and pictured his flesh slowly drying out and becoming hard as an old sponge.

His cough lessened a little and he was sleeping better, but once again his dreams were vivid. He felt he was being swept through a tunnel of light into a huge blue space, as though suspended in the sky.

One morning he was woken by the grinding of the door and opened his eyes, ready for his cup of water and piece of bread to be thrown on to the floor. The kick to his back was a shock and then he felt himself lifted off the floor. The two guards were shouting at him and kneeing him in the thigh, trying to make him stand. Tom felt his legs give way. There was no possibility of supporting himself. He was dragged out of the cell and on to the parade ground. The sun was blinding. He felt his head explode with pain. His feet dragged through the sand behind him, creating a small furrow, and he was vaguely reminded of ploughing on the farm with a pair of horses.

The guards threw him on to his bed in the barracks, face down. He felt hands slowly turn him over but the light was still too bright for him to open his eyes.

'You poor bugger, what have they done to you? It's beyond…' Sid's voice began breaking up. 'Eddie, get a cloth or something to put over his eyes.'

'Tom, it's Eddie, how are you feeling?'

'Like shit,' he croaked. It was the first time he had spoken in weeks.

'You've been in solitary for three weeks now; you look like you've been to hell,' said Sid.

They lifted Tom up a little and gave him sips of water. Eddie fussed round, trying to wash some of the thick grime from his body. Tom's back, although healed, was a mass of delicate scar tissue.

After half an hour he became accustomed to the light and opened his eyes slowly. Sid was smiling and Eddie shook his hand.

'Good to have you back.'

'Thanks, Sid, I'm glad to be back. Do I still look better than Alf?' asked Tom.

'That's good,' said Alf. 'He's taking the mick out of me.'

Chapter 22

Ivy Lodge, Stourbridge, July 1917

Madge was picking flowers in the garden and had collected some greenery and a small bunch of pink roses. Their scent was exquisite. She always made sure she lingered in the garden to appreciate its colours and perfumes.

Daisy came running across the lawn, which was now rather brown after the two-week spell of sunny weather. Madge had begun helping at the local hospital and she was still wearing her nurse's uniform, which stretched almost to her ankles. Her white starched apron flapped as she ran, clutching her cap.

'Madge, we have some news! The Swinford family received a letter from their son James, and he mentioned that Eddie was being held prisoner in the same camp. It must be true, Madge, because James knows Eddie well. They used to play cricket together at school.'

Madge dropped her flowers and stood still for a moment. She had prepared herself for news that her brother was dead, but now there was hope. She ran to hug Daisy joyfully.

'That's wonderful news. Can we be sure it's true?'

'Yes, Mother went over this morning and saw the letter herself. It was in James's hand and Eddie is mentioned as "the boy I played cricket with", so it must be him.'

'Timothy will be so pleased. I haven't been myself with him for months and I feel so guilty, but the worry about Eddie has been awful. Timothy's coming round after work to see me today.'

Madge gathered up the flowers and hurried back into the house.

The kitchen door was standing open and she saw her mother there, beaming with joy.

'I think this calls for a glass of sherry,' she said.

'I'll get the glasses,' said Daisy.

'I can't quite believe it, Mother. I feared the worst and this at least gives us hope, although I've no idea how the Turks treat their prisoners,' said Madge.

'I'm not sure either but James Swinford said that they were fed and conditions were quite good. We just have to hope the war ends soon.'

They raised their glasses and drank to Eddie's safe return.

'How was your day, Daisy?' asked Madge.

'Very busy. We had some more injured men from France admitted today. They seem so young. Most of them look as though they should still be at school. One boy had developed an infection in his leg after a shell landed in his trench, and his lower leg has been amputated. He told me he'd loved playing football before he joined up and wasn't sure how he could live without it. He just sobbed and sobbed. I felt so helpless. My training was pretty short. Sometimes I wonder whether I should be there at all.'

'You're doing a grand job, and you know how short of nurses they are. Matron says you are kind to the men and they adore you.'

'One or two try it on, they really do. Matron told me off because one man asked me to blow him a kiss when I was leaving. He was very handsome and I thought no one was looking but Matron said it was unprofessional and everyone would expect it if I wasn't careful,' Daisy said, sipping her sherry. 'Well, to spite her, I'm going to carry on nursing – and blowing kisses. Those poor men need something to cheer them up.'

Daisy laughed, her pretty face lighting up with mischief. Madge could just imagine how young soldiers fell for her and responded to her sense of humour.

Soon after tea Timothy arrived in his small car. As he drove through the gates he tooted the horn, a habit of his which had begun to annoy Madge.

He jumped out and kissed her on both cheeks. He held the car door open and she settled into the passenger seat.

'I have some exciting news, Timothy. We have heard that Eddie is being held prisoner by the Turks, so thank heavens he's alive!'

'That's wonderful, you must all be so relieved. Let's hope he's home before too long,' Timothy said, before rushing on with boyish excitement, 'I have a surprise for you too, Madge.'

'Oh, what? Do please tell me.'

'No, you'll have to wait and see,' he said, reverting to his usual prim and proper tone.

They drove on through Stourbridge and into an area Madge didn't know well. They rounded a corner and there before them was a huge funfair in the middle of a large park. Madge squealed with excitement, which made Timothy jerk the wheel.

'I'm sorry, my dear, you made me jump,' he said as he carefully parked the car.

They walked hand in hand to the funfair, discussing what they might try. There were huge crowds of people around the brightly coloured stalls, and children ran about, shouting and laughing.

In the centre was a long slide where people of all shapes and sizes were being spat out of the small hole at the bottom. Timothy and Madge walked over to the merry-go-round and climbed on to a couple of the ornate wooden horses, Madge riding side-saddle in ladylike style. The organ music started and they slowly picked up speed, spinning faster and faster.

'This is wonderful,' she shouted at Timothy, who smiled back at her. They moved on to the 'Waltzo' where they sat in semicircular seats, which rotated and spun round on a larger platform. Madge adored the speed and the force of the ride. She felt slightly dizzy as they got off and held on to Timothy for support.

'Wasn't that fun?' she said.

'Not really, I'm feeling rather sick and dizzy,' he said indignantly. They walked slowly away, Madge holding Timothy's arm as he regained his balance. One or two people gave him rather disapproving looks.

'They think I'm drunk, Madge,' said Timothy, staggering slightly and sounding outraged.

'I'm sure you'll recover in a few minutes and at least you haven't bumped into any patients yet.'

They stopped at a coconut shy where they hurled balls at old bits of china, which proved oddly difficult to break. Madge eventually shattered a teapot, which exploded into hundreds of pieces, but Timothy struggled with his technique and she thought he had what Eddie would have termed a rather 'girlie' throw.

Madge saw a candyfloss stall with children coming away holding sticks of pink froth almost as big as their heads.

'Oh, Timothy, do let's have some,' she said.

'You know it's not very good for you, Madge.'

'Surely a little wouldn't do me any harm, would it?' she pleaded.

'Very well, I'll buy you a stick,' he said in his most disapproving tone.

Madge ate it slowly as they walked back across the park but she did not really enjoy it. Timothy, who was now a little embarrassed by his own churlish behaviour, chatted about news from France. They found the car and drove back home, parking outside the gate. Timothy held Madge's hand and kissed her on the cheek.

'I hope you had a lovely day,' he said.

'I did, thank you, and I especially enjoyed the candyfloss.'

'Good. And I have a little present for you,' he said, leaning into the back of the car and then presenting her with a large coconut.

'Thank you, that's very kind,' she said slowly, wondering what on earth she was going to do with it. They said their goodbyes and Madge stood in the driveway and waved him off. He tooted the horn once again and she went back into the house, clutching her coconut.

'What has your dashing prince given you today, Madge?' asked Daisy between fits of giggles. Madge started to laugh too until tears rolled down her cheeks and her sides ached. Finally she got her breath.

'He didn't want to buy me candyfloss because it was bad for me,' she said in a serious tone, imitating him. 'He does find it hard to let go sometimes, but he is such a kind man.'

'That he is, my dear, and he dotes on you so we must be grateful for that. There may not be very many marriageable men left at the end of this war, remember.'

Chapter 23

Manor Farm, Stoulton, September 1917

It was harvest time and the weather had settled into a spell of hot, sunny days. Reg had borrowed a horse-drawn binder from a neighbour who had finished his harvest. They slowly tracked up and down the field cutting the wheat, which was then gathered into bundles and stacked into windrows to dry.

After a week of dry weather, the threshing machine came to the farm at the end of August and everyone helped to gather the windrows on to the wagons. All the neighbouring farmers came along, and Phyllis and Birdie served up home-made cakes and bread to them. The threshing machine was huge and powered by a very large steam engine. It terrified some of the younger horses.

Phyllis led her favourite horse Blackie, which she knew to be a very unoriginal name but he could hardly be called anything else. He was nearly eighteen hands and jet-black. She patted his neck and walked with her feet well away from his huge hooves. Phyllis had hitched Blackie up to a wagon and Birdie was lifting the windrows on to it using a pitchfork. Phyllis had always marvelled at her stamina but Birdie, like their father, always insisted it was nothing to do with strength but rather technique. As the wagons pulled up alongside the threshing machine, Hender and two friends helped feed the windrows into the bowels of the contraption.

It was a glorious day with a clear blue sky and a gentle breeze, which helped keep the men cool. Reg fussed around making sure all went smoothly and checking that no one was smoking. The previous summer a farmer in Gloucestershire had lost two wagons and half his crop when a fire had broken out.

The wheat was bagged up on one side of the threshing machine as a large pile of chaff and straw formed on the other. The process was slow and took most of the day. They stopped around four-thirty when Reg produced four large flagons of cider, along with fresh bread and cheese. Birdie handed round pickled onions while Phyllis passed her sponge cake and enjoyed the compliments given on both her cake and her appearance. She was now twenty and very petite, but had become used to taking charge in the family. She was very practical and matter-of-fact, and had become less tolerant of her mother's moods. The men on the farm all adored her as she was prepared to help out with anything and her language shocked even them on occasion.

'Lovely bit of cake, Miss Phyllis,' said Alf Carter, winking at her.

'Thank you, Alf.' She flashed him a smile back. Alf was now nearly sixty and helped at a number of farms during the summer. He had lost his wife to pneumonia the previous year and he missed her badly.

Later that evening the engine and threshing machine left the field to make their way to the neighbouring farm, ready for the following day's work. One or two of the men staggered home a little the worse for cider, but that was one reason why Reg never had any trouble with people helping him at harvest-time. They all agreed he served the best harvest supper in the area.

The following morning they all rose a little later and when Phyllis went downstairs she saw a letter on the doormat addressed to Birdie. She made tea and began laying the table for breakfast as her father came in from the yard.

'Good morning, Phyllis, how are you today? Another lovely day…and thank you for your help yesterday. It all went very well.'

'Yes, it did. I always enjoy harvest when the weather's good.'

Birdie came into the kitchen and poured herself some tea. She sat down at the table and picked up her letter. Phyllis was a little curious as she did not recognise the handwriting. Her sister began reading and Phyllis suddenly saw tears running down her cheeks and dropping on to the blue tablecloth.

'Is it about John?' she asked. Birdie nodded and her body began to rock with sobs as she buried her head against her father's chest.

He held her tight and kept whispering in her ear, 'You poor, poor girl,' again and again.

Phyllis picked up the letter and began to read.

31 August 1917

Dear Birdie,

I am sorry to have to tell you that our dear son John has been killed in France. We are overwhelmed with sadness but I knew I had to write and let you know as soon as possible. We had a letter from the Ministry of Defence two days ago, followed by another from his commanding officer, informing us that John had been killed. His commanding officer thought very highly of him and told us the circumstances of his death.

He was fighting near Passchendaele and the Worcesters were being held in reserve. They were ordered forward, advancing against the enemy's front line, which consisted of a series of concrete bunkers that were almost shell-proof. One brigade had captured some of the forts but was forced back. John was ordered forward and he and his men dug in opposite the strongest fort, called the Maison d'Hibou. They held firm through constant shellfire but one landed near John and he was killed along with his batman, Harold Harris. His commanding officer said how proud he was of John's conduct and bravery.

We are both so sorry to have to pass on this dreadful news.

We were hoping and praying he would come through this war so we could see you both married. I know how much he loved you, and Henry and I are overwhelmed with sadness that you will not be able to spend your lives together.

Our only comfort is that he did not suffer a slow or painful death and that he is now at peace with God. Henry and I would like to give you a memento of John as a token of your love and perhaps in a month or so you would be able to call on us to collect this.

Yours sincerely,
Henry and Edna Guilding

Birdie took the letter and went quietly upstairs to her bedroom. Phyllis thought it best to leave her, and went to tell their mother the news. She wondered if Birdie would ever recover. All through their childhood Birdie had been like a second mother to her siblings as Nora had always struggled to show her love for them. Birdie had been courted by one other man previously, but she had fallen deeply in love with John Guilding and Phyllis was certain she would now never marry.

Far too many of her friends had lost sweethearts in France and were likely to spend their lives unmarried, imagining what life might have held for them as wives and mothers. Phyllis herself had never been short of admirers but had a reputation within the family for being far too particular. Her own version was that she had not yet met someone she could fall for and was happier with her own company and life on the farm.

Chapter 24

Life for the men of the Yeomanry had reached new levels of boredom and privation. Conditions in the camp were still very poor, with limited food and frequent outbreaks of diseases such as dysentery and chest infections. Digging on the tunnels had ceased, which meant they often had little to do other than play sport in the afternoon, or in Alf's case try and maintain his supply of cigarettes.

Tom had taken nearly two months to recover from his flogging but had managed slowly to regain some weight. He was troubled by recurring nightmares, which always involved The Weasel in some form. The most distressing entailed him being held in complete darkness in his cell. At unpredictable times the door would crash open and he would be beaten until he passed out. He would wake up, pouring with sweat, and then take hours to get back to sleep. During the day he kept imagining that he saw The Weasel, and would feel anxious until he could discover the person's real identity. He had flashbacks to the flogging and found himself imagining ways in which he could take revenge for it. The Weasel had not appeared back at the camp and the fat Turkish commander was too lazy to inspect the men. He spent nearly all of his time in his office and after lunch slept for most of the afternoon.

Due to the poor diet and disease, prisoners were still dying on a fairly regular basis and the small cemetery in one corner of the camp, with its makeshift wooden crosses, was growing steadily larger. Medical care was minimal in spite of Bill the Pill's efforts to help. He had obtained a book on plant-based remedies and, when he had finished working in the afternoon, Tom would see him roaming the hills looking for plants to use in various treatments.

There were rumours circulating in the camp on the progress of the war, and one British prisoner who had been captured in May told them that Jerusalem had been taken by the British in December 1917 and that the advance was continuing steadily northwards. He also said many of the Arab tribes were now fighting the Turks and they were partly led by a British soldier called Captain Lawrence. Tom felt sure this was the man he had met in Egypt.

The guards began to talk openly of defeat. Bill the Pill told Sid and Tom that the British had captured Damascus on 1 October. For the first time the men dared to think of the war ending, and this was reinforced when one or two of the guards deserted and returned to their homes.

Finally, on 13 November 1918, the fat commander called the prisoners to the parade ground and announced that an armistice had been signed, two days before, between the Allies and Germany. The war was over.

A huge cheer went up from the whole camp and even some of the Turkish guards were waving their caps in the air in celebration.

'This is it, Tom. The war's over,' said Eddie, clapping him on the back.

'Yes, lad, I think it is,' he replied. 'Two and a half years in a prison camp but somehow we've survived.'

He said a silent prayer, thanking God for their survival and instinctively feeling for his Bible, as he had done so often since the day of his capture, only to touch his empty breast pocket. All round the camp men were celebrating. Sid and Alf were shaking hands and patting each other on the back.

'Cocker, it's over, we're off home,' said Alf, slapping Sid on

233

the back. His hair was looking wilder than usual but he seemed better than he had been for months.

'Come here,' said Sid, hugging Tom. 'Thank you.'

'Thank you too,' said Tom, his voice breaking with emotion. They both knew without saying any more how much their friendship had meant to them. Tom knew he could not have survived without Sid. His flogging, his time in solitary confinement, the friends they had both lost…he felt as though the burden had been shared. He sensed many men had developed their own ways of coping with the horrors of war and imprisonment, but he could not imagine another time in his life when he would feel this grateful or thankful to one person.

It was some days before life changed in the camp. Food supplies improved a little and the guards were more generous with cigarettes and with blankets at night. The gates stayed open but there was nowhere for the prisoners to sleep other than in their barracks.

Over the next few weeks they began to be transported by road to Constantinople, which was a long journey through the mountains. Tom did not want to be separated from his friends again so they asked to leave the camp together in one of the last convoys.

Chapter 25

Worcester, England, May 1919

The train whistled and rumbled into Worcester Foregate Street station. Every window had two or three soldiers leaning out of it, cheering and waving. A huge crowd had gathered on the platform with hundreds more waiting outside to greet their loved ones.

Tom realised he was finally home. It had been over five months since the Armistice and he had wondered, over the weeks and months since then, whether it was down to incompetence on the part of the army or if he was taking part in some strange black comedy where he had the lead role. There were endless delays with their transport but eventually a troop ship had made the slow journey back from Turkey through the Mediterranean Sea and into Southampton. Even then there were more delays before they managed to board a train to Worcester.

He had received three letters from his family while still in Turkey, which were passed on to him through the Red Cross, and he had learnt of Birdie's tragic loss. He longed to see his family again and wondered how the five-year separation would have changed them all.

The friends said their goodbyes on the train. Eddie made Tom promise he would come to Stourbridge to meet his family as soon as he was able. Sid merely said, 'See you in the Angel next week.' Alf had thrived since their release, gaining weight rapidly after a British doctor treated him for a tapeworm infection. His hair was still spiky and blond but his skin now had a healthy glow, and Sid was not the only one to think Alf must have had the infection for years.

Even before the train juddered to a stop, men were jumping from it and running into the arms of their families. Tom stepped out of the carriage and saw his father waving; Birdie, Phyllis, Hender and Ray were with him, all beaming. Tom walked slowly towards them, savouring the moment, then hugged them to him each in turn.

'It's wonderful to see you, Tom,' his father said, holding him by the shoulders. 'You look well, that you do.'

Hender hugged his brother, tears rolling down under his glasses.

'Tom, it's so good to see you.'

'You too, Hender.'

'Birdie, I'm sorry to hear about John,' said Tom, hugging her again. They were all crying. Birdie broke away to dry her eyes with a lace handkerchief.

'Thank you. It's been dreadful, but this is the best I've felt in a year,' she said. Tom looked at his young brother Ray, who was now eighteen, and shook his hand.

'How are you, Ray?'

'Welcome home, Tom. Mother is so pleased you're back. She's sorry she couldn't be here but she has a bad headache.'

The fact that his mother had not made the trip made Tom feel sad. After five years of separation her feelings towards him obviously had not changed.

The journey home was a delight, filled with chatter and gossip and Tom's father roaring with laughter at the stories they were telling each other. Tom walked up the path to the front door and absorbed the familiar sights: knocker, the scraper for cleaning boots and the worn mat. His mother was sitting at the kitchen table sewing, and looked up as he came in. She smiled and held her arms open. Tom embraced her and smelt her familiar lily-of-the-valley perfume.

'Oh, Tom, it's so good to see you,' she surprised him by saying.

'It's good to be back. I'm looking forward to some good home-cooked food again. I don't mind if I never see another grain of rice.'

She smiled but said nothing. Phyllis had told him on the way home how upset their mother had been while he was away. He wondered now whether she was simply incapable of openly expressing affection.

After a supper of roast beef and apple crumble with cream, Tom and his father sat alone in the front room and talked about the farm. It was a chilly evening but the log fire was throwing out light and warmth as they sipped their glasses of whisky.

'Well, it's wonderful to have you back. I've missed you on the farm. Hender is a good man but he's happier sheep shearing than worrying about what to plant where. We have had some luck though. You remember Lord Somers, our landlord? How he spent a lot of time in London and we always joked he must have another woman up there? Well, it would appear he liked to have a bet and got into some problems gambling. I don't know whether it was the horses or cards, and you know what I think of gambling anyway, but last year his land agent came knocking on our door. He was a bit shifty but asked whether I would ever be interested in buying the farm. I said I might be at the right price and off he goes again. I knew land prices had been dropping and soon after that they made an approach naming a sum. We haggled for a week or so but he must have been desperate because, the next thing I know, it's ours for about half what they asked in the first place.'

'What splendid news! Is that the house, the buildings and the two cottages as well?' Tom asked.

'Yes, the lot. Now I've been thinking that, with land prices down, there might not be enough men to take up the tenancies locally, so I would like you to try for a farm for yourself somewhere nearby. Hender and I would still help you out and Ray has been doing a bit as well. What do you think?'

'I always wanted to farm by myself and I suppose now would be a good time to give it a try. We can talk about it some more tomorrow.' Tom yawned widely. 'Now I'd better get to bed. Good night, Father.'

'Good night. We're all so glad to have you back. All of us, Tom. Never doubt that.'

Tom slept deeply, with no nightmares for the first time in weeks. He stayed in bed long after he woke, enjoying the sensation of being under sheets and a woollen blanket that smelt faintly of mothballs. The idea of his running his own rented farm was just what he needed to fire up his enthusiasm again and he thought he would start making enquiries that week.

He dressed and went downstairs for breakfast. The smells of bacon frying and of fresh bread wafted out of the kitchen. Phyllis was cooking and his parents were seated at the table.

'Morning, everyone, sorry I'm late down,' he said.

'Don't you worry, dear, you need some extra sleep, I'm sure,' his mother told him.

Tom poured himself a cup of tea and sat down.

'Mother, Father, there is something I need to tell you.' He stopped and took a deep breath before confessing. 'I lost the Bible you gave me when I was captured. A Turkish soldier took it out of my pocket. I tried to tell him it was the Holy Bible and I thought he would have no interest in it as a Muslim, but he laughed and took it anyway. I have felt so sad about it ever since. It had become my connection to you and to home.'

'Tom, you mustn't worry about that. The important thing is you're home safely and that is all that matters,' said his father. But Tom saw his mother looking thoughtful and realised she was not going to comment. He felt momentarily disappointed, but then his father began talking about possible farms that might be available to rent and he soon forgot his feelings.

Over the next few months Tom settled back into family life but felt a strong pull towards the friends he had made as a prisoner, in spite or maybe because of the appalling hardships they had suffered. Sid, of course, was his oldest friend in any case. They met at the pub in Pershore every week and discovered they shared similar feelings of guilt and lethargy at being back in their old lives once more. Alf appeared in the pub too but liked to spread his custom around a number of different hostelries. Dick had survived, having spent months in hospital after being injured in Gallipoli. He had a severe limp after the shrapnel injury to his back, walking with an unusual slapping motion of one foot, but was otherwise the same, still the most dapperly dressed man they knew.

One evening when Tom was in the Angel a local land agent came in and started chatting to the barman, who introduced him to Sid and Tom. The agent, Harry Warner, was dressed in a smart tweed suit and had a silver watch chain hanging across his waistcoat. He had ginger hair, a small moustache, and an air of confidence about him that grated with Tom. He stood at the bar sipping his whisky and began talking about his work and the drop in land prices. After a few minutes, Tom asked him if he knew of any farms to rent.

'I may know of one or two, but not if you spend half your time in the pub when you should be out working,' Warner said rudely.

'You've got a bloody nerve,' said Tom, grabbing the man's tweed jacket. 'I come here just once a week for a drink with my mates from the Yeomanry.'

'All right, steady on, I'm sorry. Did you say you were with the Yeomanry…was that the Worcestershire Yeomanry?'

'Yes, we were held prisoner in Turkey,' said Sid, holding out his hand and attempting to smooth things over. 'How d'you do? I'm Sid Parkes.'

'Harry Warner, pleased to meet you,' said the other man, shaking hands with them both. 'I'm sorry I was a bit hasty there, but we have a bit of a problem with some tenants enjoying their ale a little too much and not farming their land properly. Now I may know of a tenancy, Tom. Where do you live by the way?'

He explained that he farmed with his father at Stoulton but was looking to start in his own right. He added that he thought he had enough experience to manage on his own but his father lived nearby so could offer advice. They chatted about stock and the crops they had grown this summer for a while longer.

'Thank you, Tom, I'll be in touch,' said Harry Warner, draining the last of his beer.

Three months later Tom was stabling one of the horses when a car swept into the yard. He recognised Warner immediately from his tweed suit and watch chain. He was wearing a flat cap and his brown shoes shone as though freshly varnished. He flicked his small moustache with the back of one forefinger before getting out of the car.

They greeted one another and Tom introduced the agent to his father.

'Good to meet you, Mr Bomford,' Warner said. 'I've heard a lot about you over the years. Your farm always looks to be in good order.'

'Thanks, I try to keep it tidy,' said Reg, rather embarrassed by the compliment.

'Can we go inside and have a word?'

Tom led the way into the living room and offered the visitor tea, as he thought it a little too early for a drink.

'As you may have been told, I work for Lord Coventry,' Harry Warner began. 'I know you were with the Yeomanry, Tom, and Lord Coventry is always keen to help any man who fought with them. I have heard of a farm outside Pershore, at Bishampton. The tenancy is currently vacant and you may wish to consider it. The land is heavy in places, but it's about two hundred acres.

We can talk about the rent and so on later if you feel it might suit. What do you think?'

Tom knew the property and had heard the farm had become very rundown and that the tenants had been asked to leave, although they hadn't done so yet. It was a small farm with an old house; it would need a lot of work to bring it back into good order.

He glanced at his father, who nodded his approval. 'It'll need a lot of effort, but Hender could help you out.'

'Well, if he's happy to do that, it would be a grand opportunity to start on my own.'

'Good. It does need some hard graft but it would suit a young man for his first farm,' said Warner, smiling.

He said he would be back to sort everything out in the next few weeks but it would be some time before Tom could take it over.

Tom followed him out into the yard and waved goodbye as the car rattled out of the gate. He stood watching the dust and bits of straw settle back on the cobblestones and slowly absorbed the news. His father had been right when he said he needed to find a new project, and his own farm would be perfect. The amount of work involved would be huge: stock to buy, seed to plant, and only Hender to help him run it. It felt a little overwhelming, but his father would be able to advise them. A feeling of excitement built inside Tom, reminding him of Christmas Eve when he was a child. This was better. It had the potential to transform his life.

Chapter 26

Ivy Lodge, Stourbridge, January 1919

Eddie Williams had found settling back into civilian life in Stourbridge difficult. There were no other soldiers he knew in the area as most of them had been killed, and although he had been welcomed back with a lavish party he felt strangely isolated. His father had encouraged him to come and work with him in his brewing business, which was expanding rapidly. He was in the process of buying more pubs as suitable properties came on the market.

Eddie was more interested in football, and had started playing on the wing for Stourbridge Football Club in the Birmingham and District League. They were known as 'The Glassboys' as a few of the players worked in the glass-works at Brierley Hill.

His fitness had suffered but he felt stronger and had grown another inch. He was now just taller than his mother at five foot seven inches, although he realised with some sadness that he had stopped growing. After his first game of football he was so stiff he found he could only go down the stairs one step at a time. Daisy found this very amusing. She stood at the bottom, arms folded, hair coming adrift from its pins, laughing at him.

'I knew it! You were just lying around in that camp doing nothing, no exercise at all,' she said.

'It's not funny, Daisy. This hurts, you know,' he said, rubbing his stiff thigh muscles, desperate for a little sympathy.

Eddie trained once a week and they played most of their fixtures on Saturday mornings, to allow players to attend the bigger matches at Aston Villa, West Bromwich Albion, Birmingham City and Wolverhampton Wanderers. Daisy, who was a passionate West Brom fan, sometimes came to watch and would often criticise her brother after the game for not marking properly or crossing the ball too late.

It was difficult getting to training and matches, and so Eddie's father helped him buy a new motorbike. It was a small blue 250cc Triumph machine. Eddie became completely obsessed with it. He cleaned it every day and made sure it was kept dry in one of the garages at night. His mother was not at all keen on him riding it. She begged him to be careful but he always answered that he had survived far worse in the war, which gave her little comfort.

The season went well and in January Stourbridge was lying second in the league, with Eddie providing many of the crosses from which their forwards scored. He came down to breakfast one morning and found a brown envelope set on his plate. Harry always received plenty of letters but it was rare for Eddie to receive post, except for the occasional bank statement.

'I think Eddie has a lady friend, don't you, Madge?' said Daisy, winking.

'Very likely, Daisy, he's blushing too.'

'Oh, stop it, you two,' he said, opening the letter.

Then he let out a cheer, and passed it to Daisy to read aloud.

Dear Mr Williams,

This is to invite you to play for Aston Villa Reserves against West Bromwich Albion Reserves on Saturday, 26 January at 2.30 p.m. Please report to the address below and bring your own boots.

I look forward to meeting you.

Yours sincerely,

Thomas H. McIntosh

'The only bad news here, Eddie, is that you're playing for Villa and not West Brom, but that's so exciting,' said Daisy, giving him a hug.

'Well done, my boy, you must be doing well if Aston Villa are interested again,' said his father.

The following week, Eddie travelled up to the reserve team ground on his motorcycle, well wrapped against the cold. The pitch was very muddy and Eddie struggled to control the ball properly in the first twenty minutes. He was growing increasingly frustrated but then realised there was better turf nearer to the touchline where he could use his speed. He beat the fullback on a few occasions and managed to put in some good crosses, although did not get near to scoring. The match ended in a draw but the assistant manager seemed pleased with him and told Eddie he hoped he would be able to play again. But Eddie had seen the huge gap in ability between his skills and those of the regular players and knew he still had a lot to learn.

As Easter approached, Eddie decided to write to Tom and invite him to stay. They had exchanged a few letters since they had returned home, and Eddie thought about his friend every day. Tom wrote back and said he would love to come but as he was so busy on the farm he could only stay one night.

Eddie told his mother the date and spoke to the family after supper, before they began a game of cards.

'I've invited an old friend, Tom Bomford, to stay after Easter. As you know, he was very kind to me when we were prisoners together and I'm not sure if I would have survived without him, so I would like you all to meet him. Madge, perhaps you might invite Timothy over as well? Tom says he's coming on his motorcycle; I hope it's a Triumph.'

'Thank you, Eddie, Timothy would love to come, I'm sure. I'll ask him to ensure his father is on call that night. I'm rather looking forward to meeting the famous Tom,' said Madge.

Timothy was coming to the house on a more regular basis since they had become officially engaged, and Madge now felt more confident that she could spend her life with him. Her relationship with his parents was still awkward, especially with his mother who continued to make pointed comments concerning her dress sense, hair and table manners. But Timothy had asked her in front of Madge to be more courteous towards his future wife, and Madge had squeezed his hand under the table in support of his defiance. They had not yet set a date for the wedding as Madge was happy enjoying their engagement. It was generally expected to take place late in the summer.

Bishampton Fields Farm, Bishampton, September 1919
Tom had moved into Bishampton in the autumn of 1919 and had worked every possible hour to repair the roof on the house and then prepare for the planting. The land was in an appalling state with huge clumps of weeds, many of which they had to dig up individually and then put in sacks to be burnt. Hender, always full of energy, was excited about helping with the new project. They both felt it was too early to buy stock, so they repaired some of the farm buildings and carried out the cultivations, planting some winter wheat and a small field of oats. They repaired the fences around the grass fields in preparation for stock and planted vegetables in the garden at the back of the house. This took a week to clean; it was damp and smelt of mould. They scrubbed the walls and floors and, as the weather was warm and sunny, left all the doors and windows open for a week to allow it to dry out and the smell to clear. Reg had asked their sister Mary to come and act as housekeeper.

She moved into a small bedroom upstairs with her battered leather suitcase containing two brown dresses. It took her less than a minute to unpack. Hender and Tom had found some old plates, cutlery and a few saucepans, and Mary began making up a fire in the kitchen.

'Thanks for coming to help out, Mary,' said Tom, squeezing her hand.

'I'm glad to,' she told him, squinting through her thick black-rimmed glasses. 'I like being away from home for a while.' Tom felt saddened to think that his sister was only able to see a future for herself spent looking after their parents.

'Have you got all you need for the kitchen? Hender's chopped plenty of wood for the stove.'

Mary nodded and polished her glasses on her apron. Tom went outside into the yard and looked out over the fields at the back of the house. The land rolled down towards a bank and beyond lay the river Avon. A line of tall elms marked the farm boundary. Rooks were noisily flapping above their nests and flying off in search of more food.

Tom still saw Sid and Alf each week for a beer or two, and it was only with them that he ever mentioned anything to do with the war. His nightmares were becoming less common. When they occurred, there were faces of dead men such as Sergeant Vint and Walter Garland flashing before him, or else The Weasel standing over him and beating him again and again. He was excited about the farm but had days when he felt listless and depressed and experienced feelings of guilt regarding the death of Walter Garland in particular. He had visited Walter's mother, who lived alone following her husband's death, and cried with her when telling her the story of her son's last days. Sid had confided in Tom that he had similar feelings of guilt and visions of the battle before they were captured. Only Alf seemed unaffected by regret, but he always carried a hip flask of whisky with him and they knew he coped by suppressing his emotions.

Tom hoped things would improve with time and found work on the farm a helpful distraction – that was when Hender was not asking him for details of the war every five minutes. Tom lost his temper on one occasion and told Hender to shut up and stop pestering him, but apologised immediately when he saw how upset his brother looked.

Through the winter months, the land became very wet and Tom realised how difficult it was farming ground that appeared to be mainly clay. They continued tidying the hedges, repairing the buildings and trying to keep busy. He felt despondent about the long-term prospects for the farm but his father reassured him that it was a very wet winter and he should enjoy the horses and spend some days hunting.

It was now spring and the winter crops had grown, but many of the fields still had water lying in them. Tom had bought some ewes and a ram at Worcester market, and planned to build a flock over the next two years.

His sister Birdie was still grief-stricken from John's death. One night when she was staying with Tom, he walked past her bedroom on his way to bed and heard her sobs half muffled by a pillow. He knocked, went in and found her crying.

'I'm sorry, Tom, but I still miss him so much.'

He felt utterly powerless to help. His sister was one of so many women whose husbands and fiancés had not returned. He held her tight, stroking her hair, trying to give her some comfort.

'I miss him every moment of the day,' she sobbed. 'There are times when I think there is little point in my carrying on and yet it would devastate Mother and Father if I did not.'

'And me too,' he told her.

'Thank you, dear Tom. I know you still struggle with your memories of that dreadful war, but I feel as if I will never recover from this blow.'

'I know it feels like that, but one day you'll be able to remember John without so much pain.'

'Do you think so?' she said, drying her eyes with the sleeve of her nightdress. 'But thank you. Time for you to get some sleep.'

The following morning Tom received Eddie's letter of invitation. He wondered about going. He was so busy on the farm and also thought recalling details of their time in captivity together was unlikely to help his overall recovery. He showed the letter to Birdie as they sat at the kitchen table drinking tea.

'You must go, it would be good for you to see him again. Don't worry about the farm, Hender and I can cope very well.'

Tom spent Easter with his family and went to Pershore Abbey for the Easter Sunday service. For lunch they had lamb that had been reared on the farm, after which Tom and his father sat discussing the two properties and Tom's forthcoming trip to Stourbridge.

'So, Tom, are Eddie's family quite grand then?' asked Reg.

'I'm not sure. I think he said his father started a brewery in Stourbridge. I do remember him saying that people, including women, drank more beer during the war.'

'Well, he's probably done quite well. It's good you're seeing Eddie. You should not let those friendships go after everything you went through together.'

'I'll head off on Wednesday, after the Croome point-to-point.'

Easter Tuesday was the day the Croome Hunt always held their point-to-point meeting at Upton-upon-Severn. Tom never missed it. Most of the local farmers were there, and the main race featured a very large challenge cup that was always presented by Lord Coventry.

By the fourth race Tom had enjoyed a few ciders and was feeling on top of the world. Sid had tried to persuade him to back a good thing, but Tom had never liked gambling and had realised some years ago that for him the sadness of losing was far worse than the joy of winning.

They stayed until well after the last race when many of the racegoers had already gone home. Sid helped him on to his motorcycle and Tom weaved his way back down the country lanes, eventually getting home to Bishampton after dark.

The following morning he awoke with a dull pulsating headache. His mouth was dry. He drank two pints of water and washed his face in more cold water from the outside pump in the courtyard. He felt dreadful and was now in a rush to make it to Stourbridge on time.

'Morning, Mary, how are you?'

'Oh, Tom, you don't look too good,' she said, coming uncomfortably close so that her eyes seemed three times bigger than normal behind her thick spectacles.

'I had a very good day at the point-to-point yesterday. Few too many ciders,' he admitted.

'Cider doesn't agree with me either,' she said solemnly.

'Now we'd better not remind ourselves of that episode,' said Tom, shuddering at the memory of having to rescue his sister from the clutches of a local shepherd who had been plying her with the strongest brew.

Mary packed him a small knapsack, while Tom checked the oil and fuel in his bike and set off, thankful for the chill morning air, which slowly cleared his head.

After nearly an hour he was so cold he stopped to fill up with petrol and have a cup of tea. He now felt rather foolish for accepting Eddie's invitation, suspecting the family would be far too grand for him and that he would almost certainly embarrass himself. He couldn't turn back, though, so he thought it best to go for lunch and then make an excuse to leave after tea rather than stay the night.

An hour later he found Norton Road and Eddie's house, Ivy Lodge. It was a very large redbrick villa with wide wooden gates and window frames painted dark green. He pushed the Triumph through the gate and parked it. All was quiet and then he heard laughter from the garden and a shout of 'You're out!' followed by cheering. He was walking towards the back door when a young lady popped her head round the door of a shed. She was carrying vegetables in a wicker basket.

'Hello, you must be Tom. I'm Daisy. I've heard so much about you from Eddie. Follow me.' She smiled at him, and Tom thought she looked somewhat mischievous. She set off at a brisk pace across the yard to a door which opened on to a huge garden. There was a lawn of immaculate turf, the size of a small football pitch, surrounded by beautifully tended borders of shrubs with pockets of daffodils.

'What a wonderful garden,' he said.

'Oh, Deacon would be thrilled to hear you say that. He's the gardener and always muttering about his work not being appreciated. Come and meet everyone.'

She ushered him across the grass and Tom smelt a mixture of herbs and flowers drifting to meet him. There was a pause in the cricket and Eddie, who was bowling, turned and caught sight of his friend.

'Tom, I'm so sorry not to have met you at the door,' he said, shaking hands. 'Come and meet Mother and Father.'

Tom shook Harry Williams's hand and then went to shake Marian's, but she took him in her arms and hugged him instead.

'Thank you for everything you did for Eddie, it's wonderful finally to meet you,' she said, smiling. She looked very like her daughter Daisy, he thought. Tom then met Eddie's younger brother, Dick, who was a slightly smaller version of Eddie, with a cheeky face and upturned nose.

'Tom, this is my other sister Marjorie but we all call her Madge.'

Tom turned to her and held out his hand. 'I think I'll use Marjorie, if I may?' he said, blushing.

Madge looked straight into his eyes and smiled. 'Tom, how wonderful to meet you. Eddie says he would not have survived without your kindness to him. We are all so grateful. Madge is fine, by the way,' she said, and then turned and walked back to the house. Eddie saw the concerned look on Tom's face and reassured him that he had not upset her.

'She's going to meet her fiancé Timothy, who's coming for lunch too. D'you fancy some cricket?' He picked up the bat and gave it to Tom.

'Well, I haven't played for a while...maybe Dick would like to play instead.'

'No, I'll bowl, you can bat,' said the boy, walking back to his imaginary mark.

Tom had not picked up a bat for years and, although he had played at school a little, he had no style. Dick ran in to bowl and Tom was surprised by how quick he was, considering his size. The first ball he missed completely, but thankfully it also missed the stumps. The second ball hit his leg, which generated a huge shout from Dick of 'Howzat!'

Harry boomed, 'Not out,' and play continued.

Dick then bowled a slower ball, which rather played to Tom's weakness. The speed of the bat was so slow that Tom connected beautifully and the ball sailed into one of the borders.

'Mind my flowers!' shouted Marian.

'Six!' shouted Harry.

'Good shot,' said Eddie, sounding quite impressed. The play continued with Tom missing everything else before being bowled out by Dick.

He was relieved when Marian called for everyone to go in to lunch, which saved any further embarrassment. He was offered a glass of sherry, but thought that after his bucket of cider the day before he would stick to home-made lemonade. He sat down next to Eddie's mother, with Daisy on his other side and Eddie opposite. Timothy Parkes rushed in looking rather hot and flustered just as they sat down. Tom shook his hand, which felt very soft and different from a farmer's.

'I'm so sorry I'm late, Mrs Williams,' said Timothy. 'It was a very busy morning, I'm afraid.' He dabbed his forehead with his handkerchief.

Tom was intrigued by him, struck by the difference between the army doctors with their direct no-nonsense style and Dr Parkes, who seemed a very different type altogether. Madge fussed over Timothy's soup, made sure he had bread, salt and pepper, and brought him into conversation with her father. Tom was surprised to see that she wore no ring and that she seemed more tense than earlier.

He was hungry and had more soup as well as seconds of the gammon. Eddie asked him to recount stories of how they'd met in Egypt and, eventually, as the dessert plates were cleared, he was asked to tell the story of how he'd broken The Weasel's jaw.

Tom tried to make light of events, giving a sanitised version. It was the first time he had told the tale to anyone outside their immediate circle of fellow soldiers. He found it hard to continue the story after the point where he was taken to the camp prison, and Eddie took up the narration then, unaware of his friend's distress. Tom hid his shaking hands under the table but had to dab his forehead with his napkin. He was sweating profusely as flashbacks assailed him. Everyone else was fully involved with the story and appeared unaware of his discomfort.

Finally, the story finished and the whole table started clapping, before Harry proposed a toast to Tom Bomford. He nodded his head to them as he sipped his lemonade and felt himself relaxing. He was aware of Madge focusing on him intently as he stood up and thanked them for inviting him for lunch. He told of how brave Eddie had been and the support he had given to all of them, especially Tom himself.

After that they rose from the table, with chairs creaking like a prep-school orchestra, and went into the drawing room. Timothy Parkes said goodbye to everyone and left to return to the surgery.

'Seems a nice chap,' Tom said politely to Eddie.

'Pretty wet, loathes football and prefers going to the opera with his mother, from what I've heard,' muttered Eddie under his breath.

They chatted about the brewery and what beers the younger generation liked to drink. Tom confessed to liking cider and Harry said he must make a note to stock some local brew in his new public house.

After a while, Tom excused himself and went out into the garden for some air. It was still sunny although the air was a little cooler. He sat on a bench overlooking the lawn, realising that he need not feel guilty about not working on the farm today, and that he would stay the night and try to enjoy himself.

'Do you mind if I join you?' said Madge, sitting down on the bench next to him.

'No, not at all,' Tom replied, feeling he was blushing again. 'That was a very nice lunch – did you cook it?'

Madge roared with laughter. It was a throaty sound and she threw her head back as she did so.

'No, but I helped pour the sherry into the trifle. And of course I had to taste it first.'

'Of course. It might have been dangerous for us all if you hadn't.'

'Tom, do you mind if I ask you something? You don't have to say anything if you would rather not.'

'No, ask me anything,' he said, regretting his comment immediately.

'I noticed you were very upset when telling that story and I presume things were a lot worse for you than you let on. I wanted to say how much we all appreciate what you did for Eddie and now I understand a little more of what you suffered. Do you still think about it much?'

Tom nodded and paused, taking a deep breath. He felt slightly uncomfortable to be sitting in the garden with Eddie's sister, who was engaged but was also the only one perceptive enough to detect his distress.

'I was upset, you're right. I still have nightmares about it and there are times during the day when I feel anxious for no good reason. Normally if I'm busy on the farm I'm fine, but the evenings are difficult and I must admit there are times when I have a cider or a few whiskies to help me sleep. There are many worse off than me, though. Some are blind, some have lost an arm or a leg, and some were driven half mad by the constant shelling. And plenty never came back. When I think of them, I've no right to complain at all.'

They both sat in silence for a moment, looking out over the garden.

'Do you mind if I ask *you* something, Madge?' he said then.

She shook her head.

'No, go on.'

'I was wondering why you don't wear an engagement ring.'

'Ah, that question, you're not the first to ask it. I think the reason is that Timothy and I have had a very long relationship throughout the war. Not knowing whether my brother was alive or not made it difficult for me to put my feelings first. Now he's back I love being at home with all the family, but I'm sure it will not be long before we buy a ring together.'

'Well, I wish you well in your married life.'

'Thank you, Tom, that's kind of you.' And she touched his hand very lightly before she got up and walked back to the house.

Tom's hand was tingling slightly and he felt uneasy. Madge was the first person with whom he had felt comfortable talking about the war. He also realised he found her attractive. He liked the fact that she was completely independent in her thinking, too. And yet she was engaged. She was Eddie's sister and it seemed entirely wrong even to be acknowledging his attraction to her. He decided he would keep his distance tonight and return home tomorrow. Eddie could always come and stay with him, and then in time, when Madge was married, everything would be simpler.

Eddie came out into the garden and sat with him. They talked of their future plans and Eddie's hope to play more football for Aston Villa. Tom spoke of the farm and told him that Sid and Alf had settled back into country life. They walked around the large garden before Tom went upstairs to bathe before dinner. His room was small but had thick curtains and a very soft bed with three pillows, which seemed to him a little excessive. There was a small vase of flowers from the garden and a few watercolours of Scottish glens hung either side of the mirror. The whole feel of the house was one of well-to-do comfort and was in marked contrast to the more spartan style of his room at home.

He came down to the drawing room at seven and found Eddie's father reading the evening paper.

'How are you, Tom? It's good of you to come up and see us. Eddie talks about you so often. It was very hard when he told me he was going to join up and lie about his age. I knew he would find some way to go whether I approved or not, so I felt that, if he was going, the Queen's Own Worcestershire Hussars was the best option.

'His mother was furious, as you may imagine, but thank the Lord he has come home safely, unlike so many others. I know I can talk to you in confidence, as I don't want to sound unpatriotic, but the huge loss of life seems such a waste to me.'

'Yes,' Tom agreed, 'a tragic waste. In Egypt there were some very strange decisions made and, to be honest, many of the regular soldiers did not have total respect for some of the officers in charge. But I was never in France. I understand things were grim there. My sister lost her fiancé after he wrote to her of the endless shelling that went on for days. He told her also about one man who was clearly driven half mad by the noise and ran out of his trench back down behind the lines. The following morning he was shot for desertion, which seems barbaric to me.'

Harry nodded and, as he did so, Eddie and his sisters walked in. Tom jumped to his feet and shuffled them nervously.

'Hello, Tom,' said Eddie. 'Can I get you a glass of beer?'

'Thank you, I'd love one,' he said, nodding. 'You all look very smart.'

There was a pause while Dolly blushed and thanked him. Daisy realised that the remark was mainly directed at Madge. She smiled and invited Tom to sit next to her and tell her about his farm. He gulped down his beer rather quickly, which at least helped calm his anxiety a little, before they went in to dinner where he was seated between Madge and Marian, who chatted about music and her love of fishing. Tom found Eddie's mother tremendously entertaining company. After a while, as he turned to talk to Madge, he realised she had been listening to their conversation.

'Are you a fisherman, Tom?' she asked.

'No, I'm not at your mother's level. I used to fish in a pond near the football pitch at home, but that was just with a worm and float and only for tiddlers. She's caught trout and salmon. Big ones too, I hear.'

'Yes, she's very keen, but sadly it's only Dick among us who's interested. Daisy tells me you're a keen rider.'

'I rode a fair bit even before the war, but then I spent a lot of time in Egypt breaking horses with the army. Some of them were shipped from Australia and were pretty wild. One of them was mad and bucked me off and I very nearly lost my arm when it became infected.' Tom brandished his hand, still a little scarred from the infection.

'Is that where it was?' asked Madge, touching the scar. Tom nodded and moved his shirtsleeve up a little, revealing a hint of blue skin.

'Is that a tattoo? Please may I see it?'

'No, Madge, sorry. I don't think you'd like it,' he said, hurriedly pulling his sleeve down.

'Is that a tail?' she asked excitedly.

'Yes, it's a snake but it's not very pretty. I think it's best it stays covered.'

'Very well, but I shall make sure you show it to me one day,' she said as she flashed him a smile and turned away to speak to her father.

Tom felt the heat rise in his cheeks. As they had finished the main course, he slipped into the lavatory to wash his hands and face. He looked into the clouded mirror and told himself to stop blushing and gabbling like a child. After he'd splashed water over his face he felt calmer. He acknowledged to himself that he found Madge attractive. As the thought flashed into his head, it was followed by the realisation that she was unavailable and he must behave appropriately towards her. Feeling determined to be sensible and a little more relaxed, he returned to the dining room and settled back down in his chair, talking to Eddie about his hopes for the coming cricket season.

After dessert the ladies left the table, Dick was ushered off to bed and Harry produced a decanter of whisky. The men sat talking for another two hours while Eddie told stories of their time in Egypt and of playing football in the prison camp. Tom felt strangely detached as his friend talked of life there, but the whisky allowed him to laugh along as Eddie's father listened proudly and enjoyed the tales of their life together.

Tom did not sleep well and woke sweating from dreams of the camp and his time in hospital. He lay in bed feeling exhausted and arrived a little late for breakfast. Harry had already left for work with Dolly, so Tom sat eating his scrambled eggs with Madge, Eddie and Daisy, who scuttled in and out bringing toast and marmalade.

'Did you sleep well, Tom?' asked his friend.

'Not too bad, thanks,' he said. There was a moment's silence as Madge slowly put down her knife on her plate.

'Tom, I'm sorry to tell you this but I heard you shout out last night. It sounded to me as if you were having a nightmare,' she said. He was taken aback by her frankness.

'Yes, I was. Apologies if I kept anyone awake.'

'No, not at all, I just felt dreadful there was no one there to comfort you.'

'Steady on,' Eddie laughed, 'I am not sure Dr Timothy would like to hear you say that.'

'That's not what I meant. I felt sorry for Tom, that was all,' she protested.

'Thank you, that's very kind,' he said, despite his intention of avoiding any talk of a personal nature with Madge.

As soon as breakfast had finished Tom gathered up his bag and wheeled his motorbike back on to the road. Eddie shook his hand and Marian hugged him, thanking him again. Daisy and Madge stood back a little in the driveway and waved goodbye as he kick-started the motorbike. Tom gave them all a wave and the bike rumbled off down Norton Road.

It took him a lot less time to get back to Bishampton than the outward journey had and as Tom drove into the farmyard Hender came out to greet him. The lenses of his thick glasses were smeared and Tom noticed a piece of mud on one.

'How was it?' his brother asked.

'Very good, thanks. Eddie has a lovely family and they were all most welcoming.'

'No, I meant the motorbike. How did the bike go?' said Hender in an exasperated tone, as if there was nothing else more important. Tom reassured him the bike was superb and very comfortable even for a longer journey. They went into the kitchen where Mary was cleaning up the mess Hender had left at breakfast.

'Hello, Tom, would you like some tea?' she asked.

'Thanks, Mary, that'd be good. Has Hender behaved himself?'

'He keeps knocking stuff over. I'm always cleaning up after him.'

Tom smiled. He was relieved to be back on the farm with his brother and sister and busy with his plans for the rest of the year.

Tom had written to Eddie's parents thanking them for his stay and saying how much he'd enjoyed meeting them all. A letter from Eddie's mother arrived a week later, saying they would love to see him again whenever he could spare the time from the farm. Eddie had written a short note at the bottom.

> *P.S. I have been asked to add a note and post this letter, so wanted to say how good it was to meet up again, after such a long time. Family all talking about you, especially Madge who mentioned your tattoo (did not know you had shown her). Look forward to seeing you soon.*

Tom read the letter again and was drawn back to the phrase 'especially Madge'; he suspected her interest in him was only motivated by her curiosity over the tattoo. He put the letter in the drawer of the kitchen table and went to make another cup of tea. As he drank this he decided to go back and reread the letter, feeling intrigued yet confused. Finally he put it back under a pile of other papers and decided not to dwell on it any longer.

For the next few weeks he was kept very busy with haymaking. As the weather was fine he and Hender worked late, turning the hay and storing it up in the barn for winter feed for the horses and cattle that had just arrived on the farm.

After haymaking there was usually a quieter period before the wheat was ready for harvesting. Tom had checked the fields and much of the wheat was still very green and would need a lot more sun before it was ready. The cattle were looking well and after the wet weather in late April and early May there was still plenty of grass, even allowing for that cut for hay.

It was early July when he received another letter from Eddie, whose writing he instantly recognised. The envelope was of thick cream paper and of high quality, as was the writing paper itself. Tom sniffed the letter as he opened it and was reminded of the smell of books and libraries. He began to read:

> *Dear Tom,*
>
> *I hope you are well and that the farm is thriving. I am playing cricket in ten days' time at Kidderminster in a league match and hope you might like to come and watch. All the family will be there. They will be having a picnic and would be delighted if you were able to join them. Thankfully, I have made some runs recently and scored 50 two weeks ago, so we are hoping for promotion if we beat Kidderminster as they are lying second at present. The game starts at eleven and I can post a pass to you if you would like to come.*
>
> *Best wishes as always,*
> *Eddie*

Tom made a rough calculation and realised the wheat would not be ready for at least three weeks, so quickly wrote back accepting the invitation. He secretly hoped Dr Parkes would be there so that any fanciful thoughts he himself may still entertain concerning Madge would be crushed. He was annoyed to realise that he still thought about her a little too often, and felt somewhat uneasy about the prospect of seeing her again. He missed Eddie's company, though, and it would be good to see him play cricket, especially at such a high level.

For the next two weeks Tom was kept busy on the farm cutting hedges while Hender sheared the twenty ewes his brother had managed to buy.

A few days before the match, a pass for the pavilion area arrived in the post and Tom tucked it behind the tea caddy in the kitchen. He began to feel a little anxious and thought initially it was only natural he would be worrying about his first harvest. The night before the match he slept fitfully and dreamt of sitting in the garden with Madge. She talked to him about his time with Eddie until Tom took her hand and kissed it, then she slapped his face and stormed back into the house. He woke in a sweaty, anxious state and spent half an hour trying to reassure himself it was just a dream and that she had no feelings for him at all.

After his rounds on the farm and a quick breakfast of bread and jam, Tom wheeled his beloved Triumph out of the shed and set off to Kidderminster. He arrived in good time and decided to walk round the ground. One or two players were out in their whites inspecting the pitch and gazing at the sky, checking the weather. There was quite a lot of cloud although it was a warm day. From Tom's recollection of playing cricket, he thought this might mean the ball would swing. As he walked back towards the pavilion he saw the Williams family setting up their picnic.

Harry Williams was directing operations, ordering Deacon to set out the table and chairs. Marian was unpacking the hamper while Dolly stood by looking very anxious. Daisy and Madge were standing to one side, giggling and trying to secure the white tablecloth against the wind.

'Good morning, everyone,' said Tom, rather too loudly.

'Ah, Tom, very good to see you. How are you?' said Harry,

shaking his hand. Tom always felt Harry was about to stand up whenever he saw him as his head only reached to just below Tom's chin.

'Hello, Tom, it looks like a very good day for cricket,' said Daisy, placing some cutlery on the table. He spotted Dr Parkes standing just behind Madge and greeted them both. Madge gave him a wide smile and asked how everything was on the farm. Tom told her all was going well and that the haymaking had been remarkably easy for once. He was relieved when the players came out on to the field and Harry announced that everyone must take their seats ready for the start of the game.

Tom settled down in one of the deckchairs next to Daisy and was pleased when Timothy and Madge sat some way from them. Stourbridge had come out to field and Tom spotted the short, active figure of Eddie heading off to the far end of the ground. Daisy chatted away while Dolly fussed around her father, checking he had everything he needed. Marian was busy setting out the picnic with Deacon. As the sun appeared it warmed Tom and he began to feel a little sleepy. It seemed like a delightful day to be watching his friend play and to have time off from the farm…He woke from a doze to hear loud clapping from Harry celebrating the first wicket for Stourbridge. Tom started clapping a little too late and Harry looked rather baffled by his lack of attention.

A few overs later, Daisy pointed out that Eddie was removing his sweater, which she knew meant he was about to bowl. Tom was intrigued to find out how good his friend was as Eddie had always been very modest about his sporting skills. Harry had confirmed, however, that his son had a natural talent.

Eddie bowled off spin and his first over went for two runs and was otherwise uneventful. Two more overs followed before finally he got a wicket and Harry stood up, cheering.

'Quieten down, dear,' said Marian. 'That really is rather too much. It might be acceptable at a football match but not at cricket.'

Her comment seemed to quieten him instantly. Though Harry had done well with the brewery, his wife had come from a rather smarter background and occasionally this difference in upbringing became rather too obvious for Harry's liking. Eddie took two more wickets before lunch, which produced more modest applause from the family. Harry then turned to Tom and proudly announced, 'I told you he could bowl! Always could, even in the garden.'

Deacon and Dolly both nodded their approval, although Tom could hardly ignore the fact that Deacon was in no position to disagree. The players ambled off the field for lunch and Marian asked everyone to sit around the picnic table. A beautiful white cloth had been laid together with plates and cutlery along with linen napkins and even a vase of yellow roses. Dolly was dragged away from her knitting and sat down next to Tom. She picked at her bitten nails and chewed her lip nervously, already uncomfortable at having to make conversation.

'Have you been knitting very long?' he asked.

'Quite a while. I started during the war. We were asked to knit things by the Red Cross for the troops in France. I knitted all sorts…hats, socks, gloves,' she said proudly.

'You did have some problem with the gloves though, didn't you?' asked Daisy.

'That was only one pair. I'm sure the pattern book was wrong,' Dolly grumbled. Daisy leant over and told Tom that her sister had produced two pairs of gloves with only three fingers, which she had insisted on sending out to the trenches on the basis that they were better than nothing.

'I'm sure someone would have been very thankful for them,' he said diplomatically. 'That was one thing we did not need in Egypt.'

Tom was now very hungry and ate a large plate of cold beef with potatoes and some very hot home-made horseradish. Harry produced two bottles of Smith & Williams light ale, which helped calm the heat of the horseradish. Tom briefly chatted to Timothy about his cricket career, which appeared even less impressive than his own, before settling down to watch the Kidderminster team being bowled out for 142.'

Stourbridge came out to bat and appeared initially to be chasing down the score with no problems at all. The opening pair had put on 51 before there was a mini collapse where they lost three wickets very quickly, which brought Eddie to the wicket.

'Come on, my lad,' said Harry.

'Oh, do be quiet, dear. Give the boy a chance,' said Marian. Harry slid down in his deckchair sulking until Eddie hit his first boundary, which the whole crowd appreciated. Tom could see Eddie was as talented at cricket as at football. He had a good few years of competitive sport ahead of him. Tom was not envious, even though Eddie never seemed to want for anything, because he was always so modest and unassuming.

By the end of the innings Eddie was 68 not out and Stourbridge had lost one more wicket, winning the match by six wickets. Eddie came out of the pavilion to greet the family and thanked them all for coming.

'Well done, you batted beautifully,' said Tom. 'Thanks for asking me, it's been a lovely day.'

'Thanks for coming. I hope you haven't been too bored.'

'Not at all, we've had a delicious lunch and it's good to have a day away from the farm occasionally.'

He prepared to say goodbye. As he went round the small group he saw that Timothy had gone, and felt a moment's panic as he said goodbye to Madge, who was standing on her own.

'Tom, I'm so sorry, I've hardly spoken to you all day,' she said. 'Thank you for coming, it will have meant so much to Eddie. I hope you can come to Stourbridge again soon, perhaps after the harvest,' she said, touching the back of his hand.

'Thank you, I'd love to come again.' He nodded to her and turned away before his blushes became too obvious.

He set off back to Pershore, embarrassed once more by his awkwardness in social situations and especially around women. He felt more at ease in the pub with Sid and Alf, but wondered how he would ever feel relaxed at Ivy Lodge.

Chapter 27

October 1920

Tom had almost completed the cultivations on the farm, ready to plant the winter wheat, which was timely as he was sure the weather was due to change. The wind was stronger and grey clouds were being pushed eastwards; he felt sure rain must be arriving in the next day or so.

He walked over to the yard and put a bridle on his favourite workhorse, a huge grey called Bessie after his first horse in the Yeomanry. He had bought her a few months ago from a neighbour who was keen to find a good home for her. She was thirteen and had therefore not been expensive to buy, but Tom already adored her. She was perfect in the stable, ate everything and was easy to handle. He poured some oats into her manger, brushed out her tail and picked out her feet. He then put on the harness to which he would attach the plough. He opened the stable door and she followed him out. He walked her across the yard and hitched the sets of chains belonging to the two-furrow plough to the harness.

He stopped in a field at the back of the yard, and lined up the plough. Looking for a mark in the distance, he chose a tree in a far hedgerow, which would help him maintain as straight a line as possible. His father would spot any crooked line and tease him for months, as well as telling every neighbouring farmer. That said, with Bessie he hardly had to use the reins to keep her straight. Bessie set herself against the plough and Tom made sure the shears were ready to dig into the stubble.

'Go on, old girl,' he called to her, and with a shake of the reins she began pulling. The fresh brown earth peeled over as the shears cut through it. The first mark was made and Tom looked down and thought the line was fairly straight as he turned at the end. After half an hour there were two dark stripes of brown earth laid out across the field, peppered with the white of seagulls, who darted around feasting on the mass of worms brought to the surface.

It stayed dry, and towards lunchtime he unhitched the plough and took Bessie back to the stable for some hay and a rest. Mary had laid some fresh bread and cheese on the table for his lunch, and he was halfway through his first piece of bread when he noticed a letter and could see immediately it was from Eddie.

He wrote thanking Tom for coming to the cricket in July and said he was now back playing football. They were all keen for him to come and stay at the end of November as they were having a party to celebrate Dolly's birthday. There was then news of his father's brewery and some local gossip concerning a man who had taken a shine to Daisy and had been sending flowers to the house twice a week. Daisy thought he was rather ineffectual and had tried to have the flowers sent back, but the florist had refused so the house was full of a variety of roses in every colour.

Tom wrote back later saying he would be delighted to accept Eddie's invitation. He was interested to know more about Madge, and realised the letter had stirred his interest in her once more, after months when he had hardly allowed himself to think of her.

One early-November day, after feeding the horses and checking the stock, he drove into Pershore and went to Simpson's, tailors and gentlemen's outfitters. The shop window was rather dusty and featured two mannequins wearing an old suit and a blazer, which Tom thought had remained unchanged since before the war. He opened the door and a bell rang at the back of the shop. An elderly man appeared. He was wearing a three-piece brown suit and highly polished shoes. He stooped slightly and peered at Tom over a pair of small spectacles perched on the end of his nose.

'Good morning, Mr Bomford. What can I do for you today?'

'Hello, Mr Simpson, I was looking for a new suit, possibly blue, but I would like turn-ups on my trousers,' said Tom, a little unsure how this would be received.

'Well, turn-ups...very fashionable. You must be glad you're being served by me rather than old Mr Simpson. He might have asked you to leave the shop after hearing that.' He chuckled and began looking at rolls of cloth as he continued to mutter 'turn-ups'. Tom remembered that old Mr Simpson had a fearsome reputation as the man who felt it his sole responsibility to maintain correct styles of dress in the surrounding area.

Tom left the shop forty minutes later, having placed an order for his suit and with a first fitting arranged for a few days later. He also bought some new shoes and a white shirt, and felt the beginnings of nervous excitement about the party.

Three weeks later he returned to Simpson's and found the suit fitted beautifully. He bought some chocolates for Marian Williams, a large cigar for Harry, and came home to pack his small case, which he would strap to the back of the motorbike. The night before he left, his nerves began again and he slept poorly. Tom fretted over how Madge would react to him, hoping she would be pleased to see him. But then he grew angry with himself for his self-indulgence in dreaming of an encouraging reaction from an engaged woman.

He woke early, fed the horses and checked the livestock. Hender reassured Tom all would be well while he was away for the weekend. It was a cold day with a slight ground frost that was slowly clearing with the morning sun. Tom was well wrapped up against the chill in a warm hat, coat and thick gloves. He waved to Hender and opened the throttle, feeling the Triumph's grumble turn into a growl as he set off to Stourbridge. There was very little traffic on the roads and he arrived outside Ivy Lodge just over an hour later. Eddie rushed out to meet him and carried his case inside.

'Tom, it's so good to see you again. It's been far too long.'

'It has. I've been looking forward to this and to seeing all the family again. It looks like a very big party,' he said, watching men coming in and out of the back door of the house.

'Father makes a fuss of Dolly because she does so much at work, and he thinks she needs a bit of encouragement as Daisy and Madge took all of Mother's good looks,' said Eddie, smiling guiltily for raising the subject.

He took Tom for lunch at a small hotel nearby as they had been told to stay out of the way. He had briefly seen Marian but there was no sign of Daisy or Madge. Eddie said they had gone to collect flowers and some decorations for the dining room. Tom asked after Madge, and Eddie said she was well and that she still seemed very fond of Dr Parkes but they had not yet been able to agree a date, much to Parkes's frustration. Frankly, Eddie wondered if she really wanted to marry him as she was running out of excuses not to set a date.

In the afternoon Eddie showed his friend a little of Stourbridge, its main street and some of the new shops that had opened after the war. They returned in time for tea, and found Harry already settled in his favourite chair, puffing on a small cigar.

'Tom, how good to see you again. Come and have a seat, tell me all about the farm. How are things going?'

Tom was ushered into a chair next to him and soon they were deep in conversation over the price of wheat. Madge swept in with the tray of tea. She was looking as beautiful as Tom remembered. At the sight of her he jumped to his feet, knocking over Harry's ashtray.

'I'm so sorry, Harry, I'll get a brush,' he said.

'Don't worry, I do it all the time.'

Tom turned back and suddenly Madge was standing very close

to him. He caught a brief hint of her perfume and then she smiled at him.

'Hello, Tom. How are you? It's lovely to see you again.'

He shook her hand and beamed back at her. 'You look very well; it's good to see you too.'

They sat down and began discussing plans for the party. Tom found that Madge put him at his ease, and they sat talking together like old friends. It was not until one of the maids came to close the curtains that they realised tea had been cleared away and Harry was snoring gently in his armchair.

'Oh, heavens, look at the time, we've got completely carried away. I'd better help Mother with the supper for tonight. It's very informal. I'll see you later.'

She jumped up and was out of the door as Tom called after her, 'See you later.'

He went upstairs to bathe and change before supper, elated by their conversation and hopeful that Madge had enjoyed it as much as he had. It was not a deep, meaningful discussion but Tom felt a sense of relaxation in her company that he had never felt with any woman before. He wondered whether she felt as at ease with Timothy.

He found supper very enjoyable, and was more calm than usual in company. He had been seated between Dolly and Marian. He dutifully began by asking Dolly about the brewery and her work, and was genuinely fascinated to hear that she followed the stock market closely and had already invested in a number of shares very successfully. Eddie's mother was as charming as ever, with her wicked sense of humour. At one point, as Tom laughed at one of her stories, he caught Madge looking at him, but she glanced away before their eyes fully met.

The plates were cleared and Harry announced that he was off to bed. After twenty minutes everyone else retired in preparation for the following day.

Tom slept well and was woken by Eddie knocking on his door and walking in to draw back the curtains.

'Morning, Tom. You've slept well, it's past nine o'clock. Would you like some breakfast?'

'I am sorry, Eddie. I haven't slept this late in months.'

'Well, I have to tell you, Madge was worried about you,' said his friend, laughing as he left the room. Tom dressed quickly. He splashed his face with cold water from the bowl and combed his hair. He ran downstairs and into the dining room where Daisy and Madge sat giggling over cups of tea.

'Good morning, sleepy-head,' said Madge, teasing him.

'I'm so sorry. I must've been more tired than I thought,' said Tom, helping himself to some toast and butter. Daisy passed the marmalade and poured him a cup of tea.

'Tom, would you mind helping Eddie move some furniture today as we have to make space for sixty in the drawing room tonight?' she enquired.

'Very happy to help out. Are there any other jobs for me to do?'

'You can peel potatoes with me, Tom,' said Madge, grinning at him as she pinned up some wisps of hair.

'I'd be delighted to help, although my peeling is never very good. According to Mary, I seem to take rather too much potato with the skin.'

'Mary? One of your lady friends then, Tom?' asked Daisy.

'No, she's my sister. She's a bit younger than me but she's got very bad eyes. She lives at the farm and helps look after Hender and me.'

'Poor woman,' said Madge in mock sympathy.

'We try and keep things fairly tidy. Hender has a bit of a wind problem, though, and that does rather upset her, especially as he finds it so funny.'

Daisy made a small farting noise and they all collapsed into fits of giggles. They tidied away breakfast then and the rest of the day was spent moving furniture and preparing food. Tom savoured every moment spent peeling potatoes with Madge before being asked to help shift furniture. He became aware that Daisy and Madge were talking about him from time to time. There were occasions when he walked into a room to ask for something such as a hammer and they would be whispering together and would then giggle when they saw him and stop talking altogether.

During the afternoon it began to snow very lightly and a layer of white settled on the lawn. Eddie behaved like an excitable small boy and Tom was thankful, knowing his friend's skill with a ball, that it was not yet deep enough for a snowball fight. It grew dark very early due to the thick low cloud and fires were lit one by one in the downstairs rooms.

Tom went upstairs to change into his new suit, which he had laid out on the bed earlier. He stood in front of the mirror and buttoned up the jacket. It fitted him very well and he was glad he had spent so much on it, even if he doubted it would be appreciated by the one person he most wanted to impress. He sat down on the bed and breathed deeply, trying not to let his nerves get the better of him. He knew it was quite likely that if he had too much beer he would make a fool of himself and embarrass Eddie, so vowed he would be friendly to Madge and no more.

He heard the hum of people arriving and went downstairs to join the party. The hall was brightly lit and there were candles spread around the drawing room. Their flickering light reflected from the chandelier hanging in the middle of the ceiling. A three-piece band was playing in one corner and Harry was noisily welcoming his guests. Tom noticed the strong accent with which most of the visitors spoke, which Daisy had told him firmly and proudly was a Dudley accent, not one from Birmingham. Deacon was busy taking coats from people as they arrived. Some were dusted with snowflakes.

Madge swept into the drawing room, wearing a new dress that she had bought out shopping with Daisy the previous week. It was in deep blue, with a satin collar and sleeves, and finished well above the ankle. There was a murmur from a few of the couples standing nearest the door as she appeared, and Madge knew that a number of the older guests would disapprove of such daring. Timothy arrived beside her and kissed her on the cheek.

'Good evening, my dear, how are you?'

'Very well, thank you. Do you like my new dress?'

He stood back and looked her up and down.

'I love the colour, but isn't it rather short?'

'Oh, Timothy, you're so old-fashioned.' Madge walked away from him to welcome some more guests.

Tom found Eddie talking to Timothy's mother, Edith, who was looking even more austere than usual. As the room filled, Eddie introduced his friend to some more of the guests. Tom's name was already well known to most of them as that of the man who'd saved Eddie's life. Tom sipped his beer and recounted stories from the farm. At one point he found himself trapped in a corner by a man who told Tom he supplied car parts and seemed staggeringly pleased with himself. The man lectured him on politics, the war and the future of Britain until finally Daisy spotted the desperate look in Tom's eyes and came to rescue him. He then spoke to Timothy Parkes, who seemed a little flustered as he had not seen Madge for a few minutes, which seemed faintly ridiculous as Tom proceeded to tell him.

'Leave her be for a while, Timothy. You don't want to smother the poor girl.'

'I suppose you're right. I do worry, though, whether everything is well between us. Madge does seem a little distant at present.'

'I'm sure all's well. She has been very busy with the party for the last few weeks after all.'

'She's a wonderful girl and so grateful for all you did for her brother. I was hoping she would agree to set a date for the wedding now he's back and thriving, but she doesn't feel quite ready so I suppose I must respect her wishes.' He began to look around the room nervously. 'Please excuse me. I must look after Mother as she tires easily on these occasions and can't stay too late. I fear in another hour or so I'll have to take her home.'

'I'm sorry to hear that,' said Tom, trying to sound sincere.

For the next hour or two he circulated, chatting to the other guests as he sipped beer and ate some supper. There was a whole salmon and a side of beef, cooked rare, just as Tom liked it. It was very tender with a wonderful flavour and he managed to have a second helping without anyone noticing. The room began to thin out and just after eleven the band stopped playing and Harry offered some of his friends a parting glass of whisky.

Tom accepted a glass and decided to go out on the terrace for some air. He had found it very warm and stuffy inside the house. The cold night was instantly refreshing. The snow had stopped and the sky was very clear with a mass of stars flickering above. He breathed out and saw the vapour hang in the frosty air, smelt the faint aroma of whisky.

'Hello, Tom, I wondered where you'd got to.'

It was Madge's voice. He found his heart suddenly pounding in his chest.

'Yes, I thought I would come and take some air, it's quite stuffy in the house.'

'Father always likes to have the house cosy, as he puts it, but with all the fires going it does get rather hot. Have you enjoyed yourself?'

Tom saw her look directly at him and took a nervous sip of his whisky.

'Yes, I did. I was a little out of my depth at first but everyone was very welcoming. I had a talk to Timothy. He seemed to be worried about his mother.'

'She's not an easy woman,' Madge said with feeling. 'I've told him to stand up for himself but he finds it very hard. She made him leave ages ago and they were both so disapproving of my ankles being on show. Oh, sorry, you may not approve either.'

'No, I like the dress, it's very smart.'

'Thank you. I'm not sure everyone agrees with you.'

She paused and looked up at the sky. 'Do you wish for anything when you look at the stars, Tom?'

'Yes. Silly really, I think it dates back to a bedtime story my father used to read me when I was small.'

'What do you wish for?'

'If I told you it might not come true. At the start of the evening it would have been this, standing out here alone chatting with you, so it seems a wish has come true.' Tom laughed nervously, thinking he might have gone a little too far.

'What if I'd wished for the same thing? Would that make it twice as likely to happen?'

'I'm not sure. May I ask you what you were wishing for?' There was a long pause and he began to think it would be best if he returned to the house without talking to her further.

'This is difficult for me to talk about, but you may have gathered that things have been strained between Timothy and me lately,' Madge began. 'He's a kind man but I've become a little unsure about living the rest of my life with him. I realise now that I was wishing to spend time out here with you this evening, not him.' Her voice trailed off and he heard her swallow.

'Are you saying that you are not going to marry Timothy then?'

'I don't think I will, no,' said Madge, in a whisper.

Tom felt as though he had been hit by a large wave. He struggled to breathe, and then the full significance of Madge's words became clear to him. He now knew that he was hopelessly and madly in love with her, and all his denial and confusion had resulted from his efforts to suppress these feelings.

He turned towards her and fumbled for her hand, taking it in both of his. 'I hope this doesn't sound silly, and do tell me to stop at any time, but I have to say this now. I have fallen in love with you. I know you may find this ridiculous. You may not share my feelings, so if you wish me to leave tomorrow and not see you again, I do understand.'

'Tom, please, have you finished?' Madge interrupted.

He nodded, his heart pounding, feeling that his future happiness was being weighed in the balance by the woman standing in front of him.

'You may be shocked to hear this, Tom Bomford, but I believe I have fallen in love with you too.'

Tom's next thought, when his whirling brain permitted him to think clearly again, was how lovely it was to be kissing Madge. He thought he might stay outside with her, prolonging this moment, for the rest of the night.

They stood on the terrace a little longer, laughing softly and holding hands, talking about how they had both felt an instant attraction to each other, though they had been far too worried to acknowledge it. Madge wanted to say nothing to anyone else until she had spoken to Timothy. Tom was happy with that, no matter how long it took, as with the certainty of Madge's love he felt a contentment he had never known before. They went in before they were missed, agreeing to wait for the moment.

The following morning was quieter than usual in the house and at breakfast Harry was nursing a slight hangover. Tom was down early, bubbling over with joy, but realised he could share his feelings with no one. After breakfast he went upstairs to pack his small bag and carefully fold his suit. He heard the bedroom door click shut and suddenly felt Madge's arms twining around his waist.

'I have come to say goodbye properly before you go.'

'Thank you,' he said, kissing her. 'Eddie has already asked me to come and stay after Christmas for a few days, so perhaps we can stay in touch by letter until then.'

'Yes. I'll tell Timothy next week, and then after Christmas we can tell the family. Tom, this feels so different from anything I've known before. You'll never believe this but Daisy said, the second time we met, that you were in love with me.'

'Was it that obvious? She must have the gift because I'm not sure even I knew then,' he said, laughing.

They hugged and kissed and then Tom went downstairs to say his goodbyes to all the family. He secured his winter hat with his goggles and pulled on his gloves. The Williamses were lined up in the drive to wave him off. Madge stood just behind them and as he turned to wave he saw her blow a kiss to him. He drove down Norton Road, feeling his eyes fill with tears. He felt more excited about Christmas than he had since he was ten years old and had been given his first pony.

Tom wrote to Madge every few days and their letters became more expressive with each week that passed. In a jeweller's shop in Pershore he found a small brooch for her Christmas present and carefully wrapped it in bright paper, finishing it off with red ribbon. Tom was pleased with his choice; it was pretty but not too showy.

He spent Christmas Day at Manor Farm, where Phyllis and Birdie had spent hours decorating the house with holly and mistletoe from the orchard. They all went to the morning service and then returned for a glass of sherry before their traditional lunch of turkey, roast potatoes and huge numbers of sprouts. Reg tapped his glass and proposed a toast to his wife Nora as head cook, though, in reality, she had delegated most of the preparations to her daughters. Tom waited for his father's usual Christmas sprout comment, which arrived as the plates were cleared.

'What a lovely lunch. Those sprouts were good too. Lucky we've had a frost...they're always better after a frost.'

Tom smiled to himself. Every family has its traditions. Christmas was now complete, with the Bomford sprout tradition maintained for another year.

On Boxing Day morning Tom left for Stourbridge, feeling a mixture of anxiety and excitement. He knew Timothy had been well liked by the family, and was unsure as to how Madge's breaking off their engagement would have been received. His case was fuller than usual as he had tried to find small presents for all the family. He had bought a packet of cigars for Harry, some soap for Marian, and a cricket ball for Dick. Daisy and Dolly had been a little more difficult but he had decided on a more traditional book for Dolly and a newer novel called *The Age of Innocence* by Edith Wharton for Daisy. The lady in the bookshop said it was 'causing a stir', which seemed to make it suitable for her.

He pulled up outside Ivy Lodge, feeling more nervous than ever, and wheeled the motorcycle in through the gates. The yard was empty and Tom presumed Deacon would have been given Boxing Day off to be with his family. He pulled off his goggles and gloves, rubbing his hands to relieve their cold and stiffness. The back door opened and Madge ran out and into his arms.

'Tom, it's lovely to see you,' she said, talking into his coat collar.

'You too. How are you?' he said as he held her shoulders and looked down into her face. 'Are we allowed to hug like this?'

'Yes, I told all the family this morning. I couldn't wait any longer. They were thrilled, although a little worried about Timothy. He was very upset, as you can imagine.'

'How was your father? Was he happy?'

'He was delighted. Said he had always found Timothy rather wet, and that my news was the best Christmas present he could imagine. Mother was more reserved and worried for Timothy and his parents. Daisy was very happy too, but no surprise there as you have always got on so well. Dolly nodded at me and went back to doing her knitting.'

They laughed and went inside, where Marian greeted Tom with a kiss on the cheek.

'Tom, how lovely to see you. I'm so pleased to hear the news. How are you feeling?'

'I'm very happy but a little nervous. I wasn't sure how everyone would react.'

'Tom, great news!' shouted Eddie as he burst into the kitchen. 'My sister and Tom Bomford…who would have predicted that when we were in the camp in Turkey?'

They shook hands and once again Tom was surprised by how much energy and dynamism Eddie brought into a room. They went through to the sitting room to see Harry, who was even smaller than his son but just as energetic. His moustache seemed a little more yellowed by cigar smoke but he beamed at Tom and shook his hand.

'I think this calls for a drink. Tom, a Scotch for you?'

'Thank you, that'd be very welcome. I'm still thawing out after the drive.'

Harry poured three glasses and Tom felt the warming effects of the whisky slipping down. They sat and talked of the football season and Eddie's hopes of receiving another call for Aston Villa Reserves. He was playing well, but there were a good number of younger players coming through who played on the wing so it was a little more difficult than the previous year.

After lunch Tom and Madge went for a walk around the local area, which Tom had only seen briefly before with Eddie. They talked and talked, and on the way back to the house held hands. Tom told her about his Christmas. While he didn't want his own mother to sound like another Edith Parkes, he told Madge about their difficult relationship.

Madge squeezed his hand in sympathy, and as she did so he felt some of the burden lift from him.

He had two nights at Ivy Lodge and spent an hour or two each day alone with Madge, walking around the garden or the local park. On the second day Eddie and Tom took their motorcycles out for a ride to a country pub where they enjoyed a couple of pints of beer. The bond between them was even stronger now that Tom and Madge were courting Eddie felt like a younger brother to Tom. Their years together as prisoners of war had formed an enduring friendship, which had only deepened with Tom's love for Eddie's sister.

The following morning was sunny, with clear blue skies and a sharp frost. The branches of the trees in the garden looked as though they had been glazed with icing sugar, and the lawn was completely white. Tom dressed quickly, seeing his breath even in the bedroom. He had breakfast and then said his goodbyes. This time he could at least linger a little with Madge. The family left them alone in the drive. Tom promised to write and visit again soon. They kissed and he set off back to Pershore, revving the Triumph a little harder than usual as he drove down Norton Road.

Chapter 28

1921

Over the following year the couple saw each other on a regular basis, and on two occasions Madge had come to spend a few days at Manor Farm, Stoulton, under the watchful eye of Tom's parents. Bishampton was being redecorated by Hender, and Mary did not think it a suitable place for a lady to stay. There was also the danger of gossip and Tom did not want to embarrass Madge by asking her to stay alone with him, though he had taken her to see the farm and the house.

Phyllis and Birdie had liked her immediately, and had taken her off on walks and shopping trips in their car. They all had supper together in the evening. The only sticking point had been the behaviour of Tom's mother, who had been alternately distant and rude. Phyllis had asked Madge about life at home and how the business was progressing after the war. Before she could answer, Nora had said that you could not call a brewery a proper business as they were peddling drink to the poor, who could ill afford it. Tom stood up, on the point of asking for an apology, but Birdie managed to calm the situation. Later he apologised to Madge for his mother's comments.

'After Timothy's mother, Nora is nothing,' Madge said, but secretly was pleased that Tom had so quickly stood up for her.

In the summer, Tom, Birdie, Phyllis, Eddie and Madge boarded a train at Worcester and travelled to Weston-super-Mare for the weekend. They stayed in a small bed and breakfast and enjoyed themselves together with no fear of Nora's barbed comments.

They ate fish and chips, and ice cream, and played games in the arcade on the pier.

The farm was proving difficult to cultivate as the ground was very wet and weeds sprouted everywhere. Lambing had gone well this year. Tom had sold a few and kept the ewes to try and slowly build his flock. He had also found a hunter and enjoyed his days out with the Croome Hunt. His father had joined him, and they had rediscovered their old shared pleasure in riding together over hedges and post and rails that had existed before the war.

Tom's younger brother Ray had begun to help his father on Manor Farm and, at last, had something in common with Tom. They now discussed the price of lambs and cattle, often visiting Worcester market together to buy and sell stock, where Tom was able to introduce Ray to some of the other farmers in the area.

At Ivy Lodge, Madge's mother contracted pneumonia in October and was very ill for two weeks with a racking cough and high fever. Timothy Parkes came to visit in his professional capacity on a daily basis, which was a little awkward, but Madge stayed out of sight in her own room when he called. At all times he was courteous and merely said he hoped she was well. Marian made a slow recovery and was very weak.

By early November Tom had decided to buy a ring and travelled into Worcester to find a jeweller. He thought those in Pershore a little old-fashioned and was also concerned that news of his buying an engagement ring would be all round the neighbourhood in minutes if he bought one there. He had checked the size from a ring he had found in Madge's room. He visited two or three shops before finding one he thought would be perfect for her. He took it home, feeling anxious and suddenly a little unsure of himself. Tom was now certain that he wanted to marry Madge, and although they had not discussed it specifically he had every hope that she felt the same. As an old-fashioned type, Tom thought it only proper that he should ask Harry Williams's permission first, so decided to speak to him on Christmas Eve soon after he arrived at Ivy Lodge.

Having driven through heavy rain, Tom arrived soaked through to his underwear and very cold. Madge gave him a long hug and took him upstairs to run a bath for him and find him some dry clothes. He lay in the steaming water, allowing the heat to soak into his core. As the bath began to cool he got out, redressed and came down for tea and a large slice of fruit cake.

'Daisy, this is your best cake yet.'

'Tom, you can come again,' she said, smiling. 'How are things on the farm?'

'Pretty well, generally. We managed to plant all the wheat before it got too wet and we are up to fifty ewes. It's been too wet to do much the last few weeks, although Father keeps suggesting more jobs I should be doing.'

'You seem a bit nervous, Tom, is anything bothering you?' she asked.

'Just excited about Christmas really.'

Harry was still not home from the office and Tom was starting to feel very anxious. Everyone had finished tea some time before and Tom was in the kitchen talking to Madge about the plans for the following day. He knew that every house has its own particular customs at Christmas and was keen to know theirs, so he could choose his moment to swoop with the question.

Suddenly the door swung open and Harry burst in, taking his coat and hat off as he did so.

'Tom, very good to see you! Happy Christmas,' he said, shaking hands. 'Too late for tea; I think it's time for a Christmas drink. I'm frozen. Is the fire lit in the sitting room?'

'Yes, Father, it should be warm in there,' said Daisy.

'Tom, you and I will head in there and have a whisky together.'

Harry marched out of the kitchen and through the hall into the sitting room. Tom felt he couldn't have planned it better himself.

Heat blazed from behind the fireguard as he poured whisky into Harry's favourite heavy cut-glass tumblers. Tom added a little water and handed Harry his glass. They sat down in comfortable armchairs in front of the fire. After a few minutes of talking about the brewery, Tom stood up and began to pace the room nervously. He took a deep breath.

'Harry, I have something important I would like to ask you. As you know, I have grown very fond of Madge and I wanted your permission to ask for her hand in marriage.'

Tom could hardly believe he had managed to make his speech without faltering. He was still pacing the room, picking at the edges of his cuffs.

'I would be delighted if you were to marry my daughter. That's on one condition, though.' Harry laughed heartily. 'That you stop pacing and bloody well sit down!'

'Yes, sorry,' said Tom. 'I'm rather nervous about all this. As you've probably gathered, I haven't asked Madge yet so please don't mention anything to her.'

'Until then your secret is safe, but I think we need to drink to this,' said his host, topping up both their glasses. Tom thanked him again and drank his whisky quickly. He wasn't going to wait until Christmas Day. He had to ask Madge now.

He found her on the landing about to come downstairs, and ran up to meet her. 'Madge, can I have a quick word?'

'Yes, let's go down to the drawing room. How many whiskies did Father have? He looked in festive mood tonight.'

They opened the drawing-room door. The fire flickered, emitting a faint orange glow.

'He's on very good form.' Tom coughed and cleared his throat. 'I wanted to have a word with you before dinner...We have known each other a while and, as you know, I love you so much, and...

well, I wanted to know whether you would do me the honour of becoming my wife.'

He knelt down then, fumbling in his pocket, and managed to produce the small velvet box. He opened it and saw the diamonds glint. As he waited, a pulse thumped at the side of his forehead. He needn't have worried.

'Tom, of course I will! I've been praying you would ask me. What a wonderful Christmas present!'

Madge took the ring and slipped it on, holding up her left hand to the light. 'It's beautiful, thank you so much.'

'You're sure you like it?'

'I do, I really do. It's lovely and it fits me perfectly.'

They kissed and sat together on the sofa, looking at the ring for a few minutes, but Madge was desperate to tell the rest of the family immediately.

After that Christmas passed in a haze of happiness. There was a wonderful lunch and the whole family seemed delighted for them both. Eddie was thrilled that they were going to be brothers-in-law, and Marian was already beginning to make plans for the wedding day.

Chapter 29

May 1922

The weather had been dreadful for weeks and Tom was in a foul mood. He and Hender had cut the grass for hay nearly two weeks ago. Each time it began to dry they had turned it, but then the rain started again. He had got up early as usual that morning, and fed the horses before checking the sheep and cattle. The sun was shining and he hoped for a dry day. He found haymaking without doubt the most frustrating activity on the farm. The problem was, it was one of the most important as the stock needed plenty to feed them through the winter months.

He went back to the house for breakfast and as he was ready to come back out it started to rain again, heavier than ever. He cursed and kicked the gate to the yard. His father was inside, dropping off some feed for the chickens.

'I'm fed up with this weather!' Tom shouted.

'That won't do you any good, lad,' said Reg. 'It's farming. There's bugger all you can do about it.'

'I know, it's still bloody maddening, though.'

Tom decided to head down to Pershore for a pint with Alf, as he was always there on Tuesday lunchtime. As he walked into the Angel he saw his friend at the bar holding forth on a pet subject. He turned, saw Tom and stopped mid-sentence.

'Well, I never, cocker. Weather must be bad to find you in here at lunchtime.'

'You're right, Alf, too wet for making hay so I thought a pint with you might cheer me up. You're normally here on Tuesday lunchtime, aren't you?'

The barman laughed and poured Tom a pint of bitter.

'Tuesday? I think you'll find him here most lunchtimes,' he said, winking.

They sat at a small table and drank their pints, Alf smoking a cigarette as usual. He was keen to know how arrangements for the wedding were progressing. It was planned for June in Stourbridge, with a reception back at Ivy Lodge. Eddie was going to be Tom's best man and Sid and Alf both thought this was the right decision as he had been responsible for the match.

'One thing's for sure, Alf, we'll not be short of beer. Madge's father is bringing in four barrels.'

'Four? Well, that should see us through, even with your father there.'

Tom's father Reg enjoyed both weddings and funerals almost equally. He would travel the countryside attending all sorts of services. He generally only attended weddings with an invitation, but funerals caused no such difficulty and he would get Birdie to drive him all over Herefordshire and Gloucestershire to pay his last respects to the briefest of acquaintances. He once travelled down to Somerset to a man's funeral, having only met him once while out hunting. But Reg had considered him the most brilliant cross-country rider he'd ever encountered. He would normally be escorted home by his daughter rather the worse for drink, nearly always the last to leave but suitably respectful in his praise of the deceased and their memorable qualities.

Tom admitted to Alf he was now very excited about the wedding, but rather nervous about his speech. Alf told him it was just a long thank you, with one joke suitable for grandmothers. The particular joke Alf then told might well have caused a number of the older relatives to faint in horror. Tom finished his pint and headed off. The rain had stopped but it was still too wet to turn the hay so he drove to his father's farm in Stoulton.

He walked through the front door at Manor Farm and found Phyllis standing in the hall looking anxiously at him. She was holding a handkerchief, and a dustpan and brush were left on the table as if she had suddenly been interrupted at work.

'Tom, there's a telegram for you.'

He opened it and read it through twice before the news hit him. He began retching and ran to the lavatory, where Phyllis heard him vomit. She picked up the telegram and read it herself.

URGENT TELEGRAM
BOMFORD T. R.
EDDIE KILLED IN MOTORCYCLE ACCIDENT THIS MORNING COME SOONEST ALL MY LOVE MADGE

Phyllis began crying then, huge silent tears that ran down her cheeks. Eddie, so young and full of life, now dead. Tom appeared, ashen-faced and wiping water from his mouth.

'You poor, poor man,' she said, hugging her brother. Tom broke down sobbing and they stood together like that for four or five minutes. Phyllis, so much shorter, stood stroking his back and trying to comfort him. Eventually they broke apart and Tom dried his eyes. He gazed out of the window as if hypnotised. He snapped his head round and looked at his sister with an expression of utter desolation on his face.

'I'd better leave as soon as possible to be with Madge and the family. There's no way we can marry in June now. It would be wrong.'

'Yes, it may be best to postpone things for a while,' said Phyllis quietly. 'Tom, you get some things from upstairs and I'll make you a quick sandwich to take.'

When he arrived at Ivy Lodge, Deacon was standing at the gate dressed in black. Tom parked his motorbike in the road and shook the man's hand.

'How am yer, Mr Bomford? I'm sorry for your loss. The family are all inside and I have been asked to turn away visitors.'

'Thank you, Deacon. Do you know what happened?'

'It was this morning. Mr Eddie was on his way to work on his bike. He was riding down Market Street when a lorry stopped in front of him. He went straight into the back of it and died instantly. I can't believe it, he was such a wonderful lad.'

Tom knocked quietly on the back door and went into the kitchen. All the curtains were drawn and it was eerily quiet in the house. He heard someone sobbing upstairs. Just then Madge walked into the kitchen carrying a tray.

'Oh, darling,' she cried, running into Tom's arms. They stood as one, locked together in their sadness.

'Deacon told me what happened. It sounds as if there was nothing Eddie could have done when the lorry stopped so quickly.'

'That's the only blessing, he didn't suffer. After everything he had gone through in the war, to die like that at home here in England seems so tragic.'

'How are your parents?' said Tom, sitting her down at the kitchen table.

'Distraught. Father and Dolly are both in pieces and Mother has disappeared into her room, but I heard her crying all morning. Daisy is being a brick, as usual. Thank heavens you're here, Tom. We can't marry in June now, can we?'

'No, we can't. We'll wait a while and allow ourselves and everyone else the time they need to mourn.'

Tom and Madge stayed in the kitchen and made preparations for a cold supper. The cook had been sent home. Daisy came down later to help them both. Harry appeared briefly for supper but barely ate anything. He chatted to Tom and thanked him again for saving Eddie from dying in Turkey so that they could at least enjoy the time they'd had with him after he returned home. Harry poured himself a whisky then and retreated to his study. Daisy took trays up to Dolly and Marian, who had still not spoken to anybody since hearing the news.

Tom's nightmares returned that night, with visions of The Weasel towering over him. He felt drained in the morning. In the kitchen he found Daisy and Dolly sitting drinking tea with Madge.

'Good morning, Tom,' said Daisy.

'Good morning,' he said, kissing Madge on the forehead and sitting down beside her.

'We were saying that it's up to us to start planning Eddie's funeral as Mother and Father are in no fit state to arrange it.'

'What is that smell?' asked Tom, frowning.

'Lilies. Ghastly, aren't they? We have had bunches and bunches of them together with nearly forty letters already,' said Madge. 'Perhaps after breakfast we can visit the undertaker and begin to plan the service. Father, I know, wants it at St Mary's, where we were planning our wedding.'

She shook her head and tears dropped into her lap. Tom put his arm around her comfortingly. They made toast and Tom had a boiled egg and soldiers, which reminded Daisy and Madge of Eddie's favourite breakfast before the war. Afterwards they left for the undertaker's, walking out on to Norton Road, past Deacon, who was receiving more letters and flowers.

'Tom, there is one thing I would like you to promise me,' Madge said as they walked through the grey misty morning together.

'Yes, of course, what is it?'

'You must give up the motorbike.'

'Of course. I had already decided that yesterday.'

'Thank you, darling,' she said, with a long sigh.

They visited the undertaker's and afterwards called at St Mary's Vicarage where they met Reverend Shanley. He deeply impressed Tom. The Reverend was a tall man, who seemed rather severe at first but then was warm and sympathetic and full of what Tom could only describe as the Holy Spirit. Reverend Shanley suggested readings and hymns and asked who might give the eulogy. Daisy was not sure, but suggested Tom as someone who had spent more time with Eddie than anyone else in the last six years. He thought Harry would want to speak but the sisters all said he would be far too upset. Reverend Shanley said there did not have to be any immediate decision. It was a very difficult task for anyone to perform when someone had died so young and in such tragic circumstances.

The next day Harry and Marian confirmed the date of the service for the following week, and notices were placed in the local paper. Tom decided as it was a full week away he would return to the farm, but before he left Harry asked to speak to him in his office.

'Tom, thank you for coming so quickly. This is the most dreadful time and we somehow have to get through the funeral next week. I wanted to ask you whether you would say a few words about dear Eddie. You were so close and I can think of no one better placed to convey what he meant to all of us.' Harry turned to gaze out of the window, dabbing his eyes with his handkerchief.

'Yes, of course I will. It would be an honour.'

Tom drove back up to Stourbridge by car the following week with all his family except for his mother, who had developed a chest infection and stayed at home in bed. They arrived early to help with preparations for tea after the service the following day. The smell of lilies was still overpowering and he went outside to talk to Deacon.

'It's a bad day, Mr Bomford, a really bad day. Miss Daisy tells me you will be giving the eulogy. Eddie would have approved of that.'

'Thank you, Deacon. I'm rather nervous. It's difficult to do him justice in ten minutes or so. I'm worried about breaking down and not being able to continue.'

'I've heard you two went through horrors in Turkey. You'll get through this too,' said Deacon. Tom nodded and went to walk around the garden.

At ten-thirty a number of large black cars arrived to take them the short distance to the church. Tom decided to set out early and walk, in the hope of feeling a little calmer. As he arrived there were hundreds of people gathered outside the church waiting to be admitted. He walked into the graveyard at the back of the church and suddenly felt far more nervous. He thought it best to tell Harry as soon as he arrived that he felt sick and could not go through with the address. He was pacing up and down the path that led into the vestry when Sid walked up behind him.

'Hello, Tom, how are you feeling?'

'Hello, Sid. Dreadful. I want to pull out, I can't go through with it.'

'Tom, you must, for Eddie. His family and a lot of Yeomanry are here today. You'll regret it for the rest of your life if you pull out now.'

Sid patted him on the back and walked away to the main door. Tom meandered around the graveyard once more and began to feel calmer. He had a powerful sense that somehow Eddie was at peace too. He walked to the church, found Madge and took her arm. Together they walked up the aisle through the sea of black suits and dresses. He looked straight ahead, not daring to dwell on the pain on the faces of so many people gathered to say goodbye to his friend.

Tom sat down at the end of the second pew and held Madge's hand as the church continued to fill. Reverend Shanley appeared from the vestry and welcomed everyone to St Mary's, apologising that so many people had to stand at the back. The organ played the first chords of 'Praise My Soul, the King of Heaven' and the choir and congregation sang the hymn. There were two readings, one delivered by an old friend of Harry's and one read by Dick, which was followed by a further hymn, 'Love Divine All Loves Excelling'.

During the last verse, Reverend Shanley climbed slowly into the pulpit to address the congregation. He spoke of Eddie's involvement in the Yeomanry and his commitment to the local community through work and sport, and the tragedy of a man dying so young. He spoke of the love and mystery of God's will and asked everyone to pray for Eddie and his family. There was a pause then and Tom knew it was time for him to speak. The vicar descended from the pulpit, pausing at the bottom of the steps to smile reassuringly at him.

It seemed a long climb up the steps. Tom stopped and gathered his notes, looking out over the huge congregation.

'I first met Eddie Williams on Easter Monday 1916 when we were fighting in Egypt for the Queen's Own Worcestershire Hussars, or, as most of us know them, the Worcestershire Yeomanry. We had both been taken prisoner by the Turks after the battle of Qatia, where we sadly lost many friends and comrades. Eddie always had an extraordinary energy for life and an enthusiasm that was contagious. He was tough and never once complained on the long march from Egypt to southern Turkey. He always found my ignorance of football amusing, but I knew he was as talented at that as he was at cricket, and had already played for his beloved Aston Villa in the reserve team.

'We somehow survived our time together as prisoners of war and many people think that I helped Eddie through the war, but in truth he helped me.

'I, like many others, owe him so much, and the fact that

hundreds of people are here to pay their last respects says all you need to know about him.

'Eddie was responsible for introducing me to Madge, my fiancée, and for that alone I will be grateful to him for the rest of my life.'

Tom continued for some minutes, talking of his friend's strong family and happy childhood.

He paused as he felt tears welling up inside and his voice beginning to crack. He took a deep breath and carried on.

'Eddie was a superb sportsman, a loyal and brave soldier, a devoted son and brother, a true friend, and a man that I and all of us here will remember for ever.'

He made his way slowly back down the steps, feeling physically drained, and sat down next to Madge once again.

'Thank you, my love,' she whispered to him.

After the final prayers there was a hymn followed by the blessing. The family, led by Harry and Marian, filed out of the church behind the coffin. Tom saw Lord Coventry four rows back, who nodded at him. Behind him were many other members of the Yeomanry, some of them in tears. Harry had asked Tom to come to the cemetery, so while the rest of the Bomfords went back to Norton Road he joined Eddie's immediate family for the burial. He had dug graves for many soldiers killed in battle, but somehow this seemed so tragically different.

Harry had found a plot which was on the main walkway through the cemetery and very visible to anyone who entered through the large metal gates. It was a short burial service and afterwards the undertakers lowered the coffin into the ground while the vicar spread earth on top of it, uttering the words 'Ashes to ashes, dust to dust'. Marian broke down again and Daisy put her arm around her as Tom mouthed a final goodbye to his dear friend Eddie Williams.

The family returned to the house in silence and were greeted by Deacon in the yard.

'I thought it was a wonderful service, Mr Williams.'

'Thank you, Deacon,' he said with a heavy sigh.

Harry had insisted on providing a barrel of beer for those who would like it, otherwise there were countless cups of tea poured for the guests. Tom helped himself to a beer as Lord Coventry crossed the room towards him.

'Good afternoon, Bomford. That was a very moving address you gave, very moving.'

'Thank you, sir. Thank you also for the farm; all seems to be going well. I would be very happy to show you round any time.'

'I hear you are making an excellent job, which I would expect from a Yeomanry man. Good to see you again,' he said as he turned and strode back across the room to find Harry.

Madge took Tom by the arm and steered him across the room. People parted without saying anything in a form of distant concern.

'You must come and meet Aunt Frisky, she is so looking forward to meeting you.'

Aunt Frisky was leaning on the fireplace with a glass of sherry in one hand and wearing a black dress with a huge black cloak that was swept back over one shoulder. She turned and saw Madge who had hovered for a few seconds, not wanting to interrupt her.

'Madge, my darling, I am so sorry,' she said as tears welled up in her eyes. She wrapped Madge up in her cloak and hugged her.

'You must be Tom. My dear, how lovely to meet you. Poor boy, to lose your dearest friend after everything you both went through.'

She took a long drink of sherry and looked Tom up and down as if examining a horse she was about to buy.

'Well, my dear,' she said to Madge, 'you have a very handsome boy here, I must say. Do you fish, Tom?'

He shook his head. He could hardly take his eyes from Aunt Frisky's large black hat, which looked as though there was a bird nesting in the top of it.

'Pity. Still, I gather you ride beautifully and there's time to teach you how to fish. I must say, your father always serves the most delightful sherry, Madge. Now where is he?' And with that she was off, nodding to them both as she made her way in search of a refill.

Late in the afternoon, Tom's family and most of the other guests had gone, with the exception of two or three men who were a little the worse for beer. Tom and Madge left through the back door and walked out into the garden. It had been a warm day. The sun was losing some of its heat as it sank behind the pink clouds above the rooftops.

'I'm glad that's over, Tom. It feels like one small step towards a time when we will be able to marry at last,' sighed Madge.

Chapter 30

Tom looked at the date on the newspaper: 15 September 1922. It was exactly one week before his wedding day. The service was being held in St Thomas's Church.

It had been a thundery day in August when Harry had asked to talk to Tom in his study. His first thought was of the morning when he'd stood waiting to ask permission to marry Madge.

This time he was a little less nervous. Harry said it was time to think about their marriage once again, and although he did not feel like a lavish party, it was not fair on Madge or Tom to delay things any further. They discussed the date and 22 September was chosen. Invitations were sent, dresses fitted and ordered, and a reception arranged, which would be held in the garden of Ivy Lodge. Harry asked only that there should be no band and that Dolly should be a bridesmaid.

Tom now drove up and down to Stourbridge in his small Austin, which though considerably warmer than the Triumph was a lot less exciting. Hender was ecstatic when his brother asked him to be best man.

'But, Tom, what do I have to do apart from look after the ring?'

'Just make a long and very witty speech, replying on behalf of the bridesmaids,' Tom teased him.

'I could never do that,' Hender pleaded. 'You'll have to get Sid or Alf.'

'Never. Sid or Alf over my younger brother? You'll be fine.'

In reality Tom thought that Hender might well cry off with

nerves but hoped that the risk was outweighed by the boost his confidence would receive if he did it successfully. Ray and Madge's brother Dick were going to help the guests with the seating in the church. Dolly, Phyllis and Birdie would be brides-maids, and Daisy, who was adamant that she would not be, was helping to choose the dresses. Dolly had no clothes sense at all and owned only three dresses of exactly the same design. Phyllis preferred bright colours and Birdie something a little darker. In the end Daisy told them she was making the decision herself and that was that.

Ray had spent long periods with his mother, talking about Tom's time away and trying to explain to her all that he had gone through, both as a soldier and a prisoner. The result was that as Nora became more sympathetic towards Tom he found he could sit and spend time with her, talking about the farm and his plans for the future.

For the first time in months there were smiles and a little cheer-fulness around the house. Despite his sorrow at the loss of his friend, Tom was happy, deeply in love with Madge and eager to be married to her. They had met the vicar of St Thomas's, who was not quite as warm and friendly as Reverend Shanley. He seemed obsessed with the sanctity of marriage and kept reminding them both that marital relations, as he put it, were for the sole purpose of procreation, blushing as he did so. Tom and Madge giggled all the way home and Tom kept joking that they should plan to have at least a hundred children.

Madge insisted it would be bad luck if they saw each other on the morning of the service so Tom, Hender, Alf, Sid and Ray stayed at a small hotel in Stourbridge for the night. Sid had booked a table in the hotel restaurant where they each had three pints of beer and an excellent dinner of fillet steak followed by treacle tart with cream.

'Tom, old lad, how are you feeling about it all?' said Sid, after the plates had been cleared.

'A bit nervous but I'm sure Madge is the right woman for me so we'll both work hard to make sure we're happy I hope she takes to the farming and the horses; they'll be a bit of a shock for her,' said Tom.

'Madge'll be fine, although I'm not sure that hunting will suit her. She said to me she might try some riding but she didn't fancy trying to jump the brook,' said Alf.

'Rather like you,' said Sid, and then recounted the story of Alf falling in Bow Brook when it was in full flood. They all laughed despite the countless times they had heard it before. There was a pause while they ordered some whisky and toasted Tom and Madge's happiness.

Ray, who had been very quiet all evening, coughed and asked if he could say a few words. Tom had never been especially close to his youngest brother but over the last few months they had often talked together about farming, and Ray had become a bridge between Tom and his mother. They had grown closer as a result. There was still a marked difference in their dress sense. This particular evening Ray was wearing a houndstooth checked jacket over a cream-coloured shirt. He owned a wide range of hats, some with very wide brims, which Reg thought looked ridic-ulous and better suited to London parties than the Worcestershire countryside.

'Tom, I would like to say a few words before we all go off to bed. I wanted to thank you for inviting me tonight. It's been a wonderful evening and I wish you and Madge every happiness in the future.' He paused here, and Sid started up as if leaving for bed.

'Sorry, Sid, I haven't quite finished yet. Most of you know that I have an old friend who lives in Hampshire and I was down seeing him last month. He now works on a big estate there and I thought I would have a look around Southampton, as it's near to his house. I wandered around the waterfront and found a lovely little bookshop where one or two books took my fancy. One of them looked familiar, as though I might have seen it before, so I flicked through it. When I opened the front page and saw the inscription I knew why it was familiar.'

Ray reached into his jacket pocket and pulled out a small parcel wrapped in stiff brown paper and tied with string. He passed it to Tom.

'Does this look familiar to you in any way?' asked Ray, as Tom stared at the parcel.

'No, not at all,' he said, turning it over in his hands.

He undid the bow then and pulled open the paper and inside there was a small leather-bound book. Tom knew instantly it was his New Testament Bible. There was a tiny loss of gold leaf from one letter on the front, but when he opened the front cover there was the inscription written by his parents eight years before:

Tom Bomford
Stoulton
Worcester
With Father's and Mother's love and prayers for a safe return

Yet with recognition came confusion. How had the Bible ended up back in England? The room fell quiet. Tom sat opening and closing his mouth before he eventually spoke.

'This is the Bible that Mother and Father gave me in 1914 before I left for Egypt. It was taken off me when I was captured by the Turks. I just can't understand how it got here,' he said, sounding baffled.

He put the book down and looked at Ray. There were tears in Tom's eyes and he was shaking his head in disbelief.

'Thank you so much. I can't tell you what this means to me. This was with me every moment of every day until I was captured. You know I was never a deeply religious man, but I read small passages from it every night and it was a huge comfort to me. Now, to have it given back to me the day before my wedding…it's astonishing. I can hardly believe it and can only say thank you, Ray. This is the best present imaginable.'

Tom tucked the Bible back in his breast pocket as Sid wrapped an arm round his shoulders and told him, 'You always were a lucky bugger.'

Epilogue

Tom and Madge were happily married for over fifty years, farming at Allesborough, the farm they rented after their marriage until their retirement.

Tom refused ever to pay the fine he received after punching Buller Nutting on the football pitch for knocking over Hender. He received a lifetime ban from the County Football Association, but was elected President of Pershore Football Club and served for twenty-five years.

Birdie never married but continued to live at Manor Farm, Stoulton, eventually moving into a small cottage close to the farmhouse.

Mary, whose vision remained very poor, married Arthur Dunston in what was effectively an arranged marriage, moving down to Cornwall where they had a daughter, Joy. Arthur and Mary died in old age. After the death of her parents Joy lived alone, dying a complete recluse.

Phyllis lived at home, until meeting a local general practitioner, Dr Gordon Browning. He divorced his alcoholic wife and married Phyllis in 1947, and they moved to Devon where he continued to work as a GP.

Hender married Rene Simkins and they had a daughter, Margaret. They lived at Dunhampstead.

Ray lived at Manor Farm for the rest of his life, looking after his mother, Nora, until she died aged 101. He adored his garden and grew gladioli for Worcester Cathedral. He continued to dress very elegantly. Although there were many women with whom he was friendly, he never married.

Harry Williams continued to prosper, opening a number of pubs and building up the business until it was bought by the Wolverhampton & Dudley Brewery. He loved cars and eventually bought an open-topped Rolls-Royce, which was driven by Deacon. He died in 1944 aged eighty-three years old. Marian died of throat cancer in 1931 aged seventy-four, and after their parents died Daisy, Dolly and Dick lived in Ivy Lodge for the rest of their lives.

Daisy ran the house and continued to support West Brom while Dolly became housebound after having surgery for bowel cancer at a comparatively young age. She built up a huge portfolio of shares and devoured the *Financial Times* daily. Dick briefly ran a glove factory, Fitwell Gloves, but this folded after just a few years. He went on to play first-class cricket for Worcestershire and scored 81 against the touring Australians. He had one love in his life, Muriel Reading, who sadly married one of his close friends.

Sid Parkes farmed at Pinvin near Pershore and was in the Observer Corps during the Second World War, together with Tom and Dick Edwards. Alf Busk, Sid and Tom met on the anniversary of the battle of Qatia for the rest of their lives, and usually overindulged. Alf developed throat cancer and had his larynx removed, but still frequented the pubs in Pershore until he died.

Tom and Madge had three children, Edward known as Ted, John and Anne. Ted tragically died of head injuries after a fall in a point-to-point at Alcester in 1951, aged twenty-seven.

Tom and Madge retired to Elmley Castle, where they enjoyed a happy old age. Tom died in 1973 aged eight-two, having never had another day in hospital for the rest of his life. Madge died in 1986 aged ninety-one.

John took over Allesborough and farmed there until his retirement in 2004. He has two daughters, Susan and Sarah.

Anne, my mother, married a local farmer, Barry Staight, who farmed at a village called Dumbleton. They had two children:

Rebecca, who sadly died of breast cancer in 1996 aged thirty-six, and myself, a general practitioner. I rode as an amateur jockey for ten years. I married Katie Ellerington and we have three children, James, Harry and Georgina.

The New Testament Bible now sits in my bedside table with the inscription still visible inside the cover. A little more faded, but a reminder of my grandfather and his time in the Yeomanry.

Guy Staight
February 2014